THE
CHALLENGE

THE ORIGINAL SERIES

DAVID MIRAGLIA

ISBN 978-1-957220-63-5 (paperback)
ISBN 978-1-957220-64-2 (hardcover)
ISBN 978-1-957220-65-9 (digital)

Rushmore Press LLC
1 800 460 9188
www.rushmorepress.com

Printed in the United States of America

HISTORIAN'S NOTE: These novel details the little-known Federation-Harrata conflict of 2267.

The novel takes place prior to the Star Trek episode "Court Martial" and ends with a third person view of that episode.

Star date 2902.5 to Star date 2936.7: The Challenge
Star date 2947.3 to Star date 2950.1: Court Martial
Flashbacks are in the years 2220, 2252, 2254, and 2264.

INTRODUCTION

Introduction by Admiral Robert Nelson Hawke, Commanding officer Starfleet First Strike Force—Task Force Alpha, Star base Trafalgar, Gettysburg star System, Star date 9632.5. April 2296.

I have been asked by my biographer to add this forward into this account for the sake of future posterity and historical record. James Kirk, my long-time rival and friend since our academy days, has always been the greatest of us all. Not only did he outshine his predecessors on the enterprise but also put the famous Garth to shame in his accomplishments and exploits.

I still haven't gotten over Kirk's death; my wife Admiral Samantha Reynolds Hawke, myself, as well as Admiral Michael Walsh, Vice Admiral Kelly Bogle, and Vice Admiral Eric Vern Dhruva were also present at Jim's memorial service.

However, none of us really had the heart to speak at the service. It had been too emotionally devastating for us. Added to that, there were some old hands present among the crew of the Enterprise. Commodore Thaylassa Shran, Fleet Captain T'Pau, Captain of Engineering Thomas Fredrick Andrews, Captain Barbara Desalle, Commander David Russell, Commander Daniel Harris,

Commander Mariko Shimada, Commander Zari Nus Gazari Fahiri Hawke, and Ober Commander Laratay Nus Gazari Fahiri Hawke of the Constitution and the Harrata Star force were there to pay respects to our fallen comrade.

Looking back on those years, they were a true challenge, Constitution and Enterprise were the only two ships of their class of ships to return home with their ship and crews relatively intact. During the mission, I survived two attempts by Section 31 to steal my command from me and I know that Kirk suffered from similar problems.

We both had legendary missions but only one of us came out on top. Jim Kirk became Starfleets poster boy, and I was the more expendable troop inspirer but that is beside the point.

There were times over these many years when I literally had to back Kirk up. Somebody had to hold the fort together while Kirk marched out to meet the enemy.

During the Genesis crisis, despite my Commodores rank, I had to put out every single brush fire along the Federation Klingon neutral zone from Star base 12 to 27 to 41 and Starfleet always came to me first, especially when Jim, against orders, stole the Enterprise from space dock. To protect Jim and his people, I looked the other way and later during the Khitomer crisis, my squadron and I again looked the other way when Sulus Excelsior crossed into Klingon space.

Which brings me to the infamous challenge—the challenge was a real test of our skills; it was far more. Kirk and I were literally fighting for our lives and the lives of our crews. And billions of lives in the Federation were at stake.

What later transpires in this novel is the turning point in Federation Harrata relations. It also forced Jim and I to finally put aside the residual traces of our academy rivalry and grow up.

I came out of the Challenge a different and changed person. I think Jim had the same experience. I hope you will all enjoy the telling of this forgotten conflict that was the turning point in galactic affairs and began the long reconciliation between the Federation and the Imperium.

PART ONE

LEXINGTON

"A Commander is responsible for the lives of his crew." Commodore Matthew Decker: U.S.S Constellation-NCC1017, the Doomsday Machine, Star date 4202.9

PROLOGUE

PLANET HARRATA 4. HOME OF THE THIRTEEN NATIONS OF THE HARRATA RACE. CITY OF TOMAR. TEMPLE OF GOM. STAR DATE 2902.5. JANUARY 12, 2267 (OEC).

N'arita pan Marki tugged on his flowing, bejeweled robes as he made his way through the Temple of Gom—Gom the Almighty, Gom the Feared, the most powerful of all the Harrata deities. Chanting echoed in the background. A scream reverberated here and there as a worthless white was sacrificed to Gom. The glory of Gom was complete.

This year's Harrata youth—the 13th age grade—completed "the changes." Each was assigned its permanent status, an institution that emerged 500,000 years ago, after the great war of cleansing. The Great Crusade exterminated the Harrata's ancient great god Pong, the twelve other deities, and nearly all their believers. The Harr Republic passed into history. The great god Gom and its twelve deities had won. The Harrata Imperium was born. And so was the Ascension.

On their thirteenth birthday, all Harrata boys and girls pass through The Ascension. If you failed, your skin would whiten. A child's success in life and social rank are determined by its class color. The

3

highest ranks are the blacks, the religious. Scientists are the purples, the browns political, and reds and blues the military. Artists and artisans are silver. Farmers and other servers are green. The gold techies are just one rank above and the lowest: the despised whites. They are forced to work in the most polluted of trades: business and finance.

N'arita turned the corner, then entered a high-domed circular room. In the center, masses of energies swirled. It was Gom. Bolts of lightning crackled, and thunder roared. N'arita joined the Chosen standing on the center dais. He bowed his head and joined in the rest in the chant.

Suddenly, a voice boomed in his head. "N'arita. N'arita." Startled, he looked around. The voice resonated again. He was the Chosen One for the holy rite of Gur, the first in twelve kloms to be Gom's receptacle. His body began to tingle. His temperature started to rise. He felt light-headed and dizzy. N'arita screamed, "Gom!"

Pointing at N'arita, a priestess chanted. "Gom has chosen!" The other Chosen Ones on the dais cried in unison, "The Gur is coming!"

Anadaria pal Tikiri faced the possessed N'arita pan Marki. "Gom! We hear you!"

Gom/N'arita opened his cats' eyes wide. He spoke to Anadaria in Harratese.

"Federansky, Klingonasi, Gur dam Gom. No par Gur Tong Federansky, Klingonasi. Chancellor tu Gom." ["Gom sanctions war. Go forth with the Tong, the Challenge, against the Federation and the Klingons. Get me the chancellor!"] Anadaria stayed at N'arita's side.

Obediently, nearly all the black-skinned priests and priestesses rose and left the temple to spread Gom's command to the populace of the city of Tomar. Shouting "Gom Gur Federanski, Klingonaase. ["Gom wars against the Federation and the Klingons."] Rejoice!"

Anadaria turned to Valon si Ricardi. "Get the chancellor." Valon bowed and sped from the temple. Anadaria pal Tikiri turned back to the possessed N'arita pan Marki. "Gom, we hear you."

The people of Tomar cheered, celebrating the coming of a new holy war. Only the whites were not celebrating. War meant more sacrifices of their own kind, not only to Gom but to the remaining twelve deities.

Within minutes, the entire city was possessed with religious zeal. "Gom! Gom! Gom!" The chant of Gom filled the streets and alleys of Tomar. With the speed of light, Gom's word would spread to the rest of the Harrata Imperium's hundred-star systems and to all their military installations.

Chancellor Vardeck Da Banari, his staff officers, and Valon si Ricardi arrived in the temple via transporter. The chancellor could hear his people chanting. The time for holy war had come again. The Unbelievers—the Klingons and the Federation—must compete in the Tong.

The Harrata were an ancient race going back a million years before Gom appeared. The Tong, the Challenge that determines if a Gur, a religious war, will follow, had started a mere 1,000 years ago. Gom defied the other super races—the Metrons, the Organians, the Q Continuum, and the Beings—so they could test and prepare the

5

child races of the Alpha and Beta quadrants for the darkness that lay ahead. They, the Harrata, were Gom's chosen.

Obeying Gom's commands was and remains their only reason for continuing to exist. The Harrata paid a terrible price for being the Chosen. They had to rebuild their world, their civilization, repeatedly.

For centuries, the Harrata had crusaded and battled against the Unmentionables. The Tkon Empire, the Iconians—the evil sphere builders who lived in another dimension—and the evilest of all, the Horror, that existed in the great darkness, beyond the Barrier.

Lightning crackled, and thunder roared as the chanting of the remaining priests added to the crescendo. Valon led his group up to N'arita whose face now shimmered with all the colors of the Harrata race. Vardeck kneeled and gazed at the priest, his eye slits narrow in the temple's overpowering radiance. N'arita/Gom looked down at Vardeck, his eye slits wide.

Vardeck said, "We come at the will of Gom." The lightning and thunder suddenly stopped.

Putting his finger directly on the chancellor's chest, N'arita/Gom spoke softly,

"Federanski, Klingonassi Gur tong Federanski, Klingonassi." ["Federations. Klingons. Begin the Challenge."]

Vardeck could feel the power emanating from the N'arita/Gom receptacle. Vardeck turned to face his entourage. The silver-uniformed, red-skinned High Order Corp officers and the gold-uniformed, blue-skinned Star Force officers continued to stand at attention.

N'arita/Gom turned away from the chancellor, flinging himself into the maelstrom.

Anadaria stepped back. The chancellor of the Imperium approached her.

Andaria bowed to the chancellor of the Imperium. "Noble Chancellor."

"And you are?"

"Anadaria pal Tikiri."

"And the priest who was possessed by Gom?"

"N'arita pan Marki."

"He will always be remembered."

The chancellor left the Temple. He had a Holy War to plan and a Challenge to stage.

DOMAR AMID ONE. HARRATA TRADE STATION ON THE BORDER BETWEEN HARRATA AND FEDERATION SPACE. STAR DATE 2902.7.

Captain Phil Waterston walked along the colorful promenade of the Harrata trade station, past the many white-class-run merchant businesses with their colorful wares. He was on his way to Thugar's, the Harrata-run bar for Starfleet personnel.

Waterston had successfully completed transferring his bills of lading to Harrata Subjective Command, the Harrata equivalent of the Starfleet Merchant Service. Having lost the Tong twice to the Harrata, Starfleet commanders and merchants had to swallow the Harrata's contempt. And he was in a very bad mood.

Waterston detested his command, the Ptolemy, the Constitution-design transport tug he was given five years earlier. He hated being a "tug-and-tow rat." Out of his entire graduating Command School class of 2253, Waterston was the only one hauling freight. He blamed Pike, Wesley, and Noguchi. They conspired to cheat him out of a Heavy cruiser command. He wanted Constitution. Instead, they gave the ship to Robert Hawke.

What stuck in his craw was that the same thing happened to his father Henry back in 2245. Henry Waterston was given the destroyer Larson, but he was assigned to the Tribal Sectors Alpha to Zeta, a dead-end command. It was also known as the hind end of space. The rest of his father's career was dead-end backwater assignments until his promotion to the rank of Vice Commodore ten years later. Last year, Henry Waterston was killed in action when a Romulan Bird of Prey destroyed Outpost 8.

Distracted by his jealousy, Waterston overshot Thugar's. Backtracking, he arrived at the garish multi-colored neon sign flashing above the entrance. The raucous clamor resounded through the bar's heavy double doors. Thugar's was jammed packed with Starfleet personnel, all sporting the insignias of the Ptolemy, Ibn Daud, Anaximander, Keppler, Huron, and Independence. He spotted a sprinkling of independent merchant crews and a few rogue traders.

Before Waterston could reach the bar, Captain Henry Strohman, captain of the Keppler, grabbed his arm. "Hey, Phil! Come over to our table!" Strohman, a stocky, pleasant Ohioan, guided Waterston to a round table where his squadron mates were sitting. All were transport tug commanders, the grunts of Starfleet command.

Waterston pulled out the chair between Strohman and Svenquist O'Shea of the Huron. O'Shea pulled a carafe of golden Traga, the sweet-sour Harrata drink, closer to Waterston. Commodore Werner Doenitz of the Ibn Daud glanced briefly at Waterston. Captains Susan Nolan of the Independence and Alan Ben Gurion of the Anaximander ignored him.

Waterston took a sip, the sweet-sour sensation tingling his taste buds. He might not like the Harrata caste system, but Harrata cuisine was a hell of a lot better than Tellerite fare.

"Now that we are all finally present," Doenitz said in his Bavarian accented English, "Here are your next five months of assignments." He liked the personal touch.

Doenitz passed the discs and command packets to all the captains. Waterston put his disc into the viewer slung over his right shoulder. The bearded face of Admiral Peter Holliday appeared. Holliday made his usual introductions before fading from the viewer.

Waterston gritted his teeth. It was the usual—convoy duty; shuttle work between star bases; supply runs between the Delta and Epsilon outpost construction sites. What caught his interest was the chance to do a colony transport run. A new Federation colony was proposed on a class M planet near the Taurus reach.

Susan Nolan sat very still. Werner glanced at her. "Any problems?" he asked. She glared at him. "Werner, doing supply runs near Kzinti space isn't my cup of tea. I put in for freight runs in the Core systems." She paused. "Which I earned."

Ignoring Nolan's last comment, Doenitz went on. "Starfleet now has enough escorts to get the job done safely. Glancing at Captain Nolan, Doenitz added. "We should have fewer pirate attacks. The Tkarians,

Orions, Naussicans, and Kzinti will think twice about attacking our freighters."

Nolan kept her face blank, ignoring Doenitz's not-so-subtle insult.

Sighing, Strohman commented, "I don't see why everyone has to be so grim. We in Transport have a saying 'Transport and freighters get no glory.' But like our old ECS boomer ancestors, we keep the Federation running. To hell with the glory boys who command the Heavies, the snobs who command the Dreadnoughts, and the hotshots who command those Escorts. The Federation would grind to a halt if the junkyard navy stopped carrying their precious cargos."

"Hear, hear!" They all lifted their glasses in reply.

"Starfleet is right, boys." One of the independent freighter captains at the bar said. Waterston noticed that he was wearing a colorful suit of many colors, way too many colors.

"To our friends at Starfleet Merchant!" hailed a second independent, waving his tankard.

The noise level in Thugar's gradually subsided. Waterston motioned to a green Harrata waitress to come and take his order. She started to walk in his direction when she suddenly stopped. Waterston called to her again. All the Harrata in Thugar's slipped into a trance-like state, humming. Their humming became a chant.

"Gom Gur Federanski. Gom! Gom! Gom!" The Federation officers and crewmembers were beguiled. They knew of the Tong and its rituals, but this was the first time they witnessed any part of this phenomenon. The last one occurred in 2220, fifty years before.

"What the hell!" O'Shea muttered surprised.

Suddenly, the Harrata stopped chanting. Thugar's double doors swung open. Red and blue Harrata troops of the High Order Corp separated the Harrata citizenry from the Outworlders, the Starfleet personnel, and the independent traders. The blue-skinned Star Force Security blocked the doors. Two officers, one blue and one red, approached the round table.

"Who commands here?" demanded the blue-skinned Harrata Star Force officer, his neat black hair and stylish mustache gleaming.

Werner Doenitz stood up, then stepped forward. "I am Commodore Werner Doenitz, captain of the Ibn Daud, commander of unit XY 72115, representing the United Federation of Planets."

"We know who you are," the Harrata said insultingly.

Doenitz glared. "And who are you!"

"I am Commandant Hara ben Gomar, Commander of Domar Amid One." Then pointing to the red-skinned bearded Harrata standing next to him, sporting the traditional Mohawk haircut, added, "And this is Commodore Arika Fa Tal of the High Order Corp, Tomars' Legion, Ben Tams' Order."

Doenitz could practically hear Gomar's thoughts. "Now is the time to rid the station of the Federank scum, these pitiful Humass, the pathetic race who couldn't even beat the challenge."

Gomar ordered Doenitz, "You must all leave now!"

"Why!" Waterston said defiantly.

Gomar and Tal walked up to the blond-haired, white-skinned Starfleet captain.

"Are you deaf, Humass? Didn't you hear what the Commandant said!" Tal spat angrily.

"You question our authority, Federank," Gomar challenged.

Waterston could see everyone looking in his direction.

"Yes!" Waterston felt his anger surging.

"You are nothing, Humass. The Tong has come again." Gomar sneered. "We will see if your weakling race will prove itself worthy of the Challenge. You failed twice. You are pathetic. You will fail again, and we will make the Gur against your worthless Federation. At least the Klingons won the Tong. They are unbeaten."

Klingons better than humans! Never! Waterston lost all control.

"You murdered my grandfather!" Waterston lashed out at the Harrata commandant. Strohman quickly stepped in front of Waterston.

"Phil, lay off. They mean it." Strohman warned under his breath.

Gomar and Tal stepped back, affronted by the arrogance of that Humass.

"Your grandfather fells to Lothar!" Tal retorted.

"He is now consumed by the darkness!" Gomar added, affronted. "And you! A soiled, accursed descendant facing me!"

Gomar glared at the Harrata in the room.

As if on cue, all the Harrata, including the despised whites, shrieked in unison, the Scream of Purification. Glasses shattered; tables shook.

Waterston put his hands over his ears to shut out the uproar. A trader panicked and tried to run, only to be knocked to the ground by a High Order Corp red-skinned trooper.

Within two minutes, the Scream of Purification suddenly stopped. Thugar's was finally cleansed of the taint of Lothar.

Gomar looked at Waterston and said, "I knew your great-grandfather Neil Waterston, captain of the Titanic." Gomar spat out contemptuously. "And you are Philip Waterston." He sneered. Gomar's father had faced Neil Waterston in the Challenge in 2177. He had killed him during the first phase of the ordeal.

Waterston nodded, his face red with rage. His ears were ringing. He could see every human in the room glaring at him. What the hell had he done!

Gomar smiled, satisfied. Tomar was grinning. The arrogant Humass was put in his place.

"You disgust me, Humass. No Harrata would talk about a disgraced ancestor that has fallen to Lothar in the Tong," Gomar said.

"You are disgraced by your ancestor!" Tal joined in, revolted by Waterston's outburst.

"I will not continue to soil myself, Captain. You are palok," Gomar spat. "You Humass must leave now!"

Tal turned to his troops. "Ajed Soldats Humass shapa ze!" [Soldiers! Escort the Humans out!"]

Escorted by Tomar's legion and the Domar-Amid One Star Force Security, the Outworlders emptied Thugar's.

As the company strode towards their docking ports, Susan Nolan turned to face Waterston. "Now, that was brilliant, Phil. Trying to get us all killed over your lost grandfather."

"Brilliantly stupid," Ben Gurion said angrily as he brushed his silver-grey hair back. "Did you have to start your own personal war with the Harrata, again?"

Strohman continued walking. "This one, Phil, took the cake."

Waterston ignored their comments. He wanted revenge against the Harrata to avenge his lost grandfather and clear his family's disgrace. And he wanted to "get" Robert Hawke.

Robert Nelson Hawke's family was intimately involved with the Harrata. His grandmother Nicole Hawke, Alexander Hawke's daughter, and Alexander himself, were the first humans to contact this accursed alien race, back in the 22nd century.

Commodore Doenitz walked over to Waterston. "Never do that again, Phil!" Doenitz said angrily. Waterston tried to respond, but Doenitz cut him off, glaring at the young captain.

"I don't care about your ancestor, Phil. I don't care if you come from a first-generation Starfleet family. This is the reason why you command a transport tug instead of a Heavy cruiser, when we return to Federation space, I am putting you on the report."

On that sour note, Doenitz walked away. Waterston said nothing. Two hours later.

PTOLEMY WITH THE REST OF UNIT XY 72115. AT DOMAR AMID ONE:

Captain Phil Waterston stepped onto his transport tug's main bridge. It was similar in design to the Constitution-class starship bridge. "All the make-up in the world wouldn't make this pig look good." He thought with sarcasm.

Lieutenant Commander Jeffery Cooper, Waterston's second-in-command, his twenty-six-year-old Executive Officer and Science Officer, greeted him.

"All decks report ready, Sir," Cooper added, with a slight shrug. "Containers secured."

"It really stinks that we're going home empty instead of with our usual load." He continued. "And all because the Harrata happen to have some issues with us over some Tong."

Waterston nodded grimly. Cooper was a good exec, the best he could get for this ship.

"Don't worry, Captain. The whole crew is behind you," Cooper said reassuringly.

"Domar Amid One has ordered us to leave. They have retracted all moorings," said Ensign Anne Vivant from Communications.

She added, "Commodore Doenitz has ordered all transport tugs of our unit to form a defensive formation around the Huron and the Independence, and all the civilian ships."

"Acknowledged," Waterston replied. "Mister Grimes, take us to our position."

"Yes, Sir," Grimes replied as he manipulated the helm controls of the tug.

"Mister Valdez, set a course for Star Base 41."

"Aye, Sir."

Valdez laid in the appropriate heading.

Waterston smirked. Unlike Kirk and Hawke, he believed in total control. Strict adherence to the rules. Only he commanded. He would never flout the Prime Directive of Starfleet regulations, or thumb his nose at brass. Any ship he commanded would follow the letter of the law. Anyone who challenged him would be gone in the snap of a finger.

Waterston watched as Ptolemy assumed her position. The four Antares-class freighters of unit XY 71007 line up alongside the Huron and the Independence. A motley assortment of civilian ships—Class J freighters, one-man scouts, and a few updated antiques from the twenty-second century: The X, Y, and Z class clunkers comprised the ragtag flotilla. The four transport tugs of unit XY 72115 held the place of honor. They were better armed than the rest of the freighters, each containing one forward and two aft phaser banks.

Leaning back in his command chair, Waterston smiled contentedly. "Engage, Mister Grimes." Grimes nodded and swiftly manipulated the controls. Ptolemy jumped into warp.

"Good riddance," Waterston commented as Domar Amid One faded into the background.

They would soon enter the territorial zone and return to Federation space.

Cooper turned to Waterston from the science station. "Captain, long-range sensors have picked up four Neparah-class cruisers, closing on an intercept course."

The Harrata's Star Force Neparahs were equivalent to the Federation Miranda and Soyuz class ships.

"Great!" Waterston thought sourly. They were outgunned and outmatched. Neparahs were like the Hogars at half the size. But they were tough and over-gunned for their class.

"Red Alert! Battle stations!" Waterston ordered.

Ptolemy's crew jumped to battle stations.

"Reverse view!"

"Captain," Ensign Vivant said quickly, swinging her chair to face Waterston. "Just received a transmission from the Soyuz. They picked up the Neparahs and have altered course to intercept."

Waterston was relieved. If only Samantha Reynolds and her medium cruisers would arrive in time. Waterston could only hope.

"ETA of the Neparahs." Waterston inquired.

"Five minutes," Cooper replied, coolly.

"ETA XY75847."

"Fifteen minutes," he added.

Ensign Vivant interrupted, "Commodore Doenitz has ordered all Ptolemy's to disengage containers and engage the enemy. All other ships are to head for Federation space."

"Acknowledged," Waterston said. "Mr. Cooper. Disengage the container."

"Yes, Sir," Cooper said as he detached the container from Ptolemy. The ship shuddered briefly.

"Container crew signals clear," Ensign Vivant declared. "We are free, Captain."

"Alter course, Mister Grimes. And stand by on all phasers."

"Yes, Sir."

Ptolemy and her sisters broke formation. The other freighters were flying into Federation territory as fast as their warp drive engines propelled them forward. Ptolemy and her sister tugs engaged the Neparah warships.

CHAPTER ONE

U.S.S LEXINGTON-NCC 1709 NEAR THE X STAR SYSTEMS. STAR DATE 2903.1. JANUARY 13, 2267.

"Captain's log. Star date 2903.1. Commodore Robert Wesley recording. The Lexington will meet up with the Excelsior at Deep Space station K1. Excelsior's commander, Little Jack, Jacque La Liberté, was one of my academy classmates. We are to patrol between Star base 41, and Delta 4, 5, 6 construction sites. They are in the Federation corridor between Harrata Imperium and the Klingon Empire."

Wesley turned off the log recorder, then leaned back in his chair. In 2263, he had been promoted to the rank of Commodore along with Matt Decker, George Stocker, David Aaron Stone, and Jose Mendez. Wesley commanded the Avenger before becoming Captain of the Beowulf in 2251. In 2263 he was ordered to take command of the Constitution. Robert Wesley replaced Frederick Augenthaler, its commanding officer. Promoted to Commodore as well, Augenthaler, was given command of Star Base 41 and took his entire senior staff with him. Wesley did likewise. He took his people from the Beowulf when he took command of the Constitution.

In February of 2264, Wesley was ordered to turn Constitution over to Captain Robert Nelson Hawke, former captain of the Volunteer, Miranda, and the Sargon, before he transferred to the Lexington, replacing Mark Rousseau. Wesley had hoped to command the Constitution until the end of the decade, but Starfleet and Admiral Okuda had other ideas.

Going back to work, Wesley was looking over the mission summaries and the latest fleet disposition reports when the cabin buzzer sounded.

"Come."

The doors parted. Yeoman Grace Langston walked in. He smiled at her with pleasure. He had stolen her from Captain Garrison of the Pharsalus back in 2251.

"The crew status reports, Bob."

"Thanks, Grace."

"So? What's the Scuttlebutt?" Langston asked curiously.

"Standard patrol duty between Harrata and Klingon space in the infamous corridor. We will rendezvous with Excelsior and Little Jack."

"You mean the little Napoleon Bob," Langston said, smiling.

Wesley looked at Langston. Jacques always hated that name.

"Yes, Little Jack," Wesley corrected her, grinning.

"He sure beats that upstart Bobby Hawke. He was always taking risks. I'm glad you picked up Barbara Smith from James Kirk when we switched positions at Vanguard."

Wesley countered. "From what I've heard, Barbara Smith is doing just fine with Hawke and Janice Rand, doing equally well with Kirk."

"That's good, but 2264 was a mess." That was the year Kirk and Hawke took command of their starships. It had been a tumultuous, eventful year.

Wesley sympathized with Grace. The Klingons were vowing revenge for what they saw as their defeat in the Jutland System in April 2264. Matt Decker, with six starships, defeated six Klingon battle cruisers under the command of Commander Mog.

The Klingon Empire hadn't forgiven the Federation for adding insult to injury: their total defeats earlier during the Axanar Rebellion in early 2251 and the Four Years War, end of 2251 to early 2256, and the brief Federation-Klingon extended conflict of 2257. Since then, an uneasy peace had existed between the Federation and the Klingon Empire.

"Indeed, it was Grace," Wesley admitted.

The alert klaxon wailed. Wynn Samuels' voice echoed throughout the ship. Wesley sped for the bridge.

Wesley waited impatiently as the turbo lift doors opened.

Wynn Samuels vacated the captain's chair and resumed his place at sciences.

"A Hogar Class, Type 7 the Logash, opened fire on us."

The Hogar class was the famed Harrata Heavy cruiser design. It was the equivalent of the Starfleet Constitution class and the Imperial Defense Force D7 type.

The Harrata kept their design for nine generations constantly refining the class. Like the Klingons, the Harrata kept their older ships in service for a century. Wesley recalled.

Turning his command chair, he faced Mister Baila.

"Mister Baila! Open up hailing frequency!"

"Yes, Sir!"

"Mister Minh! Intercept course."

"Yes, Sir!"

"Mister Donaldson! Target her warp and impulse. I want her immobilized!"

"Aye, Sir!"

"Hailing frequencies open, Commodore."

"Harrata Imperium Starship Logash. This is the Federation Starship Lexington under the command of Commodore Wesley. Your attack is a violation of the Treaty of 2220."

Turning to his communication officer, he asked.

"Any response, Mister Baila."

"No, Sir, no audio or visual feedback."

Lieutenant Angela Donaldson interrupted, "The Harrata are firing their aft batteries."

She was filling in for Randy Pickens, Lexington's Chief Navigator, who had come down with Taylors syndrome at their last port of call at Stavros Four a week earlier.

The Lexington shuddered under the barrage.

"Overtake and pursue!" Wesley ordered Minh.

"Yes, Sir."

Lexington closed on the Hogar class cruiser. The Harrata ship maneuvered, trying to outflank the Lexington. Lexington pivoted and unleashed a salvo of phasers and photon torpedoes at the Harrata ship. Staggering under the barrage the Harrata ship withdrew out of range.

"She's withdrawing and taking up a parallel course," Samuels said to Wesley.

This was a typical Harrata behavior. Like the ancient Japanese Kamikaze pilots of World War Two, once the Harrata engaged in battle, it was all or nothing. To the death.

"Mister Baila, send a message to Star base Trafalgar. We are being attacked by the Harrata. The ship involved is the Hogar class Type 7 Logash. They refused to answer hails.

Request assistance." Wesley said to Baila swinging his command chair forward. Wesley looked at Lieutenant Donaldson.

"Our position, Mr. Donaldson."

"We are near the X star systems, Sir."

Wesley continued, "Mr. Baila, add that we are approaching the X star systems."

Wesley walked up to Wynn's station. "What do we know of the Harrata?" Wesley asked.

"They are like the Klingons. They love a good fight, and they have a streak of religious zealotry. Long before we made the first contact with them, they have been in and still are involved in a centuries-old conflict with the Naussicans, mostly skirmishes. The Federation has had two wars with them, in 2177 and 2220.

Back in the 21st century, the Ferengi and the Pakleds violated the Tong, the Harrata prewar challenge. The Ferengi had to buy their way out or be conquered. The result was a complete economic collapse. Rumors are confirmed by Starfleet Intelligence: the Ferengi are still making monetary amends to the Harrata Imperium nearly 200 years later. The Pakleds were not as fortunate. The Harrata occupied their home world for a century and stripped them of their spaceflight capacity."

Wesley was reminded of a recent Starfleet Intelligence brief he received seven months earlier. In 2266, a Ferengi Marauder raided the New Miami colony in system PK475 headed by former Excalibur commanding officer Dmitri Vlasidovich.

The Ferengi had ransacked the colony, stealing Federation technology and credits. The closest ship was Constitution, set out in pursuit of the renegades. It was fortunate that Constitution was in the nearby Zeta Maxia star system. Hawke and his crew had just completed a first and unsuccessful contact with the Children of Tama.

After recovering some of the Federation credits and most of the technology from the Ferengi Marauder, Constitution headed back for New Miami only to be cornered by three other Ferengi Kamar class Marauder ships in the Garod star system. Constitution quickly disabled the intruders. The Ferengi ships were a generation behind the Federation starships and were no match for the Constitution. The result was the second unofficial contact with that elusive race. The first had been Jonathan Archers run in with them a century earlier.

Wesley sat back in his command chair. "Mister Minh, Magnification three."

"Aye, Sir. Magnification three."

"What an ugly dog." Henry Chang groaned. Chang was Lexington's present Chief engineer. Henry had been his Chief Engineer on his two earlier assignments—Constitution and Beowulf.

Harrata ships had anywhere from the maximum of six nacelles on their mighty battleships, down to one on their scout vessels. The extra nacelles found on their bigger ships did nothing to improve their light speed factor and warp jumping or their maneuvering abilities.

"She sure is ugly," Donaldson chimed in.

Wesley looked over his opponent. Harrata ships were known to be tough nuts to crack in a ship-to-ship battle. Just as Wesley predicted the Harrata ship, Logash leaped forward across Lexington's bow and unleash her rear disruptors. Lexington shuddered again under the assault.

"All phasers fire!" Wesley commanded. This game was beginning to wear thin.

"She's making a run for that star system ahead," Donaldson warned. "Wynn?" Wesley asked his science officer as he swung his chair in that direction.

"Star system X757, one class M planet and five other planets."

"She's going to impulse," said Minh.

"Take us out of warp, Mister Minh. Mister Donaldson, keep on her tail. Are we within phaser range?" Wesley asked.

"Negative, Commodore. Secure from warp drive. Proceeding on impulse," Minh said.

Lexington swung into system X757 in hot pursuit of the Logash.

"They're heading for that class M planet directly ahead," Donaldson added. She was going to miss Lexington. And she was scheduled to transfer to Martin Callas' Potemkin at Star base 41.

Wesley sat back in his command chair. What sort of crazy game was the Harrata Commander playing?

"He's slowing to one-quarter impulse and he's coming about," Minh warned.

"Mister Donaldson, I want her immobilized. Disable her warp and impulse drives."

"Yes, Sir," Donaldson said as she manipulated the navigation controls.

On the main viewing screen, the Harrata warship slowed and turned to face the Lexington.

"Slow to one-half impulse, Mister Minh. Standby phasers, Mister Donaldson."

Planet X757- Four grew closer as Lexington closed on the Harrata warship. Lexington closed in on her quarry.

"Tactical analysis, Mister Samuels."

"Hogar class Type 7, disruptor batteries, plasma torpedoes, Tritanium-Carbonite hull."

Harrata tactics, Wesley recalled from his days at the academy, were to wear the enemy down with disruptors, then launch boarding parties. The boarding party then causes chaos and mayhem on the ship racking up a body count. The same boarding parties would then sacrifice their lives to the thirteen deities and go to paradise when the ship they boarded was obliterated by their own ship in a salvo of plasma torpedoes. The Harrata lived for death and would willingly give their lives for eternal glory.

"She's charging her weapons, Sir," Minh warned.

The Logash stood in the distance, daring Lexington to come closer.

Wesley watched as his ship closed to a firing range. A red alert sounded in the back of his head. Damn he didn't like this situation at all. He smelled a trap.

"Wynn Full sensor sweep," Wesley ordered.

Wynn immediately complied. "Commodore I am picking up multiple tachyon readings all around us."

"Cloaked what?" Wesley thought. He sure wasn't going to stick around and find out.

"Minh, Reverse course get us..." At that instant, mines suddenly appeared out of subspace and attacked his ship. Lexington shook violently as multiple explosions went off. Panels exploded. Wesley heard screams. Lieutenant Minh and Ensign Sakharov collapsed at their stations. Amidst the pandemonium, Samuels shouted, "The bastards lured us into a cloaked minefield!"

Suddenly, the explosions stopped. The smell of burnt circuitry and smoke billowed up from the damaged control panels.

"Emergency power to thrusters! Damage reports all stations! Doctor Coss to the bridge," Wesley bellowed.

Wesley felt Lexington shudder and groan as Donaldson applied the thrusters.

Lexington leveled off.

"Lexington's crippled, Sir. Our warp engines are out. The Impulse engines have been damaged. We are on auxiliaries. I just cut in the emergency battery reserve power," Chang said. His face and uniform were covered with soot.

Wesley hit the intercom switch. "Doctor Coss to the bridge medical emergency."

"Coss here," came Doctor Coss's voice through the intercom. "Bob, we are backed up into the corridors. I am sending Doctor Greir to the bridge."

"Understood," Wesley said. Leaving his command chair, he walked over to Lieutenant Donaldson.

"Minh and Sakharov are dead, Sir."

"Take Minh's station, Lieutenant."

"Yes, Sir."

Moments later, the bridge turbo lift doors opened. Doctor Greir and Nurse Shannon walked over to Wesley followed by four orderlies. In twos, the orderlies removed Minh's and Sakharov's corpses from the bridge.

Greir looked at Wesley. "We have six dead, thirty-two injured, mostly from engineering, Commodore." She turned to Nurse Shannon. "Take care of Wesley and Chang. I'll check out Samuels and Baila. Wesley watched as Shannon examined him and Chang Greir went over to Baila and Samuels leading them to sickbay. Walking out of the lift were Wesley's assistant science officer Rudy Lense and Balev a Gosh, Lexington's Tellerite assistant communications officer.

"Mister Balev. Do we have communications?" Wesley asked.

"Yes, Sir."

"Address inner ship."

"Inner ship open, Sir."

"This is Commodore Wesley speaking. Due to unprovoked aggression by the Harrata, the Lexington has been lured into a cloaked minefield. We are damaged and crippled. Within days, Starfleet will mount a search and rescue mission once they realize that we are overdue with our rendezvous with Excelsior. I have faith in all of you that we will prevail and weather this crisis. All senior staff will report to the main briefing room in two hours."

Wesley closed the intercom and then in a fit of anger, slammed the palm of his right hand against the arm of the command chair.

Donaldson and Lense pretended not to notice. Lense approached Wesley. "I have analyzed Wynn Samuels' data, Commodore," said Lense. "There is no way we could have known about the cloaked minefield."

Wesley silently agreed with his assistant science officer. "Mister Donaldson, the bridge is yours." Wesley said as he made his way to the turbo lift. Now he had to find out how badly damaged his ship was. Silently, he entered the lift; the doors closed in front of him.

LEXINGTON'S MAIN BRIEFING ROOM:

After inspecting the damage to his ship, Wesley entered the Lexington's main briefing room. None of his officers arrived yet. On the floor were seven portraits. Five were portraits of the United States Navy Lexington's. Picking them up, he hung them on the left side of the room. After that, he hung up the Lexington's Earth Starfleet predecessor and the first Starfleet Lexington on the right side of the room.

The NX class Lexington-NX-10 joined Earth Starfleet in 2155. Along with Constitution, Defiant, Excalibur, and Constellation and six others boasted a secondary hull. She was the second, improved NX class ship launched after Constitution-NX00. Lexington survived the Romulan War long enough to be inducted into the Federation Starfleet. Six years later, she was destroyed in 2166 at the battle of the Midway Star system. The First Strike Force-Task Force Alpha at an extremely high cost, defeated an unknown enemy that came from the unexplored Gamma Quadrant through the wormhole in that year.

Wesley then hung up the portrait of the NX-10's successor, the Ranger class Lexington-NCC 709. NCC 709 was lost during the second Federation–Harrata war of 2220. He then picked up the overturned chairs and rearranged the insignia flags.

Moments later, the briefing room doors swooshed open. Peder Coss, Wynn Samuels, Baila, Henry Chang, and Lexington's security Chief, Commander Patricia McCormack followed by yeoman Grace Langston and the rest of the staff.

Wesley looked at his officers; they all looked haggard. He immediately turned to Chang. "Henry."

"The main energizers are junk. The impulse engines have been damaged but are still viable. We have four holes in the ship. One in the primary hull between decks 5 and 8 starboard side. Another between decks 15-17, in the interconnecting dorsal section. And there is a hole secondary hull between shuttle bay and engineering. The final one is on decks 22-23. We are on auxiliaries, backed up by the batteries. I have Mister Ivari working on the most immediate damage right now. Which is trying to keep Lexington's hull intact. Overall? We need a month at star base to fix this mess."

"We are damn lucky we had our shields up or we would be a dead drifting hulk now," Coss added grimly.

"Peder," Wesley said as he looked at his Chief Medical Officer.

"You can increase the total to eight dead and forty-five injured."

"Baila."

"With our warp, drive down subspace is useless. We cannot contact star bases Alpha, Trafalgar, 11, 38, or 41. I was considering sending a recorder buoy, but since we don't know where the rest of the cloaked mines are, it would be a wasted futile effort to even launch one."

"Samuels."

Wynn stroked his beard for a moment, checked the library computer summarizing the data present on the screen.

"The latest information comes from Monitors Chief Science Officer, Sarah Albright, who led a landing party three years ago on Star date 0995.5. The planet below is class M. She reported that the inhabitants were humanoid similar to the Australopithecines on Earth. If we abandon Lexington, I suggest we find a place on the planet where we will not interfere with the native inhabitants."

The Prime Directive was in full force. He and his people could not interfere with the natural evolution of this planet. There were no ifs, ands, or buts about this situation, Wesley thought. On rare occasions, the Prime Directive would tie a ship captain's hands and starship captains had to be careful about how they were going to bend the number one rule on the books. It was like trying to navigate a minefield or walk on eggshells. One mistake and you could wind up being court-martialed or worse.

Wesley looked at his Chief Engineer. "Henry, what is your analysis of Lexington's chances?"

"Considering the damage, we sustained. Until help arrives, we will be taxing the ship to the limit if we kept a full crew aboard." Chang pointed out bluntly. He, Samuels, and Coss had all previously served with Wesley on Beowulf and Constitution. After almost eighteen years of service together, they knew what to expect and what was required.

Wesley turned to face Peder Coss. "What is the status of the six crewmembers in isolation with Taylors syndrome?"

"We need to keep them in isolation for another three days until the disease runs its course. Then they need to recuperate on the ship. Sending them down may cause contamination of the planet's biosphere with this alien disease," Coss warned.

Coss had a point. The last thing he needed was to have the guilt of unwittingly unleashing an unstoppable plague onto a culture that was barely out of the Stone Age. After some reflection and consideration, weighing all the information, Wesley came to a final decision.

"Wynn, I want you to find a suitable location where we could locate the crew where we will not be interfering with the locals."

Samuels nodded in agreement with Wesley.

"Chang, McCormack, Donaldson, start preparing Lexington for long-term parking orbit on minimal power to conserve resources. We are abandoning the Lexington.

This meeting is adjourned," Wesley said.

Wesley and his staff exited the briefing room.

"Captain's log. Star date 2903.11. Commodore Robert Wesley recording. We are abandoning the Lexington. Wynn Samuels will oversee the encampment on a little island located on the equator. I, Chang, Coss, and twenty other essential crewmembers are staying behind to monitor and maintain the Lexington. Coss must supervise the six crewmembers still infected with Taylor's syndrome. I hate to admit it, but old Jacque is probably cooling his heels at the rendezvous."

Wesley followed by Chang, Coss, and Samuels entered the transporter room. Samuels and Dickerson, Lexington's Transporter chief, got on the pad along with Deidre Watley, Angela Donaldson, and Victor Devereux.

"Good luck, Bob."

"If you need anything, Wynn, give us a holler."

"Don't worry, Bob, I will be calling."

Wesley, Chang, and Coss took their places by the transporter controls. Chang expertly manipulated the controls and the last of Lexington's crew disappeared as the transporter beamed them down to the planet.

"I bet Jacque is hollering a thousand French curses now," Chang said to Wesley and Coss.

"Isn't her chief engineer a friend of yours?" Coss asked Chang.

"Norlinda Vega, she's a good friend of mine. Known her since our academy days. We always like to wager on things."

"Like what?" Coss said interested at Chang's suggestion.

"You don't want to know," Chang said as he looked at Coss and Wesley with a devious smile on his face. The Transporter doors closed behind them as Wesley, Coss, and Chang broke out laughing.

Excelsior-NCC 1718 orbiting Deep Space Station K1, along the corridor between Harrata and Klingon territory. Star date 2905.4, January 15, 2267.

Jacque La Liberté shuffled side to side as the turbo lift made its way to the bridge. He had been captain of Excelsior for seven years now. Minutes earlier in his quarters, he had spoken to Commander

Douglas Kent, Commander of Deep Space Station K1 about the recent activity along the corridor. All was quiet along the Klingon disputed border, but there had been some major activity reported on the Harrata territorial zone.

Reports confirmed that a confrontation had taken place between Unit XY 75847 and a Neparah class Attack wing from Battle Group Echo near the Federation-Harrata Territorial zone not far from the battle station Bathazar One and the trade station Domar Amid One. Added to that ominous note, the Excalibur had reported increased activity on the Harrata side of the zone.

Liberté sighed Lexington was overdue. He had been looking forward to seeing his old friend again

A starship captain's work was never done. Commander Kent had transferred a renegade Vulcan named Sybok, who had been stirring up trouble at the Pengus Agricultural colony near the Federation-Harrata border from the destroyer Sargon, Commander Eleanor Sullivan's ship.

Shaking his head at the thought of a Vulcan with emotions, he had contacted the Vulcan diplomatic office at the Shir Kar colony. They had told him to turn him over to them once they had completed the patrol.

The intercom summoned his immediate attention, "Captain Liberté, Admiral Dawn Hancock of Starfleet Command is standing by."

"Thank you, Lieutenant T'Las," Liberté said in his French-Canadian accented English."

Moments later, Liberté exited the turbo lift.

Commander Bork, his Tellerite first officer, immediately vacated the captain's chair and resumed his place at the helm station.

"Put her on," Liberté said as he eased his 5'3" frame into his command chair.

Like Captain Jean Jacque Lucas of the Redoubtable at the Battle of Trafalgar, he was short in size but knew how to beat opponents twice his size. Jacque recalled. He hated being called Little Jack and despised the nickname Little Napoleon.

Moments later, a slim, tall, older woman appeared on the screen. She had her flowing dark hair in a ponytail and glasses. Hancock was a career outpost, star base officer, but unlike some of her profession, she was more understanding of the plight of starship crews than some other desk-bound prima donnas.

"Captain."

"Admiral."

Without pausing, Hancock began, "With Lexington overdue, I have ordered Commodore Fredrick Augenthaler of Star base 41 to dispatch the Lafayette under Captain Nathaniel Raines to replace her."

"Merde," Liberté muttered under his breath. Raines was an arrogant self-centered showoff; a prancing prima donna had used politics to gain command of Lafayette.

In his own opinion, Raines was a lightweight who should have stayed with his old command, the Baton Rouge class cruiser Tehran.

Lafayette was too good a ship for him. Jacque hated when undeserving political types like Raines stole commands from the more qualified, deserving officers.

"Admiral, will you be mounting a search for her?" Liberté asked Hancock.

"Starships Enterprise, Constitution, and Tori have already been dispatched to Lexington's last reported position to begin the search," Hancock said bluntly.

"I would like…"

Hancock cut him off, "Negative, Captain. Both you and Lafayette will continue with your present assignment. Be realistic, Jacques. With all the new Heavy cruiser construction going on. We never have enough Heavy cruisers to meet the demand."

"Not counting Miranda, Soyuz, Surya, and Coventry class ships mon admiral."

"They are only half a constitution, Captain. Lafayette should be arriving shortly, and you should be on your merry way. Starfleet command out."

Hancock's image faded from the screen, replaced with the view of K1.

"Captain, another ship has come out of warp," science officer Barry Blum said.

"On screen, Mr. Bork," Liberté said. Moments later, Excelsior's slightly newer sister ship appeared.

Both ships were products of the famed San Francisco Navy Yard which had constructed Twelve of the Bon homme Richards. The remainder came out of Tranquility and Utopia Planetia.

"All decks report ready for departure," T'Las said blandly.

"Course laid in and on the board," Bork said from helm.

"Captain."

"Yes, T'Las."

"A message from Captain Raines."

"Go ahead."

"Want to race?" Raines' voice came back over the speaker.

"Sacre Bleu," Liberté muttered under his breath. Raines was a fool. If only his old classmate Robert Wesley was here. At least, Bob Wesley wasn't some trumped-up prima donna. He was going to put an end to Raines' stupidity once and for all.

"Warp 8, mister Bork."

"Aye, Captain."

Excelsior jumped to warp leaving Lafayette behind. Seconds later, Lafayette also jumped to warp.

The race was on.

CHAPTER TWO

"Captain's log. Star date 2905. 8. Captain James T. Kirk recording. We have been ordered by Starfleet Command to search for the missing Lexington, commanded by Commodore Robert Wesley. Assisting in our search are Enterprise's sister ships, the Constitution commanded by my old friend and academy rival, Robert Nelson Hawke, and the Tori commanded by Akira Hirota, Constitution's former executive officer under Captain Fredrick Augenthaler when I served on Constitution back in 2257."

Kirk closed the tricorder and handed it to Janice Rand.

"Request assistance," sounded in Kirk's mind. Request assistance was Starfleet terminology for "we need help now" and was one step above the universal distress signal.

Enterprise had cut short her mission to space station Goddard in the Gamma Protus system. The destroyer Lynx had replaced her.

Constitution had come rushing out from the Versailles system. She had been involved in the prestigious Annual Federation Science Conference. Her famous passengers were now being picked up by the Saladin and her sister Xerxes to be transported back to their home worlds. Tori had left her convoy in the hands of the Paladin class destroyers Iwo Jima and Okinawa.

All three ships were in relative proximity to the X star systems and were immediately available.

"Spock?" Kirk said as he swiveled his command chair in Spock's direction.

Spock looked up from his hooded viewer. "Yes, Captain."

"Any sign of Lexington?" Kirk asked.

"Negative. According to the survey analysis done by Chandra's Monitor two years ago, there are supposed to be at least five systems that have class M planets. Constitution has about six to check out. Tori has five. So, the odds of Lexington showing up are quite probable," Spock explained.

Kirk left his command chair and walked up to Spock. "Figures. Bobby would wind up getting the most work. Robert must have raised hell when he served on this ship." Kirk just loved to take a dig at Bobby any time he got a chance. Bobby Hawke had been his number one rival at the academy.

Spock turned his chair around to face Kirk, raised an eyebrow, and said,

"On the contrary, Captain. Robert Hawke was quite a change when he came from Excalibur to temporarily replace Number One as Executive officer under Pike." Number one, otherwise known as Eunice Una Robbins and excluding her unpronounceable Illyrian name, had to return to Illyria for family matters.

"Thank you for the compliment, Spock. But I had just assumed command of the Oxford when Pike sent me a communiqué for the position." He, Phil Waterston, Andovar Drake, Samantha Reynolds, Charles Archer, and Robert Hawke had all been candidates for the temporary posting on the Enterprise in 2261 after two months serving as first officer on Enterprise. Hawke had returned to the Excalibur. Eunice Robbins resumed her place at Pike's side.

Spock reminded Kirk, "He made things interesting during his assignment on Enterprise. Hawke and Andovar Drake were your two competitors for the command of this ship."

Kirk could only nod in agreement. Andovar Drake had been given command of Yamato at the end of December 2264 after he had taken command of Enterprise. The difference was that Drake had been promoted to captain in 2263 after he and Hawke had been promoted to captain's rank in 2261 and 2262. Yamato had embarked on a five-year mission of exploration after Enterprise and Constitution had begun their Five-Year Missions of exploration in September 2264. Constitution was supposed to begin in February 2264 along with Lexington, but it had been delayed. To top it all off, Constitution was close on the heels of Enterprise in discoveries and first contacts.

"Approaching X778," said Lieutenant Vincent Anton "Mike" Desalle.

Kirk ordered, "Long-range sensors sweep, Mister Spock."

"Scanning Star System X778. No warp field emissions. No sign of any starship," Spock finished.

"Mister Sulu. Continue search pattern."

"Aye, Sir," Sulu replied as he expertly coordinated the helm controls with Lieutenant Desalle at navigation. Enterprise leaped into warp, heading for her next destination X779.

FOUR HOURS LATER:

Kirk was beginning to get frustrated. What the hell could have happened to Bob Wesley?

"Coming up on X779," Sulu said alerting him.

"Spock."

"Sensor sweeps negative. No warp fields, no contacts," Spock said blandly.

"Captain," Uhura interrupted. "Captain Hirota on visual."

"Put him on," Kirk said. He hadn't seen Hirota since Gary Mitchell's funeral.

Akira Hiruta's weathered image appeared on the main viewing screen. Hirota was no longer clean-shaven and his goatee had begun to grow grey. The sight of Constitution's former XO brought back a set of long-forgotten memories. He had served on the Soyuz class patrol cruiser Stalwart under Danilov briefly after taking a short two-month leave of absence after the loss of Garrovicks Farragut. Later that year, he transferred to Augenthaler Constitution.

Hirota had taken most of Augenthalers command staff with him when he received command of the Tori in 2265. Augenthaler had given Hirota his blessing to do it after spending nearly two years with Augenthaler on Star base 41. Hirota had been promoted to Captain after Mitchell's funeral and was immediately given command of the Tori, Commodore Edward Barstow's old ship. Eunice Robbins, Pike's old number one and Hirota classmate and contemporary was now captain of the Yorktown, another Constitution class ship.

Kirk surveyed Tori's bridge. It was like a high school reunion, most of Augenthalers old staff was present.

Lieutenant Commander Samuel Wooten was at communications and Tori's Chief of security, Commander Morris Standish, Gaynor's replacement when he left for the Potemkin, stood behind Hirota, Tori's Chief Engineer. Commander Bart Saunders sat at engineering conversing with Tori's CMO, Commander Christina Velasquez.

Standing out at tactical was Commander Jack Gaynor, Tori's first officer. Gaynor flashed a smile of recognition at him and Lieutenant Commander Brian Macpherson stood by at sciences. Macpherson was the only one who hadn't served on Constitution. McPherson had served on the Rivoli and the Radetzky prior to his posting on the Tori.

"Find anything, Jim," Hirota asked, his weathered features showing some concern between the creases on his face.

Kirk shook his head.

"If Wesley is out here, it is like finding a needle in a haystack and if I know Bobby, he's analyzing his sector tooth and nail. Never understood why he has an Andorian first officer and a Vulcan at Sciences. And to top all this off Jim, he has the youngest command staff out of all the Heavy cruisers in the fleet," Akira said showing his displeasure.

"To each his own Akira," Kirk pointed out.

"Captain," Uhura interrupted. "I have Captain Hawke. He says they have found the Lexington."

"Split screen," Kirk ordered.

Uhura switched over to split-screen. Robert Hawke's image appeared opposite Hirota. Hawke was smiling, his mixed-race Spanish, Sicilian, English, and Yemenite Jewish features were a distinct contrast to Hiruta's more weathered features. Robert had always been the butt of jokes at the academy due to his interracial heritage.

"Bull's eye, Jim, I found her," Hawke said in his Brooklyn accent.

Lieutenant Commander Thaylassa Shran, Constitution's Executive officer, sat at tactical which had been relocated next to sciences. Lieutenant Commander Francesca Martinez, Constitution's Chief of Security, stood at Hawke's left and to his right was his former yeoman Barbara Smith.

"How is Wesley holding up, Robert?" Kirk asked concerned.

"They are all safe, but the ship is stuck in a cloaked minefield. T'Pau believes that the entire system has been mined. Whoever did this did one hell of a job," Hawke explained. "Wesley beamed down nearly his entire crew to the planet and rigged the ship for station keeping." True to form, Robert was always blunt and to the point and he still had a knack for the dramatic.

"Cloaking should rule in the Romulans," Akira mentioned.

"We need to do further analysis, Akira. Our analysis is still inconclusive. My science officer is working on some leads at this moment," Hawke admitted. "We are sending both ships our coordinates."

"Coordinates received, Captain," Uhura said.

"Feed the coordinates into helm and navigation," Kirk ordered.

"Aye, Sir."

"ETA five hours," Sulu said.

"We should be there about the same time Bob, Jim," Akira said. "Tori out."

The Enterprise's screen shifted to a wide-angle view, revealing the rest of the Constitution's bridge crew.

Kirk could see Lieutenant T'Pau at sciences, Doctor David Russell, the ship's chief medical officer talking to Constitution's Chief Engineer Thomas Fredrick Andrews at the engineering station.

Lieutenant Barbara Desalle was at the helm and Lieutenant Morgan Bateson was at navigation. Manning Communications was Uhura's opposite number, Lieutenant Mariko Shimada.

Thomas Fredrick Andrews was the oldest at age 40 followed by David Law Russell who was age 38. By comparison, Scotty and Bones were in their forties. Kirk recalled.

"If anything, new turns up, Jim, we will keep you and Akira updated," Hawke said.

"Understood Enterprise out."

"See you soon, Constitution out," Hawke said as his image and Constitution's bridge faded from view, replaced by open space.

"Mister Desalle."

"Course plotted and lay in," Desalle said. He could see Sulu looking at him. His sister Barbara was the helmsman of the Constitution. Like Sulu, she was the top pilot at her Academy class at the time, but the best of the best served on the academy flight teams.

Constitution's captain, however, like Kirk were Academy legends. Both had been a year apart at the Academy and it was general knowledge to all about the famed Kirk-Hawke feud and competition that took place between both cadets at the time. Kirk and Hawke had tried to out-due the other. In the end, Desalle figured they both were equals.

"Engage Mister Sulu warp 5," Kirk ordered.

"Aye, Sir," Sulu manipulated the helm controls and Enterprise jumped into warp.

ALMOST FIVE HOURS LATER. RECREATION ROOM TWO:

Kirk walked into the recreation room two. Scotty, Bones, and Spock were already there. The ship was in the middle of a shift change from Alpha to Beta. Kirk had notified his senior staff that he wanted an impromptu meeting in one of the ship's recreation rooms.

Kirk grabbed his steak, mashed potatoes, and a sweetened iced tea and sat down next to Spock. Scotty and McCoy were already having a nice lively debate of their own.

"Hell, Scotty. I used to serve on that ship along with Jim here," McCoy said.

"And I had a hand in constructing Constitution as well as Enterprise Bones. She a damn fine bonny ship equal to our bonny lass. Thank the lord she a'nt no hard luck Lexington or Hood, if ya get my meaning, doctor."

McCoy was deep into eating his peach cobbler and looked at Scott. Scotty had a good point. McCoy took another bite.

"What's your opinion, Spock?" McCoy said looking at Spock. Spock raised his right eyebrow; the doctor was being annoying again.

"A ship is a ship, Doctor. Vulcans do not place feelings on inanimate objects like Humans. To the Vulcans who man the Intrepid, it's nothing more than Tritanium and computers in the eyes of her crew," Spock said dryly, that immediately provoked an emotional response from Scotty.

"She serves her purpose. She isn't just Tritanium and computer, Mister Spock," Scotty said upset by Spock's cold-hearted response.

Kirk cuts in, "Tell me Bones, Scotty, our rendezvous with Constitution and Tori have to do with this rumble?"

"Aye," Scotty admitted

"Yes, Jim," McCoy said, sheepishly. "I heard that Hirota called Bob's staff a gang of children."

"He did, Bones. But I think Hirota is just peeved that he didn't get Constitution." Kirk figured. "Many years ago, Hirota had told him that he had hoped to get Constitution once Augenthaler stepped down. But it didn't turn out that way in 2263. Wesley took over and in 2264. Hawke succeeded Wesley.

"Aye, But Hirota shouldn't complain, Captain. The Tori, she's a good ship with a fine reputation," Scotty added

Kirk agreed with Scott. "Robert earned Constitution by hard work and his accomplishments. His dad didn't just give him his old ship as a present." Kirk said referring to Admiral Joseph Edward Hawke, commander of The First Strike Force-Task Force Alpha at Star base Trafalgar. Fleet Captain George Samuel Joseph Kirk, his father, was presently serving as Admiral Hawke's chief of Staff aboard the Kirov.

And this wasn't the first time that his father worked with Robert's dad.

George Kirk served as first officer on the brand-new Constitution for two years in 2245-46. Fredrick Augenthaler, former first officer of the frigate Skipjack, replaced George Kirk in late 2246 after Tarsus Four. Augenthaler left in 2250, taking command of the Miranda class Rio De Janerio and had been replaced by Ann Toroyan who served as XO until 2254.

In 2250, Joe Hawke fought Starfleet to have George Kirk's rank of Commander restored. It had been repayment of Joe Hawke's friendship to George. The Valerie incident had taken place in the middle of 2249 on Star base 25. Because of that, his dad had been reduced to Master Chief and Commodore Anson had been court-martialed.

Shortly after he entered Starfleet Academy, his father's rank was restored to the rank of Commander, and he was placed at the bottom of the captain's promotion list. In October of that same year, he was assigned to the Hell Spawn outpost, near Harrata territory. Before he left for the Academy, both he and George had a major disagreement. It left a wound that wouldn't heal until 2257.

"Robert Hawke is a fine officer, Jim. T'Pau, Captain Satak's daughter, considers him to be the best captain she ever served under," Spock added. "And my experience with him when he replaced Number one for two months was a stimulating experience. Infinite diversity and infinite combination, that is the true wonder of the universe. We cannot, Doctor, expect every ship to be our Enterprise," Spock explained

Before McCoy could respond to Spock's revelation, the intercom whistled.

Kirk hit the button. "Kirk here."

"Lieutenant Uhura, Captain, I have Captain Hawke online."

Kirk took another drink of his iced tea. Bob must have discovered something important.

"Send it down here and transfer to viewer."

"Aye, Sir."

Robert Hawke's image appeared. Robert had a no-nonsense look on his face. He was standing next to the science station manned by Lieutenant T'Pau. In the distance, he could see Lieutenant Commander Shran standing near the communications station talking to their Female Korean Beta Shift Communication officer who was showing a new Edoan crewmember the ins and outs of the job at Communications.

"Running around like a chicken without a head, Jim." Hawke admitted as he turned to face his Vulcan Chief Science officer T'Pau. "Lieutenant."

"We have found evidence that that the mines are of Romulan design with phony Klingon algorithms. We also found traces of a metal Carbonite which only one race in the galaxy is known to possess," T'Pau explained.

Spock turned to Kirk, "Harrata."

"Affirmative, Spock," T'Pau said dryly.

Robert immediately replaced T' Pau on the screen. "I've already contacted Starfleet and the Tori. We have found a way to decloak and deactivate the mines around Lexington. But I need both you and

Akira in on this, Jim. Bob Wesley has confirmed that the ship he was pursuing was Harrata."

Kirk could feel the tension in the recreation room rise a notch. Silence pervaded the recreation room as the occupants were holding their breath.

The Harrata was a name that sent chills down everyone's back. With tensions rising between the Federation and the Klingon Empire, the last thing they needed was to have the Harrata come back now. The Harrata never fought a war of conquest, only a holy war, a war of attrition. Kirk had read the recent tactical analysis. A two-front war either with the Klingons or the Romulan combined with a conflict with the Imperium would lead to the destruction of the Federation.

"Put out the welcome mat, Bob."

"We will. Don't get lost," Hawke said smiling.

"We won't, Bob. Enterprise out." Kirk said as he smiled back at Hawke. Robert always knew how to make a joke out of everything. Even in the most serious of situations, Hawke came off as being not too serious.

"Later." Hawke's image faded.

McCoy looked at Jim. "Now, Jim, what was that all about?" McCoy complained.

Kirk turned to McCoy and explained.

"I might disagree with Bob sometimes but over the years, he has saved my neck on a few occasions," Kirk said recalling the infamous battle of the Savo Star system. "At the battle of the Savo star system. The Pegasus, Lydia Sutherland, Miranda, Hipparchus, Atlantis,

Atlantia, Burlingame, Pythagoras had faced off against three Klingon D7 battle cruisers and three K4 medium cruisers. Captain R.L Custer's lack of patience and sheer stupidity had cost us dearly," Kirk explained to McCoy.

"We lost the Atlantia, Atlantis, Hipparchus, Pythagoras, Pegasus, and Burlingame. Lydia Sutherland and Miranda took severe damage. Only the timely arrival of Enterprise, Constitution, Constellation, and Excalibur averted disaster," Kirk concluded.

The Federation council nearly declared war on the Klingon Empire because of the battle. But cooler heads had won out and the war was averted. He still had memories of that battle. Deaths of so many starships' crews still bothered him. Before the end of the month of December 2263, he lost the Lydia Sutherland at Ghihoge, Kirk remembered. He had then returned to command of the Sacagawea by March of 2264.

Out of the first four ships, he had commanded with the rank of Captain. The Hermes class scout Sacagawea was his main command from 2261 to 2264. Starfleet had considered sending him to the old Baton Rouge class Heavy cruisers Saladin and Hotspur. Lydia Sutherland and Oxford were Miranda class cruisers like Wesley's Beowulf.

He had taken temporary command of the Hotspur after turning Oxford over to Captain Marie Magon. Like Oxford, he was there for a month and turned over Hotspur to Captain Jose Perez.

Starfleet felt he was too junior to command a bigger ship. So, they gave him Sacagawea in May of 2261.

"Both you and Bob are like two bonny peas in a pod, Captain," Scotty said, smiling.

"Yes Scotty, we are alike, but we are also different," Kirk admitted.

Scotty turned to McCoy, "As I was saying, like Enterprise and Constitution, similar but different."

McCoy got up. "See you all later, got to tend the lunatic asylum," McCoy grumbled as he left the recreation room.

Kirk and Scotty were smiling along with some other Enterprise personnel. Spock turned to Kirk. "Lunatic asylum? I see no asylum," Spock said confounded by McCoy's response. His right eyebrow stood up. The whole recreation room broke out laughing.

CHAPTER THREE

"Captain's log. Star date 2905.9. In a few minutes, we will arrive at Star system X757. I am confident about Hawke, myself, and Hirota rescuing the Lexington. Three heads are always better than one."

Kirk closed the tricorder. So much for comedy, he thought. Janice Rand who stood next to the command chair smiled.

"Approaching system X757," Desalle said.

"On screen, take us out of warp, Mister Sulu."

"Aye, Sir."

Enterprise's engines started to decelerate. The deck plates rattled beneath Kirk's feet.

"Captain, sensors have picked up two starships, one at the system edge, and the other in parking orbit," Spock said as he looked up from his viewer.

"They are NCC 1700, Constitution and NCC 1709, Lexington," Desalle said blandly from navigation. His older sister Barbara who served on Constitution was probably watching their arrival.

"Another ship has just come out of warp," Spock added.

"Tori, NCC 1725," added Desalle.

"Get me Constitution and Tori Uhura."

"Captain Kirk, Constitution is signaling us," Uhura said.

"On screen," Kirk ordered.

Robert Hawke's image appeared again. Jim, Hirota, with his XO and Science officer are beaming over. "I need you and Spock to join us. My plan will require the resources of all three ships." Kirk always felt he should have a master plan, but Robert had beaten him to the first punch. But Bob, like Kelly Bogle, was the only other captain who would get the better of him at times. Kirk got up from his command chair.

"Spock, with me. Mister Scott, you have the con."

U.S.S CONSTITUTION-NCC 1700 CARGO BAY TWO:

Kirk and Spock entered Constitution's Cargo Bay Two. Hawke was there with T'Pau and Shran. In the distance, Kirk could see Hirota, Macpherson, and Gaynor from the Tori. He really didn't mind seeing Hirota again. But Gaynor was a different story. Gaynor had transferred to the Potemkin at the end of 57 and he had left Constitution in January of 58 to serve on Excalibur as second officer before transferring to the Thresher. He always regretted that he and Gaynor never really resolved their differences over the N'srri affair.

Gaynor spotted Kirk, turned away, and ignored him.

In the wide-open cargo bay were three deactivated mines in various stages of disassembly. Spock walked up and joined Macpherson as T'Pau showed them the components of the disassembled mines.

"Fascinating," Spock said as he ran his tricorder over the mine. Macpherson was nodding in agreement. Thaylassa Shran along with Gaynor walked over. Shran's father was Andor's ambassador to the Federation Council. McCoy had filled him in about Gaynor before they had beamed over.

"How the hell did you pull this off, Shran?" Gaynor said with Jim Kirk near. He wasn't in the mood to strike up a conversation with him. He still hadn't forgiven Kirk for the N'srri affair. So, Kirk was a captain like Hawke and he really didn't care. Hirota was a commander when both upstarts were lieutenants. Gaynor figured. In his own biased opinion, Hirota should have been given command of Constitution, not Hawke.

"With considerable dedication and zeal, Jack," Thaylassa Shran admitted. She had heard about Gaynor from a classmate who was serving on Potemkin at the time. Gaynor's performance hadn't really merited any spectacular reviews. Shran thought.

"And logic, Thaylassa," T'Pau admitted. T'Pau looked at Shran and Gaynor. Her right eyebrow went up. Between Shran's pompous Andorian iciness and Gaynor's phoniness, T'Pau wanted to give them both a neck pinch for good measure. She understood Andorians better than humans. Humans still puzzled her with their rampant illogical emotionalism.

Spock stood next to T'Pau. T'Pau's hairstyle was non-regulation loose. Her black hair flowed loosely down to her shoulders. And she vaguely reminded her of T'Pring.

"I have never seen such a hodgepodge of technology," Brian Macpherson admitted as he pointed his finger at the various components. "Romulan design, Klingon coding, Kzinti detonator, Tholian computers. These Harrata are pure genius."

"Or the greatest adapters in the known galaxy," Spock said. "Any race which uses the Challenge instead of standard declarations of war is to be feared," Spock said as he walked around the mechanism followed by the rest. "It is logical to assume that we are being tested even now. Freeing the Lexington will be such a test."

"It's daft, man," Macpherson replied in his lowland Scottish accent.

"Brian Spock is right. I have come to the same logical conclusion. The Harrata are known for their fierce standards when it comes to the Challenge. I have studied Harrata history extensively and it fits within their pattern. But we already have a solution," T'Pau explained.

At the other end of the cargo bay, the situation was different.

Kirk walked over to Hirota and Hawke. An impassioned argument was underway.

Kirk knew that he was going to have to successfully moderate this. The one thing he had learned over the years was that everyone had their own opinions and views. Even almighty starship captains had to bow to reason at some point.

"That's the craziest thing I ever heard, Robert," Hirota said flabbergasted. Why Starfleet had made Kirk and Hawke the two youngest captains in Starfleet history baffled him.

"Crazy or not, Akira, we have to try it," Hawke insisted. He respected Hirota, but Akira was beginning to get on his nerves. Hirota had been helmsman and second officer during his dad's nine-year command of the Constitution.

"Try what?" Kirk said as he coolly inserted himself into the dispute.

"The idea his science officer cooked up," Hirota said looking at Kirk and then Hawke. "The blasted idea would fry our navigational deflector dish if we tried it."

Not to be outdone, Hawke turned to Kirk and Hirota and explained to both captains his intentions.

"We will use our ship's deflector dishes to send out coded pulses. First to decloak the mines, then to deactivate them. Using our phasers, we will then blast them out of existence," Hawke said clearly pissed off, pointing to the three mines in the cargo bay. "Here is the proof, Akira."

Kirk looked at Hirota and Hawke.

"Akira Robert has a good point."

"This crazy idea is too risky, Jim," Hirota insisted.

"If you had all the facts, Akira, you wouldn't be criticizing my science officer. T'Pau next to Spock is the best science officer in the fleet. Despite her youth, she's absolutely brilliant."

Not to be outdone, Hirota replied, "MacPherson is no pushover, Robert, so let's not get all high and mighty."

"Enough of this stupidity. Let's get down to work. Robert, let me talk to Akira,"

Kirk suggested. He was getting tired of Hirota and Hawke massaging their egos over nonsense.

Hawke nodded in agreement. "No problem, Jim." Hawke stepped aside as Kirk and Hirota started to pace the cargo bay.

"I just don't like the idea, Jim. I don't question his judgment, much less his officers.

But sometimes, Bobby can play loose with the regulations."

Kirk knew that he did the same. "So do I, Akira. Before we make any rash judgments, I want to hear the full story from his science officer."

"Okay, as long as we can offer a counterproposal," Hirota suggested.

Kirk walked over to Hawke who was patiently waiting.

"Robert."

"Yes, Jim."

"Robert, are you willing to accept alternates or a combination of solutions?" Kirk suggested.

"I have no problem with that, Jim," Hawke admitted.

Kirk looked at Hirota.

"Then we are all in agreement," Kirk said

Hawke walked over to the intercom. "Yeoman Smith, please report to the main briefing room with Lieutenant T'Pau's data."

"Yes, Sir."

"Lieutenant Shimada."

"Yes, Captain."

"Get me Commodore Wesley. Have him tied into the briefing room as soon as we begin the meeting."

"Understood, bridge out."

Hawke turned to Kirk, Spock, and the rest of the group. "Folks, if you'd all follow me."

Kirk, Spock, followed Hawke and everyone else out of the cargo bay.

CONSTITUTION'S MAIN BRIEFING ROOM TWO:

Kirk and Spock followed Hawke and Hiruta's officers into the main Briefing room. All starships were equipped with two—one for the ship's officers only and the larger one when the officers of two starships had to hold a briefing.

The room was filled with portraits of ships named Constitution. The frigate, the famed USN Constitution of War of 1812 fame, began the display followed by the Civil War Ironclad New Ironsides. Kirk immediately recognized the DY 500 that followed the Naval warships.

After the DY and the SS Constitution came the United Nations Solar fleet/ UN Starfleet and the Earth Starfleet spaceships of the Cochrane, Horizon, and NX classes. NX/NCC 00 was the transition ship in the display. She was the last Earth Starfleet Constitution and the first Federation Starfleet ship to have the name Constitution.

She was replaced by the ill-fated Yorktown class Constitution destroyed by the Tarn. Finishing off the display was the famous

Bonaventure class ship Constitution. The final portrait in the display was the old Class J Heavy Cruiser Constitution decommissioned in 2240... the line of portraits spanned the entire room.

In addition to the ship's portraits were the portraits of Thomas Jefferson and James Madison.

A copy of the old United States and the Federation Constitution stood on the wall at the beginning of the room followed by the insignia flags. The briefing room hadn't changed one iota since he had served on this ship years ago. By comparison, both of Enterprise's briefing rooms were sparse and bare.

"Captain Kirk, Mister Spock."

Kirk turned to see Barbara Smith looking at them. She wore a red operation uniform, and her blond hairstyle hadn't changed since their encounter with the barrier back in early 2265.

"Yeoman Smith," Spock said. Smith had been Janice Rand's temporary replacement back in 2264.

"And how are you doing, Barbara?" Kirk asked.

"Very well, Captain. At least, Robert doesn't refer to me as Jones, Sir." Barbara let it sink in. She had wanted to nag Kirk about that ever since she left Enterprise. But she had long ago forgiven Kirk. "I'm very happy aboard this ship, Captain, wouldn't trade it even for a new tour on Enterprise."

"I see you met my yeoman Jim," Hawke said as he came over to Smith's side.

"My old yeoman Bob," Kirk reminded Hawke.

"Your loss is my gain, Jim," Robert chided Kirk.

Spock looked down to see a cat rubbing against his leg. The Siamese cat was purring.

Barbara Smith reached down and picked the cat up. Smith cuddled the Siamese cat. The cat purred contently in Smith's arms.

"I see you met the ship's mascot Max. Jim, Spock," Hawke said, "as in Maxine, not Maximilian."

"Isn't she adorable?" Smith said as she continued to cuddle Maxine.

"Okay, folks, let's get the show on the road," Hawke said as he gently took Maxine from Smith.

"Lieutenant Shimada, tie us into the Lexington," Shran ordered. Moments later, Bob Wesley's features appeared on the screen. Wesley looked tired. T' Pau sitting at the master computer station immediately tapped in the formula for the modifications.

"Fascinating," Spock said. He could only admire the brilliance of the formula.

"Efficient use of formula, T'Pau," Hirota agreed with Spock.

"Why not use star shells?" Macpherson said questioning T'Pau.

"All ships only have a limited number of them. Better to decloak them, then go through our entire inventory," Shran mentioned.

"The Lieutenant has a good point, Mac," Wesley's image said. "Wynn thinks your formula is brilliant."

"Thank you, Commodore," said T'Pau.

Kirk closely watched the conversation and said nothing. Not wanting to be left out, Kirk made his move. "Robert, to make this work, we have to go in line abreast."

Hawke nodded. "We are, but all the ships are going in at half impulse."

"That will take some time," Hirota admitted.

"I'd rather do this slow and steady. Don't want to wind up like Jonathan Archer almost a century ago," Hawke said referring to the first contact with the Romulans.

Robert's great-grandfather had been a contemporary of Archer. During his career, he had commanded two ships named Constitution. Alex had later lost his life at the Battle of the Midway Star System in 2167 when the First Strike Force had confronted a mysterious enemy that had come through the wormhole from the Gamma quadrant that year.

Hawke who was cuddling Maxine during the briefing posed one final question, "Do we have any opposition to this plan or any alternate suggestions?"

"You will have none from Spock and I," Kirk said.

Hirota looked at Gaynor and Macpherson. "None from us either, Bob, you've proven your point."

Hawke looked to Wesley's image. "The cavalry is on its way, Bob." Wesley smiled back relieved. Kirk noticed that a weight had been lifted off his shoulders.

"Understood. Good luck, Jimmy, Bobby, and Akira, Lexington out," Wesley said as the image faded.

Kirk and Spock got up. Barbara Smith came over and handed Spock a tape containing the copy of T'Pau's formula. "A pleasure to see you and Spock again," Smith said smiling.

"And you too, yeoman."

"This briefing is adjourned," Hawke said.

"Captain's log supplemental. After three hours of refit, we are all ready to implement science officer T'Pau's plan. It is risky but then our job has always been a challenge and risk. I am still surprised that Spock had never mentioned that he and T'Pau are friends. I had met T' Pau's father, Captain Satak, who had succeeded Fleet Captain Garth who had replaced Captain Spiak as captain of the Intrepid during the Four Years War. Satak had tried to lure me to the Intrepid after the disaster on the Farragut, but Augenthaler won out and I served on the Constitution. I'd hate to see what other surprises Spock would have for me and Bones over the next few years."

Kirk looked around his bridge. The tension was so thick; you needed a knife to cut through it Before leaving Constitution. He and Akira had agreed to let Bob Hawke and his crew lead the way.

"All decks report ready, Captain," Uhura said.

"Modifications tied in and are ready," Scotty said from his console. Scotty could only hope that Saunders on the Tori and Andrews on the Constitution were also ready. Kirk had been on the ship when Saunders had become a chief engineer after the Normandy incident. Saunders had succeeded Alexander. Saunders had been Constitution's fourth chief engineer after Alexander, Jankowski, and Esterhaus. Andrews at that time was serving as second engineer. Thomas Fredrick Andrews, Constitution's chief engineer, was a descendant of Andrews of the Titanic. That alone made him the butt of jokes in the Engineering corp.

On the other side of the coin, Thomas' father, Admiral Garnet Andrews, had supervised the construction of all Heavy cruiser class starships from the original Constitution class and the successor Bonhomme Richard, Trajan/ Explorer special configuration, Achenar, and the Tikopai class which were now under construction. Garnet also had a hand in the Constitution class design variations—the Coronado, Brahe/Sovereign triple Nacelle battle cruiser, and Voyager Galactic survey cruiser classes. Garnet served on the Advanced Starship Design Bureau and oversaw Heavy cruiser design and modifications.

Scotty's habit is to keep tabs on some of his fellow chief engineers and close friends. Projeff Ellis, Thomas Andrews, and Alec Macpherson were his three best friends in the fleet. They would go on pub crawl drinking binge if all three of their ships were at the Star base at that time and see who could out-drink one or the other.

Scotty looked at the monitors and checked his viewer. "Already, Captain."

"Captain, audio message from Constitution."

"On audio, Uhura."

Moments later, Hawke's voice came over the intercom.

"Constitution to Enterprise and Tori commence operations," came Hawke's voice.

"Mister Scott," said Kirk.

"Activating upgrades," Scotty added.

"Navigational deflector is running at specification," Sulu chimed in.

"Constitution and Tori have commenced phase one," Spock added.

"Activate deflector, Mister Sulu."

Sulu keyed in the deflector. The main viewing screen started to shimmer. Suddenly, mines started to decloak.

There were so many of them. Kirk thought. The mines took up the entire main screen.

"Begin Phase Two," Kirk ordered. Scotty keyed in the code.

"Mines deactivated," Spock said. "We are clear up to the outermost planet."

"Fire all phaser's, Mister Sulu, wide-sweeping pattern. Do not arc into Tori's or Constitution's line of fire."

"Aye, Sir."

Sulu quickly programmed the sequence in and fired the phasers. Enterprise joined her sisters, blasting the mines into oblivion. As the ships continued to clear the mines, at the opposite edge of the system, a spy satellite shimmered into existence and began to transmit.

CHAPTER FOUR

HARRATA STAR FORCE SPACE CONTROL CENTER: HARRATA FOUR, CITY OF HOGASH. STAR DATE 2905.12:

Vorrad Flotilar (Admiral of the Fleet) Fidel zha Dalomy, Commander in Chief of the Imperium Star force, watched with satisfaction as reports were starting to come back from the X757 system and Klingon Star base 10. The Federank were eliminating the minefield and the freighter Dogash had done her service in inciting the honorable Klingonaase. She had rammed the D6 battle cruiser Duras destroying her. In response, the honorable Klingonaase had already dispatched two battle cruisers.

Gom and the other twelve deities had already selected the Star force captains and their crews through the Von Tong Gar ritual. If they succeeded, they would join Gom in eternal bliss. If they failed, they and their crews would be damned to Lothar for all eternity.

A war with the Federank would serve the Harrata well. The testing and preparation of all non-Harrata races had to continue. The darkness was coming in the next century and they had to be prepared.

The only race they would never test were the rebel Harr of the Harrkonen Empire. Pong and the other twelve deities could burn in hell for all Gom cared. Gom had brought enlightenment to them after the pagan darkness of Pong. The War of Cleansing also known as the War of Expulsion had split them into two factions—Harrata and Harrkonen.

In his years of service, he had experienced quite a few confrontations with the Harrkonen Imperial Fleet. Compared to the Harrkonen, the reclusive Shellacki, known to the Federation as the Shelliack Corporate had not been much of a challenge. They had openly refused the challenge again. The Star force crushed their fleet in a surprise attack at the Jagva star system, effectively removing the Shelliack Corporate from the equation. Even now, the Shelliack were still rebuilding their fleet. At Jagva, a lone Federation Heavy cruiser, the Ticonderoga, witnessed the event. Ticonderoga's captain had been wise. They observed the attack and did not interfere.

The Gornaski aka Gorn however had honorably fought to the bitter end in the Tong, and they had fought to an honorable stalemate. By weakening the Gornaski, it had given the Romulanski, the Romulan Empire a chance to expand their borders. This forced the Romulanski to directly attack the Federation outposts with two warbirds.

Dalomy remembered.

"Success, Vorrad F," Chancellor Vardeck da Banari said triumphantly.

"Yes, noble Chancellor," Dalomy said to his chancellor in the traditional way. "As soon as the Federank arrives, we will begin testing the Federank and Klingonaase fleets."

It had been Harrata tradition since time immortal to skirmish with the enemy before the real slugging match begins. Once the Federank had failed the Tong, and maybe, if just maybe, the Klingonaase would finally lose, then the glorious war will begin and the Harrata will go to Gom and the other deities and live-in eternal bliss.

STARSHIP EXCALIBUR-NCC 1664, PATROLLING THE TERRITORIAL ZONE DIVIDING THE FEDERATION FROM HARRATA IMPERIUM SPACE ESTABLISHED BY THE TREATIES OF 2177 AND 2220. JANUARY 16, 2267:

"Captain's Log Star date 2906.9. Captain Anton Paul Harris recording, per treaty stipulations set down by the treaties between the Federation and the Harrata in 2177 and 2220. Two weeks earlier, Excalibur replaced the Merrimac, commanded by Igor Kranowsky patrolling the no-man's land between the Federation and the Imperium."

Excalibur. Secondary Hull. Bowling rink:

Harris stepped aside as he released the bowling ball. It rolled down the lane for a strike.

Harris had never been too fond of cards or tri-dimensional chess. Bowling and fencing had been more to his liking.

Out of the four executive officers that had served under him since he took command in 2255,

Zao Sheng had replaced Nolan who had been killed in a transporter accident in 2253. Sheng and his successor, Anthony Furillo, commander of Star base G1 had liked neither. Robert Nelson Hawke, captain of the Constitution, had enjoyed fencing. And Howard Ogden, his present number one, had loved to bowl.

Years ago, Jim Kirk had come over from Augenthaler Constitution as the second officer. He had originally considered Kirk as a replacement for Furillo but found Kirk too pushy for his tastes. So, he sent Kirk and Michael Walsh packing to other ships. Kirk had gone to the Tresher, Walsh to the Voyager, and settled on Bobby Hawke as Furrillo's replacement,

Harris hoped to have Robert replace him as captain of Excalibur in 2269, but fate had worked out differently. Hawke had Constitution now and Kirk had the Enterprise. And he had no regrets over what had happened since.

Harris did a spin as the ball toppled all the pins for a strike. "Yes! Beat that, Howard."

Howard Ogden looked up from the scorecard and tallied another strike.

Ogden was a South Carolinian from Charleston. Harris, a Floridian from Key West with the typical South Florida drawl, his hair starting to turning grey and about five feet five; Ogden was short, five feet four, built like a boxer, African American. They both were opposites not only in size but in personality. Harris was outgoing to his quiet demeanor. Terise Lo Brutto, Excalibur's Chief science officer, had referred to them as Abbott and Costello. Lieutenant Sonak, her assistant, had readily agreed unfortunately for Excalibur. Lieutenant Sonak was leaving Excalibur for the Krieger and an emergency promotion.

Ogden sighed. Captain Sanjay's Krieger had been short of personnel thanks to a plague that had devastated Star Station 007. Half of Krieger's crew along with Sanjay had died because of it.

Excalibur had been ordered to send thirty of his crew to rendezvous with Porters Kent. Along with Zarlos McRaven, they had cordoned off the sector until the quarantine was to be lifted. Three valuable Heavy cruisers were now tied down. Starfleet Intelligence believed that the Orion Syndicate was behind this.

"Your turn, Howie," Harris said as he walked over and sat down next to Ogden.

Ogden got up and picked his ball up. Expertly, he analyzed the situation. He needed one strike to match Anton and by god, he was going to get it.

Some Excalibur's crew had stopped their bowling to watch the competition.

The bowling competition was a ritual between them, Ogden recalled. He never understood why Hawke and Shran of the Constitution sparred with weapons and fenced. Bowling was so much more civilized.

Ogden released his bowling ball. The ball hit the pins squarely, plowing them over for a strike. "Yee ha," Ogden said jubilantly as he and Harris exchanged high fives.

Their celebration was interrupted when a science division ensign came running over. "Captain Harris, Commander Ogden, Lieutenant Commander Lo Brutto is calling from the bridge."

"Thank you, ensign," Harris said courteously as he and Ogden went to the intercom. "Harris here."

"Captain Jacques La Liberté send his regards. Two Klingon battle cruisers, the Suvwl and the Vorcha have passed the Delta Four construction site and are high-tailing it for Harrata space." Terise Lo Brutto, Excalibur's Chief Science officer, said.

"Thank you, Jacques Merci. Borchas, we will take it from here."

"Yes, Captain."

"Beat to quarters," Harris said. He liked that so much better than battle stations.

Excalibur's crew jumped to quarters...

Moments later, Harris and Ogden arrived on Excalibur's bridge.

"Status," Harris said as he sat in the captain's chair, while Ogden resumed his place at the helm.

"Both Klingon battle cruisers are heading toward Domar Amid 5 and Bathazar 5," Lo Brutto said from the science station.

"Mister Ogden, intercept course, then turn us on a parallel course before the Klingons enter Harrata space."

"Yes, Captain," Ogden said as he looked up from helm.

"Don't forget the treaty, Captain; all Harrata and Klingon ships have a free rein in the corridor, between Harrata and Klingon space," Lo Brutto reminded Harris.

Harris like many of his fellow Starfleet personnel hated the Corridor. It was as bad as the Borderlands, the old Disputed zone, the Phalanx, the Triangle sector, and finally, the Barrier space for lawlessness and mayhem. This was still Federation space, but the Harrata had nullified the advantage by signing a trade pact with the Klingon Empire that predated the Federation's founding.

To regain the advantage, Starfleet had recently begun construction of the new Delta series outposts.

"Intercept and then parallel, Mister Ogden," Harris ordered.

Ogden nodded and expertly manipulated Excalibur's helm controls. Excalibur headed toward the Klingon Battlecruisers and settled in on a parallel course.

IKS SUVWL- IKC 4567 AND IKS VORCHA-IKC 8888:

"We have a new contact, milord," Mara said as she looked up from the science station scanner.

"Who?" Kang asked.

"Another Constitudonu, the Excalaky," Mara said referring to Constitution's and Excalibur's Klingon nicknames.

That old rascal Harris was watching him now instead of the little Targ LaLiberté.

Harris and LaLiberté were both fine commanders. But they represented the older breed of Starfleet captain. It was more of a challenge to take on Kirk, Hawke, Drake, or Reynolds. They were younger and more innovative in strategy and tactics. Kang thought.

"They have taken a parallel course and are matching speed with us," Mara added.

"They are armed," Kang asked.

"Yes, their shields up and weapons are charged. But they do not attack," Konar, Kang's new executive officer said from the tactical station.

"They merely wish to observe us. The Federation had one of its ships already damaged by the Harrata. They will be sending their best," Kang pointed out.

The best were Kirk and Hawke, period. He had been looking to see Kirk again and seeing Hawke after all these years would be interesting.

"ETA to Bathazar 5," Kang asked the Beck who was the ship's helm officer.

"Six minutes," the Beck replied.

Within six minutes, Captain Harris had to make a choice. Kang thought. Either violate the Federation-Harrata Territorial zone or withdraw.

"Milord, Six Harrata ships directly ahead. Two Hogar Class, Type 8," Mara announced.

Meanwhile, on the Excalibur.

"Four Hogar Class, Type 7s, Captain Harris," LoBrutto said as she turned to face Harris from the science station.

"The Challenge Force, Captain," Ogden said blandly.

"Captain, I have a message coming in from Bathazar 5."

"On screen, Commander Arbuthnot."

"Yes, Sir," Martha Arbuthnot, Excalibur's Chief Communication officer, said.

Moments later, Excalibur's main screen, a Harrata female with the class skin color of the Star force blue, appeared. She was wearing the feminine version of the traditional gold uniform with the blue sash, unlike the men whose hair was worn in the Mohawk cut. Most Harrata women wore their hair in a half circle with a bald top. Harris picked out her rank, a Commandant (Commodore). And a young one at that, the Commandant was alluring in an exotic way Harris thought.

Margret, his wife, was back on Earth after serving with the famed Doctors without Borders in the New Berlin crisis. Their son, Ensign Daniel Harris, was serving on the Constitution. His younger sister Ruth was the commander of Outpost 35 at the edge of the Romulan Neutral zone. Like all Starfleet families, his family was everywhere at once. The needs of the service. Harris mused.

"Federank cruiser Excalibur, I am Commandant Shari Xa Trisky of Bathazar 5. You are within violation of treaty zone, Captain," Trisky curtly warned.

"This is Captain Harris of the Federation starship Excalibur; we were just monitoring the movements of the Klingon battle cruisers through our space Commandant. Per treaty stipulations, we will not violate Harrata space."

Harris turned to Ogden, "Reverse course, Mister Ogden."

"Aye, Sir."

"You have complied Ober Commander Harris. Bathazar 5 out," Trisky said as she signed off. The image of the Commandant was replaced by the Klingon Battlecruisers and the Imperium's squadron.

Excalibur turned away from the Klingon battle cruisers as the Harrata flotilla closed on them.

"Commander Arbuthnot, get me Starfleet command."

"Aye, Sir."

Excalibur swung away from Bathazar 5 and the Klingon battle cruisers.

"Reverse view."

Ogden switched over.

"Magnify."

The Klingon Battlecruisers were flanked in an inverted V formation and escorted into Harrata space. Excalibur sped off through the void.

CHAPTER FIVE

Starfleet Command Headquarters, Central Briefing Room. Sublevel Delta. Star date 2906.10:

Admiral Herbert Solow, Ensign Sarah Dahbany, his aide de camp, and Lieutenant Patrick West entered the main briefing room at Starfleet Headquarters. The insignia of Starfleet dominated the wall. Behind the podium were a screen and the flags of the Federation, Starfleet, and the military. On the wall to the left was a memorial of insignias of Earth and Federation Starfleet starships lost or missing in action.

"The Starfleet Liaison to the President," Dahbany said as the Admirals present stood up.

Solow walked up to the podium. Starfleet Commander in Chief Comsol and Starfleet Commander Buchinsky were on inspection tours along the Federation-Klingon border. Solow was now in charge of the show. Liaison was third in command after C in C and Commander.

Surveying the crowd of officers present, Solow began, "Ladies and Gentlemen, we have a major problem. The Federation and Starfleet are in no position to withstand a two-front conflict." He heard murmurs and gasps from all the admirals present. Only Hawke, Hancock, Hahn, Magione, and Noguchi sat in silence.

"Lieutenant West." West replaced Admiral Solow and keyed in the screen.

"Starfleet could survive separate conflicts with the Harrata Imperium and the Klingon Empire. Losses in both conflicts would strain our resources, but if we are forced into the typical Harrata war of attrition and should the Klingon Empire decide to declare war, this would be the result." West switched the screen over; another chart appeared. "We would most likely lose the Starfleet and the Federation," West explained grimly.

Vice Admiral Enrico Espana, chief of star base operations, said, "These figures are correct."

"Yes, Sir, based on my analysis of the situation and fleet status report provided by Admiral Ester De Lancey," West admitted.

"It is imperative that we contain the Harrata," Patrick Fitzgerald warned.

"Easier said than done," Hahn said grimly. "The Harrata are fanatics. They are as dangerous as the Klingons or the Romulans. All their wars are religious. Look what they did to the Shelliack six years ago for not accepting the challenge."

"The Harrata made fools of us in 2177 and 2220," Noguchi said remembering the history between the Federation and the Imperium.

Solow grimly agreed with Noguchi. If they refused the challenge, the Harrata would immediately attack.

"Dawn, which fleets are available along the Klingon-Federation-Harrata zone?" Solow asked.

"The ninth fleet under Admiral Richard Pierre Robau based at Star base 41, Commodore Augenthaler command. The First Strike Force-Task Force Alpha based at Star base Trafalgar, Commodore Gore's command under Admiral Joseph Edward Hawke. And finally, The Fourth Reserve Fleet based at the Starfleet Corp of Engineers at Star base Alpha. Commodore Koenig's command under the command of captain brevet Rear Admiral Lance Cartwright in the Ark Royal."

Admiral Dina Hawke, Chief of Starfleet Intelligence, sat in silence at the mention of her former husband's command, the First Strike Force-Task Force Alpha.

James Komack, one of the two Komack twins, cut in, "Except for Ark Royal, that fleet is composed of antiques, Baton Rouges, Ranger/ Declaration, Icarus, Einstein, Mann, and Class J starships of the Gettysburg and Canada classes and a few deathtraps of the Shepard and Nimitz classes," James Byron Komack grimly pointed out.

"And finally, Starfleet Tactical force Caesar composed of four destroyers, the Pompeii, Hathor, Ares, and Jenghiz, under the command of Vice-Admiral Vaughn Rittenhouse, attached to his squadron are units XY 75847, composed of four medium cruisers under the command of Captain Samantha Reynolds in the Soyuz and unit XY 75888 of four Heavy cruisers under the command of Commodore Harold Randolph Morrow aboard the Ari," Hancock finished.

"So, Dawn, who are the unlucky two we are going to have to send into the lion's den?"

Admiral Westervelit Franklin Komack asked.

"Here are my choices," Hancock said as she engaged the viewers. On the screen appeared Hancock's ten choices.

CO	SHIP	CLASS
Konstantin	Bismarck	2249
Anderoni	Challenger	2250
Silver	Defiance	2251
Bogle	Farragut	2252
Dhruva	El Dorado	2252
Khatami	Endeavor	2252
Hawke	Constitution	2253
Archer	Asimov	2253
Kirk	Enterprise	2254
Drake	Yamato	2254

"They are all children," Rear Admiral Tromp of Starfleet Security said surprised by the choices presented.

"And our best and brightest," Vice Admiral Alexander Marcus, Commander of the Starfleet Border Patrol added.

Herbert Solow cut in, "In 2177 and 2220, we sent in Captains Margolis, Waterston, Rayburn, and Takashi, all fifty-year old and look what happened. We had two bloody wars with the Harrata. We need to win the Tong. Only the Klingon Empire has never faced them in a total war. They have been smart enough to avoid it for a thousand years. And we sure as hell do not want to wind up like the Naussicans in perpetual skirmish mode."

Magione cut in, "They fly through our space with total freedom. Trade with us and when their crazy gods get angry, they attack."

"Ellen has a good point. Look at the corridor. That is the only part of Federation space where the Klingons could fly through our territory

on their way to Harrataland. Admiral Peter Holiday of Transport/
Logistics command said disdainfully. He was already ticked off that
four of his valuable transport tugs were damaged in a skirmish with
the Star force after the incident at Domar Amid one."

"That treaty was made long before the formation of the Federation,
Pete," Sharon said correcting Holiday.

Solow rapped his fist on the desk. "Let's cut the damn stupidity out
and get down to the important business at hand, who are the unlucky
two we have to send into the lion's den?"

"I would scratch Eric Ven Dhruva and Atish Khatami out," James
Komack said. "Both captains are assigned to critical sectors and are
unavailable"

"Endeavor is attached to Star base Vanguard in the Taurus Reach. El
Dorado is attached to Star Base Victory in the old, disputed zone,"
Hancock added

"What about Drake, Archer, and Konstantin?" Solow asked.

"Charles Archer just completed a mission to Xindi space and is on his
way to Star base Alpha to rendezvous with Kongo. Andovar Drakes
Yamato has just finished a patrol through Kzinti territory, and they
are also traveling to Star base Alpha. Petr Pavlovich Konstantin's
Bismarck has just finished a resupply mission to the Weyland
outpost line. Bismarck is now patrolling the Romulan neutral zone,"
Hancock said.

"Drake is too headstrong. Archer is like his grandfather Jonathan
Archer, too emotional at times, and Konstantin is one of those by the
book commanders," James B. Komack added.

"What about Anderoni, Silver, and Bogle?" Solow asked curiously.

"Giuseppe Anderoni Challenger and Nick Silvers Defiance are presently attached to unit XY-75888 along with Ari, Saratoga. Kelly Bogles Farragut is presently conducting an Energy barrier mapping survey," Hancock admitted.

And then there were two. Solow thought. "What about Kirk and Hawke?"

"At last report Constitution, Enterprise and Tori were searching for the Lexington, near Harrata space," Hancock mentioned.

"Now wait a minute, Herb, you want to put the safety of the Federation in the hands of those two rule-bending pains in a royal neck?" Tromp grumbled.

Dina Hawke had been sitting quietly. She glared at Tromp and angrily slapped her hand on the table startling Tromp. "My son and Kirk are not pain in a royal neck. Robert earned his command on his own merits, just like Jim Kirk did."

Tromp immediately apologized, "Sorry, Dina."

"Apology accepted."

Solow looked at Dina. "Dina, you have no problem with our choices."

"No, Robert will do his duty, Herbert."

"Dawn, you left out one captain, what about Michel Garson, class of 2250, captain of the Wasp?" Westvelit Franklin Komack added.

"Garson is too much of a prima donna Wes," Dawn said bluntly.

"Kirk and Hawke are our two best choices," Solow admitted.

"Kirk's exploits at the Romulan neutral zone and with the First Federation," Tromp said as he looked at Dina Hawke. He didn't want Dina slicing him to pieces again.

"And don't forget, Hawke's encounters with the mysterious Ferengi, the Children of Tama and the Pakleds," Hancock reminded the group.

"They both seem to attract trouble wherever they go," Fitzgerald said annoyed, cutting in and shifting in his seat. "I always dread the day I get a call from Enterprise or Constitution," Fitzgerald continued. "Because no matter what I say to both, they will disobey me no matter what."

Dina Hawke looked at Fitzgerald and smiled, "You didn't have to raise Robert. He was always running off, always disobeying me and Joe. That is why you have so many problems with him and Kirk Patrick."

"Sour grapes, Fitz," Admiral Ellen Mangione said agreeing with Hawke. "Look at it this way." Ellen got up to speak to all her fellow admirals. "Sure, Jim Kirk and Robert Hawke both can be a handful at times. But they are the best we got." Mangione paused and let it sink in. "Constitution and Enterprise are the two finest ships in the Starfleet, and they have the best crews. I will stake my life and my reputation that Robert Hawke and Jim Kirk will beat the Harrata at their own game and we will not have that doomsday scenario which Lieutenant West so graciously provided." Mangione pointed at West. Mangione looked at the other admirals who had quieted down. Dina Hawke was smiling. They both had scored a victory.

Solow got up and looked at the admirals assembled. "Ellen has a good point, folks, and I agree with her one hundred percent." Solow said looking at Mangione, "No matter what Kirk's or Hawke's faults, those two are the most qualified. Admiral Hancock."

Dawn Hancock got up.

"Since this is your sector of space, I want you to contact Enterprise, Constitution, and notify them of our choice."

"Yes, Sir."

"Since Kirk is one-year senior to Hawke, Kirk will be in overall command. Do as you see fit with the Tori and Lexington if the search has been concluded."

"Yes, Sir."

"This meeting is finally adjourned," Solow said with relief. Tomorrow, he had a bigger one, meeting with the Federation president and the council.

CHAPTER SIX

Constitution, Enterprise, Lexington, and Tori orbiting X757 Four-Star date 2906.13:

"Captain's log supplemental. Captain James Kirk recording. I am beaming over to Tori to join my fellow captains in a brief meeting aboard that ship. Hirota has notified both Hawke and I are to join Wesley and Hirota. Something is up. Something big is going to happen."

Jim Kirk stepped off the transporter pad. Commander Marvin Winters, another old Constitution hand, greeted him. "What's up, Jimmy?" Marvin asked. "Long time no see."

"Long time, too, Marv. Have you seen Hawke?"

"Arrived a few minutes before you. He was asking if you had beamed aboard. I told him no. Hawke immediately departed for the briefing room to meet Wesley and Hirota."

"Thanks for the information, Marv."

"No problem, Jim."

Kirk left the transporter room and made his way through Tori corridors. Crewmembers and officers were walking through the ship going about their business.

They all wore the Bulls head insignia of the Tori. He still wanted to get a straight answer from Hawke about Makus Three. Enterprise had made the rendezvous on time after the mess at Muraski 312. But Constitution had been a day late. Ferris had lost his temper and took it out on both captains in Enterprise's briefing room before Constitution had left at high warp speed for New Paris. Robert owed him an answer of why he was late. Thanks to Constitution's lateness, Enterprise had been late for her next mission.

Kirk stepped out of the lift and quickly arrived at the briefing room. Tori's briefing room had deeper colors and was newer than Enterprise or Constitution. The room had a larger viewing screen and triad view pod. Portraits of Tori's four predecessors dominated the room. But compared to Constitution, there were far less.

Wesley, Hirota, and Hawke were sitting at the briefing room table talking. Kirk walked over and took his seat next to Hawke. Hirota and Wesley sat opposite them.

Before Kirk could speak to Hawke, Wooten's image appeared on the triad viewer.

"Captain Hirota, Admiral Dawn Hancock is online."

"Pipe it down here, Commander."

"Yes, Sir."

Moments later, Dawn Hancock's image appeared. She was tall and lean with black hair. Hancock was in her early fifties.

"Captains Kirk, Hawke, Hirota, Commodore Wesley," Dawn said in her soft voice.

Kirk could feel a knot tighten in his stomach. Something big was coming. He knew of Hancock's reputation—a reliable administrator occasionally posted to Star base Alpha. She had served on a starship during her academy days, but instead, became a career base officer. As the commander of the Weyland One outpost in 2252, she had successfully beaten off a large Kzinti attack force. The arrival of the starships Tori and Defiance had sent the Kzinti high tailing it for home.

Hancock had later commanded Star bases 22, 25, 27, and Trafalgar before her promotion to the Admiralty. Harry Morrow called her reliable as hell and tough as nails. Never underestimate her or she would tear you to pieces.

"The Harrata are on the warpath again. The Federation has already mobilized the 9th fleet, First Strike Force-Task Force Alpha, Starfleet Tactical force Caesar, and the Fourth Reserve fleet to counter the Harrata's Star force. I have also received the following reports from Starfleet intelligence," Hancock continued.

"A few days ago, a Neparah class attack wing from Battle Group Echo attacked a flotilla composed of Ptolemy's, Huron's, Antares, and old Class X, Y, Z class freighters as they were leaving Domar Amid One. The quick response of unit XY 75847 under the command of Captain Samantha Reynolds sent them scurrying back to Bathazar One. Thanks to the work of the starships Excalibur and Excelsior, the Klingon Empire has already sent two challenge ships into the Imperium. Once you depart the system, we are sending three Bird class minesweepers, Pigeon, Stork, and Seagull to finish sweeping the system," Hancock finished.

Kirk took all this information to heart. Unit XY75847 was composed of familiar ships that he had encountered during his career. Captain Samantha Reynolds commanded the Soyuz. Anton was under the command of Captain Michael Walsh. Robert's previous command, the Miranda, was now under the command of Captain John Blackjack Harriman who had replaced him in February 2264. The Oxford was under the command of Captain Carmen Ikeya. She had taken command of Oxford after he and Hawke had returned from a mission into the Taurus reach. She had been extensively rebuilt in 2263-64. Walsh and Harriman were graduates of his academy class and Reynolds and Ikeya came from Robert's academy class.

"Commodore Wesley," Admiral Hancock said in a voice commanding their undivided attention.

"Yes, Admiral."

"Captain Hawke will transfer all of the Harrata mines and data to your ship, Captain Hirota."

"Yes, Admiral."

"You will tow Lexington back to Star base 11, then you will proceed to Star base Alpha and rendezvous with the Asimov, Yamato, and Kongo."

"Yes, Sir," Hirota responded blandly.

Kirk looked at Robert Wesley, Akira Hirota, and Robert Hawke. He braced himself. It only left him and Hawke. The big one was coming.

Dawn Hancock's image paused for a moment. From Starfleet headquarters, she looked at the three captains and the lone commodore. She had to give two of them the bad news.

"Captains Kirk and Hawke, I bring both of you bad tidings. Both of you have been selected to face the Harrata in the Challenge."

Kirk could see Wesley and Hirota looking at them surprised and shocked by the bad news.

"You will be our representatives in this great quest," Hancock continued. "I don't know if I should congratulate you both or send my condolences. You two are the Federation's up and coming, Captains, the best of your generation of captains. James Kirk, you were selected because of your enviable service record. Robert Hawke, we also selected you because of your excellent service record and your ability to work with your betters, Captain Kirk."

Kirk acknowledged Admiral Hancock, "Yes, Admiral."

"You will be in overall command of the mission. Robert's family has prior experience with the Harr. So, Hawke will be there as support, even though he is senior to you by one year."

Kirk nodded.

"Captain Hawke."

"Yes, Sir."

"I want no trouble from you. Remember, Captain. You were promoted to captain in April 2262, on your birthday. We needed someone to command Constitution and you were the most qualified. Commodore Matthew Decker, your mentor and Commodore Robert Wesley felt you were the most qualified after you cleaned up that mess at Ghihoge. So instead of giving you the Lexington, we gave the Lexington to Commodore Wesley here who had to replace Captain Mark Rousseau who had retired and joined the diplomatic Corp at Ambassador Sarek's request in February of 2264."

So that was the whole story, Kirk thought.

"Then if there is nothing more to be said, Starfleet Command out." Hancock's image faded.

Kirk, Hawke, Wesley, and Hirota just looked at each other in silence contemplating their fates. After one tense minute, Robert Wesley finally broke the silence. Wesley got up and turned to Kirk and Hawke. "If history is any guide, Jim, we don't stand a chance in hell," Wesley admitted.

"Bob, I don't think that Robert and I will suffer like our predecessor's fates," Kirk said guarded.

"Starfleet just handed both of you a death sentence," Hirota said angrily. Hirota looked at Hawke. "Well, Bobby, what you have to say for it?"

"Nothing, Akira, orders are orders. I believe Jim and I have the youth factor going for us.

Plus, I relish the challenge," Hawke said trying to be funny.

Hirota unimpressed by Hawke's attempt at humor turned to face Kirk, "And what do you have to say about this, Jim?"

"What can I say, Akira, I'm honored. How many people in their lifetime face the infamous Challenge?" Kirk was angry, but he did not show it. He never thought he would see the day that Starfleet would offer him and Hawke as sacrificial lambs. But both were the best. And Starfleet needed the best at this time. The fate of his ship, his crew, and the fate of the Federation were hanging on his and Robert's backs now. If history was any judge, humans, as members of the Federation, had done poorly. It was a disgrace they were in game parlance 0-2.

Six starships hadn't come back. That included the two scout ships sent over with the Federation News Service. There had to be a way to beat this challenge. If the Klingons could beat the challenge, then so could the Federation.

Kirk remembered that years ago in 2256, the Farragut had transported Federation Ambassador Hardin to Bathazar 12 for annual talks with the Harrata Imperium. The Harrata in their arrogance had mocked them for not beating them in the Challenge.

That same year, Robert Hawke who was serving aboard Matt Decker's Constellation had led a commando raid to Hell Spawn to rescue the survivors of the Ranger class cruiser Revere and the Hell Spawn outpost. Lo and behold, they found his father to be alive. The evil Children of Lothar had been responsible for his and his family's pain through the years. As fate would have it, both he and Robert were now coming full circle. It's fate accomplice.

Kirk got up. "I'm not going to mull over this, it would be a waste of time."

"Se la vie, Jim," Hawke agreed as he exited his chair.

Wesley and Hirota walked over to Kirk and Hawke. Wesley shook Jim's and Robert's hands. "May the great bird of the Galaxy protect you both."

Hirota came up and hugged them both. "We are rooting for both of you. Give the Harrata hell."

Kirk and Hawke left the briefing room.

Wesley turned to Hirota, "We haven't seen the last of them. They will be back."

"Amen to that," Hirota said.

Enterprise with Constitution, Lexington with Tori:

"All decks report ready," Uhura said.

"Course laid in for the Harrata Imperium," Lieutenant Farrell said.

"Our ETA is 30 hours," Sulu said.

"Constitution signals ready as always," Uhura added. She could only wonder how Mariko Shimada put up with Bobby Hawke's antics.

Sitting in his command chair, Kirk watched as Tori towing Lexington jumped to warp exiting the star system.

"Message from Commodore Wesley aboard the Lexington to Captains Kirk and Hawke, give them hell," Uhura added.

Kirk could only agree.

Spock looked at Kirk. "Give them hell?"

"An old earth term, Spock," McCoy pointed out. "Give them hell means kick them in their butt, beat the hell out of them."

"I get the point, doctor."

"Let's get the show on the road. Mister Sulu warps 5," Kirk laughed.

Sulu nodded and manipulated the helm controls. Enterprise and Constitution jumped to warp.

Next Stop, the Harrata Imperium.

PART TWO

POMP AND CIRCUMSTANCE

"Hurts worse than the uniform," McCoy to Spock. Journey to Babel.
Star date 3842.3.

CHAPTER SEVEN

OFFICE OF THE FEDERATION PRESIDENT. PALAIS DE LA CONCORDE. PARIS, FRANCE. EARTH. STAR DATE 2907.1. JANUARY 17, 2267.

"Shran, my old friend," Sarek said as both he and Shran, representatives of their own governments, walked down the corridor to the Federation's presidents' office. "We may differ in our opinions occasionally. But we do agree most of the time."

Shran nodded. "Indeed, we do old friend, more than rather than less." Shran nodded in agreement. They had come a long way since the early 23rd century.

Both ambassadors entered the President's office. Federation President Westcott got up and followed by his two aides, one an Andorian, the other Vulcan came over to meet them.

"I believe you both know my aides."

Shran nodded and Sarek said, "Yes, Mister President."

Both Sarek and Shran took their seats across the desk from the Federation President. Westcott checked his chronometer. Starfleet and the military were running late today.

"Both of you are already aware of Starfleet's choices to face the Harrata in the Tong," Westcott said.

"Spock and T'Pau will do their duty," Sarek said. He had already spoken to T'Pau's parents Captain Satak and Commander T'Lena on the Intrepid. Both had taken the news quite well. The only thing that worried T'Lena was if the Constitution or Enterprise were destroyed. They could not recover their Katras. Prior to the founding of the Federation, the Vulcan Confederacy had engaged the Harrata Imperium in quite a few Challenges over the years and had come up short. Several Vulcan ships never returned, and the crews Katras were lost forever.

"My daughter Thaylassa will do hers, Mister President. And if it comes to the worst-case scenario, she will defend her ship, the Federation's honor in true Andorian tradition," Shran said.

"Once we finish the meeting with Starfleet and the Federation Military. I have invited Klingon Ambassador Korvat and Harrata Ambassador Shari ben Gazari Fahiri to a meeting between both of us," Westcott said.

"To gauge their positions, I presume," Shran said cautiously. Sarek noticed Shran's antenna twitching. Sarek's right eyebrow went up. After all these years, he could gauge Shran's moods by his body language. He fully agreed with Shran on this matter.

"It is logical, Mister President," Sarek agreed. He looked at Shran. "Torel, we need to ascertain their positions. You saw Starfleet's doomsday scenario. If we are involved in a war with the Harrata and war breaks out with the Klingon Empire, it will spell the end of the Federation," Sarek said

"Wisely," said Sarek. "Let's hope we do not have a repeat of 2177 or 2220," Shran said carefully. The last thing he wanted was another war with the Harrata.

Shran recalled that prior to the Founding of the Federation, Andor and Vulcan had been paired in the Tong. It was typical Harrata tradition, pair two powers who hated each other in mortal combat. The Vulcans always found the Tong illogical barbarism, while the Andorians look at it as a challenge to prove their mettle. But unlike the unbeatable Klingon Empire, both Vulcan and Andor had lost a few times. And the result was the typically brief, savage Harrata wars.

Back in the 20th century, Vulcan and Andor had to forgo their differences when they had found out the Harrata's desire to conquer Earth. It had been the only time that the Andorian Empire and the Vulcan Confederacy had dropped their disagreements and joined forces. The Harrata unlike their cousins the Harrkonen did not like to conquer territory. But in the past, they made exceptions. They, the Harrata, were a touchy people, easily insulted, hard to reason with. Shran recalled.

Moments later, Starfleet and the Federation Military arrived.

"Sorry we're late, Mister President," Solow said. He followed by Lieutenant West who carried a portable screen and stand. Admiral De Lancey General Morgan Scott and Colonel Pavel Stravinsky arrived last.

"I believe you know Ambassadors Sarek and Shran," Westcott said introducing the Ambassadors.

"Yes, mister President," Solow said.

The formal greetings continued for a moment. And everybody took their seats. West set up the stand and screen as Admiral De Lancey readied herself for her presentation.

"Admiral De Lancey will start off," Solow suggested. "She wasn't able to make it the last time we had this meeting."

"I was caught up in evaluation of the new technology linear warp drive prototypes, Mister President," De Lancey said.

"And how long until we get those linear warp upgrades to the fleet, Admiral De Lancey?" Westcott asked.

"Not until 2273 at the earliest, Mister President. The Decatur was recently launched, replacing the lost Collins. She will test the linear war drive and she will be the prototype for the Belknap class," De Lancey said as she began her long-overdue fleet status report.

De Lancey's monitor screen glowed and came to life. On the screen were images of former front-line units such as the Baton Rouge, Ranger, Gettysburg, Canada, Icarus, Mann, Einstein, Malachowski, Magee, Walker, Engle, Hoover, Nimitz, Cardenas, and Shepard class antiques from the early 23rd century and the infamous and failed Crossfield class. Ten ships had been built and five had already been lost. Graphs showed all modifications done during the years.

"Presently, Starfleet is in the middle of a massive fleet buildup and upgrade program. The battles of the Savo star system and Ghihoge in December 2263 and Jutland in April 2264 showed the weakness of our fleet. Too few heavy, medium, and light cruisers, antiquated dreadnoughts of the Icarus/Baton Rouge design generation. Not enough escorts." She paused and continued.

"As for the proposed Super Constitution and the quad nacelle successors to the lost Nelson. We project at the earliest is 2275-93 for the quads, 2285 for the supers," De Lancey said as the screen showed the design studies of the two future classes.

"And Trans warp drive," Shran asked curiously.

"2284 at the earliest," De Lancey added and continued her presentation as she pointed to the display screen. On it were various offshoot designs based on the proven Constitution class.

"At present, the entire additional contract, sixty special configuration Trojan/ Explorer class Constitutions, all twenty Brahe/Sovereign class tri-nacelle battle cruisers and all ten Voyager class research, exploratory cruisers are now in service." De Lancey said as she changed the screen again. This time, the screen showed images of Constitution class Heavy cruisers.

"All the Achenar subclass Mark 9b Constitutions are now in service except for the Santassima Trinidad, Langley, Galina, Kitty Hawk, and Czar 'AK are being held in reserve at Star base 10. All the Supplemental Contract Achenar class ships are in service. Twenty-Two Original Contract Achenar class have been renumbered. We have fast-tracked the construction of the Tikopai class. They are being built out of order. The first four Tikopai are now undergoing shakedowns and modifications. All the troublesome Kirov's as well as the Kent, Kearsarge, Challenger, Defiance, and Valiant had been built with new contract numbers back in the 2250s." De Lancey changed the image. Images of the Federation, Defender, and Proxima class appeared along with a proposed design study of the massive Yamato class battleships.

"As for dreadnought availability. Ten of the twenty odd Federation class dreadnoughts except for Star Empire are also undergoing trails and crew shakedown. Star Empire will not enter service until 2270, the other nine in 2268. All ten Proxima class dreadnoughts are in service along with the other ten Defender class battleships, excluding Bismarck whose construction has been halted. Her predecessor, the Constitution class Bismarck, is still in service. The Yamato's are still in the design stage," De Lancey pointed out.

"Escorts," Westcott asked.

De Lancey switched the screen over one last time. It showed various designs on the screen—Saladin, Hermes, Nelson, Ptolemy, Miranda, Soyuz, Anton, Coventry, Surya, and Soryu class vessels.

"We now have plenty of destroyers, scouts, and transport tugs. We are doubling the cruiser force by adding more Miranda, Surya, Soryu, Coventry's, and Anton's to the existing fleet and all thirty second generation Miranda variant, the Soyuz class border patrol cruisers are all finally in service after years of delays," De Lancey concluded.

Concerned, Westcott asked, "Admiral, even with these new ships, we still not have enough ships if we have to face both the Harrata and the Klingon Empire in an extended conflict."

"Yes, Mister President, if we throw in all surviving early 23rd century ships and then we stir in some even more obsolete 22nd-century deathtraps, we still wouldn't have enough ships to survive a two-front war. Either we prevent a war with the Harrata or we don't stand a chance, Mister President," De Lancey said frankly. She was a realist. Starfleet had to quadruple in size just to meet a two-front war challenge. Contain one, finish off the other. Delancey said as she sat down. Solow replaced her at the screen.

Westcott found that reassuring. At least, De Lancey was a realist. Westcott turned to Herbert Solow.

"What fleets do we have deployed in the conflict zone, Admiral Solow?"

Solow switched the screen. On the screen in red was the Harrata Imperium. It dominated space between Star base 41 and the proposed Delta 4, 5, 6 construction sites. Deep Space Station K1 stood at one side of the border in the corridor. Star bases Trafalgar and Alpha flanked the Imperium along with the lone, abandoned Hell Spawn outpost on the other side of the Imperium's border. Star base 41 and 38 stood in the distance. All were in Blue. Along with the Klingon Empire in red. In white were the images of the Delta outposts being constructed.

"Starfleet has the 9th fleet under Admiral Richard Robau at Star base 41 consisting of 100 ships. At Star base Trafalgar, the legendary First Strike Force under Admiral Joseph Hawke with 150 ships, The Federation Tactical force Caesar, Unit XY74667 of four destroyers under Vice-Admiral Vaughn Rittenhouse along with unit XY75847 under Captain Samantha Reynolds and XY75888 under Commodore Harold Randolph Morrow," Solow explained and continued, "In addition to the above fleets, we have the Federation Fourth Reserve fleet of 30 ships at Star base Alpha under Captain, brevet Rear Admiral Lance Cartwright in the Ark Royal. Also assigned are the Starships Kongo, Asimov, Yamato, and Tori under Captain Anne Toroyan. Patrolling the corridor are the Starships Excelsior and Lafayette, backed up by Commodore Matthew Decker's squadron consisting of the Constellation, Intrepid, Defiant, and Excalibur."

"Enough ships to contain the Harrata I assume."

"Yes, Mister President. But for a small Imperium, the Harrata have at least a 2,000-ship navy. And with our other commitments, we cannot draw from any of the other fleets without compromising our readiness."

"Admiral De Lancey, could you reallocate some of the Federation's and the Achenar's to Star base 41?" Westcott asked.

"We could, Mister President, but it may take at least a week before they will be ready. Four dreadnoughts can only be allocated but only after their shakedowns are finished. In addition, we could send a squadron of the first four Achenar who are in the Tribal sector conducting war games exercises," De Lancey said.

"Hell of a lot better than the retired Four Years' War, Ranger style Achenar, and the Icarus style Tikopai class ships," General in Chief Scott said sarcastically. Starfleet had been cannibalizing the surviving antiques for parts. The loss rate of those ships had been enormous during the Four Years' War and the 2257 extension of the war. Starfleet had reissued the names, class, and numbers as Constitution class when they decided to begin new construction.

"And what does the military have for us today, General?" Westcott asked.

"At Star base Alpha, we have the following Corp assigned for the possible invasion of Harrata space. Unlike our Starfleet brethren, we all remember the results of the last two wars. Starfleet was not ready, unlike today. So, we have formed the following operation, Operation End Game. Colonel Stravinsky." Scott turned to the blond-haired, blue-eyed Russian officer.

Stravinsky replaced Solow at the display screen and switched it over. On it was a tactical layout.

"With the help of the Fourth Reserve fleet and the First Strike Force, we will hit the Harrata at their weakest point, Bathazar 5 and Domar Amid 5, the only two Harrata strongholds not backed up by a Star Force base. Once the fleet has gotten through, we will invade the Karraty Star system, a central location where a lot of Harrata trade routes converge," Stravinsky pointed out and continued.

"To invade the planet, we have the following corp. allocated to this invasion. The Andorians have graciously provided their 1st Imperial guard corp. The Vulcans, the Tal Shia corp. Earth will be adding in the following Federation Ground Infantry's 1st Army, and Federation Marines will be sending the first and second Marine divisions, the Leathernecks and the Royals, along with support troops from Teller, Deneb, and Trill," Stravinsky said.

"General Scott, all this will only go into effect if the Enterprise and Constitution do not survive the challenge," Sarek asked.

"Yes, Mister Ambassador, only then," Scott admitted.

"Starfleet also has two ships ready to be renamed Enterprise-NCC1701 A and Constitution-NCC 1700A, Ambassador Sarek. They are the Galina and Astrad. Both ships' service records outshine the rest of their mates. But this is just in case," De Lancey said.

"I hope that Starfleet is aware of the time-honored Harrata tradition of skirmishing before the actual war breaking out," Shran warned.

"Starfleet will not be caught with its pants down this time," Solow reassured Shran. "Once Captains Kirk and Hawke begin the challenge, all Starfleet forces in the zone of conflict and outside the operational area will be moved up to code two priority, defensive poster, respond if attacked. We will only move to code one if Enterprise and Constitution are lost, Mister Ambassador."

Shran recalled that in the last two conflicts, the Harrata at lightning speed had come across the border and attacked. Starfleet had no time to fully mobilize. Only the First Strike Force-Task Force Alpha had been ready.

At the Battle of the Rykar Nebula during the First Harrata war and the Battle of Star base Trafalgar during the second, the FSF took considerable losses until being relieved by the 7th, 8th, and 9th fleets.

The famed FSF had been formed during the Xindi conflict by Alexander Hawke. The FSF had been involved in every major conflict since. The Romulan War, the Tarn War, the Harrata wars, and the Tholian border skirmishes as well as supporting the rest of the fleet during the Axanar Rebellion and the Four Years' War. The FSF was the elite of the fleet and the starships Enterprise and Constitution in addition to being flagships of the Eighth and Seventh fleets were honorary flagships of the FSF. Solow had commanded the fleet at the end of the Four Years' War and Jefferies had commanded that fleet at the end of the 2240s prior to his retirement.

Westcott looked at the military and the ambassadors. "Does anyone have anything else to add?" he asked the Starfleet and the military.

Nobody said a word.

"Then thank you, ladies and gentlemen."

The Starfleet and the military took their leave. Westcott also waved his two aides off. He wanted the next meeting with the ambassadors to be completely confidential. Moments later, a tall, white-haired Quch'ha Klingon in typical imposing Klingon regalia and a brown-skinned Harrata female of the political caste wearing a black jumpsuit and a multicolored cloak entered the office.

"Mister President, Ambassadors Shran and Sarek, so good to see you," the elegantly beautiful Harrata Ambassador Shari ben Gazari Fahiri said in typical high-caste Harrata standard.

As Shari entered the President's office, she remembered that the Harrata race spoke in one of three accents, high, middle, and low.

As you rose up in the ranks or declined in them, your speech would reflect it. Only the failed whites were forbidden to speak in middle or high caste. They had failed the Ascension, so they only speak in the lower caste dialect.

"Ambassador Gazari Fahiri, Ambassador Korvat. I believe you know Shran and Sarek."

Korvat grunted, "Sarek, Shran."

"Korvat, don't be so cruel," Shari said chiding Korvat. "They are our respected colleagues."

Shran's antenna twitched. Typical Klingon, he thought. Shran bowed graciously.

Sarek however responded in his unemotional, respectful manner. Korvat and Gazari Fahiri then took their seats alongside Sarek and Shran.

"This had better not be a waste of my time," Korvat said annoyed.

"It is not, Mister Ambassador," Westcott responded. "We just need certain guarantees that the Empire would not attack the Federation if we do go to war with the Imperium."

"I cannot make any guarantees, Mister President. The battle of Star base 42 has clearly incited the more warlike members on the council."

"The Harrata Imperium takes a neutral ground on any Federation-Klingon affair, Mister President," Gazari Fahiri said plainly. "Our only concern is the challenge,"

Shari finished.

"Right." Shran wasn't convinced by Gazari's tone of benevolence.

"Conquest is not the Harrata way," she added.

"Tell that to the Ferengi and the Pakleds," Shran added.

"The Ferengi and the Pakleds violated our Tong. The Ferengi tried to have the whites rebel and the Pakleds tried to steal our technology. We had to invoke Tong VA Shar, the conquest.

Ambassador Shran. It is worse to do that than to refuse the Tong in Harrata tradition. Only then will we conquer the deceivers and blasphemers to our ritual," Gazari pointed out.

"You did have your eyes on Earth a couple of centuries ago, Madam Ambassador," Sarek said coolly.

"We did," Shari admitted. "It is a long story, but Gom prophesied the coming of the Federation. Eliminating Earth before she achieved spaceflight would have been the continuation of the Tong by all future Federation Members, Mister Ambassador. Changing the course of history. But the High Priest Annabil d' Shatar of the Temple of Gom sacrificed himself to Gom and set everything right. Gom reconsidered and decided not to pursue that course."

"That is why the Andorians and Vulcans dropped their discord and took up the Tong. We had to protect Earth," Shran recalled. It had been the only time the Confederacy of Vulcan and the Andorian Empire had ever cooperated in their long history of warfare between both races.

"When did this happen?" Westcott asked curiously.

"During your 20th century," Sarek added.

"And we never heard about your world until Broken Bow," Korvat said interjecting.

"The Harrata never discuss our plans even with victors of the Tong Korvat. It wasn't your people's business to know the greatness of Gom. Only we Harrata know the greatness of Gom and the other twelve deities," Shari said angered by Korvat's insulting arrogance.

"Lothar and Grethor will one day fight in the eternal regions, Shari. And Grethor will win," Korvat boasted.

Shari shook her head. "Grethor will lose because the barge of the dead cannot carry enough disgraced souls to fight the legions of Lothar. The legions will destroy them," Gazari shot back.

Korvat's pride had been hurt. Enough of this, he thought, the Harrata patQ had stained his honor.

Shari looked at Korvat. The idiot Klingon Palok had insulted her. She wanted to reach out to him and employ the ancient art known as Heggah on the Klingon. With a yell, Shari leaped out of her chair at the Klingon. Korvat lunged at her. Shran quickly interposed himself between both, knocking the Klingon down. Sarek moved quickly defecting Shari's blow and sent her sprawling onto the carpet.

"Enough!" Westcott said angrily as he got out of his chair. "Both of you, sit down and I will have both of you hauled out by security."

"Ambassador Gazari Fahiri, Ambassador Korvat. You are acting illogically," Sarek pointed out. Shari got up and straightened her jumpsuit and her cloak and glared at Sarek. She sat down.

"Sarek is right. Andorians, like Klingons and Harrata, are proud of our warrior class. Fighting over two gods who deal with the disgraced is most dishonorable," Shran said as he looked at Korvat and Shari directly.

Moments later, the Presidential security squad arrived.

Korvat seeing the squad arriving got up. He took his seat next to Shran. Sarek sat next to Shran, and Shari sat next to Sarek. The seating order had changed.

Westcott waved them off. It was going to be a long day, he thought.

"The next time both of you do that," Westcott said angrily looking at Shari and Korvat. "I will have you both deported back to your home worlds. Now let's get back to business," Westcott said clearly frustrated by both ambassadors' antics.

"The Harrata, Mister President, renounces the Children of Lothar. They have been doing too many depredations against the Federation and the Klingon Empire for so long," Shari said coolly ignoring Korvat.

Korvat smiled showing his white fangs. "I always wondered when the Harrata would finally renounce that group of PataQ."

"They are a disgrace, Ambassador. But we have no way to combat them, without them turning more of our people into Children," Shari said. She was still itching to teach the Palok a lesson and employ the Jaddich maneuver from the Heggah on him.

"And why do you say that?" Sarek asked. He still didn't trust Shari after what had transpired. But he had to wait and see her attitude on this matter.

"As a Follower of Gom, I know the seductive reach of Lothar's grip. Gom strives for honor. Lothar leads to the dark path. The Children of Lothar and the Slaves of Lothar are small in number compared to the Followers of Gom and the other deities. According to the Book of Creation, Gom and Lothar fight whenever there is a war. According to legend, it is always a draw. Except when the unbelievers come, and Lothar destroys us."

"Bah!" Korvat rumbled.

"The dark time is coming; the unbelievers will be returning," Shari warned. She continued to ignore Korvat.

"The Iconians," Westcott said. "Like the Continuum and the Progenitors, they were myths."

Shari nodded. "And the evil from the Tarang and Vorad regions of space."

"Gamma and Delta quadrants," Shran added translating the limited Harratese he knew.

"We call them the Borgara and the Daklenah Zh Hej," Shari said very shaken by the thought.

The Federank had fought the Daklenah at Midway in 2166 and had thrown them back to the Tarang section of space. But as Gom had prophesied, they would return at the end of this century and come in full force in the next.

"The Klingon Empire will not bow to these Daklenah and Borgara PatQ. We would face them in battle and die with honor," Korvat said proudly.

"And the Federation will not stand aside, Ambassador Gazari. We will stand with the Imperium if need be," Sarek agreed.

"But it does not change the situation today, Madam Ambassador," Westcott said.

"No, it doesn't, President Westcott. Gom wills a war against the Federansky and the Klingonasse. I am a servant of Gom and the Harrata people. I do as Gom and the Imperium wills it."

"I serve Kahless Shari and Chancellor Sturka," Korvat cut in.

Shari glared at Korvat. She wished the Klingon would stop being so rude. "We have great warriors too, Korvat, Antoi Jk Karibe who fought and defeated the Horror. Sharita Na Napari who helped stop the Iconians and Bogar Fa Taplai who helped us fight off the Tkonasi," Shari said. The Imperium had triumphed against the Iconians, the horror from beyond the barrier and had fought off the Tkon Empire and remained free. They were an ancient and proud race and had existed long before life came to this planet.

The horror, what was the horror. Westcott thought.

"The battle of Star base 42 merely balances the equation. Savo and Jutland have partially sated the Empires' will for vengeance," Korvat admitted. "But Star base 42 and Savo were only partial Klingon victories compared to the humiliation of Donatu 5. Axanar and the Four Years War. The empire will not forget its dishonor, Mister President," Korvat warned. "A reckoning is coming, Mister President, be warned. And it doesn't matter to us if you are involved in a war with the Imperium. We will have war." With that note, Korvat finished, got up, and left.

"As Gom wills it." Shari Ben Gazari got up. Westcott, Shran, and Sarek also stood up.

"It was a pleasure, Mister President," Shari said as she bowed graciously and left.

Sarek, Shran, and Westcott watched as Shari and her entourage left the president's office.

"At least we know where they both stand," Westcott said to both ambassadors.

"We must now prevent a conflict with the Harrata. It is the only way to avoid this illogical outcome," Sarek said showing a hint of concern in his voice.

"Yes, we must," Westcott agreed as he looked out the window at the first district of Paris. He had to save all of this from being destroyed. Sarek and Shran took their leave.

CHAPTER EIGHT

STAR BASE 41. U.S.S PTOLEMY-NCC 3801. STAR DATE 2907.2:

"I understand, Commodore," Waterston said calmly as he looked at the image of Commodore Augenthaler on his desk screen. Ptolemy was safely docked at 41. She had miraculously received minor damage in the skirmish and repairs were nearly complete. Anaximander hadn't been as fortunate. Ben Gurion was dead, and she was under heavy repairs. The Ibn Daud, Keppler had fared better. Both ships suffered moderate damage.

Augenthaler looked at Waterston and blew a sigh of relief. Thank god Noguchi had decided not to give Waterston Constitution. Waterston just wasn't Heavy cruiser command material.

"It won't happen again," Phil apologized.

"It had better not, Captain," Augenthaler warned addressing Waterston by his true rank. "Your stupidity is therefore why you command a transport tug instead of a heavy. You should refer to the Starfleet Alien Psychological Profile manual. Didn't you realize what would happen when you mentioned a disgraced forebear would have in the eyes of the Harrata?" Augenthaler explained. The fool had nearly caused a diplomatic incident and he had spent hours trying to calm Commandant Gomar down.

"However, Captain. Your conduct during the skirmish with the Harrata Star force light forces has balanced this out," Augenthaler said.

"Thank you, Sir." Waterston smiled.

"Don't thank me, Captain. It only mitigates your previous stupidity. Be a bit more open-minded the next time. Your sponsor Vice Admiral Rittenhouse is on his way to see you. Star base 41 out." Augenthalers image faded.

The intercom whistled. Waterston turned on the screen. The image of Ensign Mull Na Sar, Ptolemy's Tellerite assistant communications officer, appeared.

"Captain, Admiral Rittenhouse will arrive shortly."

"Thank you, Ensign Mull," Phil responded coldly. And yet, he just couldn't shake the nagging feeling he had. From 2166 until 2245, Constitution had reigned as fleet flagship. Her predecessors had also made the first contact with the Trill and many other races.

The only family member who had ever commanded a ship named Constitution had been his great uncle Hubert Waterston who commanded the ill-fated Constitution destroyed by the Tarn. Her career was the shortest career of all the Constitutions past and present.

She was launched a year after the loss of NX/NCC 00 and was destroyed a year later.

Since 2245 Enterprise reigned as the fleet flagship, Constitution was still her backup. The competition was always intense between both ships. They were like the Imperial guard of the fleet. The Ptolemy by comparison was an unsung supply corp. grunt. Sure, they were the elite of the Starfleet Merchant Service, but no glory, no guts. Somehow, life wasn't fair. The buzzer rang.

"Yes."

"Phil, it's Vaughn."

"Come in, Admiral."

The doors parted, and Rittenhouse stepped in. Looking around, he spotted Waterston sitting at his desk reviewing record tapes.

Waterston got up. "Admiral, what a surprise!" Waterston said smiling.

"Phil, cut the nonsense," Rittenhouse said as he motioned Waterston to sit down. "I know all about what transpired on Domar Amid One. That was inexcusable. The Harrata like the Klingons takes their ancestors very seriously. What you did was uncalled for," Rittenhouse said reigning in his anger.

Waterston got up, went over to one of the rooms' cabinets, and pulled out some Andorian ale.

"You know what they say about the difference between Romulan ale and Andorian ale, Phil."

Waterston nodded as he poured the ale into two glasses and handed one to Rittenhouse.

"They are both blue, but one burns, like fire, the other soothes the senses with its chill."

"Precisely."

"Your point."

"In this fleet of dreamers, idealists, and fools, we Section 31 loyalists are one percent of the blasted fleet. One percent. That is pathetic, we are the last bastion of conservatism in a fleet filled with the left wing, moderate dreamers, and idealists who placate alien scum. We do not need a Federation; we need an empire. The Back to Earth movement had it right back in the 22nd century. And our anti-Federation decedents have the same idea. Unfortunately, we are only one percent of Earth's population since the great Conservative Exodus of 2180, when the followers of Hugo Wright, an accolade of the great Henry Paxton, led the way to the Promised Land, in old, antiquated warp one ships."

"I heard that Lance Cartwright has the Fourth Reserve Fleet," Waterston mentioned.

"It is a disgrace, Phil, a right-winger of Lance Cartwright's stature is given a fleet of antiques while scum like Richard Robau and Joe Hawke have the pride and joy of Starfleet."

Waterston figured now was the time to get his just due, "That brings me to my next point, Admiral. I want the Constitution."

Rittenhouse slammed his hand down on Waterston's desk. "Are you mad! A scout or a destroyer command is realistic. Light, Medium, or Heavy cruisers are out of the question, Phillip, you don't have the service record for one," Rittenhouse said angrily. "Robert Hawke's crew would follow him to hell and back. His people occupy all the main positions on that ship. Admiral Noguchi anointed him to that position. Just like he anointed Kirk to take command of Enterprise."

"There has to be a way," Waterston said stubbornly. He couldn't believe what he was hearing.

"No way, Phil. I heard that Samantha Reynolds' cruiser squadron arrives just in the nick of time," Rittenhouse said quickly changing the subject. Sometimes, he hated Waterston's open fits of jealousy.

Waterston hated Samantha Reynolds, Robert's girlfriend. Her dad was the present Starfleet Academy Commandant for the past seven years. Arthur Reynolds had previously commanded the Hornet and was known to be a real ball-buster when it came to new officers assigned to his ship. Reynolds was a demanding commanding officer and got the most out of his crew. Reynolds had flayed him alive when he messed up on Hornet soon after his graduation in 2253. He was then transferred off the Hornet to the Trafalgar on Reynolds' recommendation. And he had never forgiven Samantha's dad for that.

How Kirk and Hawke could get along together after what happened at the academy between those two had surprised him. He hated them both. Luckily for him, Hawke knew how to keep his mouth shut over certain items of his background that needed to be kept secret. Kirk didn't know that he was a Section 31 loyalist. And for that reason, so much the better. Waterston thought.

"Let's hope that cowboy Kirk never finds out about our organization, Phil," Rittenhouse warned.

"And what if he does?" Waterston said worriedly.

"Then we can deal with him and his cohorts. Since Kirk and Hawke are good friends, it may give us the opportunity to expand our reach in the fleet. Be patient, Phil, an opportunity like that may just show up. And then you will probably get your long desired Heavy cruiser command," Rittenhouse said. To do what he was planning, he had to avoid raising suspicions in the fleet. The operation had to be clandestine and black ops.

"To my new command," Waterston said hopefully.

"To your new command," Rittenhouse agreed as both glasses clanked together in a toast.

Downing the Andorian ale in one gulp, Rittenhouse put the glass on the table. "Got to go, Phil. Captain Trump awaits me on the Pompeii. We must rejoin units XY75847 and 75888. As we right-wingers say when dealing with the Harrata, got to erase those coloreds out," Rittenhouse said as he left Waterston's quarters. Waterston closed and left his quarters. He had some more business on the star base to attend to.

STAR BASE 11. COMMODORE JOSE MENDEZ'S OFFICE. STAR DATE 2907. 3:

Jose Mendez, former commanding officer of the old Patton class destroyer Eisenhower and the old Canada class, class J Heavy cruiser starship Maine. The Canada class was the final design evolution of the old Class J Heavy cruiser class also known as the Gettysburg class. former star base commanding officer of Star bases 7 and 15, present commanding officer of Star base 11, sat at his desk. Starfleet Command had just given him clearance to take a leave of absence. Mendez had come a long way since his first command that old 22nd century antique the Eisenhower.

Sitting across from him was his temporary replacement. Commodore David Aaron L.T Stone, a fellow classmate from the Starfleet Academy class of 2230; former C.O of the Spann and the Defiant; survivor of

Donatu Five; former commander of Star base 8, and future C.O of Star base 46 Pioneer, at the border of the Taurus Reach.

"Now, Jose, don't remind me again about Donatu. It is something I would rather forget," Stone said as he recalled the chain of events.

The Patton and Eisenhower arrived to protect the colonists. They were both immediately attacked by the Klingons. Endeavor arriving on a supply mission was also attacked and severely damaged. Endeavor's sister ship Yorkshire arrived in time to assist the three beleaguered Federation ships.

Outgunned by six Klingon ships, using hit and run tactics, Patton and Eisenhower played cat and mouse with the Klingons in the atmosphere, buying precious time. Less than an hour later, the somewhat incomplete Constitution arrived and rescued the Yorkshire and the wrecked Endeavor assisting the Constitution and the Yorkshire. The Advance class destroyer Sulaco and the Ranger class cruiser Spann arrived fifteen minutes later.

Shortly after that, the Calvary finally arrived—two squadrons of ships. Captain Rollin Bannocks Baton Rouges, the Baton Rouge, New York, Los Angeles, Republic, followed by Commodore James Mays' class Js, the Excalibur, Exeter, Hood, Lakota who quickly outmaneuvered a squadron of arriving D6s. Bannock had seized the initiative and pulled his brilliant maneuver stalemating another squadron of D6s.

Finally, the Baton Rouge class cruisers Jerusalem and Rome arrived, chasing off the Raptor class bird of preys that were harassing Patton and Eisenhower. The battle was a stalemate, and the Klingons withdrew. The Donatu had been the catalyst, setting off a chain of events. The Axanar Rebellion was followed by the Four Years' War and the conflict of 2257, and it laid the groundwork for the Battles of Savo and Jutland.

After sitting in silence for a few minutes, Stone asked, "And how is Chris doing?"

"As well as he could be under the present circumstances, Dave," Mendez responded. He recalled that Pike had an enviable career. Back in 2244, Lieutenant Commander Christopher Pike had been captain of the transport tug Hevelius. In 2246, Pike was on the Aldin as temporary first officer, followed by a promotion to Commander and first officer assignments both on the York, an old Baton Rouge class cruiser and he later replaced Wesley that year who was also doing temporary duty as XO to Robert April on the Enterprise.

In 2248, Pike was promoted to captain and he became the first captain of the brand-new Constitution class Yorktown-NCC1717. Pike was replaced by Matt Decker in 2249 when he went over to the three-year-old Lexington, replacing Charles Morgan, her first captain who had died in the line of duty. In 2250, Korolev replaced him. Pike served one year at Starfleet Operations before being appointed to the captaincy of the Enterprise in 2251.

"Would you like to see him, Dave?"

Stone nodded as both men got up and headed for the intensive care ward.

Arriving at the Intensive care wing, Doctor George Hobson walked up to him, and Stone Hobson had a shock of white hair and was of medium build. Hobby as he was known on the star base had entered Starfleet Med in the year 2210. Mendez believed the old doctor was approaching the mandatory retirement age of 75.

"And how is Chris doing today, Hobby?" Mendez asked as all three men walked down the corridor of the medical wing. Hobby stopped Mendez for a moment. "We are worried that his synapse may have begun to degenerate. There may be no way of stopping it."

Mendez was taken aback. What was he going to tell Chris—Stone looked equally concerned?

The party entered Pike's room.

Christopher Pike faced the window of his room watching the comings and goings of various ships. He could feel the presence of the keeper with him. His buzzer flashed once as the Keeper told him of their plans.

Pike knew the keeper was standing next to him. He could still feel the sting in his body of the Delta's rays. Prior to that, he had had a close call on a cadet orientation tour back in 2265 when he led some first-year cadets on a tour of three old starships. The Celeste-ECS 200, an old Class J warp one freighter, Endurance- ESF 50, an old Horizon Warp three cruiser, followed by the last surviving NX class ship, the updated Columbia/Constitution class warp 5 cruiser Avenger-NX09/NCC09. The tour had been cut short when Celeste had a warp core breach.

Pike could still recall the fatal cadet cruise that happened a year later. He could still feel the Delta rays sting his wounded body. Accounts varied, but the real story was those three instructors and fifteen cadets died. In addition to that, eighteen others including him were irradiated. Seventeen recovered. He was the only one who didn't.

Starfleet was so disgusted by what had happened. Exeter was dismantled for scrap. Too many bad memories had existed on that ship and Starfleet didn't want to have two Exeter's in service further confusing everyone. All remaining Class J Heavy cruisers of the

Gettysburg class were pulled from service and retired to the reserve fleet along with most of the improved Canada class, improved Class J heavy cruiser type.

Mia Colt was now captain of the brand new Achenar class Heavy cruiser, the Sol. The door bolt creaked open. The Keeper vanished. Pike willed the chair around to face the figures of Commodore Mendez, Stone, and Commander Hobson.

"Chris, this is Commodore Stone; he will be temporarily replacing me. I have to take a leave of absence."

Pike understood. He wanted to talk and respond. But he couldn't. He wanted to say that he knew what was said but couldn't. He gave one buzz.

"I also have some bad news. The Enterprise has been chosen to face the infamous challenge along with the Constitution."

The Challenge, the damn Harrata, had prevented Enterprise and Constitution from coming to aid the Hell Spawn outpost. He also had a run-in with the Harrata Imperium when Yorktown was called in to mediate a dispute on Domar Amid 4 between the FMS and the SubCorp in 2248. It had left a bad taste in his mouth. He beeped twice.

"Gentlemen," Hobson said. "I think Pike is agitated by this news. We should go."

Stone, Mendez, and Hobson left the room.

The Keeper materialized next to Pike.

"Do not worry, old friend. Enterprise and Constitution will not suffer the fate of them predecessors," the keeper said as his voice echoed in his head.

Pike felt reassured and continued to look out the window.

CHAPTER NINE

Enterprise, Constitution, on course to the Harrata Imperium. Star date 2907.5:

James Kirk tried to sleep, but he was restless. Both ships were thirty hours away from the Federation-Imperium Treaty Zone. Enterprise was due to pass by the old Hell Spawn outpost at the rendezvous point. Hellspawn had been his father's last posting before the Children of Lothar had attacked the outpost. It was the site of a critical meeting between the Harrata and the Federation. It was a solution to open borders and foster better relations between both powers. Unfortunately for both parties, the mission had ended in disaster.

The desk intercom went off. Kirk rolled out of bed. Yawning, he made his way to the desk. Activating the viewer, the face of Lieutenant Palmer appeared. Palmer was presently serving as Gamma Shift Communication officer. She had come over from the Exeter, highly recommended by Ronald Tracey. Kirk had been hoping to move her up to Beta shift next. She would be an excellent backup for Uhura.

"Captain Kirk."

"Yes, Lieutenant."

"I have Fleet Captain George Samuel Joseph Kirk from the First Strike Force online."

He hadn't seen his father since he took command of Enterprise in 2264.

"Pipe it down here, Lieutenant," Kirk said as he rubbed his tired eyes.

Moments later, a grey-haired image of his dad appeared. He had changed much since his youth. He was no longer the dashing George Kirk who served on the Kelvin. But older, quieter, more reserved.

"Jim."

"Dad."

"I heard the bad news. Admiral Solow contacted Joseph Hawke and me directly. Those Harrata are unpredictable. Remember, Bobby Hawke will watch your back, Jim. You have been cursed and blessed at the same time."

"Why do you say that?" Kirk said tiredly.

"The Tong is a curse. The Harrata considered themselves to be superior to all the other races in mortal combat. They are like playground bullies if they don't get their way, Jim. Only the Klingons have proven themselves superior to them. They can be arrogant people sometimes," George said.

"Robert is the blessing. He, like his dad, has a lot of family history to look up to, and having Matt Decker as his mentor, gave him more baggage to haul around," George added.

Kirk recalled that during his stay at the academy. Robert commanded the famed Academy flight team, Delta squad, and they had won three Rigel cups in a row, a record still unbeaten at the academy. Robert's squadron later topped it all off with an illegal Kolvoord Starburst maneuver on Federation Day, a year before he graduated from the academy.

Robert and his cohorts had all become legends at the Academy and everyone in that squad reached the rank of captain. All five of them had commands of their own now.

"The whole family is rooting for you, Jim. Sam, Aurelian, and the three kids send you their prayers and their best. Winona also sends her love."

"Thanks, Dad."

"Give the Harrata hell."

"Yes, Dad."

George Kirk's image faded. Kirk got up and went back to bed.

"Captain's log. Star date 2907. 9. Captain James T. Kirk reporting. Enterprise and Constitution continue to proceed to our rendezvous with the Harrata Imperium. Our coordinates should take us close to Domar Amid 5 and Bathazar 5."

Kirk walked down the corridor.

McCoy ran up to him. "Morning, Jim."

"Bones."

McCoy looked haggard.

"Doing another one of those late-nighters, Leonard?"

"Yes. I've been considering some of the Harrata pre-challenge customs. You shouldn't have to worry about the food, Jim. It is edible and safe."

"You are referring to the ChaZ-Hagem ritual."

McCoy nodded. "I spoke to Doc Russell. Doc and T'Pau have been doing the same research as Spock and me. I think we should get together and figure out how to beat these Harrata."

Kirk could only agree with Bones. If they didn't survive the Challenge, then this ship and her crew's mission would end abruptly. And Kirk sure was not going to let that happen.

According to a report distributed by Starfleet Intelligence, the Harrata had one system totally devoted to all the failures whether they be Harrata, humans, or any other alien race. Known as the Graveyard, or the Lothar system, depending on who you spoke too. The Lothar system was centuries old and dated back to the War of Ascension. And that was probably going to be their first stop prior to the ChaZ-Hagem ritual and the Parida.

Only successfully surviving the Challenge would lead to another Parida and the meeting with Gom. Kirk in all his years of experience had yet to meet an alien deity, god, or goddesses in the flesh.

Sulu's voice blared over the intercom. Moments later, the red alert siren went off.

"Captain Kirk to the bridge," Sulu said over the ship-wide intercom.

Kirk walked over to the nearest intercom.

"Kirk here."

"Spock, Captain, we seem to have an uninvited guest shadowing us."

"We will be there shortly," Kirk said as he and McCoy sped for the nearest turbo lift and moments later, entered Enterprise's Bridge.

"What do you have, Spock?" Kirk said and then looked at Sulu. "Extreme magnification, Mister Sulu."

Sulu switched over. On the main screen appeared a rundown, unmarked Hogar class ship. The ship had two nacelles, which meant it was a 22nd-century ship. Early Hogar class, type one to three.

"A Hogar class, type three," Kirk said recognizing the vessel. Its more advanced nacelles were like the old NX class type. "Those ships dated back to the first Harrata war." The old Harrata ship was scarred, and the hull was pot marked with disparate replacement hull sections.

Spock nodded. "Correct, that ship is the Har Gorraty. She disappeared from the Star force over a century earlier. Her whereabouts have been confirmed by numerous sightings over the years. The most recent was a sighting by the Dauntless eight years ago. Captain Diego Reyes confirmed in that encounter that the Children of Lothar control her."

"Uhura, can you raise them?"

"No, Captain. I have tried repeatedly. They are not responding to my hails. I also have Captain Hawke on audio scrambled and secure channel."

Kirk sat in his chair. "Put Robert through."

"Yes, Captain."

"What is it, Bob?" Kirk said as he enabled the intercom switch.

"We have not been able to raise her, Jim. She must be a scout for the Children." Hawke's voice came back through the intercom. The joking, backslapping Hawke was gone. He was now the professional that Kirk had come to know, the one who had saved his neck quite a few times over the years.

He still owed Robert a promise that he had yet to fulfill. Hawke's Miranda had rescued him and the remaining survivors at Ghihoge. Lydia Sutherland had been damaged beyond repair and the Sovereign, Musashi, and the Revenge were destroyed with no survivors. Robert had saved him, Mitchell, and the rest of Lydia Sutherland's survivors. He then patched things up with the Ghihogians and the Masters, the super race that had attacked the squadron.

"We came to the same conclusion, Robert," Kirk said.

"I have a suggestion, Jim. Let's just ignore her. She's not worth the bother," Hawke suggested.

"Good idea. Enterprise out."

"Understood, Constitution out."

"Spock."

"Constitution is holding her formation, Captain," Spock announced.

"Captain, the Hogar," Sulu warned.

The Hogar suddenly swung away from both ships. Seconds later, its warp drive engaged, and it was gone.

Spock raised an eyebrow. "Fascinating."

"Why do you say that, Spock?"

"Your family has a history with the Children, their attack on the Revere when she was at Hell Spawn for diplomatic negotiations with the Harrata. They might be worried that you might seek revenge against them for the near loss of your father, Captain. And we all know the part Constitution played back in the 22nd century. Two of Constitution's predecessors commanded by the same family name as her present captain made the first initial contact with them. As you humans are fond of saying both you and Captain Hawke are coming full circle."

"Your point, Spock," McCoy grumbled.

"I have already made my point, Doctor McCoy."

"This is almost a coincidence Spock, Bones."

"Bah about coincidence, but I now see Spock's point about full circle," McCoy grumbled.

"Spock, bring all the information you have on the Harrata. Lieutenant Uhura, contact Constitution. Tell Robert I want to see him and his senior staff, including his security chief at 01000 hours aboard the Enterprise."

"Yes, Captain."

"Spock, McCoy, Scotty, and Giotto will also join me at 01000 hours," Kirk said looking at Spock and McCoy.

"No problem, Jim," McCoy said as he left the bridge.

"I will be in my quarters. Until then, Sulu, you have the con."

"Aye, Sir."

Spock, McCoy, and Kirk left the bridge.

Sulu sat back in the captain's chair, monitoring the bridge. Uhura walked down to Sulu.

"Hikaru, do you really think that Enterprise and Constitution will survive this Challenge?"

Sulu shook his head worried.

"Considering what happened the last two times, Uhura. We don't stand a chance in hell. I would hate to be in Captain Kirk or Captain Hawke's position. They are not only carrying the weight of the safety and the survival of our two ships. But also, billions of lives are at stake, and I don't want to be in Captain Kirk or Captain Hawke's position now with the responsibility they both carry."

"The Harrata are bullies, Hikaru."

"Not bullies, fanatics."

Leslie looked at him from the helm. Sitting at navigation was Farrell.

"My dad Hikaru used to run an independent freighter to various Harrata Trade stations from Earth. They always gave him trouble over the littlest thing," Leslie explained. "But it at least provided food on the table. I guess I will finally see the Harrata home world that my dad told me about," Leslie admitted.

"Tell me, Leslie. You realize what will happen to us if Captain Kirk fails the Challenge," Uhura warned.

"Indeed, I do, Lieutenant," Leslie said from the helm. "And that I am not even thinking about it."

Sulu understood. By not thinking about it, they would not lose faith.

"ETA to our rendezvous point, Mister Leslie."

"30 hours, Mister Sulu."

01000 hours, Enterprise main Briefing room:

On-time, on schedule, Kirk and his staff watched as Hawke and his people arrived from the Constitution. Kirk could see McCoy, Scotty, and Giotto all smiling. It was a reunion of sorts. David Russell: Doctor Boyce's protégée had replaced him on Constitution back in 2260. McCoy had then transferred to the Sacagawea before going to the Starfleet Teaching hospital and a short tour on the Defiance in 2263. Giotto and Martinez had served together on the Defiant earlier in their careers. Scotty and Andy had worked together on the Constitution/ Bonhomme Richard class construction program earlier in their Starfleet careers.

"Let's begin," Kirk said. "Mister Spock, what do we know about the Harrata?" Kirk said to Spock. T'Pau sat next to Spock near the library computer.

"In 2150, the Horizon class starship Constitution under the command of Captain Alexander Hawke, future CO of NX/NCC 00 was on an extended star charting mission near Omega Orrianus when she picked up an unidentified vessel on her screen. Pursuing it, she was later chased off by three unknown cruisers later identified as Hogar Class type 1s near the Midway star system," said Spock as he keyed in the desk screen. The view changed to the founding ceremony of the Federation.

"And what does this have to do with the beastie Harrata, Mister Spock," Scotty moaned.

"During the founding ceremony, an unidentified scout class ship beamed down a lone ambassador. The Ambassador was Harrata," Spock said pointing to the brown-skinned alien who wore a jumpsuit and a multicolored cloak. The Harrata ambassador was silently watching the ceremony. Taking notes, the female Harrata was ignoring all the other delegates. However, the Vulcan, Tellerite, Andorian, Denobulan delegates were talking frantically amongst themselves. She had a negative effect on the delegations. On the podium, Archer was giving his speech and noticed the female ambassador. Unflinchingly, Archer continued to give his speech.

"They sure look nervous," McCoy said. "She is even rattling, Archer."

"As soon as the ceremonies ended, the mysterious ambassador and her ship disappeared."

"I'd call that a serious lack of manners," Doc Russell said in his New England brogue, scratching his red goatee.

"That's for sure," Thomas Andrews added in his clipped English accent.

Spock manipulated the controls. On the viewing screen, the image was replaced by a slim, nicely figured brunette starship captain, wearing the uniform of a 22nd century Federation Starship captain circa 2170s—black pants and boots, white shirt with the green command band on the right arm, and captain's stripes, which were of four narrow bands on both sleeves. The UFP flag was on the left shoulder and Constitution's insignia on the right. The epaulettes had been retired. She was speaking to a multitude of people from most of the Harrata caste system. In the background, Kirk could see temples in the distance.

"Oh, hell," Hawke exclaimed surprised. "First, my granddad Alex and now my grand aunt Nicole."

"Constitution contacted the Imperium in 2175," Spock said. "The Vulcans had warned the Humans about the Harrata, about the Tong. But you typically ignored us, Captain."

"Much to our regret, Spock," Kirk admitted.

"The Harrata were clearly miffed about the Federation eliminating so many challengers," Hawke added. "They didn't get mad, just even," pointing it out.

"And that what makes the Harrata so dangerous. They don't nurse grudges," Salvatore Antonio Barry Giotto said.

"Precisely," Martinez said in her Cuban accented English, agreeing with Giotto.

"And in 2177, the Harrata had a suicide ship ram the NX class starship Curie at Star base 3," Shran added.

"Starfleet sent the Daedalus class starships Titanic and Britannic, to face the challenge, but with typical human bravado, lack of preparation. The Federation was ultimately drawn into the first Federation-Harrata war," T'Pau said blandly. Kirk looked at Hawke's Chief Science Officer. She was unfazed, just like Spock.

"What is so illogical, T'Pau, was how unprepared the Federation Starfleet was at the time, despite the recent Romulan and Tarn conflicts," Spock said.

"Only the First Strike Force at newly commissioned Star base Trafalgar was ready," Kirk added. That Starfleet could be caught with its pants down always angered him. It had become required reading at the academy to study the mistakes of the Tarn and Harrata conflicts.

"And then, we had the blundering of 2220," McCoy admitted.

"But, Doctor. The Starfleet was better prepared," Spock pointed out.

"Yes, Spock, but instead of attacking a ship to start the war, the Harrata made an example of the colony at Islandana."

"The colony was encroaching on Harrata Treaty Territory at the time," T'Pau said coolly.

"That doesn't explain the loss of 1,000 lives, Lieutenant," McCoy said shocked by T'Pau's indifference. "The High Order Corp slaughtered everyone. They didn't even spare the women or the children."

"And then we sent two more ships in. The brand-new Ranger class ships, Good Hope and Captain, and then we lost again," Andrews recalled.

"This is so depressing," Doc Russell said as he scratched his goatee.

"You said it, Doc. You hit it right on the nose." Robert looked at his officers.

"But remember, we have a job to do. It is time we show the Harrata what the Federation can really do."

Kirks and Robert's officers were nodding and agreeing on Robert's point.

"Well said, Robert," Kirk said. Hawke had summoned the right mood up. They were not going to fail. "Spock, what about the Klingons?"

"They have never lost the Tong. They welcome it as a challenge to their warrior mentality. Intelligence is spotty, Captain. But rumors point to a Harrata merchant ship, the Dogash, ramming a Klingon battle cruiser."

"That means we will have company," Hawke said.

Spock said to Hawke, "As you eloquently point out."

"Excalibur and Excelsior did shadow two battle cruisers entering Harrata Space, Spock."

"Affirmative, Captain, but which captains you will be working with, we do not know who they are," Spock said.

"Let's hope it is not Chang," Hawke warned as he shifted in the chair. "Chang would surely cut our throats as the Harrata would."

"You did encounter this Chang before, Bob."

"Yes," Hawke admitted. Constitution had crossed paths with Chang twice last year. Hawke remembered. "Chang is very ruthless, unlike you, Jim, during the Interspecies Academy program. I was one of the three officers who went to the Klingon home world for two months. Chang was one of the multitudes of Klingon warriors who I met. It was a dozy of an experience."

"Do you know Kang or Koloth?" Kirk asked curiously.

Hawke breathed a sigh of relief. "Those two are honorable, Jim. They stuck their necks out for me when I was in the Klingon home world. I owe them a debt of honor."

"That is why Captain Hawke is fluent in one dialect of the Klingon language and has a bat'leth to prove it," Shran said proudly. She would serve as number one to no other captain but Robert. His honor and his integrity had always been the key ingredient to their success together.

"We dealt with Kang and Koloth, Bob. But you are right about both," Kirk admitted.

"We do know that in both previous encounters, the Federation didn't survive past the first round during the first challenge and the Klingons didn't support them during the second time, during the second round of the second challenge," Spock said.

"So, everything boils down to both captains surviving all three levels of the challenge."

"Yes, Doctor McCoy."

"Bob, I need to ask you a question," Kirk asked.

"Go."

"Your ship had the annual Federation Science Conference hauling all of those famed scientists to the Versailles system. I heard a rumor that your science officer shook the whole conference up with a theory," Kirk asked. He immediately saw smiles appearing on all the Constitution's officer's faces, barring Shran who became aloof and tightlipped and T'Pau who suddenly became unreadable.

"I would rather not go into that, Jim," Hawke said as he folded his arms.

Spock cut in. He preferred making the matter short. "Lieutenant T'Pau successfully proposed a multiverse theory that was derided by the famed scientific experts, Captain. T'Pau should be commended for inquisitive brilliance on a subject of that matter."

"I predict between 250,000 and 500,000 combinations alone in the theory," T'Pau said. "I've been working on the formula since I joined Constitution in 2262. I prefer working on it during the crew's shore leaves," T'Pau added.

McCoy just nodded in agreement. "They should call it T'Pau's law," McCoy said.

The intercom whistled, cutting McCoy off. Kirk hit the button. Uhura's elegant features appeared.

"Yes, Lieutenant."

"An all-points fleet bulletin. Captain, Starfleet has just mobilized the 8th fleet at Star base 38."

"Thank you, Lieutenant," Kirk said as Uhura's image faded.

"Michela Harari's command," Hawke said, looking at Kirk.

"Spock, what does Starfleet now have deployed?" Kirk said as he faced Spock.

Spock keyed in the library computer. The following information appeared on the screen. 8th, 9th fleets, the FSF and the Fourth Reserve fleet, Units XY 75847, 75887, 75888, 75889, 74667."

"74667. That's Rittenhouse's destroyer Tactical command," Scotty said.

Spock nodded.

"75887, 888,889 are Morrows, Toroyan and Decker's Heavy cruiser squadrons, not including, Excelsior and Lafayette, and 75847 is Captain Reynolds' Medium cruiser squadron," Spock explained.

"Were just lucky that Starfleet has recently deployed those new Heavy cruisers. The original ships couldn't handle it alone," Andrews added.

Kirk looked at Constitution's tall, lanky Chief Engineer. He bore a striking resemblance to an English actor named John Cleese from Monty Python back in the 20th century.

"Starfleet, Mister Andrews, is taking a logical step to avoid the mess we had back in 2220 and 2177," Spock said looking at Constitution's chief engineer.

"Robert," Kirk said looking at Hawke. "We know for a fact that the first two captains barely survived the first six rounds and the second two eliminated their opponents by the seventh round, before falling in the second part of the Challenge," Kirk said concerned.

"Jim, I thank you for your concern. But we still don't know who our opponents are going to be," Hawke admitted. He didn't want to be rude. Even though they were now friends after so many years of being rivals, Kirk had a way of sticking his nose where it didn't belong sometimes. "Let the chips fall where they will fall, Jim. We will soon find out and I don't want to worry myself to death over this matter," Hawke said bluntly.

Kirk looked at Robert. Robert was getting irritated again. Hawke could be a callous, insensitive dolt on occasions. But he would rather deal with Robert Hawke than deal with stiff-necked, prim and proper Kelly Bogle. Bogle was known to be such a bore on occasions.

But both he and Robert were always opposites in personality. Robert was an out-and-out showman, to his dead-serious demeanor.

"Anything else?" Kirk asked everyone. Nobody said a thing. It was time to wrap things up.

"This briefing is adjourned," Kirk said

Wordlessly, Robert and his people left the briefing room. Kirk watched as his own people followed. Only McCoy remained.

"What is it, Bones?" Kirk asked.

"I hope the Academy rivalry between you and Hawke doesn't resurface, Jim."

"Now what is that supposed to mean?" Kirk asked.

"You know exactly what I am talking about, Jim," McCoy said as he left the briefing room.

Kirk sat back on the table and contemplated what McCoy had said.

CHAPTER TEN

THIRTY HOURS TO RENDEZVOUS. ENTERPRISE GYM FACILITIES:

Kirk punched the bag repeatedly venting his frustrations. After this, he was planning on going to the ship's pool in the secondary hull and take a swim. Spock had informed him that Hawk and Shran were sparring with Andorian, Klingon, and human weapons. Kirk thought how typical of Robert. Perspiring Kirk wiped the sweat from his brow.

Sam Fuller walked over.

"Sam."

"Yes, Captain," Sam Fuller said.

"Do you know how to use this?" Kirk pointed to the double-ended sparring clubs.

Fuller nodded.

"I need the practice."

"You always need the practice, Jim. I bet Bobby Hawke is breathing down your back now and it is really galling you."

Kirk nodded. "Spock isn't the physical type, Sam, not like Gary. Back on the Hartford, Oxford, Lydia Sutherland, and the Sacagawea, I used to engage Gary in a bout. I envy that those two have been going at it since the Sargon and the Miranda makes me jealous of Robert's luck."

Sam Fuller smiled, "What luck, Jim? More like skill."

Kirk and Sam selected one each. They moved into the adjoining room and took their places.

Without warning, Kirk swung the sparring club at Sam, who parried. The match was joined.

SPOCK'S QUARTERS:

McCoy stopped outside Spock's quarters, pausing for a moment after he hit the buzzer.

"Who is it?"

"It's me, Spock."

"Come."

McCoy stepped in. "You look like someone contemplating a major problem."

"How is ships morale, Doctor?"

"The usual, I have never seen so many depressed people in my life, Spock. A lot of the crew feels that we may not return from this mission. Doc Russell told me that Constitution's crew is suffering from the same problem."

Uhura's voice suddenly filtered through the intercom. She was singing Beyond Antares. It had become a favorite song of the crew.

"At least, Uhura knows what our crew needs, Spock."

"The Lieutenant always had that gift, Bones," Spock said as he looked up from the screen.

McCoy glanced over. "That's Harrata, Spock."

"Yes, Doctor. I decided to immerse myself in their known religious documents."

"You mean the Thirteen Scrolls, the sacred books of the thirteen deities, and the book of Creation?" McCoy asked curiously.

"The Harr centuries ago were as barbaric as humanity. But like humanity, they almost destroyed each other with their incessant wars. They have thirteen nations, and each wanted to rule the planet. Each of the thirteen nations followed one of the original deities. Pong and its ilk believed a divided Harr race was better than a united one," Spock said.

"However, 500,000 years ago, Harray Tomargura and his wife Sendai were on the plains of Homass, when they were possessed by Gom and the other new deities. Together, they spread the word uniting the fragmented Harrata race and leading to the Great Crusade and the War of Ascension, overthrowing Pong and the other twelve original deities. They became the Harrata while the followers of Pong became the Harrkonen. Doctor, did you ever wonder why all Harrata names have middle initials?" Spock said.

McCoy shook his head. "No, Spock, why?"

"Only the disgraced Children of Lothar and the rebel Harrkonen Empire, who refused to submit to Gom, left the Imperium and used the pre-Gom tradition of having no middle names," Spock explained.

McCoy whistled. "No wonder they confuse everyone. They got me baffled," he admitted.

Spock continued, "Also, when we arrive at Harrata space, we must respect all their customs concerning the Tong. They are keenly sensitive. And do not take to be trodden on by arrogance and ignorance."

"If we don't"

"They will destroy the Enterprise."

"You're not kidding, Spock, are you?"

"No, Doctor. We will be allowed to accompany the Captain at the Lothar system and during the 10 rounds of the Tong Ra Ga. We will not be able to be with him during the Tong Chavere, the first Parida, and the ChaZ Hagem. We are forbidden to be with him, and if we survive. We must complete the Tong Spac Che and the second Parida."

"So, in plain non-Harrata English, we cannot join him in the private ceremony of the combatants, or the group combat session, the first parade. But we will be together for the big Space battle and the final parade."

"Yes, Doctor."

"Well," McCoy shrugged. "It is good that I asked. See you later, Spock."

McCoy left Spock's quarters.

AUXILIARY CONTROL. TWENTY-FIVE HOURS TILL RENDEZVOUS:

Lieutenant Kevin Riley stepped into the Auxiliary Control Room. Sitting at the main control desk was Pavel Chekov.

"So, Pavel, what's up?" Riley asked.

The young Russian officer smiled. "Nothing, really, it's as boring as Siberia here," Pavel said making one of his now-famous Russian remarks.

"You heard Uhura sing. Uhura's quite good," Riley remarked as he went behind the partition checking the systems and marking his pad.

"I see the captain has you doing internal system checks."

"Yeah, that's when I'm not in charge of the forward phaser room, I had to replace Tomlinson upon his death and Styles when he left the Enterprise soon after at Star base10." No matter how good a navigator, he was still living down the stupidity of Psi 2000, and his now-infamous Kathleen rant.

"What do you think of our chances, Kevin?" Pavel asked.

"I'd say fifty, fifty. I just heard some Scuttlebutt that Captain Hawke threw a big-time party in the ship's hanger bay for his crew, just to improve morale."

"They really know how to party on that ship," Chekov said.

"That ship." Riley pointed to the main screen that showed the Constitution. "Has quite a reputation, Pavel. They are only second to us. In the number of people waiting to serve on her and next to Enterprise, she has the second lowest transfer rate in the fleet."

"I heard that you were considering transferring Kevin."

"Well, Pavel, after that stupidity I pulled at Psi 2000, I was seriously considering it," Riley said exasperated.

"Which ships?"

Riley pointed at Constitution, "And I was also thinking about Kongo, Ari, and Excelsior as possible choices, but the captain refused all of my transfer requests."

"Toroyan, she's a hard taskmaster, Morrow is pretty fair, and La Liberté is a hoot. I heard Kevin," Chekov said. Kirk had his reasons for not letting Riley transfer.

"Kirk and Hawke mirror each other, but their command styles vary. Hawke leads by example. Kirk leads from the front," Riley said.

"They will both be great captains one day."

"Yeah. They will," Riley said as he left Auxiliary control.

TWENTY HOURS UNTIL RENDEZVOUS.
CONSTITUTION'S BRIDGE. GAMMA SHIFT:

The captain's yeoman, Barbara Smith, stepped onto the bridge of Constitution, holding a pitcher and some recyclable cups. The party had gone well. They were early into the Gamma shift. Due to some of the aftereffects of the party, Captain Hawke and Lieutenant Commander Shran had agreed to loosen things up. Except in a dire emergency, Alpha was going to report one hour later. So was Beta. But when they reached the rendezvous, it was back to business as usual.

Ensign Daniel Paul Harris, son of Captain Anton Harris of the Excalibur, the temporary Gamma shift duty officer, swung the command chair around to face the captain's yeoman. Harris had replaced Lt. Commander Sandra Markowitz, the ship's regular Gamma Shift duty officer. Sandy as she was known to the crew had left the ship at Versailles for some family business on Alpha Centuri. After that, she was to rendezvous with the ship at Star base 11, assuming they survived the challenge.

"Smith, thank the captain. We are all grateful for the shot of whiskey and chips we received before going on duty," Harris said.

"I will. I am sorry you all had to miss the party."

"What do you have there?" Ensign Aret a Leek asked from communications.

"It's called Pogash."

"It's a Harrata drink," Ensign Juan Catalan at navigation pointed out.

"It's not like Traga, their traditional drink; Pogash is used at all their religious ceremonies and is highly prized," Smith explained.

"Where the hell did the captain get that stuff?" Belker, manning helm, said.

"It's a long story, but in short, the captain had just been given his first command the destroyer Sargon. Her first mission was Bathazar 11 for the annual talks with the Imperium. No heavy, medium cruisers were available. And Jim Kirk was unavailable at the time, so it fell to our captain to transport Ambassador Fox to the station. The Harrata were so pleased. They gave Commander Hawke a few gallons of this stuff."

"I heard he also had an affair with a Harrata female," Catalan mentioned.

Smith nodded. "Shari Ben Gazari Fahiri, Juan, the present Harrata Imperium ambassador to Earth."

"Whoa, Nelly," Kowalski said surprised by engineering.

"How does she look?" Dougherty asked. She was always curious about her captain's reputation as a ladies' man compared to the famous James T. Kirk.

Thallar, Constitution's Gamma shift science officer and one of three Andorians on the ship that included Shran and Thor Ahreamann Men or in short Thor ah Men, the ship's forward phaser room commander, manning the science station, punched up her picture and displayed it on all the overhead screens.

"Damn, she's pretty," Sherman at Tactical said surprised.

"Now if you boys have had your fun, let's all try the Pogash," Thallar erased Ben Gazari's image from the screens. "This is nonalcoholic. But let me show you something." Smith swirled the rainbow-colored liquid, and it became blue. "Mister Harris." Harris drank the blue liquid.

"Damn that's good. Almost like blueberries."

Smith walked down and again swirled the liquid. It became red. And he gave it out and repeated the process. Each time the liquid changed color and tasted different. "And so, the lesson ends," Smith said as she finished with the bridge crew.

"Thanks, you yeoman," Harris said graciously. "It was a pleasure."

Smith smiled. "Only doing my duty, Ensign, but I will tell the captain you all enjoyed it and the tales." The turbo lift doors closed behind Smith.

MAIN ENGINEERING. SCOTT'S OFFICE. FIFTEEN HOURS TILL RENDEZVOUS:

Montgomery Scott looked at Thomas's image. He was in the chief engineer's office. Thomas was in his opposite one on the Constitution.

"That book on impulse procedures is a gem, Scotty," Andrews said.

"Thank you, Tom," Scotty said.

"Did you update your life support system?" Scotty asked.

"Aye, eight months ago. But we haven't had shore leave since. And the captain is still moaning about half the crew wearing the

Enterprise insignia instead of our own. We are due at Star base 11 for a long overdue upgrade and an overhaul. The captain is insistent that we keep our rear phaser and photon banks regardless of what Commander Goldman at Star base 11 says," Andrews said.

During the eight months of continuous missions, the crew only had two brief shore leaves on two misbegotten space stations on the frontier. Most of the crew hadn't set foot on Terra firma since. They were supposed to go to Star base 11 for a one-month shore leave, overhaul, and upgrade after the Versailles mission, but this Harrata thing ended all chances of that. His kittens desperately needed an overhaul. The old lady needed a break from this continuous cycle. But despite this, Constitution was holding up very well. At least, he didn't have to go one year without relief that one of his predecessors Esterhaus had to put the Constitution through during the Four-Year war. Andrews recalled.

"Reminds me of Kirk, Tom, all captains are alike, they act like spoiled children. They want everything their way. Hear anything from Cordoba or Najjar." Scotty asked about the chief engineers of Excalibur and Constellation.

"Yes," Thomas admitted. "We ran into Excalibur and Constellation four months earlier on a joint survey mission to Star cluster T896 in sector 221-H not far from sector 221-G which contained the Thallonian Empire. Najjar, she's still a grouch and Cordoba still has a chip on his shoulder."

Scotty smiled. Juan Cordoba and Miriam Najjar were old-time Chief engineers, both had been instructors at Starfleet Academy when he was a cadet.

"I don't know, Scotty. Cordoba always had a temper. Any deviation from the procedure and he'd turn you into bat guano, served with him after my stint at Fleet Construction, and helped build the last four Constitutions and the first five Bonhomme Richards, served on Excalibur for two years, and back in 57, I finally made it to Constitution after the Nsrii affair."

Scotty nodded. He was just lucky he got the Enterprise, all those years ago.

"Cordoba is a procedure-driven engineer, Tom. Like those by the book captains, doesn't like innovators like us who turn procedure upside down."

Thomas nodded. Procedure, Innovator, and Technical—the three types of engineers you'd find on ships. He and Scotty were innovators. Projeff and Najjar, technicians, Cordoba, procedure-driven.

"Tell me, Tom, is ye still tinkering with ship designs?"

"Yes. Did you see my article in the Cochrane?"

Scotty nodded. The Cochrane was the fleet magazine for the engineers. Thomas had written an article on projecting the designs of ships for the next hundred years. It had caused quite a stir just like his book on impulse engine procedures.

Scotty's intercom whistled. Scotty turned away from the viewer to answer it.

"I got to go, Tom. Something came up."

"Until the next time." Thomas's image faded. Scotty left his office.

CONSTITUTION'S HANGER DECK. TEN HOURS TILL RENDEZVOUS:

Neil Sorenson, Commander, affectionately known to the crew of the Constitution as Gramps, and Constitution's oldest, longest-serving crew member, walked through his shuttle bay. Sorenson inspected every detail. The Hull, Constitution's long-range shuttle was in her usual standby position. Stewart and Bainbridge, two classes F shuttles, sat in the back of the hanger bay.

On the lower level, Constitution's armored shuttle, the Rodgers and her aqua shuttle, the James Madison and the diplomatic shuttle, Thomas Jefferson along with the Class E's Preble, and Turner and her spare class D's the Radford. Talbot was stored in the large bay. Nearby, some of the pilots were checking each shuttle, doing routine diagnostics and preflight checks. He had lost track of the time he spent on this ship. Sorensen had turned down offers to serve on some of her sister ships including Enterprise.

He could still remember her present captain as a troublesome nine-year-old who was turning ten later on that month, came aboard with his family for the Babel trip, in early April of that year. Constitution had a lot of great captains—Jefferies, Joe Hawke, Augenthaler, Wesley, and now her present one.

But there were two he didn't care for. Page was a poltroon and a fool who had used politics to do an end-run and steal command of Constitution from Augenthaler and nearly lost the ship. Fifty people had lost their lives and one hundred were injured thanks to Page's stupidity. Starfleet quickly rectified their mistake and gave the ship back to Augenthaler.

And then there was the pseudo captain, Garth, who never really commanded this ship. He hated that some reference materials were trumping that Garth had commanded this ship for ten years when Joe Hawke was the real captain. Hell, why not talk to Admiral Jefferies to confirm it?

Garth was married to his real commands during that period—Baton Rouge, Xenophon, Ares, and Heisenberg. Command of Constitution was a sideshow for Garth as well as his brief time on the Lexington and Intrepid. With the rank of fleet captain bestowed on him in 2244 when he commanded Baton Rouge at Donatu Five, he was fleet captain of the entire Constitution class division. After Joe Hawke had left for the Essex in 2254, Garth had enjoyed his only full year as Captain. After that, it was back to the Heisenberg for the rest of the decade. Even though he commanded Heisenberg until 2260 and the Antos affair, Augenthaler had replaced him that year.

The reality was that Captain Joseph Hawke and Admiral William Jefferies had put Constitution together. After Donatu Five, Garth used every means necessary to do a political end-run around Jefferies and Joe Hawke. Garth interfered with the repair and update process long enough that it delayed Constitution's official launching. Constitution was launched eight days after Enterprise.

Garth later used Constitution as his flagship during the brief Axanar Rebellion and hijacked the ship as his flagship during the Four Years' War.

During both conflicts, Garth ran roughshod over Captain Hawke and the crew. Constitution did a full year without relief during the Four Years' War. He twice threatened to have Hawke senior removed, secretly planning on replacing Hawke with West of the Bonhomme Richard.

Sorensen knew one thing. He never understood the wide-eyed mysticism some of the youngsters had for Garth. Sure, Garth was brilliant. During the Axanar Rebellion in early 2251, he commandeered the Constitution from Joe Hawke and obliterated two D5s and a D7 at the famous First battle of Axanar. But his Canada class J Heavy cruiser, Heisenberg, could have done the same job too and spared Joe Hawke damage to his ship.

Garth then washed his hands off the Constitution and went back to the Heisenberg. A week later, he brilliantly sent the remaining Heavy Cruiser Squadron along with the two medium cruisers and the lone destroyer away to intercept the Klingon relief force near the Acheron system. Using the Heisenberg, Garth's regular command, he wiped out the lone Klingon battle cruiser near the Axanar system in the second Battle of Axanar and garnered all the glory for himself.

Thankfully, he sent Constitution, Valiant, Soyuz, and Bozeman away at the end of the Rebellion, only keeping the Republic, Bon Homme Richard, Heisenberg, and Xenophon available for the Axanar Peace Mission. Sorensen smiled. He was glad just to get away from Axanar and Garth's megalomaniacal influence.

Constitution had barely resumed her exploration mission when Garth again shanghaied the ship during the Four Years' War as his flagship. Leading to two more battles above Axanar and giving scholars of both conflicts even more confusion between the Axanar Rebellion and the Four Years' War, it was eventually agreed that all four battles became known as the Axanar campaign. Constitution luckily sat out the brief Klingon-Federation conflict of 2257 at the end of the Four Years' War.

Luckily for Joe Hawke and the rest of the crew, Constitution only served two out of the four years of the conflict.

Sighing, Sorenson hoped that Constitution and Enterprise would both survive. It would be a tragedy for Starfleet and the Federation if both ships were lost.

To brighten his glum mood, Sorensen started to whistle out this old tune he knew. Some of the pilots turned from their work to listen, but his sharp eye sent them back to work. Brushing his silver-grey hair back, Sorenson continued to whistle the old tune as he headed for the maintenance bay.

NEAR THE BOTANICAL GARDENS SECTION. ENTERPRISE. FIVE HOURS TILL RENDEZVOUS:

Janice Rand, Elizabeth Palmer, and Nyota Uhura walked to the ship's Botanical area. Sulu was going to meet them. Sulu had Enterprise's favorite plant, Beauregard, present and accounted for.

Uhura showed a scanned holo photocopy of Maxine, Constitution's pet Siamese, and the captain's pet to Palmer and Rand.

"So, that's what Barbara Smith is all excited about," Rand said sarcastically.

"Isn't Maxine a pretty one, Janice? The cat has free rein of the ship. Smith told me she even flushed out an alien stowaway four months ago," Uhura explained. "The crew didn't know how the stowaway got aboard the ship. But they found the aliens' homeworld and set up the first contact."

Palmer laughed. "All thanks to a cat. You'd think we'd be so lucky."

Rand nodded in agreement.

"Isn't she a cute one?" Rand said swiping the picture from Uhura.

"Hey, Janice," Uhura moaned.

"Alright," Rand relented and handed the photo over to Palmer who passed it back to Uhura.

Moments later, the three ladies arrived at the botanical garden.

Sulu was leaning against a wall. "What took you so long?"

"This is why, Hikaru," Uhura said showing the photo of a cat.

"It's a she, am I right? That I bet is Captain Hawke's famous feline. Maxine," Sulu said excitedly.

The ladies all agreed.

"Come on, Hikaru, she's only a cat. Even your Beauregard is more interesting than that fur bag," and said exasperated.

"Now, Janice, you want to anger the entire crew of the Constitution," Palmer said.

"Yes."

Uhura folded her arms together. "Figures!"

"Why do you say that?"

"You are still angry at Smith for temporarily replacing you as Kirk's yeoman," said Uhura.

"So?"

Sulu watched as Uhura and Rand verbally battled it out between them. Palmer stayed silent.

Sulu finally cuts into the verbal discourse.

"I have an idea. Let's send Smith a photo of Beauregard. She's our mascot."

"Anybody has a holocam?"

"I do, I have one in my quarters," Palmer said.

"Go get it, Liz."

"Right," Palmer sped off toward her quarters.

Sulu followed by Rand. Uhura entered the botanical area. Minutes later, Palmer arrived back at the Botanical area and joined the group. "Breathless," Palmer said. "Got it."

Sulu quickly took the photo of Beauregard and handed it to Uhura. "You know what to do."

"Yes, Hikaru." Uhura nodded. She knew exactly what she was going to do. And it would drive her academy rival Mariko Shimada crazy.

VINCENT DESALLES QUARTERS. FOUR HOURS TILL RENDEZVOUS:

Vincent Anton Desalle also known as Mike, his nickname which he hated, sat in front of the screen looking at his older sister. He hadn't seen her since her transfer to the Constitution from the Lafayette which they both had served on.

"So, sis, how is everything?"

"Fine, has mom or pop contacted you lately?"

"No, Barbara. No word from them. If I know pop, he is too busy with the fishing trawler to worry about us," Desalle said. He and Barbara both hailed from Marseille, France. Their dad was a fisherman and mom ran a Boulangerie.

"I never understood why you never wanted to work on Enterprise, sis."

"Augenthaler dangled a nice bit of bait, Vince. And I grabbed it. I was considering Enterprise. But Pike never ran out a hook, line, and sinker."

"How is Captain Hawke treating you?" Vincent asked his sister.

"Great."

"And Kirk?"

"Same, Barbara, I saw the picture of your mascot Maxine. Someone called it a fur bag."

Barbara's image became livid. "A fur bag! Maxine's a doll, the whole crew adores her. Oh, and I saw that plant your crew worships. Someone on my ship called Beauregard an oversized Venus flytrap."

Vincent Desalle almost blew up. "C'mon, Barbara, we love Beauregard. It did sniff out a salt-sucking vampire."

"And Maxine is just a useless fur bag!" Barbara said lividly.

"No, Barbara."

"Maxine sniffed out an alien stowaway Vinny. And she did plenty of other things too which I don't want to mention since your crewmates would probably deride that too."

Vincent paused for a moment. He knew that once the conversation was ended. All hell was going to break loose all over two mascots. Barbara was going to report to her captain. And he had to do the same.

"I will see you soon, brother."

"Yes, sis." His sister's image faded. Desalle got up and headed off to find his captain and explain the whole thing.

KIRK'S QUARTERS. FORTY MINUTES TILL RENDEZVOUS:

Kirk was in his quarters when his buzzer went off. Dropping the book he was reading, Kirk called out, "Who?"

"McCoy and Spock, Jim."

"Come in." Kirk hit the open button.

Spock and McCoy walked in. Kirk noticed that Spock had an unreadable expression and McCoy was fidgeting. Which meant? Something was up.

"Now don't tell me."

"We seem to have a minor crisis concerning the morale of both crews," said McCoy.

"About what?" Kirk asked, concerned.

"Sulu's Beauregard and Captain Hawke's cat Maxine," Spock said literally letting the cat out of the bag.

"I heard a rumor. That someone obtained a photo of Bobby's cat."

"Yes, Captain. But your yeoman called it a fur bag," Spock said blandly.

"A fur bag," Kirk started to get angry.

"And in retaliation, Uhura sent a photo of Beauregard, Sulu's pet plant, calling it our mascot to the other ship. And which lead to a crew person on Constitution calling Beauregard an oversized Venus flytrap," McCoy admitted.

"Great, just great," Kirk said angered. "I'm just surprised that Bob hasn't contacted me yet on this matter."

"I think our fellow Starfleet officers are logically trying to mend wounded pride on their ship, Jim," Spock said. Human pride, Spock found, was so illogical. Pride led to error but also success if one had pride in one's own ship and crew.

Kirk hit the intercom. "Kirk to bridge."

Sulu's image appeared. "Yes, Captain."

"ETA to rendezvous."

"Less than an hour, forty minutes according to Ensign Chekov's calculations."

"Chekov." Kirk looked at McCoy and Spock.

"Captain, Mister Chekov has been on the ship for quite some time. He is doing training in Sciences and the Auxiliary Control room. This is his second time serving on the bridge Captain," Spock informed Kirk.

"Thank you, Spock, Uhura's any word from Constitution."

"No, Captain. My opposite numbers have gone silent for the time being."

"I think we all know why, Lieutenant."

"Yes, Sir, that cat on the other ship."

"Thank you, Uhura."

"Keptin Kirk." Pavel Chekov's image appeared in the place of Uhura.

"Yes, Ensign."

"Long-range sensors are picking up four Medium cruiser class starships of Federation design."

"Have you identified them?"

"Mister Desalle says they are the Miranda-NCC 1846, Soyuz-NCC 1940, Anton-NCC 1000 and Oxford- NCC 751, Unit XY-75847."

Kirk looked to Spock and McCoy. "That's just great," Kirk said annoyed. "Wait until Samantha Reynolds hears everything about us insulting Bobby's cat."

"That's if she hears about it, Jim. You did say that Bobby never liked to make a scene," McCoy suggested.

"That's not his way unless you provoke, Robert, then he will chew the furniture up," Kirk said deadpanned and turned back to face Chekov's image on the viewer. "ETA, Mister Chekov?"

"Less than twenty minutes."

"And when will we arrive at Harrata space?" Kirk asked the young navigator.

"Twenty minutes later."

"Good job, Mister Chekov. We will be there shortly."

CHAPTER ELEVEN

ENTERPRISE BRIDGE. APPROACHING RENDEZVOUS:

Kirk, Spock, and McCoy trotted out on the bridge. "Magnify, Mister Sulu."

"Aye, Sir."

On the Enterprise screen, four cruiser-type starships were approaching. Two were Miranda's; Samantha's Soyuz had an extended rear section containing her aft sensor pod and two turbo phasers, Soyuz also had the standard circumferential nacelles. The Soyuz's were also known as modified Miranda's and the Anton had a slightly different look to her. The Anton was Mike Walsh's ship.

"Captain Kirk, there is a Captain Samantha Reynolds online," Uhura explained.

"You know her, Jim."

"Yes, Bones. She's Robert's girlfriend, I nearly stole her from Bobby back during our academy days," Kirk told Bones, turning to Uhura. "Put her on Lieutenant."

"Aye, Sir," Uhura said as she switched over. Moments later, the four ships were replaced by a beautiful, long-haired brunette wearing her hair loosely. She had black leggings and boots. Samantha wore the typical feminine command gold service uniform with captain's stripes and the upside-down Constitution insignia symbolizing the Soyuz. Like Brittany Mendez, on the Exeter, Samantha had mimicked her when she had served on the Exeter as a cadet; Mendez had worn her long blond hair loosely in defiance of regulation. Samantha had been promoted to captain in December 2264, two months after her birthday and she was the youngest female in Starfleet history to reach the rank of captain.

"Hello, Jimmy."

Kirk got up. "Pleasure to see you again, haven't seen you since you replaced me on the Bonhomme Richard Sam."

"Like everyone else at the academy, I wanted to command Enterprise Jim. But instead of Enterprise, I go here and there on this Border Patrol cruiser. I have you and Bob on split-screen. We are all here just to see you both off and Harry Morrow says hello."

"Tell Harry thank you, Samantha."

"Now remember, Jim. Both you and Robert better come back alive. The universe would be a dull place without you and Robert. Love it when both of you thumb your noses at dunderheads at Starfleet Command," Samantha said to Kirk smiling.

Spock raised an eyebrow as he looked at Kirk.

"Don't worry about both of us, Samantha. We will return," Kirk reassured Samantha.

"Jim, take good care of Robert. I don't want him doing something foolish."

He could hear Robert doing a polite clearing of his throat in the background.

"And give the Harrata hell, Jim, Soyuz out," Samantha said as her image faded to be replaced by space. The four cruisers swung from a squadron formation into a line astern. Then they flanked in twos port and starboard of both ships.

"Spock."

"Soyuz and Miranda are starboard of Constitution. Oxford and Anton are the ports of Enterprise. We are being escorted to Harrata territory."

"What a woman, Jim."

"Samantha is something else, Bones. She and a senior year student Atish Khatami wound up battling over Robert back during their freshman year. That same year, I also tried to steal her from Robert. But I think Robert and Gary had something to do with that blond lab technician they sent to me."

"Hawke wanted you away from Samantha, Jim. I think I see why, she's a knockout. Have you seen Carol lately, Jim?"

"No, Bones. Last I heard in 2264, she was posted to the Mathazar Science facility at 766 Alpha."

"I bet David was with her."

Kirk said nothing. McCoy rarely ever spoke about Joanna his daughter or Barbara. So, he said nothing at all about David.

"They both broke up, shortly after their graduation from Starfleet Academy Bones. They didn't get back together until 2264. Just before I had to return to the Sacagawea, I remember Robert dropping by."

KIRK'S TEMPORARY RESIDENCE ONE DAY PRIOR TO SEEING MITCHELL. FEBRUARY 1, 2264:

Kirk sweated as he carefully mixed the ingredients for Fettuccine Alfredo sauce. The pasta was cooking and had to be exactly right. He hated overcooked pasta or burned Alfredo sauce.

It had been three months since he and Carol had that argument, and both had gone their separate ways. Sacajawea was in drydock undergoing upgrades and awaiting the return of her captain. Reluctantly, he agreed. Mitchell was still in the hospital recovering. It had been a quiet new year. Hearings on the loss of Lydia Sutherland had taken up much of his time. He had been ordered to return to the command of the Sacajawea by March of this year. And had been cleared of blame in the Battle of Ghihoge.

The doorbell buzzed. He wasn't expecting any visitors today.

"Computer, who is it," Kirk said irritated. He wasn't expecting any visitors today.

The screen above him lit up. "Captain Robert N. Hawke, Starfleet," the voice said.

That was odd. At last report, Robert was still in command of the Miranda.

"Guess who," Robert's voice chimed through the intercom.

"Hold on, Bob," Kirk said. "Computers grant access."

The door lock snapped open, and Robert Hawke strode in.

"Hello, Jim," Hawke said smiling. Kirk could see that Robert was wearing his standard Starfleet uniform where only the insignia was different, instead of Miranda's triangle. The patch he was wearing designated was Constitution's half Delta.

"Rumor has it, Jim, you might get the Enterprise," Hawke said.

"The Enterprise that would be the day. You got the Constitution," Kirk said.

"Well, here is some Eyyaian wine. Let's celebrate my new command," Hawke said as he handed Kirk the gold-edged wine bottle and looked around Kirk's trailer home. "Not much but comfy, Jim," Hawke commented.

Kirk took the bottle and placed it on the table. Walking over to the stove, he checked the pasta. It was Al dente. Quickly, he drained the pot and checked the sauce. It was exactly right. Kirk mixed the sauce and the pasta together. "Would you like some?" Kirk offered.

"Thank you, Jim," Hawke said graciously as he took the plate of pasta over to the table and sat down. Kirk sat opposite him and he opened the wine bottle up. "Eyyaian wine, didn't your dad..."

"Yes, Jim, during the two five-year missions, he commanded Constitution and the one five-year mission he commanded the Essex before his promotion to the Admiralty. During the time Constitution was under his command, they made first contact with the Kropasalins, Eyyaian, Betazeds, and Bolians. All of that despite the distraction of Garth, the Axanar Rebellion, and the Four Years' War," Hawke admitted and continued.

"And we all know that in 2254, he took command of the Essex and made first contact with the Shelliack Corporate. Despite his peace overtures to the Shelliack, we went to war with them in 2257. My dad unlike Garth localized the conflict and the war was concluded by the next year. Later, he helped Ambassadors Sarek, Shran, Fox, and Harden hash out the Treaty of Armens," Robert said between bites of pasta.

Kirk admired Garth, but then he and Robert stood on opposite fences of Garth as far as their opinions went.

"And your mom?" Kirk asked.

"She joined dad in help hash out the Treaty ,of Armens. Despite their divorce, and she even helped update the liguacode database to include Shelliack before returning to the Triangle sector and her job with Starfleet Intelligence," Hawke finished. Changing the subject, Hawke asked Kirk, "And how's your family, Jim?"

"What happened to Miranda?" Kirk asked curiously.

"While you were still at Starfleet Medical, last month, I surrendered command of Miranda to John Harriman who had previously commanded the Canopus class research ship, the Sea of Tranquility. I then spent a month working at Starfleet operations. Shran my former exec is now working at Utopia Planetia, testing new ships. She will join me on Constitution tomorrow. I got a call from Nogura two weeks ago. Wesley had approved of my posting to Constitution, replacing him as captain."

Kirk took a sip of the Eyyaian wine, reminding him of sweet Bordeaux. His old squadron commander had been given Constitution in 2263 after Augenthaler brought her home from another five-year mission.

"Congratulations are in order, Robert," Kirk said.

"Not so fast, Jim. Noguchi and Nogura agreed that Constitution needs a thorough going over and we are being reassigned to Starfleet Academy for cadet cruises and other low priority assignments. Until then my five-year mission of exploration is on hold. Potemkin under Martin Callas is going into dock for a major overhaul along with Republic-NCC 1371 and John Enright's Defiance-NCC 1617."

"Anything wrong with my pasta?" Kirk said slightly annoyed.

"No, Jim," Hawke said as he dove back into the fettuccine.

"Remember Saratoga-NCC1724. You know her nickname Sara No Go A."

Kirk and Hawke laughed.

"No go a, for a good reason, Jim. That ship has yet to be given a mission of Exploration; Saratoga is always doing border patrol work or fleet assignments," Hawke explained. "Remember Alexi Nacheyev who I succeeded as captain of the Miranda? Well, Alexi got the Saratoga."

Nacheyev had graduated from the Academy in 2250. Kirk recalled as he posed another question. "I heard Nick Silver and Phil Waterston are competing against you for command of Constitution, Bob?"

"Yes," Hawke said as he took a sip of wine. "Nick Silver commands the Ares, Phil Waterston, the Ptolemy," Hawke added. "And they both lost. Remember Ghighoge. That stunt I pulled, rescuing you and your crew as well as negotiating with the Ghihogans and the masters put me right to the top of the list. We were both equal, Jim, until Ghihoge. But you still have a more impressive service record than mine."

"Tell me, Bob, what it is between you and Phil. He was in your class, and you never liked each other."

"I don't want to discuss Waterston, Jim," Hawke said slightly irritated.

Kirk backed off. "Have you seen anyone else that we know?"

"Bumped into Andovar. He was working as an aide to Vice Admiral Ran Armstrong. Drake is also on a temporary assignment. He's angry that I got Constitution and he didn't."

Nothing ever changed, Kirk thought. Hawke had Waterston and he had Drake.

Rousseau was Lexington's present captain. Kirk had beat him to become the youngest with the rank of Captain in 2261 on his birthday. A year later in April 2262, Robert had become the second youngest, leaving Rousseau, a distant third. Rousseau had received his first command in 2253 with the rank of captain.

Hawke checked his chronometer. "Got to go, Jim, thanks for the pasta."

"Why?"

"Remember Samantha? The Bonhomme Richard is making a shortstop by Earth. Sam and I are getting back together again," Hawke said as he got up.

Samantha had replaced him as an executive officer when he left for Alexander and El Dorado and one other ship. He couldn't quite recall its name.

Kirk got up and shook Bob's hand. "Good to see you again, Bob. Thanks for dropping by."

"Any time, Jim. See you soon," Hawke said as he dashed out.

Kirk went back to the table and finished his food.

PRESENT DAY. THE RENDEZVOUS:

"Captain Kirk Unit XY-75847 is disengaging," Spock said.

"We are approaching the Federation-Harrata border," Desalle added.

"Spock, long-range sensor sweep."

"Captain, I have six Harrata ships approaching. Four are Hogar type 7s. Two are Hogar type 8s."

"On screen, Mister Sulu, all stop."

"Aye, Sir."

"Constitution has come to a full stop, Captain."

"Station keeping, Mister Sulu."

"Aye, Sir."

"Captain, shall I go to Red alert?"

"Negative, Uhura."

"Spock."

"The Harrata ships do not have their shields up. Nor are their weapons energized."

"On screen, Mister Sulu."

"Aye, Sir," Sulu said as he adjusted the controls. In two classic V formations were six ugly Harrata battle cruisers. The lead ships however looked newer. Those were probably the new Type 8s. Rumors had it that they had neutronium hull plating on the vital areas in addition to shields.

"Spock."

"The lead ships are Type 8s. Captain, the Gom de Zak and the Hajj ba Hajj. The other four ships are type 7s, the Hittati, Polaz de Visitor, Logash, and the Parmela Du Hag."

"Captain, the Gom de Zak is signaling us, a Commandant Hari Na Bogash."

"Commandant, isn't that the Harrata equivalent to Commodore Jim?" McCoy said.

"Yes, Bones. Uhura, put the Commandant on."

"Aye, Sir."

Moments later, the screen shimmered from the view of the approaching Harrata ships to a triangular gold, blue, and red bridge. Opposite Sulu and Desalle sat their equivalents. Behind them were four seats. Three out of the four were manned. Two were blue-skinned, wearing the gold uniform of the Star force. One was red-skinned and wore the silver uniform of the High Order Corp.

A tall Harrata got up. He had the classic male Mohawk hairstyle. Blue skin. His hair was blond, and he had a fancy blond mustache with curls. Bogash had the look of a veteran, and he maintained a carefully practiced air around him. This commander Kirk could tell just by observing his opponent was nobody's fool. If they survived the entire challenge, he would be a formidable opponent in the final round.

"I am Commandant Hari Na Bogash, commander of the Gom de Zak. Leader of the Bogash Attack wing of Star Force Group Alp. We come at the bidding of Gom to face the challengers of the Federanski in the holy rite of Tong," Bogash said in fluent standard with a bit of an accent.

Kirk got out of his command chair. "Commandant Bogash. I am Captain James Tiberius Kirk, captain of the Enterprise, commander of unit X-001. We come at the bidding of the Federation to take part in the holy rite of Tong. We honor your presence."

The Harrata took both of his hands, formed a fist, and touched them together.

Kirk did the same.

"You honor us, Ober Commander Kirk, in accordance with our traditions. I request you put your engines on standby and neutralize your helm and navigation controls."

Kirk looked at Sulu and Desalle. "Mister Sulu. Mister Desalle, neutralize all helm and navigation controls."

Desalle and Sulu immediately complied. Kirk looked at Scott. "Mister Scott. Put all engines on standby."

"But, Sir."

"Mister Scott."

"Aye, Sir," Scotty said as he put the engines on standby.

"Spock, what about Constitution?"

"The Harrata ships are already forming an inverted V around her and their tractor beams are locking on."

Kirk felt relieved; Robert was anticipating as he always did.

Kirk put his fists together. "It is done, Commandant."

"We stand honored, Ober Commander Kirk, Gom de Zak out."

The screen was replaced by the Hogars. The type 7s banked port and starboard of Enterprise and the type 8 flew over Enterprise. Kirk could see the neutronium hull plating and the quad nacelle configuration. Harrata ships were not known for their beauty. Enterprise shook twice.

"They are locking tractor beams on us," said Spock.

Seconds later, the Enterprise and Constitution, escorted by the Harrata attack wings, entered Harrata territory.

CHAPTER TWELVE

THE LEGATION. HOME TO THE OUTWORLDER AMBASSADORS, CITY OF TOMAR, HARRATA FOUR. STAR DATE 2908.7. January 18, 2267:

Federation Ambassador Andrea Burroughs slept soundly in her opulent quarters. After a long night of ceremonies, Andrea needed her sleep. The Harrata had a way of wearing down ambassadors with their constant religious ceremonies for their various deities.

Trumpets blared. Andrea, startled, tumbled out of her bed. "Damn," she cursed, getting up.

Burroughs tried to orient herself. "Computer, what time is it?"

A high-order female voice came back, "The time is 9 kells; the day is Nami, the month of Vorash in the year 500,000."

"Thank you," Burroughs said exasperated. In Federation time, it would be 9 o clocks, January, Tuesday, in the year 2267. She had been assigned to the Harrata home world since 2265; replacing Ambassador Neville Chamberlin who had died. Fox, Sarek, Shran, and Hardin with the approval of the Bureau of Interplanetary affairs had sent her to this crazy nuthouse. Out of all the worlds she wound up being assigned to, this one took the cake.

Her doorbell buzzed.

"Yes."

"Andrea, it's Andrew."

"Come."

A man of medium height with short black hair came in. Andrew Sutton had been her aide ever since Donna her first one left two years ago. Donna couldn't stand the craziness of the Harrata.

"The Ambassadors are gathering on the main balcony."

"Why?" Andrea said. At least, being an ambassador was more predictable than her brief career in Starfleet. She had served on the Excalibur straight out of the academy. Her C.O. had picked up that she had excellent diplomatic skills. So, after five years on the Excalibur, she transferred to the diplomatic corp. and left Starfleet for good. She never regretted the decision.

The trumpets continued to blare in the background.

"The Shawazee, Andrea, the last was . . ."

"I know when it was," Andrea said tired and irritated.

Taken aback by Andrea's response, Andrew backed off.

"Sorry, Andy. But the Celebration of Vishna really wore me out," Burroughs said. "Give me a moment and I will make a quick change. And when I'm finished, I need my schedule for the day."

"Yes," Andrew said as he left.

MINUTES LATER:

Burroughs and Sutton got into the central turbo lift. Standing next to them were two aliens with mournful expressions on their faces. Burroughs immediately recognized them to be the Pakleds.

The Constitution had made first contact with them a few months earlier. The lift stopped and the Romulan delegation stepped in. "Ambassador Burroughs," the Romulan Ambassador said courteously.

"Ambassador Burroughs."

"Ambassador Noral."

The lift took off again and stopped. Two lizard-like aliens stepped in. The Romulans' expressions of neutral benevolence darkened. The race who called themselves Cardassians had arrived.

"Ambassadors Burroughs, Noral, and what was your name again?" the Cardassians said to the Pakleds.

"I am Bomzak, Ambassador of Pak."

"Yes, Bomzak, we have much to discuss today."

"Yes, Matel, we need things," the Pakleds said meekly.

Bomzak turned to Burroughs. "We need things. We like Constitution. We need ships like her."

"Ambassador Bomzak. If I were to quote Captain Hawke's report to Starfleet, you wouldn't like what you hear. I see why the Harrata conquered both you and the Ferengi. Your people tried to steal

Starfleet's property. Captain Hawke had to put guards at all the vital areas of his ship," Andrea recalled.

"Tell me, Ambassador Burroughs," Martel cut in. "We are hoping your people stay in their side of the galaxy and leave the Cardassians' Union alone."

"None of our far-ranging Constitution class ships has yet to reach that far, Ambassador."

"The Obsidian Order tends to differ, Ambassador, at the rate of expansion of your Federation. We will have a full first contact not counting our present meeting within two years."

"Your expansions may soon bring you into contact with the region known as the maelstrom and one of our neighbors, a planet known as Bajor," Martel's aide Mira said.

"The Federation has always tried for a peaceful expansion, Ambassador Martel."

"If that isn't a lie," Noral said bitterly.

"Are you referring Noral took the Earth-Romulan War? You tried to stop the formation of our Federation. And I am aware of the recent battles of Icarus and the Hydra Nebula. When your people used our earth outposts as guinea pigs and then you send one of your ships deep into Federation space, the aggressor ship destroyed Deep Space K13, outpost Tiger, and the Malvern Research facility and you heavily damaged the Star liner Stellarford before another one of our ships destroyed the aggressor's vessel," Burroughs pointed out.

"We have a right to stop aggressive expansion, Ambassador Burroughs," Noral said as the lift stopped.

"And we have a right to stop any aggression against our Federation," Burroughs said as he and the rest of the Ambassadors were deposited into a half-circular room. "Good day, Noral, Martel, and Bomzak."

Burroughs said as he and Sutton walked toward the balcony. The sound of the trumpets blared and drums rattled in the distance. The Legation had been positioned directly on the Boulevard of the Imperium, separating the Temples of the Deities from the government buildings of the Harrata Imperium.

Exiting the room, Burroughs and Sutton could feel the blast of heat that permeated this planet. It was as hot as Miami in July on this planet for eight out of thirteen months.

Andrea looked out from the long, expansive balcony. Massive stone buildings dominated the city.

Looking around her, she made out the following alien races present: Kzinti, Lyrans, Hydrans, Mirak, Orions, Romulans, Klingons, Tholians, Xindi, and the Skorr as well as the new races the Ferengi, the so-called Cardassians, Pakleds, and a lizard race yet unidentified. The mysterious Breen and Shelliack were never seen. There were however no Naussicans.

The Harrata and the Naussicans had never gotten along. She still received occasional reports of Naussicans raiders clashing with the Star force when they were traveling through Federation space, a necessary evil provided by the two treaties with the Imperium. The Federation could patrol the territorial zone separating the Imperium from the Federation. But Harrata Star force ships had a right to come and go as they pleased into Federation space for trading and other business if war wasn't declared.

There were three buildings in the legation. The Harrata had a nasty way of showing how important you were by which building your legation stayed at. The building that she was presently stayed at was number one. Number two had the less important races and was situated to the right. Number two, with a balcony only half the length of this one building three on the left, had no balcony at all.

Andrea looked down at the multicolored masses below him. They were milling about. The silver uniformed High Order Corp and the Middle Order Corp were lining up on both sides of the Boulevard forming a wall in front of the multicolored masses.

The trumpets rang out again at the very edge of Temple of the Gods Way. A procession started to make their way down the boulevard. Suddenly, in unison, just like the madness, he witnessed when Gom had called for the Challenge against the Federation and the Klingon Empire one week ago.

The Harrata people on the street suddenly chanted in unison, "Shawazee! Shawazee!"

"Isn't this great, Andrea?" Howard said. "Not many off-worlders get a chance to see the Shawazee or the Procession that contains the mysterious Book of Prophecy."

Burroughs smiled at Sutton. He was right. "Yes, my dear. It is almost like going to Gol on Vulcan and seeing the adepts of Kolinar," Andrea recollected. Vulcan was hot but not as humid.

The Shawazee didn't pray to any of the thirteen deities of the Harrata religion of Tomargura.

The Shawazee were the masters of all the thirteen styles of prayer.

To be a Shawazee, one had to master all the prayer styles of each of the Deities. Their only role in life was to honor the book of Prophecy.

And they were protected by the special units of the Star Force and the High Order Corp known as the Shawazee Guard and the Shawazee Special Group.

Drums rolled; trumpets sang out. Andrea picked up her macro binoculars and zoomed in on the procession. Leading the procession was a troop of the Shawazee Guard in their multicolored uniforms. With Red Cross belts for the troop and in the lead was the Commore (Colonel) with her red sash. He could hear her shout, "Shawazee! TO GA!" In standard, Shawazee, make way. Behind her, was the band also dressed up in their impressive multicolored uniforms. They were tapping out a tune that reminded her of the Hohenfreidberger March of Germany back on Earth.

Following the Shawazee Guard came a procession of Blues, a small contingent led by a Vorrad (Admiral) with their blue sashes and cross belts of the Special Group. Like all Shawazee contingents, their uniforms were multicolored.

Then came the Shawazee, led by High Priest Janis VA Basar. The Shawazee carried the square stone box that contained the Book of Prophecy. Behind them, first came the high priestess of Gom, Shara Van Nesapari. And behind her in two columns were the twelve remaining high priests and priestess representing the deities Tovar to Lothar.

Another group of the Special Group followed and at the end was another contingent of the Shawazee Guard.

A green-skinned woman suddenly bolted from the crowd and kissed the casket. She was immediately dragged back into the crowd by the Middle Order Corp. The Middle Order Corp did nothing. It had been said that if one kisses the box, one will be blessed and have good fortune.

"That woman has a lot of guts, John," Howard said to Andrea.

"Yes, she does," Andrea said. He suddenly felt someone tapping on his shoulder. Spinning around, he faced Klingon Ambassador Kass and his aide Tala.

"What can I do for you, Kass?" Andrea said clearly annoyed.

The heavy-set Klingon scowled, "We heard a rumor that your people chose Enterprise and Constitution to represent your pathetic Federation in this challenge."

"I cannot confirm or deny that Kass. I will confirm to you that the Cortez with the FNS has arrived under Star force escort. And I heard that your people send the scout ship PataQ with the Imperial Information Service and has also arrived."

"You will not succeed, Burroughs. You Terrans do not have the guts to survive this challenge. I welcome the day when the empire eliminates your pathetic Federation," Kass said as he and his aide stomped off.

"Kass had better not be right," Andrew admitted.

"Andrew, we all know what happened the last two times. Let's just pray that James Kirk and Bob Hawke are up to the challenge, my dear. Or else we will be spending the rest of our lives in this crazy place," said Burroughs.

Craning over the balcony, he could see the procession was approaching the Imperium Building. Turning back to face Andrew. Andrea asked. "Let me see what I need to do today, Andrew," Burroughs said as she looked at the data pad. "Oh, boy," she moaned. Her first meeting was with the Shelliack ambassador, to spend hours debating the treaty between the Federation and the Shelliack Corporate, giving the pad back to Helen. "Let's get a bite to eat, dear." It looked like another long day at the Harrata home world. Andrew and Andrea left the balcony.

IMPERIUM BUILDING. OFFICE OF THE CHANCELLOR OF THE HARRATA IMPERIUM. STAR DATE 2908.7:

"I tell you, Vardeck. There are omens all around us," Vice Chancellor Luci Nes Nigali warned.

"She is right." Vorrad Flotior Hazar Haj Dalomey, the Commander in Chief of the Star force, agreed with her. "The sea of Gazelle has turned from blue to a black color."

"And there are constant storms on the plains of Homass," Oberst Marshal (General in Chief) Renee VA Baslone, the Commander in Chief of the High Order Corp, said.

"Foretold in the book of prophecy," Transportation Minister Osca Cah Dezel said.

Vardeck suddenly looked up as his aide Donas ne Zekal ran in.

"Noble Chancellor! Noble Chancellor!" Donas said as the gilded doors parted. "The Shawazee! The Shawazee! Harr Chancellor," Donas said panting for breath.

"The Shawazee!"

"Yes, Noble Chancellor."

"Luci, gather the Noble Council, the Harrata Council, and the Supreme Imperials in the Great Hall of the Imperium."

"Yes, Noble Chancellor," Luci said as she spun around and left.

"The rest of the chancellors and ministers will also attend. And assemble the military staff and the Imperium governors, Renee."

The General bowed. "Yes, Noble Chancellor."

Not wasting any time, Da Banari and his remaining entourage made haste for the great hall of the Imperium. Bells rang out and gongs sounded. Quickly, they made their way to the hall, passing through the corridors of the Imperium Building.

Banari and his entourage finally made it to the enormous Great Hall of the Imperium. Statues of Former Harrata chancellors lined the ends of the walls. At each of the sections were paintings of the thirteen Harrata Deities or as the Outworlders called Gods. Orderly pandemonium raged as officials of the Imperium took their places in their required spots.

Banari, Negali, and Prator Fa Cosha, Viceroy of the Imperium, took their places in front of their required seats. Behind them sat the Supreme Imperials. To the right was the House of the Harrata and in front of them was the House of Lords. The ministers sat to the left of the Supreme Imperials and in front of them sat the Military Staff. At both ends of the central path were columns and two sets of seats manned by the governors that were present from the one hundred systems of the Imperium. Guarding both sides of the governors were the omnipresent High Order Corp troops interspersed with the Star Force Security.

A Shawazee soldier ran up to Cosha. Cosha nodded and stroked his red beard. Bowing, the Shawazee soldier ran out. Picking up his staff, he tapped it on the metal that lay below the staff. The bells stopped ringing and the gongs suddenly stopped.

"The chancellor of the Imperium!" he yelled out loud, his voice echoing throughout the hall.

Silence prevailed. Banari got up.

"By the Grace of Gom, Shawazee!" Banari's voice echoed through the great hall. On cue, all the Harrata officials stood up. The great doors parted. The procession began to make its way in. The band immediately stood to the side of the doors and continued to play. The Shawazee Guard and the Special Group officers and troops immediately took their places in front of the already-present High Order Corp and Star force troops.

The Shawazee marched forward carrying the stone box that contained the book of Prophecy. High Priest Janas VA Basar led the Shawazee carrying the Stone Box containing the book of Prophecy.

Behind them was the high priestess of Gom Shara Van Nespari and the twelve other priests and priestesses representing the other twelve deities.

The procession arrived at the stairs leading up to the chancellor.

"Shawazee!" Basar said. The entire room repeated in unison. Then everyone sat down, except Banari. Basar clapped his hands twice. The Shawazee gently put the box down, with a soft bang.

The Shawazee opened the stone box. Basar reached in and pulled out a heavy ornately designed book. He gently placed it on the dais that stood in front of the chancellor and the rest. All the other priests and priestesses immediately prostrated themselves, except for Nespari who glided over effortlessly to Basar. Basar touched his fists together. Nespari did likewise. And then he stood away from the podium.

Putting her right hand on the heavy book, Nespari recited, "Alkal VA sha, Alkal Shawazee, Vo Nespata Harrata, Harrata to Gom, Harrata to phasy. To Pha, Harrata, Photash Photash."

The book glowed and flung itself open.

Nespari looked at the page. She shook her head. She could hear the officers of the Imperium suddenly murmur. It was as the book predicted. She began.

"The beginning, Chapter one, Page Thirteen verse one. Two crusaders will come. Challengers who had faced the celestial temple of our gods, one, a survivor of the trials who slew his best friend in search of the missing. Another who succeeded in passing through our temple into the great expanse, who found the eternal battlefield where our ancestors fought the horror and then passed into the doorway to the Immortals and the Infinite and so returned? They will overcome the greatness of the Harrata. Darkness is coming! The Infidels are coming! Prepare! Prepare!"

The entire great hall exploded in pandemonium. She could hear the Viceroy slamming his staff against the metal. Moments later, the hall again quieted down. She looked at Banari. "Noble Chancellor, you may come up." Nespari motioned her hand. Banari walked up to the dais and stood next to Nepari as she showed him the verse. "Praise Gom. It can't be," Banari said shocked at the discovery.

"It is true, Noble Chancellor. The dark times will return. We must prepare."

"And the Federank and the Klingonasse?"

"The Challenge must continue, chancellor. The honor of our people is at stake. You must fulfill the Tong or face Desta."

"Understood, High Priestess." Banari bowed and kissed the right hand of the priestess. Banari returned to his seat. Basar clapped his hands together. The procession with military procession fell back into line. The trumpets sounded, and the drums rolled. The procession made their way out of the great hall. Banari turned to Luci.

"Luci, contact the Federank president as soon as we return to my office."

"Yes, Noble Chancellor," Luci said. Something was bothering the chancellor, something that he had seen in the book of Prophecy.

OFFICE OF THE FEDERATION PRESIDENT. STAR DATE 2908.9:

Kenneth Westcott breathed a sigh of relief; he finally had some peace and quiet from the daily grind of hardball in the council. With the upcoming Harrata war and the specter of another shooting war with the Klingon Empire looming soon, Westcott sipped a glass of red wine. He smiled; the Burgundy was from Chateau Picard in Labarre France. He looked at the vintage year. It was 2220, the last time the Federation had gone to war with the Harr. Closing his eyes, Westcott tried to relax. He had sent both of his aides and his chief of staff to lunch and wasn't expected to be bothered.

Getting out of his chair, he went to the window and looked at the city of Paris. Since he was a kid, he had always been fascinated by the city of lights.

Back when the Federation was first formed, Paris along with London, Washington DC, and Moscow had all been considered the capital of the nascent Federation.

Paris had won because it made the most violent Andorian relax. Vulcans liked the logical symmetry of the city and the Tellerites preferred French Cuisine over British, American, and Russian cuisine.

Geneva, Switzerland, and Federa-Terra Florida which was north of Magonia Park were the backup capitals in case anything happened to Paris and held additional Federation government offices.

The desk intercom buzzed. Westcott huffed. Now what? He thought.

He hit his desk intercom.

"Yes."

"Mister President. I have a priority call from the Harrata Chancellor Vardeck da Banari. He says it's urgent and is only to be taken by you with no other government members present."

"I'm alone. You may put him through and transfer to my desk screen," Westcott said as he put the glass down and sat back in his chair. Moments later, a brown-skinned Harrata of the political caste appeared. He was about Westcott's age. But he had a black mustache and atypical wavy black hair instead of the traditional Mohawk.

"Chancellor Banari, so good of you to call," Westcott said putting on his best political look.

"President Westcott. We have much to discuss."

"You are not calling about ending your Challenge."

"No. It will continue, Mister President. And we are aware of the buildup of Federansky forces at our borders. The Star force will continue its hit and run raids on your units when the Tong begins. It is tradition. As we test your champions, we test your forces."

Westcott understood. They had only four real choices. Accept the challenge and fail, a war. Accept a challenge and win. No war. Accept a challenge and betray, war and conquest. Do not accept the challenge and there would be war.

"Have our challenger's ships made it to your space, Banari?"

"Yes, they are heading to the rendezvous with the Klingonasse challengers and then to the Lothar system."

Westcott looked at Banari. He didn't call him up for this. There was something else. He was hiding something.

"Vardeck, you didn't call me to state the obvious."

"No. Just send two of your best ambassadors to Planetoid X on the Federation-Harrata border. We will be sending two of ours."

"That is all."

"Yes. Do it and do not waste any time," Vardeck said almost desperate. Something was really eating away at him.

"You have my word, Chancellor."

"Keep it or else, Westcott." Banari's image faded. Westcott opened the desk intercom. "Get me Starfleet and Ambassadors Sarek and Shran immediately," Westcott said urgently.

"Yes, Sir."

STARFLEET COMMAND FLEET OPERATIONS CENTER
(MAIN MISSIONS). STAR DATE 2908.10:

Solow and Starfleet Commander Marcus "Bull" Buchinsky entered
the operations center. With Robert Comsol on an extended fleet
inspection tour, Buchinsky was in charge until he returned. From
here, the chief of Starfleet operations controlled the whereabouts of
hundreds of starships.

"Thanks for holding the fort, Herb," Buchinsky said.

"How was the Star base, outpost inspection tour along the Klingon
borders?"

"All our facilities are up to par, Herb. I've already issued orders to
start mobilizing our reserve fleet ships just in case the Klingons act
up. Captain Henry Leedson of the Hornet was most cooperative."

Leedson, if that captain wasn't the biggest ingrate in the fleet and a
supporter of Vaughn Rittenhouse to boot. Solow thought. Leedson
had a reputation for being a martinet. He was hoping to replace
Leedson with Jason Welles, captain of the Rahman later.

Mattea Hahn walked up to Buchinsky and Solow.

"Marcus, Herbert."

"Mattea."

"All fleets and squadrons except for Harari's are now in position
along the Federation-Imperium border. That squadron of the new
Federation class dreadnoughts and the squadron of the Achenar class
Heavy cruisers are now heading for a rendezvous with Rittenhouse's
Tactical command."

Hahn turned to a controller. "Get me Augenthaler at 41."

"Yes, Admiral," the Tellerite controller said.

After a momentary lag, Augenthalers image appeared on the screen. "Fred."

"Mattea."

"What is your status on your non-allocated ships?"

"Commodore Doenitz's Ptolemy squadron is still here. Doenitz's three tugs are still under repair. Only Ptolemy is available. Commodore Darion Pages, Constitution class Heavy cruiser, the Victorious is undergoing major repairs after being attacked by the Children of Lothar near Pyrrhus. Commander J.T. Esteban's Bozeman is nearly finished with upgrades. The destroyers Samson, Cochise, and De Ruyter are awaiting overhaul."

"I'm sending the Galileo, Ulugh Beg, Newton, and Messier to Delta three, four, and five construction areas to evacuate the construction crews. Keep Doenitz's squadron in reserve," Hahn said.

"Understood Mattea." Augenthalers image nodded.

"Do we have an SCE Daedalus class ship at the Magellan Deep space array?" Hahn asked.

"Yes, the Masao-NCC 179 commanded by Commander Richard Hawke. They are doing upgrades and routine maintenance on that array, Admiral." The Masao had been one of the three Daedalus class ships reactivated by Starfleet. The Thomas Jefferson, Daedalus, and the Discovery were museum ships.

Great Hahn thought. It was bad enough that Richard's older brother Robert was facing the challenge. His father commanded the FSF. And First Lieutenant Roger Hawke of the Federation Ground Infantry was with the Xindi regiment at Star base Alpha. And finally, Elizabeth Hawke was serving as an aide to Ambassador Shran. Even Admiral Dina Hawke, commander of Starfleet Intelligence, was involved. She had been present at the Admirals meeting selecting the candidates to face the Tong.

"Send Captain Esteban's Bozeman as soon as she has finished upgrades to the Magellan array to ride shotgun in case the Children of Lothar or the Star force gets that far out."

"Understood, Star base 41 out." Augenthalers image faded. Hahn looked to Buchinsky and Solow.

"Now, what can I interest you gentlemen in?"

"We need a starship."

'For both of you?" Hahn asked curiously.

"No," Solow explained. "One that could transport two ambassadors via Vulcan, Andor, and Planetoid X and she could supplement the existing fleets if necessary."

That only meant a Miranda, Soyuz, Constitution, or Coronado class starships. Hahn thought. Hahn went over to the computer and punched up the list of Federation ships in Earth orbit. Two Archer class scouts, the Aries and the Capricorn. One Hermes, the Carson, and two transport tugs, Al Rashid and Hayashi, as well as two Heavy cruisers Hornet and Littorio remained in orbit.

Only the Heavy cruisers were really fit for this sort of mission and despite the massive Fleet Construction program, they never had enough of them. The Kirov class variants were all assigned to the fleets as flagships and the rare Coronado's were hardly ever seen.

"We have two, the Hornet, which I just reassigned and the Littorio under Captain Svetlana Ivanova."

"Good. Tell Ivanova to expect two ambassadors and their entourages," Bull said as he kissed Mattea Hahn on the cheek in front of all the officers assigned to the Center.

Buchinsky and Solow left.

"What are you all looking at? Back to work. Ensign Nagumo, get me Captain Ivanova."

"Yes, Admiral."

Now to the next problem, she thought.

LITTORIO-NCC 1727, IN EARTH ORBIT. STAR DATE 2908.10:

Sarek, Amanda, and their entourage materialized in one of the transporter rooms of the Littorio. They had no time for the usual shuttle craft ceremonies on this trip.

Sarek stepped down from the platform. In front of him stood a woman. She was in her mid-fifties with closely cropped blond hair.

"We come to serve," she said in Russian-accented English, closer to Moscow and Saint Petersburg. Sarek thought.

"May I present my first officer Commander Victor Godunov, my science officer Lieutenant Silvia Guzman, my ships doctor Commander Louis Voight, and my chief engineer Commander Sharon Hoyt."

"My wife Amanda, Captain, and my aides Sutal and Shas," Sarek said.

"We are honored, Ambassador Sarek, Ambassador Shran, and his entourage already on board."

"Captain Ivanova, due to the nature of this trip, I would like to skip all formalities so Shran and I can prepare for these negotiations."

"Understood, Mister Ambassador, Commander Godunov will see to your accommodations."

Sarek, Amanda, and their aides left the transporter room following Commander Godunov. He could hear Captain Ivanova ordering the ship to leave orbit.

Littorio swung away from Earth passing her sister ship the Hornet which was heading in another direction.

CHAPTER THIRTEEN

ENTERPRISE RECREATION ROOM FIVE. STAR DATE 2909.1:

Ben Finney toyed with his meatloaf and mashed potatoes. So many years in the fleet and he still hadn't gotten past his lieutenant commander's rank.

After the affair on Republic, he had stayed a little while longer at the academy before, getting a berth on Harris's Excalibur. Later, he transferred to the Asimov and the Bismarck before Kirk had asked him to come here to the Enterprise. The Enterprise, Republic, or Yamato should have been his. Starfleet wouldn't even give him a lowly transport tug command or even an Archer class scout. It just wasn't fair, all because of one error.

"Is this seat taken?" came a familiar voice. Finney looked up to see Lieutenant Madge Sinclair looking at him.

"No. But I prefer eating alone, Madge."

"And wallow in your guilt, Ben. You still haven't gotten over what happened aboard Republic," Madge said as she emphasized with Finney and sat down opposite him anyway.

"You will make a good captain one day. You can't take no for an answer. I heard you are leaving Enterprise."

"Yes, Ben. A promotion to second officer on either the new Antares class survey ship or a hospital ship post."

"Oh."

Bigger than the small Ariel class vessels, but smaller than the new Oberth class science vessels, if there wasn't enough confusion in the fleet with the old Antares class freighters as well, give it to ASDB and Fleet Construction to confuse the hell out of everyone. Like the two Suraks Starfleet had. One was a Constitution used by the Vulcans; the other was an Oberth used by Starfleet. Finney thought.

"Ramart had a lot of gall whipping the F letter off Antares contract number," Finney pointed out.

"The crew of the destroyer Jenghiz wasn't so pleased, Ben."

Madge decided to change the subject. Fleet Scuttlebutt didn't always interest her. "I heard a rumor you were once offered a first officer job."

"Yes once, a few years ago. Bobby Hawke who had just assumed command of the Sargon reached out and offered me the job."

"What happened?" Madge asked curiously.

"Starfleet got word and threatened to take Hawke's new command away. They got back to me and Hawke. That one stink in error I made stood against me, Madge. I could have been Hawke's first on Volunteer, Sargon, Miranda, and Constitution. But no, Starfleet ever lets you forget an error!" Finney said upset.

Madge reached over and comforted Finney. She had heard of Bob Hawke's selflessness. He had taken many dead-enders and turned them back into productive officers and crew.

"Ben, we all have our purgatories. We need to look forward, not back. If I ever get my own command, Ben, I will put you on my list."

Finney looked up. "Thank you, Madge."

Madge finished her food. "Only trying to help," she said as she got up. "Must get back to the rear phaser room. Kirk wants us to start practicing simulations against Harrata Hogar class, type 8s," Madge said as she left the rec room. Finney for a moment considered Madge's offer.

But he would be like that fellow Gramps on the Constitution on the Enterprise. The Enterprise's Gramps, he thought sarcastically. Never! No! If Enterprise survived this Challenge, he had to find a way to get even with Jim Kirk. Somehow, someway, he would find a way to disgrace James Kirk. He only needed the opportunity to present itself. Finney quickly finished his meal and left for the computer core. He had to spend the rest of the day updating all the logs.

ELBA TWO. FEDERATION PENAL COLONY FOR THE
INSANE. STAR DATE 2909.2.

JANUARY 19, 2267:

Donald Cory wiped the sweat from his face. He had received word
from Starfleet about Constitution. The ship Garth had used as his
flagship at Axanar Rebellion and again during the Four Years' War
was being sent into the Harrata Imperium along with the Enterprise.

Garth had been a recent arrival here; his previous location of
incarceration had been the Federation Psychiatric Facility on
Dementia Three. The Antos affair took place in 2260, after the end
of the Four Years' War. Garth due to his dementia always thought
it took place months after the end of the Four years War. Garth had
not been involved in the Shenzhou stupidity that had flared up latter
on.

Heisenberg made first contact with the Antosians in 2256. But it was
on the return visit in 2260 that the infamous accident and mutiny
happened.

The reality was that Garth's megalomania began to manifest itself
during the Four Years' War and the horrific mutilation that Garth
suffered at Antos brought the madness to the surface.

But repeated escape attempts and his lack of any progress toward
normalcy had forced Governor Salk to have him recently reassigned
to Elba Two instead. Salk, an old colleague of his, had called Garth
an incurable megalomaniac. What a comedown for the victor of the
Axanar Rebellion and the Four Years' War.

"Anders, Williams, come with me," Cory said as his two aides
followed him through the force shields to the cells.

"You are coming to see the magnificent Lord Garth," Mara said from her cell.

Cory ignored her. Mara was again spouting delusions over Garth. Moments later, they arrived at Garth's cell.

Garth was facing the opposite way looking toward the wall of his cell. He wore the typical Izarian clothes that he would wear off duty. Starfleet had stripped his regulation uniforms when he was incarcerated.

"What is it, Cory?" Garth said still looking at the wall. He sounded bored. Which meant trouble.

"Enterprise and Constitution have been sent into the Imperium to face the Challenge," Cory said.

Garth still looking at the wall said nothing. Cory, Anders, and Williams began to walk away

Garth suddenly leaped out of his chair and ran to the edge of his cell. "Constitution! Enterprise!" Garth yelled as the shapes shifted into the form of Joseph Hawke, Constitution's original unsung full-time commanding officer. "That self-righteous traitor! He would never follow the greatness of Garth the first!"

Corey followed by Anders and Williams quickly returned to Garth's cell.

"Kelvar, you must control your emotions," Corey said as he was cut off.

After the Four Years' War, Garth had launched a propaganda campaign to eliminate any trace of Joe's achievements. Most reference works touted Garth as commanding officer of Constitution. He occasionally took command of Constitution using his rank of fleet captain as a prerogative, making Joe the number two on his own ship.

Joe Hawke/Garth looked at Corey. "Who are you to speak to the great Garth the first, master of the universe, lord commander of the Constitution, Lexington, Intrepid, Baton Rouge, Ares, Heisenberg, and Xenophon? Ruler of the Axanar and Antos."

"As your doctor, Kelvar. You tried to escape from Dementia. You were outsmarted by the son of the commander who you now appear to be. Captured by Robert Hawke of the Constitution."

Garth's shape shifted again. This time, he appeared as Robert Hawke. Garth pointed a finger at his chest. "Sacrilege," Garth said venomously.

Garth morphed again, this time into the figure of Jonathan West. "Now John was never disloyal to me. He believed in Garth's greatness. Just like my loyal minions on the Xenophon and Heisenberg." Garth's voice was calm, too eerily calm.

"And what about the rest, Kelvar?" Corey said.

"Damn them all to hell! They are all traitors!" Garth yelled as his shape shifted into Kor, Korolev, Spiak, Bannock, and then back to Joe Hawke.

"Why?"

"They followed Hawke, that is why," Garth said. "Go, Cory, I have no need of the likes of you and your drones."

The other prisoners in the other cells started to clap.

Garth bowed down in his cell. "Thank you, my loyal subjects."

Cory, Anders, and Williams immediately left to the lunatic laughter of Garth and his new minions.

ENTERPRISE. DOCTOR MCCOY OFFICE:

McCoy scanned all his medical reports and went back to his focus. Every time Enterprise had to serve with another ship, he always made sure he checked up on the service records, psych profiles of the other ship Enterprise worked with. So, he could advise Kirk if there were any rough patches to be found. McCoy looked up to see Spock walk in.

"What can I do for you, Spock?"

"I assume you are checking the profiles of the senior officers on our sister ship," Spock said.

"Correct, Spock, when we served with Decker's Constellation a few months back, I did the same."

"And what have you found out about our present companions, Doctor?"

"I have never seen such an incompatible bunch in my life, Spock, all brilliant, all competitive. Everyone has their own agenda. And yet, Bobby has somehow gotten this group to work together. Even Kelly Bogles' staff on Farragut is more harmonious than this bunch," McCoy admitted.

"And ours, Bones."

"Don't bring Enterprise into this, Spock."

"Are we not considered to be brilliant, harmonious compared to Hawke's gang of children?"

"We still haven't resolved the battle of the Mascots, Spock," McCoy said plainly.

"We are on a critical life and death mission, and everything is devolving into a battle over which mascot is better? The human preoccupation with matters of no importance, I have always found to be quite fascinating," Spock said as he sat down opposite McCoy.

"It is almost an obsession, Doctor McCoy," Spock added. "That humans would spend endless time and energy on non-critical matters, completely ignoring the more important ones until it is too late."

"Tell me, Spock, it appears to me that Vulcans are masters of efficiency. Trivial matters like the present battle of the mascots would hardly register between those two-pointed ears of yours," McCoy said.

"Yes, Doctor, Vulcans do not believe in wasting energy on matters of little or no importance," Spock admitted.

"No wonder some humans consider Vulcans to be boring."

"I will take this as a compliment, Doctor."

"Now tell me, Spock. We all know that Jim Kirk is the most highly decorated captain out of all the present Heavy cruiser captains. But who are the next two?"

"Is that a question, Bones?"

"Dammit, Spock! Just answer the question," McCoy said exasperated.

"Both Roberts, Wesley of the Lexington and Hawke of the Constitution are the other two."

"That is my point, Spock. Jim and Bob have been competing against each other since their academy days. Kirk does one thing and Bob tries to out-due him. At least, Kelly Bogle isn't like those two."

"Kelly Bogle is a by-the-book captain, Doctor McCoy," Spock pointed out.

"Not Jim or Bob. We have a cowboy and a swashbuckler, Spock, two rule-bending, independent damn all to hell captains."

"As you probably recall, Spock, I served with Jim on old battlewagon many years ago," McCoy said recalling one of Constitution's better nicknames. He sure as hell hated old Duranium sides, the old bucket of bolts, that old rust bucket, the old rattletrap. Hell, even the Enterprise had a better nickname, Lucky E or the Big E.

"Let us first start with comparing Jim and Robert's careers, Spock."

"Their career records speak volumes, Doctor."

"Ever hear of a nebula called Beta Porthos?" McCoy quickly changed the subject. He didn't want to bother with Jim or Robert's service records.

"Affirmative, Bones, discovered by Captain Archer in 2155. Named after his pet beagle, a month after that discovery, the Battle of Beta Porthos took place, the newly launched NX00 along with NX01 and NX02, Napoleon, FDR, Patton, and the Republic intercepted a Kzinti task force that was heading for Earth Colony 7. The Earth Starfleet was victorious," Spock said and then continued, "It had been the first time the Kzinti had gone on the offensive since losing the four Earth-Kzinti wars among the fleet that had won the battle, NX00 was the prototype for the second generation NX class."

NX00 had been revolutionary. She was the first NX class ship built with an interconnecting dorsal, secondary hull. Constitution was a special appropriation NX starship. She had been launched at the end of 2154. Constitution then spent part of 2155 for the testing and shakedown of the new design. The success of Constitution led to the launch of her sister ships Lexington, Excalibur, and Defiant in 2155. The launch of the three improved NX class ships coincided with the launch of Challenger, Atlantis, and Discovery during that year.

By 2159, the remaining NX class ships NX06-09, 16 and improved NX class ships NX 14-15, NX 16-20 were finally completed.

Enterprise had been the first off, the original class to be updated to Columbia/Constitution class specifications.

During the Earth-Romulan War, the original NX class had lost Columbia, Challenger, Discovery, Atlantis, Intrepid. Only Enterprise, Endeavor, and Avenger of the original class survived the war.

Most of the second generation NX class led by NX00, NX10-NX 15, NX 17 -NX 20 had survived the war with the loss of Excalibur and Defiant being the only war losses.

The Intrepid class out of 30 ships had lost 10. The Daedalus class lost fifteen out of fifty. The older Warp 3 Horizon class lost ten out of twenty and the Marshall class destroyers lost twenty-five out of sixty. It had been a terrible war.

The destructive Tarn conflict of 2169-79 had been a decade-long border war. That flared up on and off over the years. The conflict was still ongoing when the Federation got involved in the Federation

Harrata conflict of 2177-78. Luckily for the Federation, the Tarn and the Harrata never decided to combine forces since the Harr had angered the Tarn centuries earlier, in a long-forgotten conflict. And the Klingons had gone into isolation along with the Romulans for the remainder of the century.

Later, the Federation went back to war with the Harrata in 2220. The war was even more violent and destructive than the previous conflict.

The unfortunate Tholian border conflict of 2230-35 was a vicious border war, over the limits of the borders between the Federation and the Tholian Assembly.

The Axanar Rebellion in early 2251 led to the Axanar Peace Mission but at the end of 2251, the Klingons went back on the Axanar peace mission and the destructive Four Years' War broke out. The Four Years' War had ended in 2256 and was then extended into 2257. It had been a limited war on a single front. Spock figured another war with the Klingons would be on a wide front.

Later in 2257, the short but destructive Federation-Shelliack war broke out. Luckily for the Federation, the Shelliack Corporate had no appetite for a long war. And the war was quickly resolved by the treaty of Armens that year.

A new war with the Romulan, Klingon Empires, or the Harrata Imperium would exceed the level of savagery.

Spock had no illusions; the conflicts all spoke for themselves. War was illogical waste and was to be avoided at all costs.

"War is a waste doctor, an illogical waste of lives and resources. During our careers in Starfleet, we did witness two wars."

McCoy nodded. "The Four Years' War and the Shelliack war. In both cases, Spock, I didn't arrive on Constitution until 2257. Constitution and Enterprise did not participate in the Shelliack conflict. That was left to the newer Bonhomme Richard class ships."

"Enterprise missed the Four Years' War. We were involved with the problem with the Borderlands which took place shortly after the Axanar Rebellion. The Klingons were looking for an excuse to ignite a war after failing with the rebellion."

"They did succeed, Spock. We had four grueling years of war. But the Klingons localized it between the borders of Star base 12, 24, 25, and 27. Fortunately for us, it didn't extend past there."

"If we go to war with the Harr, that means we will not be here to witness it. I predict that the Klingon Empire and the Romulans may decide to combine forces and hit the Federation together."

"That would be an unfortunate scenario, Doctor. Federation strategists have already predicted that scenario. It was called Armageddon. We must do all we can to prevent this from happening. We do not have the resources for a war of that magnitude."

"Which brings me to the present day. Back in 60, I was still on Constitution just before I transferred to the Sacajawea. I ran into Jim when he was serving on the Eagle Spock. Both ships were assigned to do deep-space survey mission of the adjoining systems near Beta Porthos, which Starfleet had finally got around to doing after a century. Jim was mighty upset about that nickname he was given as a XO."

"Mister Fill in, Doctor McCoy," Spock reminded McCoy.

"Yes, Spock, I forgot how many ships Jim served on as a temporary XO until he got the XO position on Eagle. Kirk was everywhere,"

McCoy said. Kirk admitted to him later that he wanted Excalibur, but he was satisfied with his position on the Eagle.

"Bones, Harris served as Brittany Mendez's XO on the Exeter. Jim was on the Republic, not Exeter. And Robert Hawke along with Samantha Reynolds and Charles Archer served on the Exeter."

"I know, Spock, they were known as the Exeter Three. And that is where our future problems lay, Spock. Those two are under enough stress as it is. They are both very good friends, but that competitive streak from their academy days will ruin everything. It could blow up in our faces, jeopardizing the mission, Spock."

"I see your point."

"I referred my concerns to Doc Russell, and he fully agrees on this. Shran and T'Pau were also informed. They will support us all the way if Jim or Bob go over the edge. The critical points will come during the first part of the Challenge, and we all know what will happen to the loser's ships."

"The High Order Corp will slaughter the entire crew and the Star force will slice this ship up with surgical precision, Doctor, leaving Enterprise a wreck. They have also slaughtered their own people, Bones, and wrecked their own ships."

"That is barbaric, Spock."

"It is their way, the Harrata prefer death to dishonor."

"No kidding just like the Klingons and the Romulans," McCoy said sarcastically.

"Thaylassa told me that if that happened, she would fight Constitution to the bitter end, Bones. She is much like her famed ancestor," Spock mentioned.

"The Shran who helped Archer helped pave the way for the formation of our Federation. Yes, Spock, indeed she is. She is Robert's Andorian Gary Mitchell in a way."

Odd, Spock thought. Mitchell had been in the same class as Kirk together. Gary could have been near the top of his class if he had applied himself like Hawke and kirk and would have had his own ship by now. But Mitchell had slacked off and finished much further down in the standings.

"You did the right thing, Doctor, by informing me," Spock said as he got up. "We will keep this between ourselves and our opposites on Constitution, Doctor. Billions of lives are at stake. The Federation will not survive a two-front war if we are involved with the Harrata and the Klingons decide to enter the fray. We cannot have Jim Kirk or Robert Hawke losing total control.'

McCoy nodded. "Because if that happens, we will lose everything."

"Yes, Doctor, everything." Spock left sickbay.

CHAPTER FOURTEEN

CAPTAIN KIRK'S QUARTERS:

Kirk sat at his desk. Enterprise hadn't had a break in a few months. Luckily, his ship was in better shape than Bob's. Enterprise had recently been resupplied by the freighter Meredith.

Robert's ship, however, was long overdue for an overhaul. They had been in deep space without relief for almost eight months. She was overdue at Star base 11, but the Harrata crisis had quashed that notion. Sorting through his reports, Kirk tried to catch up with the paperwork, an obsolete term still used by the fleet, even though everything was now digital. His desk intercom whistled.

"Yes."

Uhura's image appeared. "Captain Kirk, Captain Hawke wishes to speak with you."

"Put him on."

Moments later, Robert's image appeared on his desk screen. He was in his quarters. Robert was cuddling his Siamese cat Maxine.

"Jim."

"Bob."

"Catching up on paperwork, Jim?" Hawke asked.

"Same," Kirk said and then continued, "You didn't call me just for the mundane, Bob."

"No, let's resolve this Battle of the Mascots once and for all, Jim. Both our yeoman's are guilty for rubbing both our crews the wrong way over this matter."

Kirk could only agree; Rand had called Robert's Siamese a fur bag and Smith had retaliated by calling Beauregard an oversized Venus Flytrap.

"I agree, Bob, want to barter?" Kirk asked.

Robert smiled. "I thought you would never ask. What do you have to offer me, Jim?"

"And what do you have, Bob?"

"I got this Harrata drink called Pogash. It is pretty rare, Jim. And Klingon Blood wine."

Kirk smiled. "I don't want to ask where you got that stuff. But I have a drink called Tranya and Romulan ale if you are interested."

"Tranya, wasn't that the drink Balok offered you when you contacted the First Federation, Jim?" Hawke recalled. Constitution had to do two follow-up missions later that year with the First Federation and none of the commanders had even offered his people some Tranya.

"Yes, Bob, Balok gave us quite a few gallons of this stuff and I had to clear out most of Enterprise's wine collection in exchange for it," Kirk recalled.

Kirk's door buzzed. "A moment, Bob."

"Yes."

"Rand, Captain, I have your lunch and the rest of your reports."

"Come."

Kirk turned back to his desk screen to see that Bob was also talking with his yeoman.

"A moment, Jim," Hawke said.

Rand was looking at Kirk watching as Hawke gave Maxine to Smith.

"De jà vu, yeoman."

"Yes, Captain. Here are the rest of your reports and your lunch, Sir." Rand placed Kirk's sandwich, salad, and coffee in front of Kirk along with the report tapes.

"Thank you, yeoman."

"Understood, Captain." Rand left looking back knowing that Kirk and the image of Hawke were watching her.

Hawke picked up from where he left off. "No hard feeling, Jim. Tell Rand that."

"I will and tell Smith the same, Bob."

Kirk said, "Bob, I'll give you a bottle of Romulan ale and some Tranya for the Pogash and a bottle of Klingon Blood wine."

"You have a deal, Jim. But we need to do one more thing; we should formally speak to both of our crews on this matter. I got some people on my ships who still feel their pride was rubbed the wrong way on this matter," Hawke said as he took a bit out of his sandwich.

Kirk listened as he dove into his sandwich. "Starfleet Communications Protocol 272."

Hawke nodded. "II, Jim."

II or aye, aye as it was jokey referred to by wags was better known as Intraship-Inner ship that had been developed by Hoshi Sato of NX01 and Patricia Neal of NX00 back in the 22nd century. It was a way for a commanding officer of one ship to speak to the crew of another ship. Simply, the captain would be talking to two crews at the same time: his own ship and the other ship or ships. Fleet Admirals would use the protocol to address all the ships in the fleet. Kirk could only agree. Even his crew had been rubbed the wrong way by this trivial matter.

"Agreed. And one more thing, Bob, if we survive the first round, to ease tension between both crews, we should have visitation rights for both ships. We should have a two-day break before the second round."

"I totally agree. It should go a long way to ease the tension between both of our crews. I really don't think the Harrata would mind if we did this."

"Not at all, Robert, so when do you want to wrap up this matter?"

"Before we get to the second rendezvous and the Lothar system."

"One hour, Bob, we'll be calling."

Hawke nodded, and his image faded.

ONE HOUR LATER:

Kirk stepped onto Enterprise's Bridge. "Uhura, contact Constitution, also prepare to use protocol 272."

Uhura looked up at Kirk. "272, Captain?"

"Yes, Uhura."

Uhura swung back to her board. Putting the Feinberg receiver in her ear, she opened up a channel to Constitution as she prepared protocol 272 for implementation. "Constitution, come in. Please respond."

"Constitution here. Nyota, Mariko speaking."

"Mariko, ready to implement 272."

"Yes."

Uhura swung her chair to face the center of the bridge. Kirk was conversing with McCoy and Spock. "Captain Kirk, Constitution is ready."

Kirk hit his intercom button. "Robert, you will go first."

"Agreed."

Uhura initiated 272. An unfamiliar voice suddenly boomed through the corridors of Enterprise at the same time as it resonated through the familiar corridors of Constitution. Chekov in Auxiliary control, Finney in the computer core, and Riley in the forward phaser room looked up from their posts as Captain Hawke began to speak.

"I do not need any introductions. Some of you may remember my brief service on Enterprise years back. This trivial matter must be put to rest. We are on a critical mission for the Federation. Billions of lives are at stake. We have the two finest ships in the fleet and the best crews. Twice in our history, we lost to the Harrata. Jim Kirk and I want to prove them wrong. We cannot do that if our attention is being diverted by trivial matters or rivalries. As of this Star date, I declare the battle of the mascots over."

"Your turn, Jim," Hawke's voice boomed through the intercom.

Kirk began as his voice sounded through the familiar corridors of Enterprise and resonated through the unfamiliar corridors of Constitution. Gramps in the shuttle bay, Harris and Catalan, who were in one of the recreation rooms playing Gin and Morgan Bateson who was conversing with Smith in the Constitution's officers lounge, took notice.

"I do not need to reiterate what Captain Hawke has so eloquently pointed out. Some of you might still remember my service under Augenthaler. We are on a critical mission; our pride and our passion have interfered with this mission on this trivial matter. If we are to survive, both of our crews need to work together. This is not the time for petty rivalries; we have a job to do. The battle of the mascots is now resolved," Kirk said as he nodded to Uhura who disconnected 272.

"I'm glad that is over with," McCoy said relieved.

"Yes, Doctor, the battle of the mascots was so trivial; it will go down in history as..." Spock said as he glanced at his viewer. "Captain, long-range sensors are picking up two types 8s, four type 7s, and two Klingon battle cruisers. One is a D6, the Suvwl, the other a D7, Vorcha."

"Kang."

"Yes, Captain. However, I am unfamiliar with the other ship."

"Uhura, get me Constitution."

"Aye, Sir."

Moments later, Robert's image dominated the main view screen. He was sitting in his command chair. T'Pau was visible from the science station. Next to T'Pau, Shran sat at the relocated Tactical station.

"Sorry to bother you, Bob, but we are unfamiliar with the Vorcha."

Hawke smiled. "Jim, that is Khod's ship. I ran into him a few times. He got this U.S. Grant complex about him, but he's a worthy adversary, Jim. Don't let his scruffy looks deceive you. He's that good."

"Understood. Enterprise out." Robert's image faded from the screen.

"The stage is set; the actors have arrived and now the play begins," McCoy said.

Spock could only nod in agreement. The play had now begun.

The combined fleet jumped to warp.

CHAPTER FIFTEEN

KIROV-NCC 3300. FLAGSHIP FIRST STRIKE FORCE. TASK FORCE ALPHA COORDINATES CLASSIFIED. STAR DATE 2909.3:

George Kirk woke up suddenly. He was bathed in sweat and his heart was pounding. He was having another nightmare about Hellspawn. Hellspawn was supposed to be a birth of a new era.

The Federation and the Imperium working together. Hellspawn became a disaster all thanks to the Children. The Revere with Ambassador Sharif, Captain Arnold Halsey, and her crew wound up crashing on Hell Spawn. The Ranger class cruiser was wrecked with nearly her entire crew killed. The Harrata cruiser, the Nasba, a Hogar class, type 5 was destroyed with Ambassador Nos Cal Kiraay. Commodore Barry Hansen Sr., Commandant Rulla SA Trira, and nearly the entire outpost crew were massacred.

George got up and went to the bathroom and splashed some water on his face. He was glad that Matt Decker and Constellation risked themselves to save him and the thirty remaining survivors of the disaster. Seeing Winona again had been the happiest day of his life only to be marred by the disaster at Tycho Four that had led to the near loss of the Farragut later that year. He had almost lost Jimmy. Because of that, he decided to take a leave of absence from the service. It lasted two years before he returned.

Promoted to captain, Starfleet gave him his old ship back, the old Kelvin. Kelvin had seen better days. Richard Robau his old captain, now a Vice Admiral, had told him. He commanded Kelvin for three years, even working with his son on one mission when James commanded the Sacagawea. When Jimmy finally received the Enterprise after beating off completion from Robert Hawke and Andovar Drake, it had been the proudest day of his life. Shortly after Jim had been given command of Enterprise, he had been promoted to fleet captain.

The intercom buzzed.

"Yes?"

"It's me, George," came the voice of Joe Hawke. "I'll be calling the fleets Co.'s in an hour. Starfleet Commander Comsol has appointed me supreme commander of all Federation Fleets assigned to this conflict, George."

"Congratulations are in order, Joe."

"Indeed, they are. Get all the Intel you have on the rest of the fleets and meet me at the central briefing room."

"Understood." George Kirk quickly finished up and left his quarters.

Kirov's Central briefing room. 1200 hours.

George Kirk slipped by the one hundred and forty-nine captains, commanders, and Lt. commanders that commanded the various ships in the Federation's largest, most prestigious fleet.

The famed FSF was sometimes derisively known as the Elite of the Fleet, but the moniker was well-earned. No other fleet in the Federation had so many battle honors. The fleet was also the edge of the sword, the first to go into combat in nearly all the wars since the Xindi conflict. Kirov's briefing room did not show her predecessors, but depictions of the famed battles the FSF fought in.

Joe Hawke was present along with Stanley Fairchild. George came up and gave Joe the information.

"Now that we are all present, this briefing is now in order," Hawke said. The assembled officers went mute.

"Engage the screen," Fairchild ordered.

Joseph Hawke walked up to the screen. "As of this star date, I am now the supreme commander of all Federation Starfleet forces assigned to this conflict. That includes the 8th, 9th fleets, and the Fourth Federation Reserve fleet, the tactical fleet, and the assigned XY units. General Simmons commands the invasion force poised at Alpha. We all know that my son and Fleet Captain Kirk have been chosen to face the infamous Challenge. Some of us here have friends or relatives serving on both ships. We can only hope that they return to us safely. If not, then we will have a full-scale war on our hands at that time. However, the Harrata don't sit around, they will attack us; they will test our resolve and our mettle. We will be engaged in a quasi-war. Never underestimate the resolve of the Harrata race, caste color aside; they will stop at nothing to achieve the ultimate bliss of sacrificing their lives to join with their deities. Only when betrayed would they conquer; they are not the Klingons or the Romulans. Territorial gains do not mean anything to them, the only glory."

Kirk stepped forward. "As you can all see, except for the Achenar and Federation class squadron reinforcements, Starfleet cannot spare any more ships. We still have a possible conflict to deal with the Klingon Empire and the Romulans will not be sitting put. Success simply boils down to the Enterprise and Constitution surviving the Challenge. This is our present deployment in conjunction with the other Federation forces." Kirk showed the assembled commanders the deployment of the respective fleets and squadrons.

Fairchild walked over and replaced Kirk.

"Intel provided by Starfleet intelligence, the Harrata Star force fleet totals 2,000 ships of various configuration and age. 80 are in reserve, 37 are presently unaccounted for. The remainders are deployed into Star Force Groups Alpha to Hotel. Star force Special Group and Star force Lotharian Group are at the home world. The other Special Groups, Gom to Chiss, are unaccounted for; most likely, they are guarding the special systems set aside for their deities. We also believe that the unaccounted-for ships are on various missions outside the Treaty Zone. Starfleet Main Missions has notified all starships, bases, and installations of their whereabouts. And then we have the random factor of the Children of Lothar," Fairchild concluded.

That didn't fully satisfy Captain Mush Morton of the Miranda class Wahoo.

Morton scratched his blond beard and looked at George Kirk.

"Fleet Captain Kirk."

"Yes, Captain Morton." Kirk faced the captain of the Wahoo.

"Why is the fourth Starfleet Reserve Force deployed?"

"Starfleet cannot spare any more frontline fleets. All other Federation fleets from the First- Sixth and the Tenth-Fifteenth cannot be spared. Starfleet however has just reactivated the First, Second, and Third reserve fleets. And they have just begun searching the five surplus depots for any 22nd-century antiques for reactivation."

"The joke is on us, Sir," Captain Miriam Fox of the Boston said. "All those deathtraps returning to service, can't Fleet Construction build us enough ships?" Boston was another Miranda class cruiser.

"No, Captain Fox. If it weren't for the Battle of Savo, we'd be even less prepared," Vice Admiral Fairchild explained.

Hawke stepped up. "Ladies and gentlemen, the facts are clear as daylight. Everything boils down to the Enterprise and Constitution surviving the Challenge. Starfleet Intelligence believes that unless we stop the Harrata within a month of the beginning of the conflict. The Romulans and the Klingons might use the opportunity to move in on us from their borders."

"That would mean the end of the Federation," Captain Hunter said. "We could never survive a conflict like that."

"That is correct, Captain Hunter," Admiral Hawke said. "Any more questions?" Hawke said as he scanned the room. "FSF Beta will deploy with Vice Admiral Fairchild. FSF Alpha will remain with me. You are all dismissed."

The commanding officers all departed. Only Fairchild, Hawke, and Kirk remained. Hawke looked to see Hunter waiting. "Yes, Rachel. What can I do for you?"

"I pray to god that they return safely."

"Yes, I hope Robert and George's son Jim return to us, Rachel." Hawke and Kirk along with Fairchild walked Hunter to the door. "God speed, Captain Hunter."

Hunter saluted the three senior officers who returned the salute. Hunter left. George Kirk looked at Hawke and Fairchild. "Officers like Hunter give me hope, Joe."

"Yes. George, they are the strength of our organization. But having Rittenhouse and Cartwright assigned fleet commands bother me. Those two are two self-serving prima donnas."

"I once had to reprimand Cartwright when he was in command of the old Indomitable," Fairchild recalled.

"And Rittenhouse with that super Federation class ship that he is building is no better. Vaughn has an ego a quadrant wide," Joseph Hawke said.

"Sometimes I wonder if we have all outlived our usefulness," George Kirk mused. "Starfleet now belongs to the likes of Jim and Bob."

"To be young again," Fairchild said remembering.

"A long time ago, far away," Kirk added.

"Would you gentlemen like to join me for a drink? I got some Orion ale," Hawke mentioned

"Why not?" Fairchild agreed.

"Certainly," Kirk approved.

The officers stepped out of the briefing room. Kirov followed by her ninety-nine charges sailed majestically through the void.

LEXINGTON, ORBITAL DRYDOCK ONE. STAR BASE 11. STAR DATE 2909.6:

Deidre Watley patiently waited as Angela Donaldson completed the final packing of her clothes and personnel items.

"How long, Angela?" Watley said impatiently.

"Another minute."

"Wallaha that it lets go, Deirdre," Angela said as she swung her duffel bag over her shoulders.

"Do you always wait until the last minute to pack?"

"Yes."

Both officers left Angela's former quarters.

Angela noticed that Deidre had a smaller carry-on with her. "So where are you going?"

"Wrigley's Pleasure planet. The Astral Queen is making a stopover at 11 to pick up Starfleet personnel."

"You realize that Potemkin is due at the base in two hours."

"I know."

Deirdre and Angela walked to the turbo lift. Seconds later, Commodores Wesley and Stone stepped out of the lift followed by Commanders Chang and Goldman. Wesley turned to Deidre and Angela. "Good luck on your new assignment, Lieutenant Donaldson, I forwarded a glowing recommendation to Captain Callas. We are all going to miss you here on the Lexington."

"I'll miss this ship too, Sir. Lexington was my first assignment out of the academy."

"Do make Lexington proud. Lieutenant Captain Callas always keeps an eagle eye on promising officers."

"I will, Sir."

With that, Watley and Donaldson entered the lift.

"Deidre, what do you know of Potemkin?" Watley asked.

"She's had seven captains since her launch; her XO Louisa Strauss has served with three of them. She replaced Anderson who retired ten years ago and is one of the few execs in the fleet who doesn't want her own command. Her present CO Martin Callas has commanded Potemkin since 60."

"Sounds like Spock, Godunov, and Ogden."

"She's happy at number two. Not like Shran or Takesheweda."

"Shran, she's Hawke's number two and Takesheweda is Decker's," Donaldson remembered.

"Yes, they are like two peas in a pod. Rumor has it Takesheweda might be getting one of the new Achenar's in 2268."

"And Shran."

"Will have to wait until 2270. She's a real go-getter, Hawke's right hand, they been working together since the Sargon. Like Mitchell was to Kirk. Despite her Andorian iciness, she's well-liked by the crew of Constitution."

The lift deposited both of them at the appropriate deck.

"I heard Randy Pickens is transferring to the Exeter," Donaldson mentioned.

Watley checked her chronometer. She still had time. "Angie, you will be reporting to the star base fleet assignment area."

Angela nodded.

"I was thinking." Diedre gave a smile

"Oh no," Angela could only moan. Deidre was up to one of her little games again.

"Don't worry, Angela. I can still make the Astral Queen. I'll put in a request to transfer to the Enterprise."

"Enterprise! Deidre, that ship is even harder to get than the Lexington."

"Yes, well, I did serve on the old rust bucket," Watley said. "And next to Enterprise, she is just as hard to get."

"You want the notoriety of saying I served on the two best ships in the fleet," Donaldson admitted.

Watley nodded. "You only live once, my dear," Watley said. "And my sister serves on the Enterprise."

"So, you have a possible leg up."

Watley nodded. Either way, she was still going to be assigned to the Enterprise, unless Starfleet had a special reason for assigning her to that ship.

Both women arrived at one of Lexington's transporter rooms. "Tell me, Angela, what is Potemkin doing anyway?" Watley asked.

"Potemkin was assigned to the Taurus reach to fill in for Defiant which was assigned to Matt Decker's squadron. Along with the Endeavor and the Coronado, we are to do an extensive survey mission around Sectors TR001-TR17, which Constitution did an initial benchmark survey of back in 2265 after the rendezvous with Lexington and Farragut at Star base Vanguard."

"Thanks for reminding me, Angela," Watley said as she and Donaldson entered the transporter room. She had almost forgotten about that. Except for an encounter with a Tkarians marauder near Echo Vega, Lexington's survey mission near the barrier was pure boredom. By comparison, Constitution's mission in the Taurus Reach had been full of challenges.

"Where to?" Dickerson said.

"The Star base, Dickey."

"Good luck on the Potemkin, Angela."

"Thanks, Walter."

"The star base it is. See you two weeks, Deidre."

"Until then, Walter."

Watley felt the transporter grip her as she vanished from the Lexington.

CHAPTER SIXTEEN

Enterprise-Constitution under tow by Star force. January 21, 2267.

"Captain's log. Star date 2911.2. We have been heading to the Lothar system for the past two days. Despite the presence of the Klingons and the Harrata, the ship's routine is normal."

Kirk walked onto the bridge of the Enterprise. The Alpha shift was present, and Spock was at the science station looking up at one of the overhead screens. The screen was blank. A glaring warning was posted on it.

"Constitution's captain's log. Star date 1015.5 to 1107.3. Classified by order of Federation council. Black level priority only."

Kirk walked up to Spock. "Frustrated Spock."

"I was attempting to find out about Constitution's mission to the barrier and I got this, Captain," Spock said as he pointed his finger at the screen above the science station.

"If we cannot delve into the classified, Spock, what about what we do know?" Kirk said posing a question at Spock.

"According to Harrata legend, Gom and the other twelve deities came from the barrier. Only three ships have attempted to break through the barrier, the S.S Valiant, this ship, and Constitution. Constitution was four days behind us, Jim."

"When Constitution didn't return after a month, Starfleet dispatched the Hornet, Monitor, and Merrimac to search for Constitution, Spock," Kirk recalled. They had already completed their assignments at Vanguard and Star base 33. When the Merrimac found Constitution drifting powerless near Alpha Vega, the ship was on minimal life support and the crew was in a hibernation state. Enterprise was almost home on the final leg of her nine weeks return trip to Earth.

"Kranowsky and his staff revived the crew and towed the Constitution to Star base 33 where Captain Hawke and all of his officers were also debriefed by Admiral Saylor and Captain Francis Damon," Spock said. Damon and Saylor had also briefed Kirk when they had returned from Delta Vega.

"Rumor has it that Constitution discovered six extragalactic solar systems and they had found a hyper warp conduit that led to the Barnard's galaxy," said Kirk.

"Seventeen crewmembers transferred off the ship. Ten at Star base 33 went to the Tori and the other seven went to the Lexington at Vanguard. And five crewmembers remain unaccounted for, Jim. The five missing all had ESP abilities. And Constitution's entire crew were all sworn to secrecy on what happened out there," Spock explained.

"Barnard's galaxy, that's poppycock," McCoy said as he joined in the conversation. "It would take generations for her to get back," McCoy said as he leaned against the railing next to Kirk. "And what the hell is hyper warp?" McCoy interjected.

Spock looked at McCoy. "Hyper warp is theoretical, Doctor, it will take another ten centuries minimum until we have the capabilities. The official word from Starfleet is that we are the only ship other than Valiant to encounter the barrier. Constitution's mission is Apocrypha. It never happened. Constitution never made it through the barrier," Spock said.

"Why all the deep cover secrecy, Jim?" McCoy said.

"I don't know why, Bones, but whatever happened out there, the council want a lid on it," Kirk admitted.

Scotty walked over and jumped into the conversation.

"When I tried to talk to Andy about what happened out there, Andy gave me a look and cut the transmission. I have never seen him so spooked, Captain."

Because of her late return, Admiral Mattea Hahn had ordered Constitution to take Enterprise's place at Star base 20 and receive her updates at the Antares yards along with Hood and Kongo.

Hahn then ordered Enterprise to be being updated at Earth after Mitchell's memorial service. She had followed the Republic into the San Francisco Navy yards for her updates. During this time, Kirk had sent Barbara Smith to the Lexington, since Wesley's newly updated Lexington was already heading for Vanguard. Kirk recalled.

"Gentlemen," Spock said changing the subject. "According to Harrata legend, the Progenitors and the Continuum were both involved in creating the barrier between a billion and 600,000 years ago."

McCoy grunted, "More tall tales, Spock, the Progenitors and the Continuum are myths."

"Not according to the Harrata. Doctor McCoy, in the book of Gom around 50,000 years ago, there is a mention of a great battle in the great beyond, past the barrier where the Harrata, Skorr, and a now-extinct race known as the Rogar defeated the Horror from another galaxy with the help of gigantic planet-killer monsters. The Harrata deities parted the barrier to let the fleet led by Antoi Jk Caribe to pass into the great beyond. They never returned."

"More legend and poppycock, Spock," McCoy grumbled. Spock was spinning tales again, he thought.

"Captain Kirk."

"Yes, Uhura."

"Commandant Bogash, Sir."

"Put him on."

The blond-haired Harrata Commandant appeared on the Enterprise's main screen. "Ober C Kirk," Bogash said referring to Kirk in the traditional Harrata slang.

"Yes, Commandant."

"We will be approaching the Lothar system shortly. You can only beam down with your closest compatriots. Do not interfere with us. We will be in Harrakie. As outworlders, you would not understand. Once we finish with this, it is less than a day's journey to the ChaZ system where we will hold the ChaZ-Hagem. Your ships will have remained within our tractor control until the end of the first part of the Challenge. If you survive, you will be under escort for the second and third rounds, Ober Commander," Bogash said warning Kirk.

"We understand, Commandant."

"Gom de Zak out."

"Captain Kirk, I have a visual sighting on the Lothar system," Sulu said.

"Spock."

"Multiple metallic readings, the Lothar system captain are spectral class M, six planets. Two are class C; one is class G, one class L and one class Y."

The combined fleet entered the system.

"Mister Sulu, enhance grid 20," Kirk ordered.

Sulu nodded and complied.

Everyone on the bridge suddenly quieted down.

On the main screen, the hulks of the Titanic, Britannic, Captain, and Good Hope that appeared next to them were the remains of the ill-fated scout ships Discovery and Mercury.

Spock broke the pall that had descended over the bridge. "Captain, there are numerous ship types here, Vulcan, Andorian, Romulan . . . the list of races is endless. Some ships date back to 1 AD when the Harrata regained their warp capabilities after the Tkon, Iconians, and the Horror space eras."

"Uhura, get me Constitution."

"Aye, Sir," Uhura said. Moments later, Robert Hawke's image appeared.

"Yes, Jim."

"I want your opinion, Captain," Kirk said.

"It makes my blood boil, Captain," Hawke replied tensely.

McCoy looked at Spock. Spock only nodded. The sight of these hulks was affecting both crews. It was depressing, to say the least.

"Opinion noted. Captain Hawke Enterprise out." Hawke's image disappeared.

On the main screen, more hulks appeared. One looked like a smaller version of Balok's ship. It was of Fesarian origin. The hulk looked like it had been torn open. The first Federation that appeared also had contact with the Harrata and had lost the Challenge.

"Captain, we are now entering orbit of Lothar three," Sulu said.

Kirk turned to Spock.

"Mister Spock."

"Lothar three-class L, two landmasses, two small seas. Oxygen nitrogen atmosphere suitable for human life within class L tolerances for humanoid colonization Intermittent life form readings."

"Captain Kirk, we now have beamed down permission courtesy of the Star force," Uhura said.

"Acknowledge them, Uhura." Kirk turned to Spock and McCoy. "Let's face the music, Bones, Spock. Scotty, the Enterprise is yours."

"Aye, Sir."

LOTHAR THREE. HOME TO LOTHAR. DEITIES OF DEATH AND BETRAYAL. STAR DATE 2911.9:

Kirk, Spock, and McCoy materialized in a clearing. Mountains jutted out in the distance. Sand whipped at their feet.

"I don't believe it, Jim, we are the first ones here," McCoy said surprised. "What a depressing planet."

"Spock."

Spock had already taken out his tricorder. The Harrata had given them the right to record down on this planet.

"Multiple Harrata life form readings bearing 045, I am picking up massive stone structures in the same direction, Captain."

"So, Jim we just wait," McCoy said impatiently.

"Yes, Bones."

Seconds later, the air shrieked, the sound of Federation transporter materialization. Four figures appeared. Two were human, one Andorian and one was a Vulcan. The landing party from the Constitution had arrived. Hawke and T'Pau immediately opened their tricorders up and started to scan. Kirk and his party walked over. "Bob."

"Yes, Jim," Hawke said as he looked up from his tricorder.

"Three tricorders?" McCoy asked as he looked at Constitution's executive officer Shran. "Isn't that excessive?"

"We do things in triplicate, Doctor McCoy. The captain likes to lead, but he also likes backup. If one tricorder is lost or destroyed, we have an extra copy," Shran explained to McCoy.

"Logical commander, very logical."

"Thank you, Spock. This is the way the captain and I have used since the Sargon," Shran said as she looked at McCoy. "You did serve on this ship once, did you, Doctor?"

"Yes, Thay, I did under Augenthaler."

"And so, was Jim Kirk your captain?"

"Yes, Shran."

"Then I am honored to be with you, Bones. No small talk, McCoy. Andorians don't like having their time wasted on trivial matters," Shran shot back.

McCoy looked at Shran. Boy, he thought, she's lethal.

"I told you, Bones, watch out for Shran," Kirk said as he came over. "She has been known to slice up all her foes."

"And she is gorgeous too, boot," McCoy added graciously. "I noticed it earlier, Commander, but I didn't have time to comment on your beauty."

"Thank you, Doctor McCoy. To be called beautiful by a human is a compliment. Have you ever been to Andoria?"

"Yes, once, when I served on the Constitution. Have you ever been to Georgia, Shran?"

"Yes, many years ago. It was very, very hot," Shran said recalling the long-forgotten memory.

Hawke, T'Pau, and Russell came over.

"What's taking the reception committee so long?" Doc Russell growled.

"How should I know, Doc?" McCoy said exasperated at Russell's nagging.

"This planet gives me the creeps," Hawke admitted.

"Ladies and gentlemen, I don't believe the reception committee would arrive until the Klingons arrive," Spock added. The illogic of this planet astounded him and the waste.

"A logical point, Spock."

"Affirmative, T'Pau. Quite logical."

Seconds later, the air suddenly pulsated as the Klingon transporters' effect rendered the air. Six Klingons, four males and two females, appeared. In unison, they walked over to the group of Federation officers.

"Kirk! Hawke!" Kang said as he approached the two captains who stepped aside from their officers. The heavy-set Klingon next to Kang looked at Kang and said, "They look like fat Federation Targs Kang."

Kirk and Hawke walked up to the Klingons followed by the rest. Kang and the other Klingon commander stepped up to face Kirk and Hawke.

"The Federation chooses wisely," Kang said as he looked at Kirk and Hawke. "Both you and Hawke have gracefully aged, Kirk."

"So, this is the infamous James T. Kirk," Khod said as he looked Kirk over. The heavy-set Klingon with the bushy eyebrows and the sparse beard said. Looking at Hawke, Khod made another comment, "I am not scruffy-looking Hawke. I still remember your snide remark."

Hawke faced Khod. "A figure of speech, Khod, you could never get any of my jokes."

Khod growled annoyed. Hawke had done it to him again.

Kang smiled. "What do you have to say for yourself, Kirk?"

"What is there to say, Kang? We are here, aren't we?" Kirk said noticing the squabble between Hawke and Khod. Out of all the captains the empire the Klingons had to send, it had to be Kang.

"Yes, Kirk. We do not want to be here. But the Harratas are honorable people unlike you Federation types. The Empire has never lost the Challenge. The Challenge hones our warrior skills to perfection. The Harratas might be fanatics, but they fight like true warriors. If you and Hawke perish, they will bleed your Federation dry as we conquer and crush you, Kirk."

Kang paused for a moment and remembered. "I was at Savo, too, Kirk, I was the captain on the battle cruiser Doj at the time. Under the leadership of the Dahr master Captain K'mentoc of the Vor'Tak. Both of your ships, the Lydia Sutherland and the Miranda, destroyed the three medium cruisers while that fool Custer wasted his pathetic scouts and destroyers against our three mighty battle cruisers that tore them to pieces. Only the last-minute arrival of your battle cruisers changed the battle, Kirk," Kang said reminding Kirk and

Hawke of that glorious day. The Doj, Mekleth, and the Vor'Tak had won true glory. The empire was still singing songs about that battle.

"So, it was you, Kang."

"Yes, Kirk. Both you and Hawke battled us like angry beasts. That is why when we last met, I did what I did," Kang said as he looked at Kirk's and Hawke's officers. "Now tell me, Kirk, who in the Empire wouldn't know the officers of the Enterprey or the Constidonatu, the finest that your fleet has to offer."

Kang said and then introduced his officers. "This is Mara, my science officer," Kang said looking at the pretty Klingon woman behind him. "And this is Konar, my first officer," Kang said pointing to the clean-shaven muscular Klingon, looking over to his left. "This scruffy-looking proud Klingon is none other than Khod Sutai Katal, Son of Mosh of the Klingon Great House Klod. The woman to his right is Mira, his science officer, and finally, this is Korag his first," Kang said pointing at the wild-looking, narrow-faced Klingon who had sharp upswept eyebrows.

Spock, observing the whole meeting, looked at McCoy. "Are you troubled, Doctor?"

"No, Spock. This whole scenario is so unreal."

"Indeed, Doctor, it is."

Shran, Russell, and T'Pau walked over. "Never underestimate Khod, Spock," Shran warned.

"Kang is no pushover, Shran."

"My captain met Kang and Khod on the home world as you recall during the Interspecies academy program in 2256. Hawke will let

Kirk do the talking, Spock. Your ship is still better known to the Empire than us."

"Constitution is no pushover herself, Shran. I heard that her repute nearly equals the infamy of Enterprise," McCoy admitted.

"Tell me, Leonard," Russell spoke up. "Doctor to Doctor, which ships do you prefer, Constitution or Enterprise?" Russell was clearly in a provocative mood.

"Now, don't get nippy with me, Doc. You know that we both cannot choose fairly between both ships," McCoy said exasperated by Russell's suggestion. McCoy knew Doc's repute in Starfleet, a brilliant, somewhat driven medical officer.

His mentor was none other than Phillip Boyce, former CMO of the Enterprise. His dad had served as CMO of the Potemkin for three five-year missions; Donald Russell was now serving as a Commodore in charge of the highly secret contagious disease storage facility Null Omega which had replaced Cold Station in the early 23rd century. Donald Russell had been a perfectionist and had passed his driven personality onto his son.

At least, Doc wasn't as annoying as Jack Carter on the Exeter who had the award for most annoying CMO in the Heavy cruiser fleet. Carter had served with Tracey going all the way back to Tracey's first three commands, the Retribution, Republic, and the Lafayette, much in the same way that Peder Coss had served with Wesley on the Avenger, Beowulf, and briefly on the Constitution before going over to the Lexington. McCoy remembered. Old Jack Carter always complained about everything. McCoy recalled.

Shran squinted as she scanned the area. She spotted a lone figure in a black robe with a hood over its head approaching.

"Jim! Robert! I think we have company," Shran warned.

Russell walked up to McCoy. "Finally! The reception committee has finally arrived," Russell grumbled.

Kirk, Hawke, Kang, and Khod walked over to the group. Spock came by Bones' side, his tricorder humming away.

"Harrata, Captain, most likely a priest of Lothar," Spock said blandly.

Russell and McCoy had pulled out their tricorders.

"Definitely Harrata, Jim," McCoy said.

Russell just nodded as Hawke came to Russell's side along with Shran and T'Pau. They were comparing their findings as Hawke just silently nodded as they spoke. McCoy watching the crew from Constitution in action could only remember that famous line "different folks, different strokes" or as the Vulcans said IDIC, "Infinite diversity, infinite combinations."

The mysterious figure was wearing a black robe. Ornamentation glittered on the black hands that extended out of the robe.

Kirk, followed by Hawke, Kang, and Khod walked up to the mysterious figure. The figure dropped the hood revealing a black-skinned female with blond hair in a half-circle and red eyes which glowed almost catlike in appearance. For a moment, Kirk thought he was looking into the eyes of Mitchell and Dehner again.

"I am High Priestess Daviney Ma Caralty, Lord of Lothar Three, Keeper of the Temple to Lothar, the mighty. You all must be the challengers coming to face the will of Lothar if you fail the Tong."

Kirk decided to speak up, "I am."

"You are Kirk, this is Hawke, and the Klingonasse are Kang and Khod," the priestess pointed to the four captains. "And coming up behind you are your weak underlings," she said as the other officers started to come up to join them.

Kirk looked at Kang and Khod. Both Klingons said nothing at the insult. He looked at Hawke, but Hawke was distant. His mind must be wandering, Kirk thought. Kirk looked as Spock and McCoy came alongside him.

"Now that we are here, follow me," Caralty said as she led the group toward the temple. As they proceeded forward, Kirk and the rest could hear screaming, groaning, singing, chanting, crying, and growling coming from the distance. As they walked over the desolate landscape, the noises became louder and louder. The enormous temple of Lothar in its grotesque glory jutted out of the landscape like a monster consuming all before it.

"Talk about taking forever, Jim," McCoy mumbled.

"Soon, Doctor McCoy, soon," Spock reassured McCoy.

Kirk looked back to see that the party from the Constitution had gone silent. Nobody was really talking. The Klingons however were chatting to themselves in their native language; it struck him that the Klingons were treating this as though they were on a stroll in a park.

"Unreal, Jim. Never thought I'd see the Klingons treat this like a lark."

"Bones, never mind. It is totally irrelevant," Kirk waved Bones off. What seemed like ages, they passed over a hill, and lo and behold stood the Temple of Lothar. It was ugly. Kirk had never seen such a grotesque garish monstrosity. Hawke walked up to Kirk. "Jim, that building is uglier than the old Soviet architecture on Earth," Hawke said finally breaking his silence.

"I was wondering when you were going to shake off that stupor, Bob."

"This planet is depressing, and we haven't reached the temple yet," Hawke repeated again. He really hated this planet.

"The captain has a good point, Jim. The illogic of this place astounds me," Spock admitted.

"Lothar is like our devil, Jim," McCoy said.

"Maybe worse, Lothar has no honor," Shran added.

In the distance, the voices became louder. The party descended the hill. Appearing before the temple in a section off to the right of the main path were the Harrata Star force commanders. Some were crying, others were chanting, while some others were growling, singing. All were prostrated or bowing down. Only the screamers were standing.

Kirk went up to the high priestess. "High Priestess, what are they doing?" Kirk asked.

"The unbelievers in Lothar are repenting their souls in their blasphemous prayer styles of the other twelve deities, Captain Kirk. The screaming Harratas are true believers in the might of Lothar. They are the slaves of Lothar." Kirk looked at the Harrata Ober Commander. He was one of the three who he had to face in the Challenge. He recognized Bogash who was chanting and was prostrated on the floor with his officers along with a Flolitor Commander (fleet captain) and his officers. At the ChaZ, he would find out who they were. The Lotharian Ober Commander smiled evilly at Kirk as he screamed out the words in Harrata.

"They are in Harrakie, the repentance, Captain Kirk," the high priestess said. As they started to climb the stairs up to the entrance to the temple, two imposing guards flanked the entrance to the temple. They were of the High Order Corp wearing a variation of the uniform of Silver and black with Red Cross belts flanked at the entrance. The priestess turned to face the entire group. "Past this point, only the challengers may pass."

"But we thought," McCoy spoke up.

"McCoy, you are not chosen by your people. This is as far as the loyal ones may go past here. Only the chosen go and Captain Hawke."

"Yes."

"No recording devices."

Hawke handed his tricorder to Shran.

"Now, if you four would follow me."

Kirk, Hawke, Kang, and Khod entered the temple. Kirk could smell the stench of death. The temple was poorly lit.

Kirk grabbed a torch that was handed to him by one of the Lotharians. He could hear water tapping on the rock as he followed the priestess deeper into the temple. Hawke, Kang, and Khod who held the rear made up the rest of the group. Screaming echoed through the walls as the Lotharians prayed. They walked past a corridor with a circular room, flame shot up through the circular opening. A scream not of the Lotharians sounded. A helpless white female was sacrificed into the flames of Lothar. Kirk could only hate the barbarity of the Harrata because of that. But then, he realized it was their way.

They descended deeper into the temple.

Outside Lothar's temple.

McCoy sat on the steps of the temple. The rest of the officers from the Constitution were sitting near him. The Klingons as usual sat a distance away from them, considering the deteriorating relations between both powers. McCoy really couldn't blame them. Spock was up on his feet with T'Pau scanning the neighboring area and both were discussing their findings. Russell and Shran walked over and sat next to McCoy.

"We figured you need some company since Spock and T'Pau are preoccupied," Shran admitted.

"That pointy-eared, devil. Spock can never catch his breath. Sometimes, I think your T'Pau is just like Spock," McCoy said.

"They are Vulcans. Rest is meditation, not a vacation, Bones," Russell pointed out. "However, I do admire their analytical skill. No pun intended, Shran. But T'Pau's logic sometimes trumps Andorian passion."

"There you go again, Dave. Remember one hundred years ago, Andorians and Vulcans did not get along," Shran said a little bit annoyed by Russell's candor.

"And Shran, I know you like Robert," Russell said.

"What was that again?" McCoy said incredulously.

"Thay likes the captain."

"But isn't Robert engaged to Samantha?" McCoy said.

"Yes. But Thay doesn't care. Isn't that right, Thay?"

"Yes, Doc. I admire my captain for his skills. He might belong to Samantha Reynolds, but I can admire him just the same," Shran said smiling. She really wanted to avoid the subject altogether. Robert was her captain and a good friend. But Doc could be so annoying at times.

"You will never admit it, Thay, would you?" Russell pressed.

"No, Doc. Never," Shran said still smiling.

Spock and T'Pau walked up. "Doctor McCoy, did we miss anything?" Spock said.

McCoy, Shran, and Russell just smiled.

"No, Spock, nothing," McCoy said still smiling.

T'Pau folded her arms. "That is not logical. When humans—" T'Pau was the model of Vulcan seriousness.

Spock cut T'Pau off, "T'Pau, do not try to figure humans or Andorians out. They are most illogical."

McCoy slapped Spock in the back. "You bet your pointy ears, Spock."

It almost provoked a human reaction from T'Pau. "Doctor McCoy, how—"

Spock put his hand up, cutting T'Pau off.

"Understood, Spock." T'Pau became stony-faced again. Spock and T'Pau sat down next to the other officers.

"Humans are so illogical," T'Pau admitted and looking at Shran. "And Andorians are nearly as bad."

"They are not perfect, T'Pau," Spock said sitting next to T'Pau.

McCoy said summoning everything up and got in the last word. "And proud of it, Spock."

Kirk followed the high priestess deeper into the temple. The stench of death and rotted corpses had become more pronounced as they neared the end of their journey.

"The stench of failure, Kirk, Hawke," Kang said. "You will find no Klingons among the dead."

"No Klingon has ever joined the pit of Lothar," Khod added. Before he and Hawke could add a word in response, they entered a wide rectangular room. Corpses, captains from all known alien races, filled the pit in various forms of deterioration. Uniforms dating back centuries in various forms of deterioration covered the respective corpses. The stench of death was horrible.

"High priestess, what about the crews?" Kirk asked.

"Entombed in the hulks that float above us, Kirk. Both you and Hawke will lie in this pit if you fail."

"We will not fail, High Priestess," Hawke said holding back his emotions.

She looked at Hawke. "You are a descendant of the Hawkes who contacted us."

"Yes."

"And Kirk's father was at Hell Spawn."

"What does that have to do with us, Priestess?" Kirk said angrily. "You show us death. Isn't there any compassion?"

Kang and Khod laughed.

"The Lotharians have no compassion for failure, Kirk," Kang said.

"It has to do with everything, my challengers." A devilish, conspirator smile appeared on her face.

"It is your destiny."

Robert Hawke looked surprised at the priestess. "Our destiny?"

"Yes, Captain, yours, Kirk's, Kang's, and Khod's. You are all intertwined one way or the other. All of you will see the next century. How you arrive there is another matter."

"How?" Kirk asked. "Do you know our destiny?"

"It is not your time, Kirk. Both you and Hawke touched our celestial temple. Kang and Khod however did not, but they are great warriors, not weakling Humass. In the lying book of prophecy, it was foretold that warriors would come defeating our greatness and summoning the coming of the unholy."

"Iconians," Kirk mentioned.

"Do not speak those words, Kirk. They like the Borgara and the Daklenah are horror to all Harrata. It is blasphemy to speak it."

The ground started to shake beneath Kirk's feet. He had to steady himself to prevent himself from falling.

"Lothar is displeased."

"Jim, did you have to make Lothar angry?" Hawke said as he held onto a stone supporting him. The Klingons rode the shock out as the ground shook beneath their feet.

"What the blazes," McCoy said as the temple started to shake, "is going on here?"

"Someone, Bones, made Lothar angry," Russell said.

Spock was looking at his tricorder. The emanations come from at least one kilometer down. "Doctors."

"Confirmed, I am picking up two humans, two Klingon, and one Harrata reading," T'Pau added.

"They are all still alive," Shran added.

"Yes, Commander."

"Look at the Klingons," Shran pointed out. The Klingons were just standing there looking at them. The two female Klingons Mara and Mira were looking at them. They were not pleased.

"Spock, I think we stirred up a hornets' nest."

"A what?"

The Klingon party started to move toward the Federation party.

"Jim, now would be a good time to apologize," Hawke suggested, still braced against the stone.

"Lothar, I apologize," Kirk said aloud.

The shaking stopped.

Spock and the rest of the Federation party watched as the Klingons suddenly turned away from them and walked in the other direction.

"Now what was that all about?" McCoy wondered.

Kirk felt relieved; the shaking had finally ended.

"It is time to leave," High Priestess Caralty said.

The group followed her out of the temple.

Kirk rejoined Spock and McCoy.

"Well, Jim, what happened down there?"

"I don't want to discuss it, Bones." Kirk flipped open his communicator. "Let's get the hell out of here, Kirk, to Enterprise three to beam up."

The Enterprise party disappeared.

"I said it once before and I will say it again," Hawke said agitatedly looking at his party. "There's nothing to talk about."

"But Robert, we need to know as you're—" Shran said.

"No!" Hawke said adamant flipping his communicator open. "Constitution four to beam up, pronto."

The Constitution party disappeared.

Kang watched as Mara and Konar came over. "Khod's people have just left Kang," Mara said. "Did one of the Earthers anger Lothar?"

"Yes, Mara. It was Kirk."

"They are so arrogant, those Federation types. They think they could control the galaxy."

"Milord," Konar asked. "Didn't the Earthers learn the last two times not to offend the Harratay gods?"

"The Earthers never learn, Konar," Kang said speaking in his native Klingon. Kang's party shimmered out of existence.

CHAPTER SEVENTEEN

"Captain's personal log. Star date 2911. 10. Captain James T. Kirk recording. Death, destruction, what future do I have? Or do we on the Enterprise have a future at all? And what is this mysterious book of prophecy? Are our destinies already written in stone? I do not know."

"Captain's personal log. Star date 2911.10. Captain Robert Nelson Hawke recording. How did they know? Mine and Jim's past, how? It doesn't make any sense. How did they know? I have too many questions and no answers. I cannot let my crew down; they are my responsibility, my family. Ces't la vie."

STAR BASE VANGUARD. ADMIRAL NOGURA'S OFFICE. STAR DATE 2911.11:

Starship Captain Atish Khatami and her XO Katherine Stano entered Nogura's central office. Endeavor had just finished a four-month patrol and research mission. The ship was in for resupply and shore leave. With Defiant detached to Matt Decker's squadron due to the Harrata crisis, Endeavor had taken up all the slack. Khatami was happy that Potemkin was on her way and Coronado had arrived.

Sitting opposite Nogura was the familiar figure of Doctor Carol Marcus and two familiar Asians.

"Sun! Kenji!"

The two Asians came over and hugged Khatami.

"Finally made it, Captain, heard about Zhao's death, Atish. Belayed congratulations are in order," Sun Lee Manchu said as he adjusted his uniform.

Khatami remembered that Sun was always spit and polish in his mannerisms and dress. Nothing ever missed Sun's eagle eye. Her time on Coronado had been fulfilling until she transferred to Endeavor. Unlike Jim Kirk or Bob Hawke, during her career, she hadn't been sent everywhere and anywhere.

"Indeed, they are," Kenji Nakamura, Coronado's slim, athletic Japanese first officer said.

"Sun, Kenji, I would like you to meet my XO. Katherine Stano."

Stano shook hands with both officers. "A pleasure," she said in her southern drawl.

"Atish, sorry about Zheng. He was a good officer and a friend."

Nogura and Marcus walked up. "Sorry to break up the reunion, folks, but we have a business to attend to. I believe you all know Doctor Marcus."

"I was three years ahead of Doctor Marcus at the Academy," Khatami said. She had graduated in 2252 with the likes of Sean Finnegan, Kelly Bogle, Eric Ven Dhruva, and Hallie Gannon.

Carol smiled. Just like old times, she thought.

Sitting at the end of Nogura's desk, Carol watched as Khatami, Stano, Manchu, and Nakamura took their seats next to her.

Nogura finally settled into his seat. "The reasons why I called you here, Atish and Carol, is because both of you know the commanding officers of the Enterprise and the Constitution."

"How is Jim involved?" Carol suddenly said concerned. She hadn't seen Jim in almost four years.

"Oh, I bet you called me here, Hirohito, because of Bobby Hawke," Khatami added.

Stano looked at Khatami surprised. "You knew Bobby Hawke."

"Yes, Katharine, during my senior year. Bobby and Samantha Reynolds were in their Junior year. Samantha eventually beat me out for Bob's affections. But I found Robert and Jim so sexy, Katharine, I had to try."

"I served on the Miranda under Hawke's command back in 63," Stano mentioned. "We were at Ghihoge and Savo." Stano looked surprised at Khatami. "I didn't know that you almost dated him."

Nogura cut in, "Atish, I received this list from Solow." Nogura handed Khatami the pad. She looked at the names. "Konstantin figures, Silver, Kirk, and Hawke," Khatami said as she found her name near the top of the list. The classes of 2253 and 2254 were below her class.

"You were considered for the Challenge, Atish. But Endeavor is assigned here. Solow told me that Hancock said that Starfleet cannot spare Endeavor or you."

"The Challenge! Starfleet sent Jim Kirk and Bob Hawke. That is a death sentence. The Harrata will destroy the Enterprise and Constitution if they lose," Marcus said aghast.

"The reality, Carol, it is that the Harrata are on the warpath again. Jim and Bob are the best we have," Nogura said.

"With Defiant assigned to Decker's squadron, Manchu's Coronado is replacing her. Potemkin should be arriving soon," Nogura continued.

"Here we go again. Another war with the Harrata," Manchu said resigned.

"Yes, Captain Manchu. But I believe that Jim Kirk and Bob Hawke will pull off the impossible and there will be no war," Nogura reassured everyone present.

Marcus wasn't so reassured by Nogura's statement. "Hirohito, how can you say that? We lost the last two times," Carol pointed out astonished at Nogura's casual manner.

"Now, Carol, I admire your opinion. But we both know Jim Kirk. If anyone can survive the Tong, it is Jim Kirk."

"And don't forget about Bobby Hawke," Khatami reminded the group. "Robert is no slouch either."

The intercom whistled. Nogura answered it. "The Potemkin has arrived. Manchu, Khatami, you have your orders," Nogura said.

Khatami, Stano, Manchu, and Nakamura got up and left.

"I hope you are right, Hiro," Marcus said.

Nogura looked at Carol. "Let's hope that they come back alive."

"Amen to that," Carol said as she left Nogura's office.

"Captain's log. Star date 2911.12. Captain James T. Kirk recording. In less than an hour, we will be arriving at the ChaZ system. And so, begins the next part of pomp and circumstance."

"Captain's log. Star date 2911.12.1. Captain Robert Nelson Hawke recording. Here goes nothing. When we arrive at the ChaZ system, it is time for ceremonies and a lot of hoopla's."

Kirk adjusted his dress uniform as McCoy looked on. Putting his medal of honor on, Kirk could only feel the importance of this ceremony.

"One down, two to go, Jim."

Kirk nodded. "Right, Bones."

"Jim, I don't know what you and Robert saw in the temple. But do not put your personal feelings ahead of your duty. You and Robert are no longer at the academy, Jim. This is life and death."

"Dammit, Bones! Don't you think I know that?" Kirk said angrily. "Robert knows too."

"And that is my point, Jim. He saved your neck at Ghihoge and, at a risk to his ship and crew, patched up the situation there. He is going through the same emotional stress that you are experiencing."

The intercom interrupted the conversation. "Yes."

"Captain, we have entered the ChaZ system," Spock said.

"Understood, Spock."

McCoy and Kirk left his quarters.

Moments later, Kirk and McCoy arrived on the bridge. In place of Desalle, Harrison manned navigation.

"Spock, what do we have on the ChaZ system?"

"Spectral class K orange. Three class M planets, 3, 4, 5. One classes A, one class F."

"Spock, this system houses a Star force base."

"Yes, Captain, planet five. Planet four is the Harrata's equivalent of Risa and Planet three is our destination."

Minutes later, Enterprise and her escorts entered the orbit of ChaZ three.

"Spock, you have the bridge."

"Affirmative, Captain."

Kirk stepped into the lift.

CHAZ THREE. A HARRATA CEREMONIAL PLANET:

Kirk materialized facing an opulent building that almost reminded him of a French Chateau back on Earth. A cool spring breeze whipped at his face. Multicolored trees rustled in the distance. Alien chirpings sounded in the background.

Moments later, the sound of transporter materialization sounded the arrival of another. Bob Hawke appeared in his dress uniform. Kirk could spot his medals of Honor and Valor hanging on his chest. They both had the Karagite order of Heroism, Grankite order of Tactics, and the Silver Palm with cluster. Robert's Silver Palm however had oak leaves and clusters, but that's where the similarities ended. Robert had his Andorian Battle star, the Legion of Honor, and his civilian honor won years back, given to him by the Federation President at the time. And he had one more than Bob Wesley and Robert Hawke.

Seconds later, Kang and Khod appeared in their formal Klingon dress uniforms.

Seconds after that, the air hummed as yellow shimmering fields formed and the Harrata champions appeared. Commandant (Commodore) Bogash flanked by one Flotilar commander (fleet captain) and one ober commander (captain) made their way toward him. They all wore a variation of the Star force gold uniform. A blue cloak hung over each Harrata, and they all had a gold sash studded with their required honors.

Bogash walked up to Kirk.

"Ober C Kirk. I would like to present two more of your challengers," Bogash said as Kirk was introduced to a heavy-set, silver-haired, older Harrata who had grey eyes and a graying beard. "This is Flolitor C. Napari JA Fakari of the Hittati. You will face him if you survive, in the second round."

The older Harrata bowed to Kirk and touched his palms together. "I am honored in the name of Chiss to meet you, Kirk."

Kirk did likewise.

"And this is Ober C. Goraday van Sant, commander of the Logash," Bogash pointed to the thin, lanky Harrata who had red hair and cat-like silver eyes.

Kirk looked at the Harrata captain. Kirk realized that he was looking at the Lotharian who had smiled at him on Lothar three. The Harrata captain said nothing and didn't bow to Kirk. The Harrata commander was showing complete disregard for protocol. He was deliberately being snubbed.

"Yas va Humass Bogash Patx uu sa far. No sazaer," Van Sant said angrily at Gorady in Harratese.

"What did he say?" Kirk was baffled.

"You do not want to know, Ober C. Kirk," Fakari told him.

"He is Lotharian. They will not speak in your standard unless it is necessary," Bogash said. "Now that we have all met, let us go and celebrate the ChaZ," Bogash pointed out. He then slapped Kirk on the back. His back ached. Fahiri had a more potent back slap than Hawke.

Together, the four ship captains set off for the main building. Moments later, they entered the posh building. In the center of, at the heart of the building, lay an enormous square room. Light reflected into the building from the overhead windows casting a wondrous glow as the light reflected off the multicolored rocks that lined the inside of the building.

Four tables were laid out to the center. Behind the tables lay a group of Silvers, playing Harrata musical instruments. The band was playing Harrata folk music and then switched into a Harrata military

March music when they all entered the room. Greens hustled around making the final arrangements for the feast.

The Klingons sat down first with Khod's group at the far end, followed by Kang's. Kirk and his group sat down next followed finally by Hawke's group.

On cue, they all stood up. The Harrata band swung into the Harrata Imperium anthem. After that was finished, the anthem of the Klingon Empire blasted out and finally, the Federation anthem finished off the finale.

The greens started to pass out the food. He never really tasted Harrata food. Farragut's stay at Bathazar 12 had been too short. He had been confined to the Farragut during the visit and had no time to visit the Battle station.

"Try the Mazga root stew, Kirk, it is quite good," Fakari suggested.

Kirk ladled the white soup into his bowl and took a taste. It was quite good, reminding him of potato soup back home.

Bogash poured him some wine. Kirk took a taste of it. "This reminds me of Eyyaian wine, Commandant."

"It is Vasgi wine, far better than Eyyaian Kirk," Bogash said. "Who gave you Eyyaian, Kirk?"

Kirk pointed to Robert Hawke. Compared to his group, Robert and his competitors were roaring with laughter and making enough noise to wake up the dead.

"His dad contacted the Eyyaian in that ship that he now commands, Commandant."

"I did not know," Bogash admitted.

Kirk leaned over. Compared to Hawke's and his own. Kang was singing in Klingon as the Harrata responded in their native dialect. And next to Kang's, Khod's table was silent as a tomb. Khod and his Harrata companions were eating in silence.

"Bogash, I do not understand," Kirk said as he bit into the slab of Jambat meat. "Why many gods, not one?"

"It is our way, Kirk. Many centuries ago, we Harrata had one god or goddess that ruled each of the thirteen nations of Harrata Four. We warred and fought. We were divided. And then Gom and the other twelve deities came. We reached ascension."

"Ascension?"

"You do not understand, Kirk," Fahari said.

"Ag SA Humass, No Harratay hiisba, Ja sav nee sav," Van Sant muttered.

Fahari turned to Van San and spoke in Harratese, "Lothary cha za Va saya Humass."

Van San quieted down. Fahari then turned back to Kirk. "As you were saying, Kirk."

"On my world, the Greeks, Romans, and other pagan civilizations had many gods. But then we went the other way," Kirk explained. "Hashem, Mohammed, Jesus, and Buddha are the sole deities on Earth, not counting other religions such as Hinduism and Shintoism and many other ones. Some of our gods and goddess are male or female," Kirk explained.

"So, your world is ruled by many single deities and multiple deities together. Doesn't that lead to wars?" Bogash added, "But our deities are male and female combined."

Kirk nodded. "We had many Bogash all over our religious differences. And I am surprised that your deities are multisexual."

Bogash took another sip of his Rattay beer. The Humass was becoming interesting. It would be a pity that they had to kill each other.

"That is our way," Fakari added.

"A question, Bogash, why the specific skin colors? On Earth, we have white, olive, black, reddish, brown, yellow for each of our regions." Kirk asked.

"It is our caste color, our permanent career occupation. We all have a place in the greater good of the Harrata Imperium, and even the worthless whites must contribute in a way."

"So, if I went on a Harrata space liner, the Blues run the ship. The whites take care of financials, the greens are the culinary crew, and the silvers provide the entertainment."

"Almost correct, Kirk," Fakari said. "Occasionally, we have overlaps."

"We have Star force security and the Order Corps. Blues doing the work of Reds, but that has been agreed upon by all thirteen deities," Bogash added.

"So not everything is set in stone."

"Yes, Kirk. We are starting to undergo a fashion revolution. In thirty years, Harrata males will no longer wear their hair in what you Humass term as Mohawk style. And women will no longer be wearing the half-circle style. Our hairstyle will be as varied as any alien race. Gom decreed it so."

"Gom decreed it after agreeing with many of the deities, Kirk," Fahari said.

"That is why we have thirteen," Bogash added.

The noise in the room suddenly grew to a crescendo as everyone turned to Kang's table. The three Harratas had stood up and been singing.

"Gomas, Gomas, Harratay, Gomass, So Annady Gomass Harratay Harratay, Harratay Gomass."

The Harrata repeated the song. Their feet pounded on the floor in unison.

Khod's Harrata champions joined in. Finally, Hawke's champions joined the spectacle.

Kirk watched as Bogash, Fakari, and Van Sant stood up and joined in the celebration. The band continued to play, and the silvers joined in dancing and singing, contributing to the spectacle. Finally, the greens finally dropped what they were doing and joined in.

Kirk could only smile. He could see Robert swinging his tankard of beer back and forth. After the hellhole of Lothar, this was truly an eye-opener. Kang and Khod oddly enough had joined in singing with their Harrata opposites. This whole scenario was unreal. Wait until he told McCoy and Spock about this.

ONE HOUR LATER:

Kirk clenched his fists and said goodbye to the three Harrata officers. Robert walked up to him after saying goodbyes to his own champions.

"Never a dull day in Starfleet, Jim," said Hawke.

Kirk noticed that Robert looked slightly stoned. Too much beer or wine. Hawke could never hold his liquor. Kirk remembered; the famed almighty brought down to earth by too much liquor. Kirk could still feel his head buzzing from the Rattay beer he had consumed.

"Like our days at the academy, Bob."

Hawke could only nod in agreement. "I'm really going to hate to have to kill them, Jim."

"No doubts, Robert. Either they die, or we die."

Hawke nodded. "Understood. Au revoir, Jim."

"Au revoir, Robert," Kirk said as Hawke dematerialized. "Kirk to Enterprise, one to beam up."

Kirk watched as ChaZ faded from view.

CHAPTER EIGHTEEN

January 22, 2267

"Captain's log. Star date 2912.3. Captain James T. Kirk recording. We are on a final approach to the Harratay Star system. The final part of Pomp and circumstance will be played out here. Then it is do or die."

"Captain's log. Star date 2912.5. Captain Robert N. Hawke recording. The last act of this part of the play is about to unfold. Then it gets serious from here onward."

Kirk sat in his command chair. The final part of pomp and circumstance was going to be played out at the Parida. Then, the infamous challenge would begin. There was no turning back now, on his and Robert's shoulders lay the survival of their ships and billions of lives. Kirk could only think of his predecessors that had failed. It was not going to happen this time. Not if he and Robert could help it.

"Captain, we are approaching the Harratay star system," Sulu said.

"Thank you, Mister Sulu, Spock."

"The Harratay star system is a dual system of two suns overlapping with sixteen planets. Six are class M. Our destination is Harrata Four, home world and the heart of the Harrata Imperium."

Spock looked back at his scanner. "I am picking up numerous warp fields, multiple metallic readings."

"Captain, my board just lit up. Multiple, overlapping transmissions, some I recognize. Orion, Kzinti, Skorr, Tkarians, to name a few," Uhura added.

If the Kzinti and Orion pirates weren't bad enough, the Tkarians Marauders took the cake. A vicious people. Tkaria, one hundred years ago, had its central government slip into anarchy. It was now ruled by warlords whose ships preyed on all. Kirks Sacagawea and Robert's Sargon had both drawn patrol duty near Tkarians' space back in 2262.

And the results were not positive. Kirk recalled that both he and Robert had to turn tail and run from the swarms of raiders that had attacked them. Luckily for them, Matt Decker's Constellation had been nearby along with the Santa Domingo, a Canada class cruiser. Both ships had chased the raiders off. It had been a sobering dose of reality for him and Bob. Starfleet had seven Class 1 ships captured by the Tkarians over the hundred years of conflict. Despite the advances made, Starfleet still could put an end to the Tkarians raiding. Kirk thought.

"The advantages of not having to trade at their stations, Mister Spock," Scotty added.

"Indeed, Mister Scott. Direct trade and no neutral zone will benefit the Federation and the Imperium immensely," Spock agreed.

The combined fleet swung deeper into the home system.

"Captain Kirk, I am receiving a signal from the Cortez," Uhura said.

The Cortez, Kirk thought, was a Saladin class destroyer, the replacement for two other ships named Cortez. One of her predecessors had been the unpopular Larson class. The Larson class had the highest loss rate in the fleet, so some of them had been replaced by the more durable Saladin-Hermes, Constitution design ships.

"Spock."

"Have her on my sensors, Captain. It is the Cortez."

"Captain, the Cortez is signaling us. She is requesting visual."

"Patch her CO through, Uhura."

"Aye, Sir," Uhura said as she switched over. Kirk almost sunk into his seat when he saw her commanding officer shimmer into view.

"Hello, Jimmy boyo." A slightly older Sean Finnegan appeared. He was wearing commander stripes and the classic Cortez circle with points insignia of the ship that graced her two ill-fated predecessors on his shirt. Kirk was also surprised to see that he had grown a goatee.

"Remember me, Jimmy boyo," Finnegan said sarcastically.

"Yes, Sean. So, what brings you here?" Why, Finnegan, he thought. They could have sent any other captain but Finnegan. It must have been the luck of the draw.

"Got stuck with the FNS, Jimmy, we are here to record you and Bobby in all yer glory. I have a reporter on board, Jennifer Jennings. She wants to give an interview to both you and Bob before you participate in the Parida."

"Tell her to contact Mister Spock over here to arrange the details."

"Understood, Jimmy, Cortez out." Finnegan's image faded. Kirk blew a sigh of relief. "Spock, the bridge is yours. I leave the details of our interview in yours and Shran's hands."

Spock nodded.

"Captain's log. Captain James T. Kirk recording. Supplemental entry. An interview? And Finnegan. What did I do to deserve this?"

"Captain's log. Captain Robert N. Hawke recording. Additional entry. FNS and Finnegan, what else could go wrong? Why did it have to be Finnegan?"

SPOCK'S QUARTERS:

Spock strummed on his Vulcan lyre as Shran played her Andorian flute. Her image was visible on his desk screen. They played together for a little bit longer before Shran stopped. Spock figured it was Andorian impatience that was nagging Shran.

"Are you concerned about your captain, Shran?"

Shran nodded. "This interview is such trivial nonsense."

"Indeed, it is, Shran. Another ill logical distraction, but we need a place to hold it."

"I would lean toward Enterprise. She is the flagship."

Spock considered Shran's proposal. "It is acceptable. But I think that we should hold the interview on your ship since the briefing room is so much more exhilarating than Enterprise's."

"You must have logical reasons, Spock, for this change of venue."

"Our captain's history with your ship, plus, I lean toward your ship on the account of her standing in our fleet. Next to this ship, she is the most famous. And it would be good not to have the press not hounding this ship and her crew," Spock said recalling the missions he served under Pike when the press had bothered them at the end of her missions.

"So, we get a little spotlight, Spock."

"Yes, Shran, Constitution and her sisters rarely get to shine in the face of Enterprise's fame."

"It is as you Vulcans say logical. I will contact my captain and after the interview, it would be appropriate to have a reception in the officer's lounge on this ship," Shran suggested.

"It is most agreeable, Shran. We will contact you soon."

"Understood. Shran out." Shran's image faded. Spock picked up his harp and started to strum a melody. He paused for a moment and then contacted the bridge. "Spock to bridge."

"Bridge here, Lieutenant Palmer."

"Lieutenant Palmer, contact the Cortez. I want to speak directly to Miss Jennings."

"Yes, Sir."

Starship Constitution orbiting Harrata Four flanked by Harrata Star force ships:

Kirk, Spock, and McCoy materialized in one of Constitution's transporter rooms. Kirk could see Robert and all his senior officers present. Standing next to Andrews and Dorvil was Commander Finnegan and a medium-sized redhead wearing a blouse and a skirt. She had a radiant smile and perm haircut. Opposite her stood her cameraman.

Robert stepped up. "Jim, this is Jennifer Jennings of FNS."

"A pleasure to meet you," Jennifer said. "And this is Spock and McCoy."

McCoy was almost speechless, and Spock fidgeted. "Who wouldn't know the famed crew of the Enterprise?" Jennifer added smiling.

Kirk could hear Robert sighing.

"No pun intended, Captain Hawke. I know that Constitution is right up there with Kirk's ship, in fame," Jennings responded. "Your ship too is famous, just overshadowed by Enterprise."

Hawke smiled graciously. "If you can't beat them, join them."

Jennifer nudged Robert to the surprise of his and Kirk's officers. Robert was taken aback, regaining his composure. "If you'd all follow me." The group left the transporter room.

CONSTITUTION'S MAIN BRIEFING ROOM:

When they finally arrived at the main briefing room, Kirk could see two security guards posted at the entrance and Lieutenant Commander Martinez was present. Evidently, Robert was taking no chances even on his own ship.

Kirk, Hawke, and Jennings and her cameraman entered the briefing room. Shran went up to the intercom. "Bridge, secure the main briefing room. No incoming communications except in an emergency."

"Understood," came the voice of Lieutenant Barbara Desalle.

Shran turned to Spock. "Now we wait."

Hawke and Kirk showed Jennings the long line of ships named Constitution framed on the walls of the room. Also, in the background next to the Federation flag, the Starfleet flag and the Constitution's insignia flag were a duplicate copy of the Declaration of Independence and the United States Constitution and the portraits of presidents James Madison and Thomas Jefferson.

"Kirk sits here," Jennings said. "Hawke here." Jennings pointed to the two seats opposite her. Both captains sat down. Jennifer and her cameraman double-checked the equipment. Her voice and visual recorder were present. The portable holoprojector was at spec. Constitution's chief communications officer Mariko Shimada had done a professional job of tying the equipment into the Harrata subspace array. And into the Harrata subspace relay system relaying into the Federation Subspace array system past the border. With only slight delays, she would be present at all Federation member planets' colonies and all Starfleet faculties within hours of this interview. Anyone further out would receive a time-delayed already-recorded interview.

"Are you both ready?" Kirk and Hawke nodded. She checked her chronometer, 1759.

"In three, two, one," she said. "Reporting live from the briefing room aboard the Constitution, deep in the Harrata Imperium, at the home world of Harrata Four. This is Jennifer Jennings. With me is Captain

James Tiberius Kirk of the Enterprise and Captain Robert Nelson Hawke, commanding officer of the Constitution, Starfleet's two choices to face the infamous challenge, win or lose. It is the luck of the draw," Jennings said. "What do you both have to say about that?"

Kirk immediately spoke up, "Miss Jennings, both Captain Hawke and I don't believe in luck when you are cut off from Earth for months at a time in deep space, relying on your own resources. It all boils down to the ship's CO. Either you make the right decision or the wrong one."

"What's your opinion, Captain Hawke?"

"Luck has nothing to do with it, Miss Jennings. My dad, Admiral Joseph Hawke once said. A captain stands alone and only he or she is accountable for the right or wrong choice they make."

"My dad fleet Captain George Kirk told me something similar. There are too many unknowns when you are involved in deep space exploration that Enterprise and Constitution are presently involved in."

"Captain Hawke," she asked.

"We are the tip of the sword in deep space exploration followed by the Coronado's, Miranda's, and other such classes," Hawke added.

"Risk is why we are out here," Kirk said looking at Hawke. Hawke nodded in agreement.

"We in Starfleet have a saying, never a dull day in the fleet," Hawke added. "Win or lose, I wouldn't trade my job as captain for any other."

Jennings looked at Kirk. "And you?"

"I agree wholeheartedly with Robert here, Miss Jennings. Since I was a kid, I dreamed of being a starship captain."

"And what about you, Captain Hawke?"

"Same, but it is also family history and legacy."

"Robert's family is one of the first-generation families, miss Jennings, along with the biggest one the Roddenberry. My family didn't join up with Starfleet until after the Romulan war. Samuel Kirk was first to join. Before that, my cousin Benjamin Kirk, we were a MACO family."

"Ground pounders, third-generation Starfleet," Hawke added.

"Your family treats this ship like it is an heirloom," Jennings pointed out.

"We are not the only family whose descendants have commanded ship with this name. We have the Taggerts. Presently, David Taggert has been succeeded as Captain of the Repulse by his daughter Laura five years earlier. And then we have the Wangs who command the freighters called Nissan Marus and the Winstanley's who command any ship named Ticonderoga."

"Miss Jennings, way back when the Enterprise was going to be built, Commodore Henry Archer Jr. felt that it was time to cut the strings to the new Enterprise and Robert April was given the job."

"My dad as well as April had a say in the specifications of the Constitution class during the design phase," Hawke added. "To get Constitution into service faster, he and Admiral Jefferies installed old pre-duotronic technology."

"That is why this ship is slightly different than Kirk's Enterprise."

"Yes."

"Enterprise set the base standard for all newer ships. Constitution is the prototype,"

Kirk said. Through numerous upgrades, Constitution has caught up with Enterprise, Miss Jennings."

"No ships are alike, Miss Jennings. Even among Enterprise and Constitution's later sister ships, they all have minor differences. We are the only Constitution class ship in the fleet to have an experimental captain's ready room, the only one," Hawke mentioned.

Kirk could remember reporting to Augenthaler in the ready room on deck two during his time on this ship. Enterprise didn't have it. Just a bigger officer's lounge that became fleet standard.

She changed tack on them. "Captains Kirk and Hawke, both of you are considered mavericks and risk-takers by the brass. What are your views on this matter?"

"We are not by the book, Miss Jennings," Kirk answered.

"We like thinking outside the box," Hawke added.

"Both you and Captain Hawke were a year apart at Starfleet Academy and both of you stood out in your classes with the amount of first you both accomplished. Kirk becoming one of the youngest instructors at the academy and became the only student ever to beat the Kobayashi Maru and the Bug spot," Jennings said as she turned to look at Robert. "And Captain Hawke here, who stalemated the Kobayashi Maru, won three Rigel cups with Delta squad and pulled off a successful but illegal Kolvoord Starburst maneuver."

"Our solutions were quite original. Wouldn't you agree, Bob?"

"Yes, they were. But you beat the Maru and the bug test. I barely made it halfway through the course, and I stalemated the Maru," Hawke admitted.

"But Bob, you commanded the academy flight team Delta Squad. You won three Rigel cups and pulled off a successful if illegal Kolvoord Starburst maneuver on Federation day," Kirk added.

"And the brass wanted to kick both of us from the academy," Hawke admitted.

"They reconsidered, Miss Jennings. And here we are today."

"Who were your sponsors, Kirk, Hawke?"

"Captain April, Admirals Mallory and La forge. Captain Morrow sponsored me for my first command," Kirk said.

"Admirals Jefferies and Noguchi. Captain Nogura and Captain Chandra sponsored me for my first command," Hawke added.

"Your dads had nothing to do with it," Jennings asked. "Even you, Captain Hawke, your father did command this very ship."

"And thanks to him and Starfleet Regulation 233, I received no preferential treatment," Hawke admitted. "My dad did the same with my younger siblings. No favoritism, you succeed on your own merits."

"I had the same treatment, Miss Jennings. Isn't better than having our way to our commands paved in hard work and not given to us. Robert nearly became captain of Enterprise and I was even considered for the command of this ship."

"Would you both trade places if it came to it?"

Kirk shook his head; Hawke had his arms folded and had an eyebrow risen at the suggestion.

"You have got to be kidding," Hawke said slightly brusque. "I'm glad it worked out this way. Enterprise is Jim's and Constitution's mine. Not in your life would I switch places. Jim could keep the flagship. I like my ship just the way she is."

"I agree, Robert, it worked out for the better."

"Do you believe that both of you will survive and beat the Tong and we will have another war?"

"I don't want to answer that question, because if we are wrong," Kirk said.

"Neither do I. Overconfidence can kill," Hawke said.

He didn't want to play his hand and give false hope. Robert was holding back, his own defense mechanisms were cutting in. Kirk thought.

"So, citizens of the Federation, there we have it, win lose or draw. In two weeks, we will know if we are at war or at peace. Jennifer Jennings signing off from the Constitution in Harrata territory." Jennifer waved to her cameraman who shut his feed off.

"Both of you could have been a bit more forthcoming."

"I'm sorry, Miss Jennings, but we can't. Starfleet security, some things are best left under the rug," Kirk said. Robert was already on the horn. Moments later, the staff of Enterprise and Constitution walked in.

"So, Jim how did it go?" McCoy asked, curious.

"As well as it should have gone, Bones."

"Figures."

Hawke walked over to Miss Jennings. "We have a reception in the officer's lounge if you would like to attend."

"Certainly, Captain Hawke." With Finnegan trailing, the group left for the officer's lounge.

CONSTITUTION'S OFFICERS LOUNGE, OPPOSITE THE CAPTAIN'S MESS AND THE READY ROOM:

Kirk, Spock, and McCoy entered the lounge following Robert's people, Miss Jennings, and Commander Finnegan. The lounge was just as he remembered. Simply furnished, but it was cleaned up with new furniture. And it was smaller than Enterprise's.

"This is much roomier than the one we have on Cortez," Finnegan admitted. "Unlike Jimmy and Bobby, I spent my entire career on destroyers and scouts, never cared for the big boys. If you get my meaning, Miss Jennings."

Yeoman Smith came in along with two attendants. They laid out plates and silverware for everyone present and some glasses. Moments later, Smith came back holding a pitcher of yellow liquid. "Jim, this is Pogash," Hawke said as he swirled the liquid. It started to change into different colors.

"Swirl yours to whatever color you want," Hawke advised.

Kirk swirled the liquid which changed to green. Tasting it, he was nodding in approval. Jennifer was nodding too as she drank her purple liquid. "Isn't this Harrata, Captain?"

Hawke nodded. "It is this drink they use at all religious ceremonies. It is not as common as Traga. But it's rare."

The attendants were already laying out the Andorian rice swirls, Tellerite moback meat sandwiches, and Vulcan plommek soup. T'Pau had already joined them and was silently eating her plommek soup. Spock had joined her, and he too was eating silently.

"I've had Traga, Rattay beer, and Vasgi wine," Jennings admitted. "This is in a league apart."

"On the Enterprise, we have Tranya, Miss Jennings," Kirk said.

"Call me, Jennifer, Captains Kirk and Hawke. The interview is over," Jennings said. "Tranya, I heard you contacted the First Federation, Captain Kirk."

"That is correct. When we complete the Challenge, we could send you a bottle of Tranya. If you wish," Kirk offered.

"I accept, Jim, and not to sell Robert short, I would also accept a bottle of Pogash."

"No problem, Jennifer."

"Tell me, Jim, how you and Robert see each other in historical context," Jennifer asked.

Kirk paused for a moment. "If this was the Royal Army of Queen Victoria, I would probably be Garnet Wolseley, our only major General."

"Not so fast, Jim, I would wind up being Fredrick Roberts, our other Major General."

"Interesting point yet accurate, considering the historical context," Spock said.

"Most illuminating," T'Pau added.

"Where it rains, it pours," McCoy added.

Russell huffed, "Bones, I don't see any rain."

"Don't get nippy with me, Doc. You New Englanders don't have any fun," McCoy responded in his Georgia drawl.

The civil war had started. Hawke thought.

"We have plenty of fun, Bones. At least, we don't swelter like you good old Southern boys do," Russell responded in his New England drawl.

"Doc, stow it," Shran cut in. "And you too, Bones," Shran said as she looked at both doctors.

McCoy and Russell went mute when they met Shran's gaze.

Shran turned to Kirk. "Mission Accomplished."

Kirk could only smile. Hawke was also smiling.

"Thank you, Thay," Kirk said

Shran nodded. "Just doing my job, Captain."

"You are most effective, Thaylassa. Not many people can shut Doctor McCoy up," Spock said.

"When you must deal with irascible doctor David Russell here, you learn ways to minimize negative fallout," Shran said.

Bones and Doc got up. They both had pained expressions on their faces.

"Where are both of you going?" Hawke asked curiously.

"Doc wants to see his old ship, our Enterprise," McCoy said. He needed an excuse, so he and Doc could continue their feud with less interference.

"No problem, Doc," Hawke added.

"Go right ahead, Bones," Kirk approved.

McCoy and Russell left the officer's lounge. As the door closed, Kirk could hear both of them continuing their feud.

Jennifer looked at the remaining group. "Now that was something."

"Two different ships, two different commanders, Jennifer. I do things my way on Enterprise and Robert does his way on Constitution," Kirk explained.

"Legends all," Jennifer admitted. "The two most famous ships in the fleet, the two youngest starship captains, the best staffs."

"And the biggest responsibilities," Finnegan said. "Jennifer, while Jimmy and Bobby are getting all the fame, Cortez is slugging it out, with little fuss. Enterprise and Constitution along with their lesser-known sisters get all the press. My kind as Jimmy and Bobby might recall in their younger days also slugged it out on ships like Cortez. The destroyer, scout gang, doesn't believe in all the pomp and circumstance that floats around the big boys."

Jennings looked at Kirk and Hawke. "You both did a little time in the little boys."

Kirk nodded. "Served on at least two destroyers and a scout in my career."

Hawke added, "My first command was a destroyer like Finnegan's. And in my career, I served on one destroyer, a scout. And I even worked a transport tug and did some outpost duty earlier in my career." Hawke admitted trying to get the better of Kirk.

"It is always good to have variety in one's career," Shran admitted. "Until I became the first officer on this ship, I never served on a Heavy cruiser."

"Heavy and Medium cruiser duty is the most strenuous in the fleet," Finnegan admitted.

"Destroyer and Scout duty less so. My choice was the above. I didn't want a heavy. Not everyone in Starfleet wants to serve on Kirk's or Hawke's commands. Not everyone is cut out for that sort of work."

Kirk could just look at Finnegan. His tormentor had grown up.

Finnegan got up and yawned. "I don't know about you but I'm ready to pack it in."

Jennifer Jennings got up. "I agree. Captain Hawke, it was a pleasure."

Hawke kissed Jennifer on her hand. "I am glad you enjoyed it."

Kirk came over and did the same.

"E tu, Kirk," Jennifer said surprised.

"If you can't beat them, join them," Kirk said smiling.

Jennings and Finnegan left. Spock looked to Kirk. "Captain."

"I'll meet you in the transporter room, Spock."

Spock nodded and left with T'Pau and Shran. Robert was just about ready to leave when Kirk stopped him. "Bob, we need to talk."

Kirk sat down. Robert sat opposite. They finally had time for a one on one.

"Robert, you realize that after this upcoming Parida, everything boils down to you and me. Our ships, our crews, billions of the Federation's lives are resting on our shoulders."

"If that hasn't been weighing on my mind since we were given our orders, Jim, you are senior to me. You oversee the success of this mission."

"I also want your advice, Robert. At this point, if you have any brilliant ideas, don't hold back. I am still relying on my own staff, as you rely on yours. But if we get to the second and especially the final round, those Hogar class, type 8s, really worry me. And I don't care how crazy they are."

"Same, Jim, since we entered the Imperium, all of my weapons' crews have been drilling for type 8 combat. We also have a contingency suicide plan if the worst happens. Shran has seen to that."

"We have the same, Bob. If I lose my life, Spock will destroy the Enterprise."

"I don't want to wind up in that hole in the ground, despite what the priestess said."

"Neither do I."

"I'll be watching your back, Jim," Hawke said.

"And I will watch yours, Bob. I will see you one day from now."

Hawke nodded, shook Kirk's hand, and departed the lounge. Kirk glanced at his chronometer and left the room.

CHAPTER NINETEEN

"Captain's log. Star date 2912.8. Captain James T. Kirk recording. Today is the day, the Parida, the final saga of the prelude to the Tong."

"Captain's log. Star date 2912.8. Captain Robert N. Hawke recording. Looks like Jim and I are going be displayed like trophies to the Harrata race and the galaxy at large."

Kirk materialized on a podium in the center of the city of Tomar. Heat beat at his uniform. Luckily, he was wearing his green command shirt with the rank on his shoulders. The humidity was terrible, reminded him of Brazil. Moments later, Robert materialized next to him. He was also wearing his green command shirt but with the rank on his sleeves.

"Hot as Vulcan," Robert said.

"More like Brazil, Bob."

A tall, elegant brown-skinned male Harrata of the political caste walked toward them. He had a red beard and a Mohawk haircut.

Carrying a staff, he was dressed in the more traditional Harrata outer garments.

"I am Prator Fa Cosha, Viceroy of the Imperium. You must be Ober C's Kirk and Hawke."

"We are."

"Follow me."

They followed the Viceroy around the back of the building. More buildings appeared. Laid out before them was the Harrata parade. In front was a band followed by a troop from the Order Corps and the Star force champions. Behind them were another band and Kang and Khod. Awaiting them at the end was another band and a brace off Star force security and the High Order Corp made up the rear.

A male and female Harrata, also brown-skinned, approached Kirk and Hawke. The man had wavy black hair and the woman wore her black hair long.

"Harr Chancellor, Herr Vice Chancellor, may I present Ober C's Kirk and Hawke representing the Federansky."

"A pleasure," Kirk said as he and Hawke shook their hands.

"You honor the Imperium by coming. It takes real courage to face the Tong Ober C. Kirk," Banari said.

"The only thing you need to do is follow the troops and the band. Once you have finished, you can beam back to your ships and proceed to the Omarti Tong system," Negali added.

Kirk and Hawke walked to their places between the Order Corp and the security.

"Just follow the parade," Negali reminded them.

Kirk and Hawke waited for the parade to start.

ORION MERCHANT SHIP OMARZ ALLAH ON THE PERIPHERY OF THE CHALLENGE FLEET. STAR DATE 2912.9:

"This is as close as I could get us," Omark Ek said as he turned his big green bulk backward to face the three humans present. "Any closer and the Kocaka class type 4 gunboats watching the fleet would immediately intercept."

"I have the feed. Hawke and Kirk should be present at the parade."

On one of the three screens present in Omark Ek freighter, one showed the Harrata politicians making speeches. The other one showed the Challenge fleet and the third showed the gunboats patrolling at the periphery of that fleet.

"Magnify Enterprise and Constitution and split the screen, Omark."

Omark nodded. The human's employers had better pay him well for the trouble. The ship had been fitted with a camouflage screen projecting the three humans as Orions since the Federation could not directly trade with the Imperium.

"How I hate those two ships," the female human muttered, looking at the Enterprise and Constitution.

"Our people should be commanding those two ships. Not Kirk and Hawke," one of the two males spoke up.

"Rittenhouse says that Waterston isn't ready, and we have no window of opportunity," the other male said.

"In time, we will have our revenge on the Hawke family. And Kirk will pay too. Section 31 never forgets."

Omarz Allah continued past the Challenge fleet.

ENTERPRISE:

Spock was sitting in Kirk's command chair and watched as the politicians finally finished their speeches. McCoy was standing next to him and so was Rand.

The parade had started. Spock was just fascinated with the archaic stone designs of most of the city.

"Nothing to say, Doctor." Spock turned to McCoy.

"No, Spock, I just don't like it that Jim and Robert are being paraded like so many cattle."

"It is their tradition, Bones."

"Humbug with tradition, Spock."

"Aye, Mister Spock, Doctor McCoy is right. Blast those beastie Harrata," Scotty chimed in.

"Gentlemen, there is nothing we can do. The logical thing to do is wait."

McCoy could only agree.

CONSTITUTION:

Thaylassa Shran watched as the bridge crew of the Constitution waited as the parade started.

She hated to see her captain and Kirk being paraded in front of the entire population of the city of Tomar as trophies. The bridge elevator doors swooshed open as Doc Russell entered.

"Did the parade start?" Russell grumbled.

"Yes, Doc," Shran answered. She scanned the bridge and noticed that Bateson was looking gloomy and Desalle was equally depressed.

"Mister Bateson, Mister Desalle, anything wrong?"

Morgan Bateson straightened up. "No, Commander."

Barbara Desalle said, "No, Sir, but this is so exploitive, Commander," Desalle said revealing her true feelings.

"It is but we have no choice, once we get past here, it becomes harder," Shran said as she swung the command chair around the bridge. "And I don't want this bridge's crew looking like they came out of a funeral home. Captain Hawke will not let us down."

Voices of agreement came from everyone present.

"You hit it right on the nose, Shran," Russell agreed.

Shran nodded in agreement at Russell's statement.

"Indeed, I have," Shran said smiling.

THE LEGATIONS:

Jennifer Jennings and her cameraman Victor had finally made it to the main legation building. They had gone to the other two buildings to conduct interviews and find out other people's opinions concerning the Challenge.

It had been frustrating. In the third building, the Kropasalins had given a short interview. The other minor races except for the offensive, rude Tkarians had given them a cold shoulder with the Tkarians venting their rage about the evils of the Federation.

In the second building with the more powerful races, she had met with the same reluctance. Only the visiting Dolhman of Elas and the Troyian Ambassador Petri had given interviews. Considering the ongoing conflict between both races they had given their interviews with considerable distance involved.

The Dohlman wanted to see the warrior prowess of the two Federation captains. She had thought that Kirk and Hawke were fine specimens of manhood. The Troyian ambassador had gone on an opposite tack to the Dohlman. He was betting that the Dohlman was wrong, and the Federation would not have a war with the Imperium. Both races had been given rides on the Harrata Subjective force, the Harrata merchant fleet to get to Harrata Four, no other races had come forward in that building.

They had finally arrived at the main legation building where the major players were. Jennings was finding it equally frustrating. The Romulans had avoided her. Orions, Kzinti, Lyrans, Hydrans, Mirak, and an unknown lizard race had gone the other way on her approach. The Tholian and the Shelliack ambassadors had been rude. The four Xindi ambassadors wished them good luck. A race called the Ferengi had hounded her all over the balcony on buying some Ferengi trinkets. The Pakleds ambassador following the Ferengi ambassador kept reaching for her voice recorder and Victor's camera.

And the Klingon ambassador was too full of himself being interviewed by his opposite in the Imperial Information Network and didn't want to be bothered. Finally, she had caught up with Ambassador Andrea Burroughs and her aide Helen. "Ambassador Talbot."

"Yes, Miss Jennings." Burroughs and Andrews stopped. They were next to the balcony overlooking the parade route. Jennifer swung back to the harassing Ferengi and Pakleds ambassadors. "No, I don't want your trinkets! And stop trying to steal our stuff!" Jennings lashed out at them. The Ferengi Ambassador Quall looked hurt. The Pakleds Ambassador Bomzak looked even more mournful.

"Give me a moment. Quall, Bomzak." Andrew went over to them. "Here are five credits for that trinket. Quall and Bomzak, I have a surprise for you." He then pulled out an antiquated Earth Starfleet scanner and gave it to Bomzak.

"Five credits!" Quall complained.

"Nice," Bomzak said. "We like things." Bomzak was pulling the classic idiot act that his race was so good at. It suckered many races in.

"I don't like this, Andy," Quall growled.

Andrew turned back to Burroughs and Jennings. "I'll fix this." He looked at the Ferengi and the Pakleds.

"I'm in the mood to deal, are you?" Andrew said as he led the Ferengi and Pakled Ambassadors off to another part of the balcony. Jennifer blew a sigh of relief. The parade with the champions and the challengers was now approaching the Legation.

"You want my view. Isn't it right, Miss Jennings?" Andrea said.

"Yes, Ambassador Burroughs."

"Shoot."

"Victor."

"Yes, ma'am."

"This is Jennifer Jennings reporting from the Legation in the city of Tomar. With me is Federation Ambassador Andrea Burroughs. How many years have you served as Ambassador to the Imperium, Madam Ambassador?"

"Seven, Miss Jennings. Prior to that, I was Ambassador to Calabria."

"What chances do you think Captain Kirk and Captain Hawke have in surviving the Challenge?"

"Nil Miss Jennings we lost the last two times," Andrea said bluntly.

"What if Kirk and Hawke do survive?"

"Then we will not have a war. And it would truly be a miracle."

"There you have it. The view of a Federation Ambassador, this is Jennifer Jennings signing off from the city of Tomar."

Jennifer and Andrea looked over the balcony to see Hawke and Kirk passing by the legation with the Parida.

Kirk looked up as they walked past the Legation. They were now approaching the Temple way. The heat was still stifling. He could see Robert waving to the crowds and going with the moment. For all they knew, they were being broadcasted to all the worlds of the Federation, Klingon Empire, etc.

He hated this. Soon, the crowds disappeared as they entered the row of temples. Kirk couldn't believe the myriad designs that dominated both sides of the road. At the end was a circle rounding the temple of Gom. The many priestesses and priests lined the steps of the temples as they passed by. Kirk walked over to Robert who was still showing off by waving his hands.

"Bob, how can you act like this at this time?"

"Jim, are we back at the academy again? Stop acting like a stack of books with legs."

"Yeah, there goes raving Robert again."

"I will do what I want, Jim. By not being so serious, I could get through this torture."

Kirk smiled. "Remember Gary."

"Yeah, Gary had a way with nicknames," Hawke said as he almost started to laugh but kept his composure.

Kirk felt like laughing but restrained himself. Kirk wiped his brow as they circled around the magnificent Temple of Gom and entered a side road. The Parida was over.

CHAPTER TWENTY

STARSHIP ENTERPRISE FLANKED BY THREE HARRATA CRUISERS. ORBITING HARRATA FOUR:

"Captain's log. Captain James T. Kirk recording. Additional Entry. The Parida is over. We are now awaiting the Lotharian Attack wing."

"Captain's log. Captain Robert N. Hawke recording. Additional. Jim and I survived the Parida. The Lotharians are coming, the Lotharians are coming."

Jim Kirk paced the bridge of the Enterprise. They were waiting for the execution squadron to arrive. Execution as in if he failed. They had to join them and complete the trek to the Omarti Tong star system to begin the Challenge.

"Anything, Spock?"

"Negative, Captain. They could be cloaked."

"Captain," Sulu said

Kirk and Spock swung to face the viewing screen, just as Spock had predicted. Three Harrata ships suddenly decloaked. Two were midgets by comparison. They flanked the ugly monster that lay in the center.

"Spock."

"The ship in the center is a Varrah class battleship type three, four plasma batteries, six disruptor batteries, and four cutting lasers. The other two are Spedy class scout ships type six, one plasma battery, two disruptor emplacements," Spock said.

"Captain, the Lothar GaZ is hailing us," Uhura added.

"Put them through."

Kirk sat back in his command chair. The screen flicked and coalesced into a dark, dank bridge. Compared to the bridges of the Challenge ships, this bridge was dark and dreadful.

A tall, thin, gangling Harrata Admiral appeared. He had a long full beard and a gaudy-designed Harrata Gold Star force uniform with excessive trinkets attached.

"I am Vorrad (Admiral) Palmery Na oo Tagazy of the Tagazy attack wing of the Lotharian fleet. I welcome the champions and challengers to the Tong. Any deviation or cowardice will be rewarded with the instant destruction of said vessel. The two scouts present are here to inform the challengers' fleets of your future status. You will now follow us."

The screen rematerialized showing the three Harrata ships.

Before Kirk could say anything, the Enterprise towed by the Harrata ships jumped to warp.

The combined fleet left the Harratay Star system.

PART THREE

THE TONG OR
THE CHALLENGE

"To the dead, Captain Kirk," T'Pau to Kirk. Amok Time. Star date 3372.7.

CHAPTER TWENTY-ONE

ROMULAN SENATE. ROMULUS (RIHANNSU). KI BARATAN. STAR DATE 2913.1. JANUARY 23, 2267:

Newly promoted Commander Liviana Charvanek along with newly promoted sub commander Che'sik Nerul d'Tal followed Commander Augustus Pardeck to the entrance of the Senate. Inside, she could hear arguments and bitter acrimony being spilled back and forth between the members of the senate.

"This is a nest of Vaprine," Pardeck warned the two officers. Despite Charvanek Royal upbringing, the senate would be a cesspool of corruption at the time. Vaprine was used as a curse word in Rihannsu.

The Praetors Praetorian guards opened the door to the senate.

Two senators were bickering back and forth. The Praetor Vrax and his successor Praetor Gaius had two proconsuls sitting to the right of them. The Honor blade stood beside them.

The emperor's chair was empty.

Empress Neranah and Legate Torval had passed away the year before. Their successors had yet to be appointed by the senate.

"We lost the Bloodied Talon in the Taurus Reach, the Gal Gathong destroyed by the Starfleet at the Battle of Icarus by the Enterprise. The Van Hashem wiped out after our most glorious penetration of Federation space at the Hydra nebula by the Constitution and the Val Redeck destroyed by the Klingon ship D'k' Tahg at Commadus. Four of our glorious birds of prey were wiped out of existence. Tell me, Senator Banock, how are we so fortunate that two of the guilty ships Enterprise and Constitution are in the Harrata Imperium?" Senator Toloth said.

Toloth was one of the older senators in the senate. Toloth served as Senator for the wandering ship clans' faction and had served in the Earth-Romulan war a century earlier.

"My esteemed Senator Toloth, Enterprise and Constitution now face the Challenge in the Imperium. Ambassador Noral has notified me that they are there. The humans have never won the Challenge. If we are to be so fortunate, they will lose again. And with the relations deteriorating between the Federation and the Klingon Empire, a Federation-Harrata war would benefit the Romulan Empire. The Harrata do not conquer. They are fanatics. They will bleed the Federation dry-sapping its strength. If the Klingons decide to attack the Federation, then we should join them and expand our empire," Banock responded.

Banock was of a noble house and had never served in the military. He was also young by senatorial standards. "Simply Toloth the Harrata will solve our problem."

Praetor Vrax suddenly stood up. Banock and Toloth ended their debate as the Praetor of the Romulan Empire took the floor. "Commander

Pardeck, Commander Charvanek, and Sub Commander Tal, welcome," Vrax said as he walked up to the three officers who bowed.

"Aren't these discussions most illuminating?" Vrax said as he stood with the three officers.

Turning to Chavernack. "And how are Ael and Miral?"

"They are presently engaged in the Harrkonen campaign," Livianana said.

Vrax stroked his angular chin. "Ah, yes, the Harrkonen, the Harrata orphans who refused to follow the teachings of Gom and left the Imperium to form their own government following the teachings of Pong instead."

"The Harrkonen have never been conquered by us. They remain a thorn in our side," Pardeck mentioned.

"Two of our greatest captains Keras and Valeria fought them only to be defeated by the Federation," Vrax said. He looked at Charvanek. "You did serve under them, did you?"

Chavernack bowed. "It was an honor to serve under Keras and Valeria, my Praetor."

"Has the Honor Blade been refitted?" Vrax asked.

"Yes, Praetor. The new improved cloaking device and the updated plasma torpedoes have been installed."

Vrax looked around the senate and said, "Honored Romulans of the Senate, Commander Charvanek has been chosen by the highest echelons of the government to spy on the Klingon dogs and the Federation in the area calls the corridor, deep within the outmarches where no Romulan has ever gone. We need to assess the strength of the Federation, Klingon, and Harrata forces. If the Federation is drawn into a war of attrition with the Harrata, we will attack the Federation. We will not wait for the Klingon dogs to move. But take the initiative. Commander Chavernack and the valiant crew of the Honor Blade will lead the way!"

The senate resounded with clapping and cheering. The stage was set.

In the rear of the senate, three senators of the old Preatorate class joined in. Soon, they would wipe away the sham of a sole Praetor and the lackey emperor/ empress injustice that contaminated the greatness of the Romulan Empire. Soon, the Preatorate of Twelve run by three will return.

KLINGON COUNCIL, KRONOS (QUONOS). FIRST CITY OF THE EMPIRE. STAR DATE 2913.3.

"Really?" Commander Chang said as he turned to face Commander Kumara. "We are Klingons, not Ferengi!"

Kumara could only smile. Chang was a typical blood-thirsty PataQ. His benefactor was none other than Lornak the insane.

"Commander Chang, we are all followers of Kahless. Attacking the Federation while our champions Kang and Khod face the Tong is disgraceful," Kumara said as he walked around the council floor. Half of the members were HemQuch and the rest were Quch'ha. Kumara looked at Chancellor Sturka who was flanked by Lornak, Kesh, and Korval.

"As you said before, Chang, we are Klingons, not Ferengi, and to attack the Federation when our champions are facing the Tong is a disgrace," Kumara repeated the line again, looking directly at Chang.

Councilor Gorkon watched as the charade played itself out.

He had faced the Federation before, dealing with the starships Constitution and Dauntless earlier in his career. He had also served in the diplomatic service on rare occasions. Not many warriors were capable of both in the Klingon society. That was why he had risen so fast to become a Councilor in the High Council.

Chang was underestimating the resilience of the Federation and the Starfleet. The Empire had fought to a draw at Donatu. Never had a chance with the Axanar rebellion thanks to Garth and then fought to another defeat during the Border war known to the Federation as the Four Years' War and the 2257 extension after a very brief period of peace caused by the fools of the Shenzou. And the infamous battle of Knek Star System known to the Federation as Savo nearly drew the Empire into a war which they were not prepared for.

War would come, but only when the empire was ready, not before. A war with the Federation was a big possibility, sooner rather than later. Gorkon thought.

Chancellor Sturka suddenly rose from his chair and spoke.

"Commanders Chang and Kumara the council is enlightened by your two different views on what we should do with the Federation. We will wait, we will be patient, and there is glory for all warriors of the Empire," Kahless once said. "Only a fool rushes into war without a plan, without honor. We are not Romulans; we are not Ferengi nor are we deceitful Cardassians. We are Klingons!" Sturka stepped down followed by Logash, Kesh, and Korval.

Sturka continued, "Even now, Admiral Kerra and General Koord watch our borders for the glorious attack of the Harrata Battle Groups which is sure to come. The Harratay and the Harrkonash have always been honorable foes. Go back to your ships and join Korrd and Kerra and bathe yourselves in glory," Sturka said as he and the entire council walked out. Chang looked at Kumara who said nothing and walked off.

Kumara realizing that he was now in the chambers walked off the council floor singing an old Klingon war song.

CHAPTER TWENTY-TWO

TONG OMARTI FOUR. THE CHALLENGE WORLD.
January 24 2267.

"Captain's log. Star date 2914.2. Captain James T. Kirk recording. "Per Harrata tradition, I am beaming down to the planet with my closest confidants. It finally begins."

"Captain's log. Star date 2914.2. Captain Robert N. Hawke recording. "With my four closest confidants, we are beaming down. The time for games is over."

Kirk flanked by Spock, McCoy, and Robert's officers sat at a half-circle table in a majestic stone arena. Sun shone through the arches providing natural light. To the right of him were the Klingons and to the left were the four half-circle tables containing the Harrata champions.

Behind them, Kirk noticed some High Order Corp soldiers of Lothar's Legion had taken position behind each of the tables. They were carrying lethal-looking scimitar-type swords. Kirk could see that the ring was divided into four separate mini arenas. A heavy-set Harrata male sporting a red Mohawk and what looked to be

299

an archaic mutton style mustache and wearing a multicolored robe walked up to the center of the arena.

"I am ringmaster Pokash ji Hittay. Welcome to the Challenge, the ultimate test of survival. I honor the Federansky and the Klingonasse who have come with honor to face this Challenge. This is only the first part, five rounds of hand-to-hand combat and five rounds of weapons combat. All to the dead, the victor survives and with their vessel passes onto the next level. The loser and their ship, well, if you would all look behind you," Hittay said as he pointed to Lothar's Legion. "Are here to stop any cowards and will slaughter the loser whether they have fought honorably or not. Then the Lothar GaZ will massacre the losers' crew. It doesn't concern us if the loser is Harrata, Federansky, or Klingonasse. The results will be the same."

Hittay clapped his hands. A gong sounded. Fourteen Harrata priests and priestesses filed into the area blessing the combat areas.

"Not again, Jim," McCoy muttered in resignation.

"Yes, Bones, again," Kirk said resignedly. He could see Bob Hawke sighing impatiently.

"Bob."

"Yes, Jim." Hawke looked at Kirk.

"Relax."

"I am relaxing."

STARFLEET COMMAND HEADQUARTERS. EARTH. STAR DATE 2914.3:

Admiral Gene Roddenberry, Chief of Public Relations and Media affairs, hurried through the corridors. He had some important matters to discuss with Buchinsky and Solow and that couldn't wait. Arriving at the flag officers' dining room on the twenty-sixth floor, he walked in. Buchinsky, Solow, and Hancock were sitting down having a meal.

"Well, Gene, are you going to join us?" Dawn Hancock said.

"Yes, Dawn," Gene said as he sat down next to Hancock, opposite Solow and Buchinsky.

Gene quickly ordered his meal and got down to business.

"If you haven't already heard, the Challenge has started," Roddenberry said.

"Then we've just entered the first phase. The quasi-war will start, and our fleets will be engaged with the Star force," Dawn added as she ate her food.

"Gene, you didn't come by here just to announce the opening of another conflict. You have another agenda in mind," Herbert Solow said.

"Correct," Roddenberry said as he put down his cup of coffee. "It concerns the Enterprise and the Constitution."

"Let's hope that both ships survive," Dawn added.

"Knowing Kirk and Hawke, they will, Dawn," Buchinsky said.

"Marcus, Herb, Dawn. I'm talking about the public record. Starfleet needs to put its best face forward in the eye of the public. Both ships have legendary records and legendary crews. But one ship seems to seamlessly have little negative exposure, while the other one despite her best intentions continually winds up leaving us with controversy," Roddenberry explained.

Buchinsky could only agree. He knew which of the two ships Roddenberry was talking about.

"Every time there is a command change on Constitution, we have a bloody donnybrook over who is going to command her. On top of that, Garth, even though he commanded Baton Rouge, Xenophon, Aries, and Heisenberg. Used Constitution as his flagship only, he never was her permanent assigned CO like Joe Hawke, Fredrick Augenthaler, and Robert Wesley. Garth is now in the Elba nuthouse. And then we have Page, who again after years of shore duty pulled strings to get the Victorious, a poltroon and lightweight that nearly destroyed the Constitution under his command. The ship has a record of fantastic discoveries just like Enterprise. And we know that her predecessors were Flagship of the Federation Starfleet between NX01 and 1701," Roddenberry pointed out.

"And now to the Enterprise who, despite a few minor abrasions, has a flawless record. She has discovered more than Constitution and the rest of her sisters. None of her captains are in the nuthouse. We need to advance Enterprise over Constitution; Kirk is already ahead of Hawke in discoveries. Kirk's mission should be our number one priority," Roddenberry said.

Hancock looked at Roddenberry concerned. "But Gene Kirk didn't make it through the barrier. Hawke did—"

Roddenberry cut her off, "I know, Dawn, but we all know what they discovered which for the sake of Federation security has to be kept under wraps."

"Gene, you do realize that one day long after we are gone what Constitution discovered may come out," Solow pointed out.

Roddenberry nodded. "Bobby Hawke is a fine commander, just like his dad. But I think Jim Kirk is better."

"Why?" Hancock asked.

"Kirk cheated on the Kobayashi Maru and beat it. Hawke stalemated it."

"They are both different Co's, Gene."

"They are both risk-takers, Dawn. And despite losing the Lydia Sutherland at Ghihoge, we all know that Kirk should have been cashiered, but he was the hero and Bobby Hawke wasn't."

"I tend to differ, Gene," Buchinsky said. "Hawke arrived three days later, rescued the survivors, salvaged the Lydia Sutherland, and patched up the entire mess."

"But he wasn't a hero," Roddenberry said.

"Gene, he should have been. Instead, Starfleet gives his command to John Harriman and sends him to main missions," Dawn argued passionately.

Roddenberry put his hand on Hancock's shoulder. "Dawn, this is how I will work this out. Enterprise, Constitution, Valiant, Asimov, and Yamato were all issued five-year exploration orders at nearly the same time. Valiant had changed commanders and has been lost in the line of duty. Charlie Archers Asimov is doing a Jonathan Archer revival tour; Yamato under Drake has done nothing at all except give us more heartache than Constitution, leaving Constitution and Enterprise to grab all headlines," Roddenberry pointed out. "Jim Kirk will be our poster boy for Starfleet. Hawke, he will fill in as the number two guy, and he will go and inspire our troops in the field. That is if both captains survive their five-year missions."

"Makes sense, Gene," Buchinsky said.

Solow nodded in agreement. Hancock reluctantly gave in. "Good point, Gene."

Roddenberry got up. "I will see all of you later."

Roddenberry left the flag officers' dining room.

TONG RA UNNA. TONG ROUND ONE. STAR DATE 2914.5:

The gong sounded, and Kirk took his place opposite Van Sant. The Harrata Captain was glaring at him with malevolence in his eyes. He was wearing his gym clothes with the Enterprise insignia on his shirt and was shoeless.

"So, Humass, we finally battle," Van Sant said in standard.

"So, Van Sant, you finally decided to come out from your cave."

"Don't joke, Humass, you will be as easy to destroy as the Lexingtany. Weslasly was no match for my plan," Sant said egging Kirk on.

Kirk paused. So, he was the bastard who lured Lexington into the mind field. Kirk could feel his anger rising up within him. He wanted revenge for all the dead on Wesley's ship.

"A pity his shields were up. Another wrecked Federansky ship is no loss. Wouldn't you say, Kirk?" Sant relished every word he stuck at the Humass. He enjoyed toying with Kirk.

"We have a saying on Earth, Sant. Don't count your chickens before they hatch," Kirk said.

He could feel the anger grow within him. Don't get mad, get even. Kirk thought.

"What?"

The gong rang and Hittay yelled, "Nacht!"

Kirk launched himself into Van Sant. Slamming into the Harrata, they both went flying. Crashing into the sand, both men rolled around as they each tried to fight for an advantage.

Sant and Kirk staggered up. Kirk seeing an opening pummeled Sant with repeated punches. Sant screamed and went flying backward. Sant moved like lightning and quickly regained his footing. Grabbing some sand, he flung it in Kirk's face.

Blinded, Kirk staggered back. Sant leaped onto Kirk. Both went crashing into the sand. Rolling free, Kirk recovered from the Harrata's attack, grabbed Sant's arms, and twisted it. Sant let out a scream as Kirk slammed him into the wall. Sant quickly recovered and drop-kicked Kirk. Kirk rolled over avoiding Sant's foot as he tried to flatten Kirk's face. Kirk swung clear, leaped up, and punched the Harrata captain in the stomach.

"Nacht, JA!" Hittay yelled as the gong sounded. The round was over. Kirk followed by an equally tired Hawke staggered back to their table. McCoy and Russell ran back to their captains and brought them over to the table.

"Bones."

McCoy said as he ran his medical scanner over Kirk. "You'll live."

"Just nine more to go, Captain," Spock said.

"Very funny, Spock," McCoy grumbled.

Spock raised an eyebrow.

STARFLEET MAIN MISSIONS. STAR DATE 2914.6:

Hahn was running back and forth as reports started to come in. Buchinsky and Solow were present. Hancock had caught the first available ship to Star base Alpha to report on any progress.

"Bull, Herb, you might be interested in this."

"What do you have?" Marcus asked Mattea.

"The Exeter, Ron Tracey's ship was traveling to Star base 11 for upgrade, overhaul, and refit. Ran into a Hogar class, type 5, the Niparty San Solari near Hiroshima quasar. In a running battle, Exeter scared off the Harrata ship. But Exeter received damage."

"Only Lexington, Constitution, and Enterprise haven't been upgraded or refitted," Solow mentioned.

"She will be the last if she survives the Challenge, Herb. All other cruisers including our new ships all have the upgrades."

"The Farragut under Captain Kelly Bogle was surveying the barrier ran into a Nacht Mat class battle cruiser type 3, the Fortunata Mat near Delta Vega. She was able to beat them off and the ship disappeared into the barrier. Farragut had to return to Star base 20 for repairs," Hahn added.

"The children of Lothar attacked Barmus colony. But they were thrown back by a garrison of Federation Ground Infantry, suffering heavy losses. And Augenthaler reports that Victorious and the three destroyers are ready for service. Estebans Bozeman is escorting Masao back to Star Base Alpha. Excelsior also reports that the Klingons have amassed two battle groups near the border," Hahn said.

"The Klingons won't attack. They are too involved in the Challenge," Solow said. "Those forces are for defense when the Harrata Battle groups attack the Empire."

"What about the Romulans?" Buchinsky asked.

"Outposts one and thirty report slightly larger than normal concentrations of ships in their sectors," Hahn added.

"Have all ships, outposts, and star bases along the Federation-Romulan border increase surveillance activity on the Romulans," Buchinsky ordered.

"Just in case, Bull," Mattea figured.

"Yes, Mattea, just in case. And what is the status of our fleets?"

"All fleets are in position. Commodore Serling's Federation class dreadnought squadron has arrived and Fleet Captain Rice's Achenar class Heavy cruiser squadron is in position."

"Notify us if the main Harrata Star Force Battle groups twitch."

"I will, Marcus," Hahn said as she returned to her job.

CHAPTER TWENTY-THREE

TONG RA TRE. TONG ROUND THREE. STAR DATE 2914.6:

Kirk rolled in the sand as he and Van Sant fought desperately. He had to win. Too much was at stake.

Kneeing the Harrata in the groin, Van Sant fell off Kirk. Sant grabbed Kirk's shirt and dragged him over. Breaking free, Kirk staggered up.

Van Sant got up and screamed in anger as he slammed into Kirk. Both toppled over again.

"Nacht, JA!" Hittay yelled. McCoy and Russell hauled their commanding officers back to the table.

McCoy ran his scanner over Kirk's face. "You will live, Jim." Pulling out a hypo, McCoy adjusted it as Kirk poured himself another cup of Jamba juice. The hypo hissed as McCoy injected Kirk.

"Bones."

"A vitamin supplement, Jim. The strain is beginning to show."

Kirk took another sip of the Jamba juice. It was bitter, yet oddly refreshing. Hawke however was chugging it down.

"How can you stand that stuff, Bob?" Kirk looked at Hawke.

"I picked up a taste for this when I commanded Sargon, Jim. That trip with ambassador Fox to Bathazar twelve, we were the only ship available," Hawke recalled.

Kirk could only agree. He had just transferred from Oxford to Hartford when the mission came up. He hadn't been ready and instead of sending the usual heavy or medium cruisers, the fleet had been stretched to the limit. Westcott's predecessor had halted all construction in an attempt to placate the Klingon Empire. Because of that bad decision, ships like the Sargon had drawn assignments they usually wouldn't get. Robert had lucked out.

"You were lucky, Bob."

"Luck of the draw, Jim. Shran was on Sargon when I assumed command. Starfleet refused my first choice and my other two choices couldn't make it in time and I didn't have time to find another."

"In desperation, he chose me, Jim. I was serving as second officer at the time and Sargon's Captain Chandra had transferred to command the Kongo before going to the Monitor and her first officer was promoted to a command of her own," Shran admitted. "And the rest is history."

"They are both inseparable," Russell said adding his two cents in. Shran hit Russell in the arm with a punch.

"Hey!" Russell said as he rubbed his aching arm.

"Don't start, Doc," Shran warned.

"She's got us both beat Dave," McCoy said smiling, clearly seeing that Russell was getting the short end of the stick for once.

Russell grumbled, "At least you don't have to deal with Shran Bones."

McCoy smiled. "And you don't have to deal with Spock."

Russell pointed to T'Pau. "I have to deal with T'Pau and my captain's ego to boot."

McCoy looked at Kirk. "Tell me, Jim, how that big macho ego of yours is doing."

"Same as Bob's." Kirk smiled.

"Bones, Jim Kirk and I possess a macho galaxy-wide ego. If we didn't have that, how would we ever be able to manage four hundred and twenty-nine independent thinking, self-centered crew persons who also have their own agenda?" Hawke said.

"Here! Here!" Kirk said as he and Hawke clanked their mugs together. "Captain's prerogative, Spock."

Spock looked at T'Pau. "A perfect example of Human weakness, T'Pau. Vulcans are not prone to exaggerated human emotions."

"Want to bet, Spock," McCoy said as he remembered Psi 2000. Spock had been reduced to an emotional wreck. But he really didn't want to bring it out. Bobby's people probably knew all about it. Nothing ever really stayed private in the fleet.

"No, Doctor, betting and wagering are entirely illogical," Spock responded.

"Challengers! Champions! Resume positions!" Hittay said as he exhorted the champions and challengers back to their positions.

Hawke and Kirk jumped to their appropriate circles.

"Here we go again, Spock," McCoy muttered. When was this insanity going to end?

"Nacht!"

The Challenge resumed.

PLANETOID X, FEDERATION-HARRATA NEUTRAL ZONE. STAR DATE 2914.7:

Sarek of Vulcan looked at Shran of Andor as they along with their aides waited for the Harrata delegation to arrive. The Littorio had arrived without incident, and the Hogar class type 6 cruiser, the Palama Van Takairi, had joined them. But just like the first time he had been here, the Harrata delegation had taken their sweet time arriving.

"Nothing has changed, Sarek; this place defies time and space," Shran said.

"Indeed, it has, nothing has changed," Sarek said he could still remember the first time he had been here. He had been called here out of desperation.

STAR BASE TRAFALGAR. SECOND FEDERATION-
HARRATA WAR. APRIL 1, 2220:

"If you would follow me, Ambassador, the Commodore is waiting," the young Japanese aide said. Sarek followed the aide who was wearing the old white uniform that was now being replaced and followed the ensign.

Trafalgar, Sarek recalled was one of the ten special appropriation star bases authorized after the original fourteen that had been set up for specific purposes only. That included Alpha, Pendleton, Victory, and two secret ones, Null Omega and the Yard. Trafalgar had gone into service in the year 2176, a year before the First Federation-Harrata War. Home to the legendary First Strike Force-Task Force Alpha, the elite of the fleet.

Trafalgar had been the homeport to this famous fleet. Under Alexander Hawke during the Earth Romulan War, the FSF had taken the brunt of the fighting. In battles of desperation, the FSF had fought the Romulans, fell back, regrouped, and attacked again, buying time for Archer and Larson to inflict the killing blows.

The FSF had early in the war ambushed a Romulan fleet and had later stopped a Romulan fleet from attacking Earth at Wolf 359, which then led to the famed six-day battle. Starting with Wolf 359, the FSF fought the Romulan invasion fleet all the way back to the border. The FSF was so depleted from the battle. It was pulled out of line for rebuilding. The FSF returned to combat in the third year of the war.

Because of that, during the second year of the war, the Romulans had attacked Earth but were thwarted by the first fleet.

Entering a sparse, plainly furnished office, he could see two Starfleet officers present. One was female, the other male. Both wore the new blue command uniforms, and both sported the two broad stripes of Commodore. One wore the insignia of the Constitution, the other the standard Starfleet Command insignia. Behind the desk were two models—one Mann class, the other Class J.

"Ambassador Sarek, welcome," the female commodore said.

"Nice for you to join us," the male commodore added.

"Commodores Hahn and Jefferies, so glad to meet you," Sarek said to both officers.

"Would you like anything to drink? Tirra juice, mister Ambassador?" Hahn asked.

"Why not?" Sarek said as he filled his cup with the green Vulcan liquid. Sipping, he could feel the refreshing liquid revive him. Sitting down, he sat next to Jefferies and across from Hahn.

"I was traveling to Dionysius when Constellation was diverted here," Sarek asked.

"Ambassador Stillwell will replace you. Sarek, you are the best we have. The Lexington was destroyed by the Children of Lothar, and according to Federation intelligence, the Harrata cruiser Hogar class type 5, the Lom Bak was also destroyed," Hahn said.

"It is that serious."

"Yes, if you probably noticed, the FSF took a beating at Rasgul. Admiral Holland with the Cumberland and Vice Admiral Hood of the Chesapeake were destroyed. My flagship, the Constitution took severe damage. We also lost six other ships," Jefferies said. "Starfleet is promoting me to Vice Admiral and Hahn will take Exeter back and be my second in command with the rank of rear Admiral."

"It is a sad day when the Flagship of the Federation is damaged," Sarek said.

"Starfleet is rushing additional Ranger class Achenar's and the Icarus class Tikopai into service. The Class J starships of the Gettysburg and Canada classes as well as additional Baton Rouges however are slowly making their way into service," Hahn added.

"With Ambassador Toval and Murphy dead, Commodore, who will be my second?"

"Do you know, Captain Torel Shran?"

"He commands the Eagle. And Andorian manned ship like the Vulcan manned Surak," Sarek recalled. "A fine warrior and an excellent diplomat."

"Former President Jonathan Archer and Ambassador T'Pol have vouched for you. You come highly recommended, Sarek. Torel has been vetted by the Andorian diplomatic corp. The Eagle will be escorted by a full squadron this time. Kelvin, Tiberius, Einstein class starships, and the Hawke and Archer, both Mann class, will be detached from the FSF to escort Eagle to Planetoid X," Hahn explained.

"President Richard Morvehl wants you and Shran to expedite the talks with the Harrata. This war needs to be ended before the fleet is irreparably weakened and our security is compromised," Hahn explained.

"Since our second disastrous contact with the Klingon Empire after the Klingons went into seclusion after the Earth-Romulan war, the Klingons have been raiding along our borders, sapping our strength even further," Hahn added.

"Lucky for us, Sarek. All is quiet on the Federation-Romulan border," Jefferies said.

"Indeed, Commodore, we are fortunate. But according to the profile, the Harratas are very stubborn people. They did drag negotiations out the last time," Sarek said.

"Negotiations during the first Federation-Harrata war had lasted eight months dragging the conflict into 2178. The last thing the Federation needed was this war lagging into 2221," Jefferies said.

"The president wants both you and Shran to use every ethical means possible to shorten negotiations and expedite an end to this conflict,' Hahn added. "We cannot have a repeat of the first time, Ambassador." Hahn stopped for a moment and answered the intercom. "Well, ambassador, looks like the Eagle has arrived here ahead of schedule," Hahn added.

Moments later, the Japanese officer came in.

"Lieutenant Nogura, see that the ambassador's luggage is expedited to the Eagle."

"Yes, Commodore Hahn," Hirohito Nogura said.

Sarek faced Hahn and Jefferies. "Live long and prosper, Commodores Jefferies and Hahn," Sarek said as he saluted both of them.

"Peace and long-life, Ambassador," Jefferies said.

Sarek looked at his chronometer. Those were heady days back in 2220. He and Shran had come a long way since that time. He was now married to Amanda. Spock his son served in Starfleet, and Sybok however had been banished. He however hadn't spoken to Spock or Sybok in years. Both had disappointed him.

Jefferies was now retired. Hahn was Chief of Starfleet Operations and was approaching retirement age. In forty Terran years, everything changed. But this dreadful planetoid remained immune to the vagrancies of time.

The antiquated, unchanged features remained, relics of a bygone era dating back three centuries when Vulcan and Andor had faced the Challenge before joining the Federation.

The door facing Sarek and Shran suddenly clanked as it spun open. Sarek and Shran along with their aides stood up. Two brown-skinned Harratas of the political caste walked in. One was a tubby, heavy-set male Harrata with lazy eyes and graying hair. The other was a short, busy-looking female whose hair was white.

Shran looked at him. His antenna was twitching. The Harrata ambassadors were very familiar. Only age had changed them.

"Sarek! Shran! So, we finally meet again," the male Harrata spoke in a reedy voice. "It has been too long."

"Takaras Val Hattari and Dana Gi ToZak," Shran said surprised.

"Yes, Torel, it is us. Do you think the Imperium would send anyone else? We dealt with you and Sarek back in 2220 and we also dealt with your predecessors in 2177. By the highest of Chiss and the honor of Tovar, we still remain in this existence," Dana said. "At age 150, I am as those Humass say no spring chicken."

"The Imperium did choose wisely," Sarek said.

"Sarek, as you know, we Harrata must pray before we start these negotiations," Takaras said.

"Understood, you may proceed," Sarek agreed.

Takaras broke into mumbling and Dana started to spin in circles yelling.

Sarek and Shran sat down. Soon, the negotiations would begin.

TONG RA FAV. TONG ROUND FIVE. STAR DATE 2914.7:

McCoy shifted in his seat restlessly. Nobody had died, no ships were destroyed, no crews massacred.

McCoy glanced over and watched as Spock and T'Pau were both calculating the odds.

Russell had quieted down. He was scratching his goatee and looked impatient. Shran looked bored to death.

The Klingons were however through this entire match yelling Kahless at the top of their lungs and the Harrata officers appeared to cheer their captains on by invoking their deities.

He wished that his nightmare was over. It had been the longest hour in his entire life. Everything hinged on Jim and Bob.

McCoy heard a scream. Jumping up, he thought that Kirk or Hawke had bit the dust. A Harrata captain strangled by Kang suddenly slammed to the ground. First blood.

"Nacht Je SA!" The ringmaster called. The fighting stopped for a moment.

Across the arena, one table suddenly erupted in screams as the Lotharian Legion's swords came down on the unlucky captain's officers. Yellow blood was everywhere around the table. Seconds later, the yellow transporter beams whisked the dead officers off to their doomed ship.

The Klingons were shouting "Kahless! Kahless!" as Kang walked back to his table victorious. The Klingons broke out into a song that McCoy did not recognize.

"Nacht!" Hittay said.

The fighting resumed.

Everybody at the table had woken up out of their stupor. One mistake by Kirk or Hawke and they too would be dead. McCoy realized that reality had just set in.

CHAPTER TWENTY-FOUR

FEDERATION COUNCIL. SAN FRANSICO EARTH. STAR DATE 2914. 9:

"Gentle beings! Gentle beings! This Council will come to order!" Westcott said raising his voice as pandemonium gripped the chamber. "There will be order!"

"How can there be order, Mister President?" the Tellerite councilor yelled out. "When the Harrata dare to dictate to us how to wage war?"

Moments later, Ambassadors Korvat and Gazari Fahiri walked in. Boos and jeers resounded from the council.

"Enough!" Westcott yelled. "Of this nonsense, the council will come to order!"

Westcott's Chief of Staff, an Andorian named Tox, came over and spoke in his ear. "The Klingon ambassador and then the Harrata Ambassador want to speak and there will be order!" Westcott said angered at Tox's information and the general pandemonium of the council.

On that note, the council began to quiet down. Westcott could breathe a sigh of relief. "The Klingon Ambassador has the floor."

Korvat strode to the center of the chamber. "Mister President, honored councilors," Korvat said as he looked at the council. The heart of the decadent Federation, the council reminded him of bickering PatQ who couldn't make their minds up.

"The Klingon Empire will not violate the Tong. We may be future enemies, but we will not dishonor Kahless. We have never lost the infamous Harrata Tong, unlike some member races here who recall their prior defeats at the hands of the Harrata," Korvat said as he strode back and forth watching the councilors. "You are being tested as are we. The mighty Federation is cowered by a little Imperium of only 100-star systems. You should all be ashamed." Korvat followed by his aides quickly departed the council.

Before anyone could respond, Westcott made his move. "The Harrata Ambassador may speak."

Shari Ben Gazari Fahiri glided to the center of the council. Shari looked around and watched the Federation councilors. Her every word would be dissected, analyzed. The honor of the Imperium was at stake.

"Gentle beings of the Federation, to renege on the Challenge will only condemn your challengers Kirk and Hawke to death. It is dishonorable."

"So is preventing us from declaring war! We are now in a quasi-war, just the way you Harrata like it," the voice of an anonymous councilor rang out.

"Let the Ambassador speak, Councilor!" Westcott said lividly. "Continue, Madame Ambassador."

"Thank you, Mister President," Fahari said as she thanked the Federation President.

"It is dishonorable to even consider it. You will be notified of their status. If they are lost, we will refrain until you have confirmation. If they win, we will withdraw."

On that note, Gazari Fahari left the council with her aides.

"The council is adjourned," Westcott said. This council meeting had been a bomb and a bust. Quickly arriving back to his office, Westcott slumped in his chair turning to both of his aides. "I do not want to be disturbed for the next hour."

"Yes, Mister President." Westcott's Vulcan aide said. Both aides stepped out. Westcott stood up again and paced his office, looking out his window again. He said to himself, "Jim Kirk, Bob Hawke doesn't let me down."

TONG RA SEV. TONG ROUND SEVEN. STAR DATE 2914.10:

Spock watched as Kirk expertly used his sword and shield. Expertly, Kirk held off the Harrata captain. Earlier in the sixth round, Khod had finished off his champion. With the same bloody results, the opposing ship captain's officers had met an untimely end. Now it was down to Kirk and Hawke.

Within an hour, they would either be back on their ships or dead.

Jim Kirk however after six punishing rounds was starting to feel the strain. His body ached, and he was perspiring. His sword slammed into the shield of his opponent. Quickly, he blocked the sword thrust of his enemy which rattled off his shield. Keeping his guard up, Kirk desperately searched for a weak spot. He had no time to glance over and check on Robert's status.

"Afraid, Humass," Van Sant chided Kirk.

"No, Sant," Kirk said. "I am not afraid, and we humans are not weaklings," Kirk said as he could feel his body perspire from the strain. He had to succeed and there had to be a better way than just killing each other. He had changed the conditions of the test during his academy days during the Kobayashi Maru. If he changed it and still won, Bob would follow suit only to keep his honor intact. Robert hated being one-upped, and that was his old academy competitors' weak point.

Kirk's sword parried another thrust from Sant. Kirk brought his shield up to block the blow that came from Sant's sword. Falling back and giving himself some maneuvering room, Kirk's sword chopped into Van Sant's shield. Seeing an opening, Kirk slammed his shield with all his strength into Sant's shield.

The blow was powerful enough that it nearly stunned the Harrata. Seeing his advantage, Kirk used his shield as a battering ram. The impact cracked the shield and sent it flying. Using his sword, he stabbed the Harrata in the left side. Van Sant let out a scream, dropped his sword, and collapsed on the sand. Yellow blood poured from his side. Kirk immediately kicked Van Sant's sword away.

Hittay yelled "Nacht JA!" and walked over to Kirk. Kirk could see Hawke and his opponent Ober Commander Nomard Ze Fahiri had stopped their fighting. The Klingons all stood up and looking over his shoulder, he could see McCoy, Spock, and Robert's officers also standing.

Hittay pointed to Van Sant, "Kill him!"

Kirk shook his head. "No." He refused.

"Kill him!" Hittay demanded turning to the Lotharian legion. "Aje! Humass!"

The Lotharians put their sabers up to Spock's and McCoy's throats and pushed Hawke's officers to one side.

Kirk threw his sword to the ground. "No!"

"Jim, what the hell are you doing!" Hawke yelled from his challenge circle. "Are you trying to get us all killed!"

The priest of Gom ran down to Hittay's side. "There is a way, not done in ages past when the Challenge was young." The priest then whispered into Hittay's ear who immediately understood what he meant. "HiJa Waka Mass!"

The High Order Corp released the Starfleet officers. The fourteen priests and priestesses left, passing by Kirk and Hawke, just staring at them as they entered a room that was situated in the rear of the arena.

ONE HOUR LATER. STAR DATE 2914.11:

Kirk could feel his knees buckling. They had not let him sit. Robert wasn't allowed to speak either. What had he done? Van Sant was still crying in pain, occasionally screaming out to Lothar in Harratese.

The door opened as the retinue of priests and priestesses made their way back to their seats. The priest of Gom got up.

"What do the holy of the holiest honor us with?"

The priest of Gom stepped down to Hittay. He looked at Kirk and Hawke.

"It says in the Book of Gom, mercy is superior to cold-blooded murder. If one faces the Challenge with honor, they deserve mercy. If one does not, then they too must die. Mercy for cowardice cannot be condoned, so says the holy one."

Kirk could feel his legs sink. Had he really condemned them all, all on a hunch—his ship, Robert, the Federation, all, because he had to stand on principle?

"And what have thee decreed?"

"In a judgment out of the fourteen, ten have ruled in favor of the Humass, Kirk, four against," the priest from Gom said.

Hittay walked over to him. "Now kill him!"

Kirk turned to face Hittay. "No." He refused again. He wasn't a cold-blooded killer.

"Then witness true honor Lothary Ha je va nasgul."

"Va pa nasgul! Honer Nacht!"

Kirk watched in horror as the Lotharians brought their sabers down on Van Sant who screamed, "Lothary!" Van Sant was hacked to pieces. His mangled body lay on the ground.

McCoy, Spock, and Hawke's officers watched in horror as Van Sant's officers were mercilessly slaughtered.

McCoy and Russell helped Kirk and Hawke back to the table.

Kirk noticed that Robert was furious at what had happened. Shran, T'Pau, and Russell were conferring to themselves as Robert grabbed a jug of Jamba juice and poured a glass. Hawke slammed the jug on the table, spilling some of the contents. "Damn!" Hawke cursed angrily. "Jim, what were you thinking! The Klingons will be laughing at our weakness!"

"What am I supposed to do, Bob? I am not a cold-blooded murder! Are you?"

"No. You just put me on the spot again, just like at Ghihoge and at the academy!" Hawke fumed. "Fahiri has matched my every move. There may be a draw," Hawke admitted as his temper started to subside.

Hawke could see Russell saying, "Another cliffhanger!"

McCoy responded, "Yes, Doc, another one," looking at Kirk. "Jim, sometimes I think you make a bad example. You got Robert tied up in knots."

"Sorry, Robert," Kirk apologized. "Maybe you were right, but we are better than being a bunch of barbarians."

Hawke sighed. "Sorry about the temper, but aren't we here to stop a war?"

"The remaining champion and challenger will resume their places!"

"Got to go, Jim."

"Give it your best, Bob."

Hawke silently nodded as he resumed his place opposite Fahiri.

Hittay yelled, "Nacht!"

The clash of arms resumed.

CHAPTER TWENTY-FIVE

ORGANIA. COUNCIL OF ELDERS. STAR DATE 2914. 12:

"What do you see, Trefayne?"

"Horrible, most horrible, barbaric. The Harrata super beings are playing with the Klingon Empire and the Federation using them as toys in a game," Trefayne said shaking his head.

"They never learn. They banished Pong and the others many years ago and they think they could be ringmasters to all the child races," Claymare said.

"We should contact the Q. Teach Gom and their minions a lesson. We should call the Coalition of Light together and sanction Gom," Trefayne added.

"The Q will ignore us. We are forbidden to go there. Only Polwheal who nursemaids Trelayne is even allowed there," Ayelborne said resigned.

"Polwheal and Enowil are embarrassments to us," Trefayne said shaking his head.

"That is why they were banished. They did not want to conform," Ayelborne admitted.

"He reminds me of that Q, nothing but trouble," Claymare added scathingly.

"Because Polwheal was called away on an errand, Trelayne got loose and played with an Earth ship. Luckily, Trelayne's parents caught up with him," Claymare said as he got up to stretch his legs.

"What was the name of that ship?" Trefayne asked.

"Enterprise," Ayelborne added. "Polwheal I heard doesn't like her. He prefers another ship, one of her lesser-known sisters."

"He once went to Earth using full form projection that appeared on this USA ship during her three most famous battles during an Earth war," Claymare said infuriated. "Interfering with a primitive society just to see a historic event instead of following proper edict."

"Will both captains survive the Challenge, Trefayne?" Ayelborne asked.

"If the continuality is to remain in normal flux, they will," Trefayne said. "Gom and its minions will not get their war."

"We cannot be so sure. Trefayne, are there any other barbaric conflicts coming between the Federation and the Klingon Empire?" Claymare asked.

"Yes. A ship called Enterprise will arrive followed by the Klingons. Soon, Organia will be orbited by Federation ships with names like Constitution, Lexington, Republic, Exeter, Yorktown, and Klingon ships with the names Suvwl', Vorcha, D'k'takg, and Klothos that will appear in orbit overhead."

"We have plenty of time. The children will come to us," Claymare said.

"Indeed, they will. Now we must go to a meeting with the Thasians, Excalbians, and the Metrons. We need to use the Coalition of Light to ask for equal rights with the Q against possible invasion of the Infinite and the Totality," Ayelborne said. "The Immortals cannot hold back the Infinite for all eternity and with the likes of O and the Totality in the deep reaches of the void. They need to be stopped. The children's races will never survive without us," Ayelborne admitted. If only the Q would listen.

Moments later, the council chamber on Organia dissolved in a flash of light. Nothingness remained.

ROMULAN WAR BIRD HONOR BLADE APPROACHING THE OUTERMARCHES. STAR DATE 2914.13:

Chavernack stood next to Tal and Centurion Bacakra watching the screen. The main screen had been added during the refit. However, the officers and crew still had their controls on the centrally located control area with their hood viewers.

Honor Blade had been notified by the Flavius outpost that Klingon patrols along the border had been decreasing. Instead of the usual eight Klingon vessels that patrolled the Klingon-Romulan Conflict zone, only three remained. Of the three, one of the battle cruisers was the infamous D' k'Takg, Captain Koloth ship. Takg had more bird of prey kills than any other battle cruiser in the Klingon fleet. Her infamy equaled the Enterprise and Constitution in the Starfleet.

They were now in the neutral zone heading for Federation space under cloak at minimum speed. Chavernack watched intently as the swift lethal battle cruiser kept its constant presence. Her commander was no fool.

However, the new cloaking device was holding up and the improved quantum singularity drive had kept fuel problems to a minimum.

"He's withdrawing," Bacakra, short, somewhat heavy-set, graying-haired Romulan said.

"The new cloak works, Commander," Tal said as he stood next to the helm officer, checking the hooded viewer. "She is now out of range."

"How long till the Federation Outer marches?"

"Two shevs, Commander. Tal Shiar intelligence says that this is the endpoint of the Federation Sierra outposts. Our operatives also report that the Federation is now constructing a new set of outposts facing the Klingon Empire. Most are still far from completion," Tal said.

Luckily for the empire, after the Earth-Romulan conflict, the Tal Shiar had trained Romulans to act as Vulcan traders posted to every critical outpost or star base that affected the empire.

"I will be in my quarters. Contact me when we enter Federation space."

"Yes, Commander."

Chavernack headed for quarters. She had a lot more planning to do.

TONG RA DAS. TONG ROUND TEN. STAR DATE 2915.14. JANUARY 23, 2267:

Hawke's and Fahiri's shields slammed together. Swords clashed. And the noise of metal on metal shrieked through the area. Hawke was frustrated. No matter what he did, Fahiri countered his every move.

Both he and Fahiri were reaching the point of collapse, neither could hold on much longer. They had been at this for nearly ten full rounds, not including Kirk's delay. It was all or nothing. Both were going all out to finish each other and yet, they were still at a tie.

Hawke swung his sword at Fahiri. Fahiri countered blocking the blow.

Hawke spun around keeping his shield protecting his body. Fahiri had done the same as both collided. The sound of two metal shields colliding filled the air. Hawke and Fahiri had reached their breaking point as they spun out of control. Both he and Fahiri collapsed on the sand dropping their swords and shields. As Hawke hit the ground, he could see Fahiri lying prone, his sword had been wrenched clear of him. Exhausted, he closed his eyes.

Minutes later, Robert found himself looking up at Kirk. McCoy and Spock were looking at him. On his right stood T'Pau and Shran. Doc Russell was examining him. "What happened?" Hawke said weakly.

"A draw, Robert, both you and Fahiri knocked the hell out of each other," Kirk said.

Robert slowly got up.

"Now take it easy, Bob," Russell said as he hovered over him. Pulling out his med kit, Russell injected him with some Clarazin.

McCoy asked, "Clarazin, Doc? Cordrazine is more effective."

"Robert has a bit of an allergic reaction to Cordrazine, Bones. Clarazin is not as strong and it doesn't cause delusions or mania if I accidentally give too much of a dose," Russell said as he gave Robert a vitamin supplement pill which he downed with a cup of Jamba juice.

Kirk could see Hittay, Fahiri, and the priest of Gom approaching them. Something must be up.

Feeling stronger, Robert hopped off the table. Joining Kirk, they walked up to meet the three Harratas.

"Ober C Hawke and Fahiri fought valiantly. However, this is the first draw in 500 years," Hittay explained.

"There is a solution however," the priest of Gom said.

"And what will that be?" Kirk asked.

"It is called the Nom Bat ritual. Both captains must enter a pit where poles are suspended in the air. They will pick up one pole only and bring it back. If it is smaller than you, it means instant death. Same size or larger, you will not die," Hittay said.

McCoy looked at Spock. "Spock, ever hear of drawing straws?"

"Yes, Doctor, the Nom Bat appears to be the Harrata equivalent."

Hittay looked at Hawke and Fahiri. "Refusal to accept the Nom Bat will mean instant destruction of said vessel."

"I accept," Hawke said reluctantly.

"And I agree," Fahiri agreed.

Hittay turned to the remaining groups. "The Klingonasse may go; you have three days to prepare for the next round."

Kang and Khod nodded and let their officers back to their ship.

"Follow us, Kirk, Hawke, and Fahiri," Hittay said as he led the three remaining groups through a labyrinth of corridors. Arriving at an open pit, a circular stone walkway surrounded the pit at the bottom. Suspended by tractor beams were multicolored poles all at the same height.

"It is deceivingly fascinating, Spock," T'Pau said as she walked over and stood next to him.

"Yes, T'Pau. By suspending them at the same height, it is a trick. Your captain must choose wisely," Spock said.

"Indeed, the odds are against Captain Hawke and Ober C Fahiri. It will be close," T'Pau added as she calculated the odds.

Kirk watched as Robert and Fahiri mounted their primitive personal hovercraft. "Robert, remember to choose wisely, no quick decisions," Kirk said as he spoke to Hawke who had just gotten the craft into hover mode.

"Don't let us down, Robert," Shran added.

"I won't," Hawke said as he and Fahiri pointed their personal hovercraft into the center of the pit.

"We're counting on you," Russell said.

Kirk turned to see a squad of the Lotharian legion walk in. The legion pushed Kirk, McCoy, and Spock back and separated Fahiri and Hawke's officers from each other.

The fourteen priests and priestesses immediately surrounded the pit. Kirk could see Robert in the distance. Kirk felt his throat muscles tense up. He did what he rarely ever did. Worry.

Hittay said, "Nacht."

Looking down, Hawke released the hover mode and hit the decent switch. The hovercraft plunged toward the levitating pylons. Reaching the right attitude, he and Fahiri slowly hovered over the numerous multicolored pylons. Attaching the support line around his body, he could see Fahiri doing the same. The colors were deceivingly beautiful as they reflected off the glasslike walls generating a rainbow hue. Red, orange, blue, black, etc.

Hawke knew that he had to make a choice. Jim and his people were counting on him and so were Shran, Russell, and T'Pau. His own people's lives depend on his choice. Hawke paused for a moment and remembered his crew. He could not let them down either. Nearby, he could see Fahiri already slotting his green pole into the slot.

Damn! He cussed. He was running out of time. Hawke swore a couple of curse words and decided to use an old earth trick. "Enney meeeny Miney mos catch a right size pole by the toe. If it wanders let it go, my mother says to pick this one enney meeney miney mo."

Drawing a deep breath, he grabbed the purple pole and put it in the slot. It looked bigger than him. Holding back his fear, Hawke released the hover mode and hit the ascent button.

Kirk watched as Hawke and Fahiri arrived with their poles. The Lotharians had released them.

Hittay came over to the two captains. "The poles," Hittay ordered. Hawke and Fahiri released the slots and grabbed them. Hawke watched as Fahiri tried to measure up to his pole. It was shorter than him. He stood next to his pole. It was taller than him. Hawke breathed a sigh of relief. He could see Kirk giving him the thumbs-up signal. Russell had a rare smile on his face. Even Shran looked relieved. T'Pau and Spock merely nodded.

McCoy however was beaming.

Hittay came over to him and handed him a sword. "Now kill him." Hawke walked up to the Harrata captain. Fahiri was looking at him meeting him eye to eye. "Shari is my wife, Ober C," he said. Stunned, Hawke halted his swing. Fahiri nodded. His past had caught up with him. Hawke looked at Kirk and then looked at Fahiri. Turning to Hittay, Hawke threw his sword down. "I will not kill him."

Hittay, instead of turning to the Legion, faced the priests. "Your vote."

The priest of Gom looked at Hawke and then at Kirk. "We have come to the same conclusion. Twelve favor Hawke, two Fahiri."

On that note, with no more than a whisper or a suggestion, the Legion's swords came down on Fahiri who yelled "Toval!" before being sliced to pieces in front of Hawke. Fahiri's officers met the same violent death.

In orbit above, the crews of Enterprise and Constitution watched as another ship met its demise.

Hittay looked at Kirk and Hawke. "It is nearly finished, Humass."

"I thought this concludes the first round," Kirk said.

"You Humass are indeed ignorant," the priest of Gom said. "Do you not know the consequences of your actions?"

"What the hell do you mean? Are we being still dead?" Hawke said confused.

"No Ober C's, because you chose mercy over outright killing their captains, by Harrata law, you and Hawke must inherit their wives and offspring," the Harrata priest explained.

Kirk looked at Hawke. Hawke looked at Kirk. Both were dumbfounded by the news. What the hell was he supposed to ever tell Carol about this?

Robert was equally confused. This complicated matters. He had been hoping to marry Samantha in two years and now this?

Kirk could see McCoy rolling his eye around at this. Spock's eyebrow was raised. Russell was mumbling about something. Shran had gone coldly silent and T' Pau had folded her arms together.

"However, this is still not final, you must first survive the last two parts of the Challenge," Hittay explained.

Kirk felt relieved. Hawke smiled faintly.

"Go back to your ships. You have three days to prepare for the second round."

CHAPTER TWENTY-SIX

KIRK'S QUARTERS:

Kirk had cleaned himself up and had changed into a fresh uniform. He had just inherited a wife and children. And he wasn't ready for it.

Kirk heard the intercom go off. "Kirk here."

"Uhura, Captain, Captain Hawke is online."

"Put him through."

Hawke's image came through. Hawke looked spotless but he had a concerned looked on his face. What was bothering me was also nagging at Robert.

"Don't worry, Jim. I'm not going to want to have a battle royal between us over this issue,"

Hawke said referring to what had transpired during the first round. "I just wanted to tell you that the welcome mat is out for your people on my ship, Jim. I'm just going to have a hard time trying to explain this to Samantha when we meet up again."

Kirk smiled. "I agree, Bob, we'll finalize this issue when we finish this Challenge. Tell your people the welcome mat is out."

"Understood. Hawke out." Robert's image faded.

Kirk headed for the bridge to attend to ship business.

U.S.S SOYUZ-NCC1940 WITH UNIT XY 75847, NEAR THE PATRELLIAN NEBULA. STAR DATE 2915.15:

Samantha Reynolds sat back in her quarters reading. The Soyuz and her squadron mates were presently ten parsecs from Harry Morrow's squadron. Watching over the Harrata, hoping and praying was all she could do. None of the main battle groups had even moved yet. And yet she knew this could not continue.

Except for one minor skirmish. Excelsior and Lafayette had chased off a squadron of class of Speedy scouts near Dorval. Things had been quiet.

Kirk might have been a pain in the neck at the academy. Jim and Robert were always competing over something, but she respected them both.

Recently, she had just received news of Robert's old Delta squadron mate Arthur T. Marshall. He had been promoted to command a Federation class dreadnought, the Star League. Art had previously commanded Soyuz's sister ship, the Dunkerque. Marshall was deployed with Josiah Serling's Federation class dreadnought squadron assisting Rittenhouse's Tactical Fleet.

Art might have a bigger ship, but size wasn't everything. Her border patrol medium cruiser was still more agile than Art's clumsy battleship. She never understood the male predilection for size. It was usually the smarter captain who won the battle.

And they're all supposed to be one big happy fleet. The fleet was filled with enough factions to make one's head spin. And occasionally, there had been power grabs and struggles within the Starfleet. And she knew one shining example of one.

Robert and that jealous nitwit Phillip Waterston as an example. Phil had been such a phony during their time at the academy. His dad constantly violated Starfleet Regulation 233 to get him all the chosen assignments while her dad and Bob's had refused.

She really didn't blame her father, trying not to show favoritism. And he had given her dad major heartache when he was assigned to the Hornet. It had gotten so bad that Phil at her father's request had to transfer off Hornet. Her dad later got an earful from Phil's dad over the issue.

A few months earlier, she had run into Waterston when Soyuz had to convoy three Ptolemy's and four Hurons to Star base Victory for a supply run. Waterston had acted like a spoiled brat giving her and Commander Esteban of the Bozeman nothing but heartache and complaints.

And did Waterston ever really wonder why he had a tug instead of a heavy?

Waterston, like the infamous Darion Page and the equally infamous R.L. Custer, had graduated at the bottom of their command school class.

The desk intercom buzzed. Samantha hit the switch.

The shuck of white hair and the neatly trimmed white mustache of her XO Henrich Van Dietrich appeared. Like Gramps on the Constitution, Henry as he was known to Soyuz's crew had been on this ship since her launch in 2250 as her XO. He had served every one of Soyuz's former CO's and had turned down command of this ship every time there was a command change.

As first officer and First mate, Dietrich was her right arm. Henry was old school, but she always counted on his excellent advice. She might have wanted someone her own age, but she really couldn't find a good candidate to replace Henry. Plus, Henry was too good to pass up. In 2270 when Soyuz completed her five-year patrol and interdiction mission, he had told her that he was retiring.

"Stefano reports that a Speedy class scout ship the Noob is heading our way. She's using her running lights flashing white," Dietrich said in his Dutch-accented English.

White on the ship's running lights meant parley or surrender.

"Tell Baines to signal the squadron to plot an intercept course. We'll rendezvous with that Harrata ship and bring the ship and fleet to yellow alert," Reynolds ordered. "I'll be there shortly," Samantha said as she quickly left her quarters. The yellow alert started to flash on the walls as she made her way to the bridge.

SOYUZ BRIDGE:

Samantha quickly replaced Dietrich in her command chair as he took his place behind her at the mate's station.

"Stephano," Reynolds asked her young science officer.

"She's making no overt moves, Captain," the young blond-haired and blue-eyed Italian officer said. Stephano hailed from Rome and lived in Octavio.

"Mister Riggs, magnification three," she ordered her helmsman.

"Yes, Captain," Susanna Riggs said. Riggs was Soyuz's chief helm officer. Samantha really hated to lose her. She was being promoted and given command of an Archer class scout at the end of this year.

"Sometimes, Captain, I'd wish Starfleet would give us a better science station than that excuse for one that we have," Henry said wishfully.

Samantha could only agree. Compared to Oxford, Miranda, and Anton, her three squadron mates, the Soyuz class scientific capabilities were virtually nonexistent.

Being Border patrol cruisers, the Soyuz's sacrificed scientific capabilities for an expanded military sensor suite that in one case was more efficient than Constitutions' classes legendary sensor layup. The Soyuz's sensors could spot an enemy ship long before a Constitution would.

Soyuz only had two science labs compared to ten on the multi-mission Miranda and the research-driven Anton had eleven. She could only feel a bit of pride that the Ptolemy's only had one.

"Captain," Ensign Gabriel Bush said as he looked at his CO from navigation. "Do you think the Challenge is over?"

Samantha smiled. "We'll soon see, Mister Bush."

"Captain, the Noob is hailing us," Baines said.

"On screen."

Replacing the small agile Harrata vessel was the typically triangular gold, blue, and red bridge. However, unlike the bigger ships, this one only had two sets of seats. Two blue-skinned Star force officers were present, one female, one male. The female got up. She was tall and thin, plain-looking with the traditional half-circle hairstyle.

"I am Nav Commander (Commander) Ida D'taz of the Noob, assigned to the Special Group Lothary. I bring word for your leaders," the Harrata captain said in English.

"I am Captain Samantha Reynolds of the Federation cruiser Soyuz, commanding unit XY- 75847. Will you convey it to us here Nav'C?" Samantha was relieved that they didn't have to use the universal translation matrix.

On rare occasions, Starfleet captains had encountered some races that taught their people standards. Years in advance of Starfleet first contact, she had over the years ran into Vulcan's and other founding members who didn't need translation via the matrix.

"No, I will beam aboard alone, and we will meet alone."

"Understood, five minutes aboard Soyuz, Nav'C."

"Agreed." The screen went blank, replaced by space and the little scout vessel.

"Is it wise, Sam?" Dietrich asked. "Meeting her."

"It is Harrata tradition. Henry. A face-to-face plus I need to find out what Bob and Jim's status is," she explained.

"Understood, Cap." Henry nodded. She was right.

Samantha left the bridge. Moments later, she arrived at transporter room one.

"Energize, Ensign," Samantha said. She had started to worry what if the worst had happened.

Her Harrata opposite materialized on the platform. "Ober C. Reynolds, I'm Nav C' Ida D'taz," she said as she left the platform. "For your leaders." She handed her a disc.

"Questions, Nav'C, does Kirk and Hawke live?"

"They do," the Harrata captain said as she walked back to the platform.

"Energize, Ensign."

"Yes, Cap."

The Harrata female shimmered out of existence. Suddenly, the red alert siren blared out.

Henry Dietrich's voices resounded through the ship. "Red alert. All hands, man your battle stations!"

"Henry, what's happening?"

"Long-range sensors are picking up Harrata Battlegroup Echo leaving Bathazar six. They are on the move."

"Understood," Samantha said as she bolted for the bridge. Moments later, she arrived back on the Soyuz's main bridge.

"Henry tactical," Reynolds said as she went over to Communications. "Mister Baines, dispatch this message to Earth: Kirk and Hawke survived the first round. Reynolds commanding Soyuz," she said as she gave him the tape. Stepping down, she surveyed the screen.

"Captain, long-range sensors are picking up one hundred ships. One Verrah class, three Nacht mat, Hogars, Neparahs, Deparys, and Speedy's, Sir," Stephano said.

"Dietrich, overlay our position and the nearest fleets."

"Yes, Captain." Dietrich tapped in the information.

Reynolds stepped back. "Baines, contact the following fleets, FSF, Unit XY 75888, and the Fourth Reserve fleet. Battle group Echo on move. Reynold's commanding XY75847."

"Yes, Sir."

"Captain, six Hogars have broken off and are heading our way."

"Message sent, Captain. They are jamming us."

"Signal the squadrons, follow my lead. Helm alters course 225-mark 15 warp eight."

XY 75847 began their retreat.

CHAPTER TWENTY-SEVEN

FIRST INTERLUDE. THE BATTLE OF CARON. STAR DATE 2915. 16.

FIRST STRIKE FORCE. NEAR THE VOLA QUASAR:

Admiral Joe Hawke paced his bridge. George Kirk could only watch as Joe's frustration mounted.

"Are you certain, George?"

"Yes, Joe. They are heading for the Caron Star system. Cartwright's Fourth Reserve is there," George Kirk confirmed. "Sam Reynolds' Cruiser squadron was driven off by six Hogars. Harry Morrow's four Heavy cruisers have fallen back on Rittenhouse's combined fleet. Rittenhouse says that Battle group Hotel has made feigns in his direction."

"Commander O'Hara, tell Cartwright to fall back to sector Alpha six."

"Sir, we are being jammed," O' Hara warned.

"Tactical." The main bridge screen shifted from space to a grid. "Damn! O' Hara, order all ships' maximum warp to Caron. All ships' battle stations!" Joe Hawke said angrily.

Joe turned to George. "Let us hope we are not too late."

George Kirk looked at the tactical display and he could only agree with his friend.

FOURTH RESERVE FLEET. CARON STAR SYSTEM:

Lance Cartwright paced the bridge of the Achenar class Constitution, the Ark Royal.

Compared to his old ship the Indomitable, his first command and a Ranger class clunker, Ark Royal was a marvel. She was virtually brand new compared to the twenty-nine other antiques that made up the fourth reserve fleet. Starfleet had posted them here to supplement the main fleets. If the Federation lost the Challenge, Ark Royal and the Fourth Reserve would be the escorts to the invasion fleet.

"Sir, I picked up two garbled messages," Willis, Ark Royal's Chief Communication officer, said.

"From where?" Cartwright said concerned.

"The FSF and Unit 75847."

"Play it."

The speakers were suddenly filled with static and barely discernible words.

Commander Victoria Simmons came over to Cartwright's side. "I don't like this, Lance," Simmons said as she brushed her red hair back. Simmons had served as his XO on the old Indomitable.

"We were ordered to return to Star base Alpha two hours ago, Rear Admiral," Simmons said addressing Cartwright by his brevet rank.

"Mister Travis, long-range sensor scan."

"Aye, Sir, scanning." Travis turned to Cartwright. "Sir, long-range sensors are picking up one hundred unidentified ships closing at high warp speed."

"Admiral, the Thresher just picked up one hundred Harrata ships closing on our position," Willis added.

The Thresher was an old Advance class destroyer assigned to the reserve fleet.

"Tactical!" Cartwright ordered. On the display, one hundred foreign objects were closing on the thirty ships that made up the reserve fleet.

"All ships' battle stations, jump to emergency warp rendezvous!" Cartwright quickly stammered out his orders. Hopelessly, the fourth reserve fleet began to retreat as the massive Harrata Battle group closed on the helpless fleet; it was every ship for themselves.

"Squadrons one and two with me."

Cartwright said as his two main squadrons composed of Ark Royal and seven various class J, Icarus, Baton Rouge, and Einstein class ships swung around to face the onslaught. They didn't stand a chance. He had to buy some time.

KIROV WITH FIRST STRIKE FORCE-TASK FORCE ALPHA:

"Admiral, the jamming has stopped, I'm picking up multiple distress signals coming from the Caron Star system," O'Hara said.

"Tactical."

George walked over to Joe who sat in the Kirov's command chair. Joe looked worried.

"Are we not too late, Joe?"

"We will soon see, George. O'Hara, signal all ships attack, attack!" Joe Hawke ordered.

"Yes, Admiral."

The First Strike force-Task Force Alpha swung into action, slamming into the already engaged Harrata Battle group. Taken by surprise, the Harrata Battle group staggered and tried to disengage.

As some of the stragglers tried to retreat to Harrata space in disarray, Unit XY 75 847 which had evaded the six Hogars entered the fray picking off some of the Harrata ships.

A massive melee ensued. Space was lit up as phasers and photon torpedoes from the Federation ships retaliated against the Harrata vessels which responded with disruptors and plasma torpedoes. The dance of death continued in the vast expanse of space.

STARFLEET MAIN MISSIONS. STAR DATE 2915. 17:

Hahn turned to the screen to see Dawn Hancock's image on it. Next to her was Commodore Koenig. At main missions, Hahn was flanked by Starfleet Commander in Chief Robert Comsol who had finally joined them after returning from a fleet inspection tour on the Klingon-Federation border aboard the Eagle. Marcus Bull Buchinsky, Herbert Solow, and Lieutenant West were also present.

"We just had a major battle at the Caron Star system. The FSF, 75847, and the Fourth Reserve were involved," Dawn said.

"What are our losses, Dawn?" Robert Comsol, Starfleet's grizzled, veteran commander, said.

"The FSF suffered four ships damage, the Miranda class ships, Wahoo, Boston, Concord, and the Soyuz class ship Royal Oak. Unit XY 75847 suffered some damage to the squadron. Anton needs to be dry-docked, but the fourth suffered the worst, Robert."

"How bad, Sharon," Comsol said, his voice betraying major concern.

"Class J starships Bellerophon, Excalibur, Baton Rouge class starships Saladin, Churchill, Republic. Einstein class Starships Tiberius, Einstein, Kelvin, Icarus class starships, the Hera, and Prometheus were lost. Ark Royal has been crippled with 200 dead; Thresher, New York, and Paris have been damaged beyond repair. The rest of the fleet is serviceable only after repairs."

Comsol cursed under his breath, this was a quasi-war and already, Starfleet had lost irreplaceable ships and crews. The only bright spot was the news that James Kirk and Robert Hawke had survived the first part of the Challenge.

"And the Harrata."

"Echo lost four ships, seventeen were badly damaged."

Comsol again cursed under his breath, damn Cartwright! If he had returned to Alpha when he was supposed to. Comsol looked at Hahn and the rest of the staff.

"If Cartwright had gone back to Alpha when he was supposed to, none of this would have happened," Comsol said infuriated.

"Yes, Bob," Dawn admitted.

Comsol looked at Hahn, Buchinsky, and West. He had to make a major decision. "Where is Cartwright?"

"Sickbay on the Kirov," Dawn said.

Comsol looked at Solow. "Herb, isn't Commodore Carlos Florida of Star base 29 reaching retirement age?"

Solow looked at Comsol and nodded silently.

"As soon as Cartwright is recovered, post him to Star base 29 and have Ark Royal's five-year mission cancelled. She will be the flag for the 13th fleet assigned there."

Solow could only smile at the order. The 13th was the least important main fleet in the Starfleet. To be given command of the 13th was like being punished.

Comsol turned back to face Hancock's image. "Dawn, notify Cartwright that he is being removed from command of the fourth; he will be given command of Star base 29 and the 13th fleet. I am also giving you command of the fourth, Dawn. You are the only officer I know who could get that fleet up and running in a record time," Comsol said confidently. Hancock had proven herself over time and time again.

Dawn's image smiled back. "Thanks for the word of trust, Robert."

"Any time, Dawn. Starfleet Command out." Dawn's image faded.

Comsol turned to Hahn, "Mattea, I don't care if you have to move heaven and earth. The four Constitution class ships assigned to the reserve fleet at Star base 10, I want them crewed and activated."

"I'll get right on it," Hahn acknowledged.

Comsol followed by Solow, Buchinsky, and West left main missions.

KIROV SICKBAY. STAR DATE 2915.17:

Cartwright's vision focused as he slowly opened his eyes. His head was still ringing, and he had some pain in his right side. Looking at him were Joseph Hawke and George Kirk. Neither looked pleased.

"What happened, Joe?" Cartwright said painfully. Kirov's chief surgeon, a gruff Tellerite, injected him with a pain killer.

"Now you may talk to him," Doctor Orel le Saj said.

"You are just lucky to be alive, Lance, we thought you were dead."

"My ship and crew," Cartwright asked.

George Kirk spoke, "Ark Royal was severely mauled. You lost 200 dead and another 86 injured."

"Simmons, Wills, Travis, Lee."

"All dead. You are the only survivor of your bridge crew, Lance," Hawke said.

Cartwright wanted to scream inside.

"Not counting the eight hundred dead from the other ships," Kirk added.

"What other ships did I lose? Joe?"

"Excalibur, Tiberius, Einstein, Kelvin, Bellerophon, Saladin, Churchill, Republic, Hera, Prometheus," Joe added.

Cartwright could feel nothing but guilt. The fleet was his responsibility. The combined losses from those ships amounted to almost 1,000 dead and it was all his fault.

"When will I return to the Ark Royal Joe, George?" Cartwright said concerned.

Joe Hawke looked at Lance. "You are being reassigned."

Cartwright almost jumped out of bed. But Hawke waved him off. "Lance, Robert Comsol, our illustrious and veteran fleet commander, has let you keep the Ark Royal, but you are being reassigned to Star base 29 and the 13th fleet as her commanding officer."

"The thirteenth! That fleet is the biggest joke in the Starfleet. Useless officers are always given that command. It's a great fleet to run one's service down if one has to retire, but for an active command, it's a joke!" Cartwright said angrily. "It's purgatory!"

George Kirk gave Cartwright a "what me" expression and Joe Hawke waved him off.

"Lance, those are your orders and to top it off, guess who is replacing you?"

"I was hoping for Lieutenant West's father."

"No, he is back on Earth and retired," Joe said.

"Then who?"

"Dawn Hancock."

Cartwright again wanted to explode. "She's a career star base, outpost officer. She never commanded a fleet." Cartwright paused. "She's a desk-bound paper pusher."

"Who has, in my experience, Lance, pulled miracles with what she has," George admitted.

"As they say in French, Lance Se la vie," Joe Hawke added.

With that, George and Joe left sickbay. Cartwright could only curse at his bad luck. Someway, somehow, he will escape the purgatory of Star base 29 and the 13th and roam the stars again. Someday.

CHAPTER TWENTY-EIGHT

TONG. PART TWO. OMARTI TONG STAR SYSTEM. STAR
DATE 2916. 6. January 24, 2267.

ENTERPRISE. TRANSPORTER ROOM TWO:

Pavel Chekov eagerly awaited the arrival of one of his academy
classmates along with other Enterprise crew members. He could see
Ben Finney and Janice Rand among the group.

"And what brings you here, yeoman?" Pavel said as he looked at
Janice Rand.

"Barbara Smith is bringing Captain Hawke's feline aboard, Pavel.
Your captain suggested that Maxine and Buregard Koom ba ya for
the interest of peace between our crews. And who are you waiting
for, anyway?"

"A classmate of mine, Steven Harris."

"Anton Harris's son," Ben Finney chimed in. "As in Captain Harris
of the Excalibur."

"How did you know, Captain Harris Ben?"

"Served on Excalibur back in the 57, Harris is a stern one, but he gets the job done."

"And who are you expecting, Ben?" Rand asked.

"Cheryl Beaumont. She's Constitution's record officer. Like me, she served time as an instructor at the academy way back when."

"Constitution to Enterprise, this is Renee Dorvil. Kyle, are you ready," came the voice of Constitution's Haitian Creole transporter chief.

"Enterprise is ready," John Kyle said as he swiftly manipulated the transporter controls. Six starship crewpersons materialized.

"Steve," Pavel said surprised.

"Pavel," Harris said in his South Florida brogue.

"Welcome to the Enterprise," Pavel said excitedly. "I haven't seen you since the academy. I thought you were posted to the Lexington."

"Dad had other ideas, Pavel. I transferred to Constitution at Vanguard," Harris admitted.

Pavel turned to see Barbara Smith conversing with Janice Rand. She was holding what appeared to be a Siamese cat. Standing next to Finney was a full-figured blond whose hair was longer than regulation and had streaks of white in it.

"So, this is the Enterprise. Reminds me of my own ship. Don't see the difference, Pavel?" Harris said egging Chekov on.

"Don't start, Steve."

Harris put his hands up in surrender. "Just kidding, Pavel, just kidding." Harris gave a devious smile.

"Let me show you my quarters."

"Lead the way, Pavel."

Kirk walked onto the bridge, so far so good. The crews were enjoying the visitation rights which had gone a long way to defusing the tension brought by this mission and the infamous Battle of the Mascots.

Uhura who was sitting at Communications turned to Kirk. "Captain, I received a faint transmission from Starfleet. A battle had taken place."

Kirk looked at Uhura concerned. "Any details, Lieutenant?"

"A little Mister Spock has them."

Spock who had manned the command chair walked over to him, "Details are vague, Captain, but it took place in the Caron Star system."

Kirk recalled from memory that the Caron Star system lay outside the Harrata Imperium. The Lydia Sutherland had laid over there for a rendezvous years ago. The system had little value and was virtually worthless from a strategic point of view.

"Doesn't make any sense, Spock."

"Considering that the Harrata are testing us as well as testing the Starfleet, it is logical, Jim."

"Why do you say that Spock?"

"We are not in a full-scale war with the Harrata but a quasi-war that may or may not become a full-scale war depending on the actions of her captain. The losses the Harrata inflict on us at this time may also determine how long a real war would last if we failed, Captain. It happened the last two times."

"I see." Turning to Uhura. "Lieutenant, I am surprised you don't want to visit Constitution," Kirk asked.

"I am content here, Captain."

"That is no answer, Lieutenant."

"I have no interest in visiting, Captain. Mariko Shimada was a year ahead of me at the academy and well, Sir, we never saw eye to eye. Don't get me wrong, Captain. We were both at the top of our Communication class, but she has her own ideas and I have mine."

"Uhura, Bobby Hawke, and I didn't see eye to eye at the academy. But Robert and I appeared to have outgrown our rivalries. Plus, I'd rather deal with Bob's flamboyance than put up with Andover Drake's arrogance or Kelly Bogles' stuffiness any day, Uhura. Why don't you invite her here? Maybe you both can mend the fences," Kirk suggested.

"The captain is pointing out a logical solution, Lieutenant," Spock added.

"I will take the suggestion, Captain. But don't tell me that I warned you both."

Turning back to Spock. "Did Robert leave Constitution yet, Spock?"

"Yes, Captain. An hour earlier, the Shuttlecraft Stewart left the hanger bay."

"Mister Scott, report to the bridge," Kirk said into the intercom.

"The Einstein is also ready."

McCoy stepped on the bridge followed by Scott. "So, where are you two off to?" McCoy said grumbling.

"We need to do a survey of the Challenge area for the next part of the Challenge, Doctor McCoy."

"And I'm not invited," McCoy huffed.

"No, Bones, Robert only took T'Pau with him. So, I'm bringing Spock. And Scotty the ship is yours."

Kirk said as he and Spock entered the lift.

"Jim, just remember one thing," McCoy warned as the doors closed on Kirk.

"What is that, Bones?"

"Don't try to outfly Bobby. He'll run circles around you."

"I'll keep that in mind." As the turbo lift doors shut, McCoy turned to Scott. "I'll bet you a bottle of single malt Scotch, Scotty, that Jim will disregard my advice and lose to Bob."

"Now that is a deal," Scotty said as he shook McCoy's hand. Scotty knew that he was going to win this bet.

IKS SUVWL. KANG'S QUARTERS:

Kang, Mara, and Konar sat a sumptuous banquet that Kang's cook had laid out.

Opposite to them sat Khod, Mira, and Korag. In front of them was wartnog, blood wine, Tarak ale, along with the main courses of Gagh, Tongue of Borta, Klomga intestine broth, and meat bread. Khod could only lick his chops at such a repast. His house was great, but it stood at the bottom of the pecking order of great houses in the Empire.

"This is most impressive, Kang. You shame my cook with this festive extravagance," Khod admitted.

"I know of your houses' place in the Empire. An honorable, old house, but never blessed with riches Khod, but great warriors and even a Chancellor in its history."

Khod took a bite of Gagh and washed it down with blood wine. "If you are referring to Chancellor Temoc who reigned at the beginning of this century, you are correct. He reined forty odd years until the infamous Battle of Donatu V. Only to be treacherously assassinated by the Duras who installed Durek," Khod said. "It was he who ordered the Klingon Empire to rise out of its doldrums and face the humans again. This time, no human patQ was going to set foot in the great hall like Archer did. Thanks to him, we bravely face the plaque that is the Federation."

"If we are victorious, no one can stop the Empire," Mira added. "Let's hope that the Empire is again victorious in winning the Challenge."

"Success," Korag chimed in as he stood up and raised his mug.

Kang and his people joined him in the salute to the Empire. Sitting back in his seat, Kang took another bite of the tongue of Borta. Soon, the second part of the Challenge would start and he already had a plan on how to win. But Khod wasn't going to like what he proposed. But it had to be done and it was the only honorable way to maintain face despite the very real chance of war with the Federation.

"According to the Daher Master council of Strategy, they predict war with the Federation in three months," Konar said.

"And this time, we will be ready," Korag added. "The Empire can build two Drells for every Constidonatu the pathetic Federation can launch."

"Numbers help, Korag, but it is the skill of the warriors that really count," Khod said looking at his first officer.

"Our Drell 6 and 7s can out-turn their Constitution. Surely, we are superior to the Starfleet," Mira added.

"Never underestimate the Federation, Korag," Kang said. "Kirk might be a patQ, but he is formidable."

"And what about that Targ Hawke?" Korag said. "Surely, he is no equal of your greatness, Milord."

"Hawke is no fool, Korag," Khod warned. "He might not be a patQ like Kirk, but he stayed two months on Quonos and is one of the few Earthers who know our ways."

Korag smiled. "You jest, Milord Khod."

"Don't be a fool, Korag," Mara said.

Without warning, Khod whipped out a dagger and rammed it into Korags hand. Korag let out a scream of pain.

Grabbing Korag, he pulled him close and said, "Never jest about Hawke or Kirk, you young, arrogant fool."

With that, Khod pulled the dagger out of Korags hand.

"Take him to my surgeon," Kang said. "Khod, we need to talk."

Khod grunted, "Mira, once Korag is cured of his disability, take him back to the Vorcha."

"Yes, milord."

Kang turned to Mara and Konar. "I need to speak to Khod alone."

Mara and Konar nodded and left. Khod was wiping the purple blood off his ceremonial dagger as he took another helping of Gagh and another drink of blood wine.

"He's young and green, Khod."

"And an arrogant fool. He has the temerity to boast to me in private that his house is greater than mine," Khod said. "If he'd only tamper his stupidity, he would be a great warrior."

"Konar is closer to his own ship than what he realizes," Kang admitted. "Korag however has a way to go."

"Yes, Kang, but this isn't what you wanted to ask me."

"I intend to cooperate with Kirk and Hawke."

Khod leaped from his seat. "What! Cooperate with the Earthers! The Empire has never had a better chance of ridding itself of those two and their accursed ships!" Khod came to Kang's side. "Think of the glory of the Empire if Hawke and Kirk are no longer problems."

"No, Khod, we both know Hawke, and he is one of the few humans who don't consider us to be dogs or animals. Kirk, however, is a devious tin-platted dictator with delusions of godhood. If we go to war with the Federation in the next few months, I would rather kill them in glorious battle than give the Harratay the glory."

"But Mortha and Dennar refused and the two Earther captains were eliminated in the second round."

"Yes, they were, Khod. Didn't Tomec salute them and then he had them both executed for not being true warriors, followers of Kahless?"

"Yes, they won the Challenge, but dishonored the empire."

"We will cooperate, Khod. The humans have a saying the enemy of my enemy is also my friend."

"Wise saying for an Earther," Khod admitted.

"Ever read Shakespeare, Khod?"

"He translates well into Klingon along with the Greek tragedies."

"Then we are agreed."

"Yes, Kang, we are." Khod said as he left, "Keplach."

"Keplach," Kang responded as Khod left.

Kang sat back down in his chair and grabbed some Tarack ale. Mara walked in. "It is done."

"Yes, one day, the day will come when I kill them both and garner glory for the empire. One day."

"Korag is back on the Vorcha."

"Yes, Kang, and all the wiser. What is it that you and Khod were discussing?" Mara asked.

"The humans, Kirk and Hawke," Kang said as he took another sip of Tarack beer.

"You are cooperating with them," Mara said.

"Yes. It is the only honorable thing to do. I will not disgrace the empire like our predecessors did."

"You hope to kill them in battle."

"Yes, Mara. We will be at war with the Federation. Then we will gain our glory."

"You are truly wise, Kang."

CHAPTER TWENTY-NINE

ENTERPRISE HANGER BAY. SHUTTLECRAFT EINSTEIN. STAR DATE 2916.8:

"Einstein, you are clear for launch," Scotty's voice came back.

The light at the top of the bay switched from red to green as the hanger bay doors opened. Expertly manipulating the controls, Kirk flew the Einstein clear of the hanger bay. As they shot out, Kirk could see the two Harrata Hogars flanking his beloved Enterprise. The tractor beams were no longer restraining his ship. To port lay the menacing form of the enormous Verrah class battleship.

"Spock, scan for the Stewart," Kirk said as he flew over the Constitution and her escorting Hogars. In the distance lay the two Klingon battle cruisers and their Star force escorts.

Banking the Einstein, Kirk flew as near as he could to the two Klingon battle cruisers. Since this was neutral territory, the Klingons couldn't do squat. Swinging back, he swung by the Constitution again.

Spock looked from his scanner. "Sentimentality, Jim."

"Yes, Spock. Next to Enterprise, Constitution and Farragut are the two ships I am most fond of. A lot of good memories when she was under Augenthaler."

"I see."

"Don't get me wrong. I just missed serving under Robert's dad since I was posted to Farragut, instead of Constitution after leaving the Academy; she is still a fine ship."

"And she is in the capable hands of your academy rival Captain Hawke Jim," Spock said.

"I still found him to be a fascinating person when he did his brief service under Pike as her XO. He had his moments; he might be a bit more hard-nosed than you, a bit less reflective and philosophical. But he is he and you are you, Jim," Spock finished.

"Well, no one is perfect."

"I wasn't implying that, Jim."

Kirk smiled. "Just a metaphor, Spock."

"I have the Stewart, Captain. These are her coordinates," Spock said as he transferred Stewart's coordinates to Kirk's console.

"Captain, you can never outfly Captain Hawke. He has one of the highest piloting scores in academy history."

"Want to see me, Spock?"

"Just warning you, Captain."

"Understood," Kirk said as he banked the Einstein to starboard and swung down toward the planet.

Shuttlecraft Stewart NCC 1700/4

T'Pau walked back from the service compartment with a pad in her hands as she checked the computers on the shuttle. So far, the survey of the Challenge area had gone as planned.

She had also picked up numerous life forms in the vicinity. It was all fascinating. The only catch was that they couldn't land and do a ground survey. The Harrata had forbidden it.

Robert walked back from the aft compartment and gave her a tray of greens and Tirrah juice while he would feast on a sausage calzone and blood orange juice that he had packed in the rear compartment's service area.

"So, T'Pau, another planet, another survey," Hawke said casually as he bit into the calzone and took a drink of Sicilian blood orange juice.

Munching on her greens and sipping the Tirrah juice, T'Pau nodded. "Affirmative, but we came close the last time when you fought that draw to losing our ship. This part of the Challenge is even tougher."

"I haven't forgotten, T'Pau. Jim and I still need to prevent this war."

"It has already begun, Robert, the news about the Battle of Caron."

Hawke could only nod and agree. The Harrata true to form were testing them at the same time as the Federation was being tested.

"To sacrifice our lives, T'Pau, in the service of the Federation is a high honor."

"As is to know when you are doing it honorably, not throwing your life away. You are my captain and my friend, Robert. I believe in you as Shran does. She has been your right hand since the Sargon. She is your passion; I am the voice of logic, of reason. Your logical side and Doc Russell, he is your devil's advocate. Logic dictates that the needs of the many outweigh the needs of the one."

"We will succeed, Jim and I. Life is too precious to waste."

The bosun's whistle went off. "Shuttlecraft Stewart, come in."

Hawke hit the intercom. "Yes, Lieutenant Desalle."

"The Einstein has just overflown us."

"Thank you, Lieutenant. Stewart, out," Hawke said as he jumped back into his chair followed by T'Pau. Who immediately began scanning?

"Jim never learns, T'Pau." Smiling. "He never learns," Hawke said shaking his head as he disengaged the shuttle from hover mode.

"Strap yourself in. It's going to be a wild ride," Hawke warned.

T'Pau nodded and refocused her scanner. "Got him, Robert. Einstein just entered the atmosphere and she's heading our way."

"Standby, T'Pau, on my mark."

SHUTTLECRAFT EINSTEIN. NCC 1701/6:

Einstein continued her flight toward the surface. Kirk knew he had Hawke, Hawke the god of the famous Delta Squad and poor Kirk, shuttle captain of a glorified ferry. Einstein was much like the shuttle he had commanded at the academy minus the warp sled.

Hawke back then had called his first command a glorified ferryboat much to his disgust. They had disagreed a lot back then. Only in their post academy careers did they start forging a bond and having mutual respect. But Jim still had an occasional axe to grind, just as Bob had.

Kirk checked his scanner as Einstein swung through the clouds.

Spock turned from the scanner. "Jim, I just lost Stewart on the scanner."

Kirk looked at Spock concerned. "We'll fly visual," Kirk said as he activated the switch and the three windows opened revealing the forest and a mountain range nearby.

"There is an unknown metallic substance in the mountain range that is blocking my scans."

"Damn," Kirk cursed. "He could be anywhere in those mountains," Kirk said as he swung Einstein's nose up. He wasn't going to fall for Bobby's trap. The Stewart was probably out of scanning range of his shuttle by now. Einstein climbed, gaining altitude as they cleared the clouds.

"Jim," Spock warned.

Plunging at them was the Stewart. Kirk quickly banked Einstein to port as Stewart banked starboard. Hawke's voice rang through the Einstein, "Jim you never learn!"

"Where is he, Spock?"

"I have him, Captain," Spock said as he fed the coordinates into Einstein's nav computer, swinging Einstein spaceward. Einstein pursued the Stewart as both shuttles swung into the orbit of Tong

Omarti. Hawke had swung his shuttle toward his ship as Kirk swung Einstein in pursuit. To Kirk's surprise, Hawke swung Stewart over Constitution doing a barrel roll as she plunged toward the Enterprise.

Robert's laughter came back. Kirk could almost laugh with him. This was insane, two grown men acting like children. But after what they had gone through in the first round, they needed to let off steam.

"Hang on Spock." Spock quickly fastened his belt. Kirk flipped Einstein into a barrel roll mimicking Hawke as they flew over Constitution. As Kirk steadied Einstein out of her barrel roll, Spock could see Kirk smiling. Kirk, he was back at the academy again. Einstein flew in pursuit of Stewart.

ENTERPRISE COMPUTER CORE:

Ben Finney sat across from Cheryl Beaumont as they discussed the latest shop talk.

"Get real, Ben," Cheryl said pointing out the facts of life to her fellow records officer. "We'll never see the center seat of any ship. We are Starfleet's version of librarians."

"Librarians, Cheryl, have you lost your mind."

"No, Ben. I'm just realistic, like you. I have a successor that I am training. He's from Kirk's class, Lieutenant Adam Timothy. Do you really think I'm going to stay a records officer all my life?"

"Then what do you suggest I do?" Finney said.

"Well, forget about commanding a starship like Archer, Ptolemy, Antares, or even a Huron Independence class ships."

"Then what?"

"Starfleet and the Federation are planning on expanding the Memory Alpha complex into at least six more locations. I intend to become one of the commanders of those facilities."

"Another ground assignment."

"Yes, Ben. Starfleet and FGI will even station a brigade of troops to defend those facilities."

"This is all hypothetical, Cheryl. Those facilities are about five years away from completion."

"So, tell me, Ben. After Kirk stuck it to you on the Republic, I am surprised you are actually serving with Kirk."

"Kirk offered me the post. I took it."

"And what happened with you and Bobby Hawke?"

"I was offered a XO job on the Sargon," Finney said. "Hawke always has a soft spot for hopeless cases."

Beaumont smiled. "Bobby is like that. Constitution despite being second to this ship is a halfway house for Starfleet's lost unwanted rejects and basket cases. Either you make the cut, or you are out."

"Starfleet came down on both of us hard. Hawke was forced to drop me or lose his first command and be reassigned to outpost duty. It was the only time that his dad ever protected his kid. The Hawkes do not believe in favoritism. But this was the exception. Again, I took the fall," Finney admitted.

"Have any regrets?"

"No. It wasn't Hawke that put me at the bottom of the command promotion list. It was Kirk."

"How's Jamie doing, Ben?"

"She's at Star base eleven now. With school being out, she's spending her Christmas-New Year's break traveling via Starfleet on an officer's travel pass. Figures she needs the freedom instead of being stuck on Earth or confined to sector 001."

"Heard from her lately."

Finney nodded. "Before she arrived at Star base eleven, she hitched a ride on an Archer class ship the Hawke; she said she was getting tired of riding with the dullards who command Ptolemy's, Huron's, and Antares' class ships."

Beaumont smiled. "I hope she likes living in a sardine can because that is what duty on those Archers seems to be."

"She found it interesting, Cheryl," Finney changed the subject. "I need a change of scenery."

"Let's go to the Constitution, Ben."

"You have a deal."

Finney and Beaumont left the core.

CHAPTER THIRTY

PLANETOID X STAR DATE 2916.9

"Unacceptable! It is unacceptable," Torel Shran said making his feelings know. Day in and day out, both he and Sarek had sat here with no real agreement in sight.

Sarek could only sympathize with Torel. Never had the Harrata called for negotiations while the Challenge was still underway. They were hiding something, but the Harrata could not be forced or bullied. Sarek turned to see Shas his aide walk up to him. The aides to the Harrata Ambassadors were talking and Liz Hawke was conferring with Shran.

"A recess, Ambassadors," Sarek said.

"Agreed," ToZak agreed. "Five minutes."

Sarek and Shran along with their entourages quickly entered the anteroom that was adjacent to the conference room.

"It's Captain Ivanova," Shras said as he handed the communicator to Sarek.

"Yes, Captain."

"Ambassador Sarek. We have been recalled by Starfleet. We have been ordered to join up with the starships Excelsior and Lafayette. After the Battle of Caron, Starfleet needs every cruiser she can get a hold of."

"And what about us, Captain? The Children do lurk in this section of space," Shran said bitterly.

"Star base 41 has dispatched the Ptolemy to replace us. The Bozeman will provide distant protection in our place," Ivanova said.

"It is reasonable, Captain," Sarek said.

"She will arrive within the next hour; Bozeman will be doing a picket patrol less than one parsec from Planetoid X. Ivanova out."

"Two for the price one, Sarek," Shran said.

Sarek nodded another human metaphor. Instead of one multisession Constitution class ship, they were now stuck on a transport tug and were to be backed up by an unglamorous border patrol ship.

Such was the way of the universe.

Both Ambassadors reentered the room. ToZak and Hattari didn't look to be pleased either.

"The Palamas has been recalled Sarek," Dana said irritated. "And in her place, the Imperium has sent two Wha bat class transport tugs to fill in."

Sarek and Shran sat down.

"Rest assured, Madame Ambassador, we have received the same treatment," Sarek said.

"And what is that?"

"The Littorio has also been recalled, Ptolemy and Bozeman replace her," Shran added.

"The deities must hate us," Hattari said in his reedy voice.

"As does the universe," Shran added

"We are ready to resume negations, Madame Ambassador."

The negotiations resumed.

ENTERPRISE BRIDGE. STAR DATE 2916.10:

Scotty shifted in the command chair. The bridge had become crowded. In addition to the regular bridge crew, they had been joined by visitors from their sister ship. Chekov manned the science station and was conversing with Harris. Next to them at communications, Uhura had been joined by a Japanese beauty who had long black hair and an air of quiet elegance around her. She was Constitution's Chief Communications officer Lieutenant Mariko Shimada. Near the turbo lift stood Rand and Smith who was carrying the supposedly infamous feline Maxine in her arms.

McCoy walked up to Harris and Chekov.

"So, Mister Harris, how's the old bucket doing these days?" McCoy asked.

"She's still holding together, Doctor; I heard you once served on her."

"Yes, Ensign in the late 2250s. How's your dad doing, son?"

"Well, Doctor McCoy, Defiance saved the day when you developed a cure for that plaque that infected the crew of Excalibur back in 2263."

"Just doing my job, son."

At that moment, the Shuttlecraft Stewart flew over the bridge doing a barrel roll. Moments later, the Einstein did the same thing.

Scotty let out a few Scottish epitaphs which caused Sulu and Desalle to look back in surprise.

McCoy walked down to Scotty. "Did I tell you so?"

"Aye, you did."

"Those two think they are back at the academy, all fun and games," McCoy growled.

"I warned Jim about this," McCoy said exasperated.

"Doctor McCoy." Smith holding Maxine walked over to him. "Our captain has wanted to do this for years; he and Kirk back at the academy again."

"Well, you're not alone, Barbara," Rand said. "Kirk has been looking forward to this too."

McCoy grunted. "How typical."

SHUTTLECRAFT EINSTEIN:

Spock braced himself as Kirk did another barrel roll as they flew over Enterprise's Bridge. Calculating the odds, Kirk was a good pilot but just not in the league of Hawke. Kirk's rolls were sloppy compared to the precision rolls that Hawke did.

"Jim, you will never match Captain Hawke on the finesse of his barrel rolls."

Kirk smiled back. "I don't care about finesse, Spock; I'm just having a good time."

Einstein did one more barrel roll as they cleared the Enterprise.

Spock's eyebrow went up. Einstein then tried to do a Yeager loop mimicking the Stewart.

Spock felt his stomach turn.

"Jim, my digestive system is out of alignment. We should stop."

Kirk became serious again. "You're right, Spock."

Einstein swung away from Stewart and headed back to the Enterprise.

SHUTTLECRAFT STEWART:

"Einstein is breaking off, Robert," T'Pau said as she looked at him from the scanner.

Before Hawke could reach for the switch, T'Pau stopped him.

"No boasting. It would be counterproductive."

Hawke nodded. She was right.

"Stewart to Einstein."

SHUTTLE CRAFT EINSTEIN:

"Stewart to Einstein," Hawke's voice boomed over the speakers.

Kirk hit the switch. "Yes, Bob."

"I'm impressed you have improved much since our days at the academy. Not bad for a glorified shuttle captain."

"Thanks for the compliment, Robert. You are still very impressive. Are you ready for the next briefing?"

"Yes. We'll follow you in and land on your ship. I'll notify my senior officers to beam over."

"Understood," Kirk said as he switched over." Einstein to Enterprise Request landing clearance.

ENTERPRISE BRIDGE:

"Einstein, you are clear to land," Scotty said.

"Einstein complies," Kirk's voice resounded through the overhead speaker.

EINSTEIN:

Kirk eased the Einstein into the shuttle bay. The doors closed behind him with a thud. Moments later, the shuttlecraft swung around on the turntable. Kirk watched as the pressurization lights shifted from red to yellow to green. Kirk followed by Spock exited the shuttlecraft and were met by Lieutenant Commander Diana McLane, Enterprise's hanger bay chief. McLane didn't look too pleased.

"A problem, Commander?" Kirk asked.

"Yes, Sir. Captain Hawke is requesting a manual landing."

Spock had his eyebrow raised.

"Let's get to the control room." Kirk, Spock, and McLane headed for the control room.

ENTERPRISE BRIDGE:

"The captain wants what?" Scotty said surprised at the idea.

"A manual landing, no tractors, no auto," Uhura said surprised.

Scotty looked back to see the three visiting crewmembers smiling.

"And what is so bloomin' funny?" Scotty said as he looked at the visitors from the Constitution.

"You don't practice manual?" Harris said.

Sulu looked at Harris. "No."

Desalle turned to Sulu. "My sister told me that every qualified pilot on his ship is required to be able to do a manual as well as an auto or a tractor landing."

"The captain wants no ifs, ands, or buts. No excuses," Shimada added.

Uhura keyed in the overhead speakers.

"No, Robert, we don't do manual on my ship," Kirk's voice came back.

"Jim, I've never scratched the paint on my ship. I sure as well won't harm the Enterprise."

Sulu turned from his position at the helm as the battle of wills resounded through the Enterprise's bridge.

"Tell me, Mariko, what part of Japan you are from?"

"Kobe."

Desalle turned to Sulu. "I wouldn't go there if I were you."

"Why?"

"I'll tell you why." Shimada walked down and whispered into Sulu's ear. Sulu looked back surprised.

"My sister and Mariko are having an affair, Hikaru," Desalle admitted.

Shimada kissed Sulu on the cheek. "For trying, I had to disappoint many boys. If I were straight, you would be at the top of my list," Shimada said as she walked back to Uhura.

"You got burned, Hikaru," Uhura said.

"I had to try," Sulu admitted.

Scotty cleared his throat. "Mister Sulu, if you are finally finished playing Romeo, could you give me an aft view of the shuttle bay and the Stewart's position?"

"Aye, Sir, aft view, shuttle bay," Sulu said as he switched over. The Stewart was hanging just outside the bay. Hawke had her lined up with Enterprise.

"Your captain is some pilot," Sulu said looking at Harris.

"Told you so," Harris said.

"Scotty, I'm going down to the shuttle bay and have a talk with Jim. They are both playing academy games again."

"I'll go with you," Smith said, still clutching Maxine in her shoulders. "It's time like these he need his feline."

"Come on, Smith." McCoy and Smith departed the bridge and headed for the shuttle bay.

The battle of wills continued the speakers as the turbo lift doors closed behind them.

McCoy followed by Smith entered the hanger bay control room. Kirk, Spock, McLane, and two shuttlecraft pilots were present.

"Jim, we need to talk."

"Robert, stand by," Kirk said as he faces McCoy. Noticing that Smith was carrying Maxine, he asked, "What's the cat for?"

"To avoid a donnybrook. I know my captain; he will come storming out of that shuttlecraft like the devil himself," Smith said.

"Jim, you should quit playing academy games with Bob. You are not at the academy anymore," McCoy said.

Spock came over. "The Doctor is right, Jim. You always spoke highly of Robert, compared to some of your other academy cadets."

"Yes, Spock, I do remember," Kirk admitted. Compared to Andovar Drake, Robert was harmless. Drake had refused to come to Lydia Sutherland's aid. The Hector had been ten parsecs from the Miranda and Robert had told him the Drake had refused since Miranda was closer.

Both were three days from Ghihoge. Drake's excuse had been that someone had to patrol the sector. Kirk had never really forgiven Andovar for that. Drake had copped out just like he did at Savo the year before. Drake had refused to come to the aid of Lydia Sutherland and Miranda. The Hector and the Jenghiz could have been there before the four Heavy cruisers arrived. But Drake again refused. Starfleet took no action against Drake in either instance.

Kirk looked at McLane. "Clear the Stewart for manual."

"Aye, Sir."

A FEW MINUTES LATER:

Kirk, Spock, McCoy, Smith, and Maxine stood outside the shuttle bay entrance door. The door light shifted from red to green. Smith made a beeline for Hawke as he stormed out of the Stewart followed by T'Pau. Smith handed the cat to Hawke who looked like he was going to rip his head off. T'Pau and Smith conversed with him for a moment. Kirk could see that Hawke had relented.

He walked over meeting Robert halfway.

"You're just damn lucky that Smith had my kitty here, Jim," Hawke said as he cuddled his cat.

"I'd wish you'd quit playing games, Jim," Robert added.

"Jim, Robert is right, and I'd wish both of you would grow up," McCoy said.

Without a pause, Hawke immediately handed Maxine over to Kirk. Kirk grabbed the cat and felt the Siamese cat's claws cut into his uniform as she growled.

"What the . . ." Kirk said almost speechless.

Hawke was smiling. "Your punishment, Jim. Hold my kitty until we get to the briefing room or I'll deck you for holding me outside your ship."

Kirk relented, "Sorry, Robert, but I like dogs over kitties."

Years earlier, Hawke recalled, he had visited the Kirk ranch in Iowa. It had been shortly after he had led a commando raid to Hell Spawn from the Constellation, rescuing Jim's father.

Jim had a leave coming so he joined him at the family farm in Iowa after leaving the Farragut. It had been the first time that he and Jim had spoken since they had worked together to prevent the Klingons from opening a new front during the final year of the Four Years' War.

It had been an interesting experience. The family had two Great Danes, Bueller and Beatrice. Jim's Mom Winona had been very cordial and had reminded him of his mother Dina.

Unfortunately for him, his mom and dad were in the middle of divorce proceedings that year. Later, he and Kirk had taken the Keppler. He had to make his rendezvous with the Constellation and the Farragut. Robert remembered. A few months after that, they were both assigned to the Interspecies Academy program.

Kirk went to Anzar Five and spent two months with a Klingon named Kumara and Hawke had lucked out and was assigned to Quonos with Kang and Khod for the same two-month period.

"Jim let's stop wasting time," McCoy grumbled. "Bobby's people are waiting in our briefing room."

"Right, Bones," Kirk agreed. Holding Hawke's cat, Kirk led them all out of the hanger bay.

CHAPTER THIRTY-ONE

ENTERPRISE BRIEFING ROOM:

Kirk followed by Spock, McCoy, and Robert's people entered the briefing room. Kirk quickly handed Maxine back to Hawke.

Doctor David Russell came storming forward. "Are you both crazy, pulling antics like that?" Russell pointed his finger at Kirk and Hawke. Kirk could see Rand and Smith smiling as they both got the hell kicked out of them. Kirk looked at Hawke. Russell made McCoy look almost cerebral by comparison. "I pity you, Bob. Doc is the devil on wheels."

Hawke smiled. "Never get Doc on the wrong track, Jim. He'll burn you alive."

"Aren't you both listening to me?" Russell grumbled in his New England brogue.

"We are, Doc. I was wrong. Are you satisfied?" Hawke admitted.

"When did you two first meet?" Spock asked.

"Starfleet Academy, Spock. The year Jim graduated was also Doc's graduating year in Starfleet Medical School. That year after Jim pulled his miracle on the Kobayashi Maru, Command school decided to repeat the experiment and let a few non-command students have a go at the no-win scenario," Hawke said.

"I hold the record of incompetence on that scenario," Russell admitted. "I took it on the Tori, destroyed her in record time." Russell looked at Kirk. "That is why I let you and Bob make all the big decisions."

"Welcome to the club," Kirk said as he patted Russell on the back. Kirk looked at everyone present. "Let's begin the meeting. As Kirk sat down, he could see it was the same group like the last time, with the inclusion of Martinez, Giotto, and the addition of Rand and Smith.

Spock keyed in the computer. "We all know that the second part of this Challenge is one of survival, not only against the elements but the wildlife, the flora. This part of the Challenge will run between five and twenty days, a record held by the Klingons in the late 22nd century. Both captains must survive. Injuries are accepted. But death by the elements, wildlife, flora, or being killed by a Harrata champion, will still result in the destruction of the said vessel."

"They have the deck stacked against us, Mister Spock," Salvadore Antonio Barry Giotto said.

"Yes, Mister Giotto."

Spock engaged the screen. "There is a number of life forms not lethal which could be used for food or substance," Spock said as the screen showed various plant and animal life.

"Jam bats, roty plants, Kakaras, Techanos, Umbats, and Oobary fish," T'Pau pointed out, "are not lethal. The sap of the Techanos can be used as a natural band-aid, wound cleaner."

"However, the planet has numerous lethal life forms," Spock said as he keyed in the required images.

"Do not go into the caves," T'Pau warned.

"Why?" Kirk asked.

"This is why, Captain."

Spock keyed in the image. In the darkness, a single eye stared out at them.

"This is the only known recorded image of a Drakma. Captain Takahashi sneaked an old-style tricorder into the Challenge. What we do know is that Takahashi and Rayburn were fleeing from the dreaded Knabra. Takahashi ran into a cave and was never heard from again."

"That reminds me of an incident that happened back in 2260," Hawke said.

"This should be interesting to hear," McCoy said.

"I was on the Excalibur serving as her XO under Harris when we received a distress signal from the Potemkin. At that time, she was under the command of Captain Leonard Wingate. Potemkin had been surveying the first of the X star systems. They were under attack by an unknown one-eyed life form that materialized out of nowhere and wiped-out Wingate landing party. Strauss was barely holding her own when we arrived. Harris had our shields up and those creatures couldn't get through them. We latched a tractor beam onto the Potemkin and pulled her clear of the planet."

"My dad was still on the Potemkin when that happened," Russell mentioned. "He still has occasional nightmares about that day."

Hawke continued, "We beamed over two squads over to the Potemkin. Harris in the meantime extended Excalibur's shields over to the Potemkin. I led a landing party over with Chief Science Officer Stannis. The ship looked like a scene from a horror movie. Bodies were everywhere."

Kirk remembered the incident. Eagle had been the closes ship to the Excalibur. To solve the problem, Harris had turned Excalibur's phasers on the derelict fleet that included the missing Klingon battle cruiser Cha ditch. By destroying the ships, it sent the monsters running in panic.

"Lucky for us, Eagle had arrived. But not until over half of Potemkin's crew had been wiped out and we lost Stannis and twenty crewpersons," Hawke said as he looked at Kirk.

"You still owe me one, Jim."

Kirk nodded. "I know, Bob. Starfleet then quarantined X1313."

"Captain Kirk and Captain Hawke if I may continue," Spock said.

"Continue, Spock," Kirk said as Robert silently nodded in agreement.

"Exhibit B, the Knabra," Spock said. The screen showed a large, almost beastly creature that had four thin legs and spider-like mandibles.

"The Knabra tries to avoid the caves where the Drakma lives. These creatures are fast and very agile."

"We could find a cave, Bob, and find a defensible site above it, using the Knabra fear of the Drakma to our advantage."

"Are you both crazy?" Russell said stunned.

"You're both nuts," McCoy added.

"I agree with Jim. Anywhere else, we'll be open prey for the Knabra," Hawke said.

Spock continued, "Exhibit C, when you are near any river, beware of the Nobry."

Spock switched the view to a river. The turquoise river remained calm for a few moments when an enormous thick-scaled fish jumped up. It was huge and had three eyes with a jutting pincer-like jaw.

"Remind me never to go fishing on this world," McCoy said sarcastically.

"Are there any more dangers that we need to be aware of, Spock?"

"These are the most lethal. T'Pau and I have prepared a disc of all the life forms that inhabit the planet for your study."

Kirk looked at Hawke and his people. Robert was still cuddling his cat.

"Any questions?"

Hawke shook his head. "None, I will take my people back in the Stewart. Jim and I will all see you within a day."

Spock handed Hawke a disc as he and his people left.

Kirk said, "Don't be late, Bob."

"I won't."

CHAPTER THIRTY-TWO

January 25, 2267

"Captain's log. Star date 2917. 3. Captain James T. Kirk recording. Today begins the longest part of the infamous Challenge. We will be left to our own devices, no modern equipment allowed. Luckily for Robert and me, we both survived the Starfleet survival course. The only random factor is the Klingons."

"Captain's log. Star date 2917.4. Captain Robert Nelson Hawke recording. The Tong Chavere begins. This reminds me of the survival course all cadets took on Minius V in our junior year at Starfleet Academy. We are at the mercy of the elements and the wildlife. If Jim and I survive this, we only have one more to go. My crew is tired but game and we are all looking forward to our appointment at Star base 11. Once this is completed, the end of the Challenge is in sight."

TONG OMARTI FOUR. TONG CHAVERE. STAR DATE
2917.5. DAY ONE. 0900 HOURS:

Kirk, Spock, and McCoy materialized at the coordinates provided
by Hittay the ringmaster. Multicolored grass rustled beneath their
feet. Alien noises filled the air. He could see the officers from all the
remaining ships were present. The heat was awful and the humidity
even worse.

Kirk trudged up to the group of officers present. In the center of
the group was Hittay in his unique robes, silver skin, and his red
Mohawk and his mutton chop sideburns.

The Harrata ringmaster began, "Now that we are all present, I
will spell out the rules of this part of the Challenge. No modern
equipment allowed. This is a survival test where one lives off the
land. If you are killed by the life forms, poisoned by the flora, or
killed by a Challenger or Champion, the results are the same. Your
ship and crew will be massacred."

Hittay continued, "For complete anonymity, the second part of the
Challenge will take place in the mountain ranges beyond where no
sensor or scanner can penetrate."

McCoy looked at Kirk and Spock. "They are stacking the deck, Jim."

"Right, Bones." Kirk thought McCoy did have a good point.

"You may now say your farewells," Hittay said as a Harrata shuttlecraft
roared overhead and touched down. "We will be watching," Hittay
warned.

"Good luck, Jim," McCoy said as he tried to hold back his emotions.

"Thank you, Bones."

Spock made the Vulcan symbol. "Live long and prosper, Jim."

"Thank you, Spock."

Moments later, Spock and McCoy shimmered out of existence.

Hawke walked up to Kirk.

"Ready when you are, Jim."

Kirk could see the Harrata champions all four of them heading for the mountain range as the Harrata shuttle lifted off.

"First priority, Bob. Let's look for shelter," Kirk said as they both started to head for the mountain range when Kang bellowed out. "Kirk, Hawke."

Kang and Khod walked up. "In the interest of honor, Kirk, we are joining you and will work with you in this part of the Challenge."

"And what if we do not want your help, Kang?"

"It would be a mistake, Kirk; we Klingons are used to challenges like this and with the rumored war between both of our governments, we would rather face you and Hawke in battle than give the Harrata any satisfaction with your demise."

Kirk could feel his natural distrust for the Klingons kick in. How could he work with his future enemy when it came to this?

Hawke cut in, "Jim you asked me for my advice. We need to talk. Kang, Khod, give us a moment," Hawke said as he let Kirk aside.

"I don't want to work with them, Jim, but if it wasn't for Kang, I wouldn't be here now," Hawke said as he remembered his time on the Klingon home world.

"Robert, they are our enemies to collaborate with them," Kirk said angrily.

"I am not a collaborator, Jim; you know me too well. We didn't come this far just to throw it all away. Without the Klingons, we are as good as dead. Ask Takahashi and Rayburn. Because they didn't work with their opposites, they lost their ships and their lives. At Ghihoge, who came to your aide, not Drake but me, and who fought beside you at Savo? Custer was a fool. Remember how he put us down and refused to take our advice," Hawke said passionately.

Kirk paused for a moment and remembered. He did ask him for his advice and Hawke made some good points.

"Jim, my ship and crew are exhausted. I want to make it back to Star base 11. I do not want to commit suicide and throw it out the window all because of our prejudices against the Klingons. Didn't you tell us that we need to show the Harrata just how good the Federation is and that we humans are not weakling pushovers?" Hawke said. "And don't forget about your precious Enterprise, Jim, do you really want to lose her because I will not sacrifice my precious Constitution so we may all lose the Federation over a war we did not need to fight?"

Kirk realized that Robert had given him his unbiased, unvarnished opinion. Hawke was right, without the Klingons they were as good as dead. He had let his prejudices cloud his judgment.

"We could always go back to hating Klingons after this mission is over, Jim," Hawke finished.

"Tell me, Bob, were you this annoying with Harris?"

Hawke smiled. "I never gave Anton an inch, just my unbiased opinion."

"You made a good point. Let's go see Kang and Khod," Kirk said as they walked over to the Klingons.

"Kang, we will work with you."

"Excellent since we need to find shelter. I propose we split into two groups. I will go with Kirk and Hawke and Khod will work together," Kang suggested.

Khod grumbled at the thought of having to work with Hawke.

"We will rendezvous at the edge of the mountain range in four hours," Kirk suggested.

"Agreed."

Both groups of captains split up making their way toward the mountain range.

STARFLEET MAIN MISSIONS. STAR DATE 2917.6:

Comsol, Buchinsky, Solow, Hahn, and West were huddled over the Tactical board that had a layout of the Quadrant where the Harrata Imperium was located. On the board were the designated units that were assigned to the conflict.

"We need to consolidate our fleets, gentlemen," Hahn said.

"What are you proposing?" Comsol asked.

"Rittenhouse's Tactical fleet will be split up. His destroyer squadron will join Harari's 8th fleet. Josiah Serling's Dreadnought squadron will join up with the FSF. Mary Ann Rice's Achenar squadron along with Ann Toroyan, Harry Morrows, and Matt Decker's Constitution squadrons with the addition of Littorio, Excelsior, Lafayette, and the reassigned Wasp will form FSF Charlie and support the FSF. The three destroyers at Star base 41 will replace the three cruisers mentioned above patrolling the corridor. The FSF will patrol between 41 and Delta 4 construction site, Robau's 9th fleet will patrol between 41 and Star base Alpha, and Harari's 8th fleet will patrol between Alpha and Delta 4. Doenitz's recently repaired transport tug squadron along with the newly joined Al Rashid and Hayashi will standby add logistic support to the three fleets. Commodore Pages Constitution class Victorious will escort Doenitz's flotilla," Hahn explained.

"Wasn't Littorio assigned to Ambassador Sarek and Ambassador Shran?" Solow asked Hahn.

"Yes, but the Ptolemy and Bozeman have replaced her. Captain Waterston will take the ambassadors home once this conflict concludes and Commander J.T. Esteban's Bozeman is providing escort and picket duty."

"And Maseo," Buchinsky asked.

"She and her sister ship are on standby at Alpha. We dare not let them go on any missions due to the extreme danger in this quadrant."

"So, Lovell and Okagawa have to pick up the slack," Comsol added.

"I have contacted Okagawa. He told me he understands. And he will do whatever he can," Hahn said.

West spoke up, "Admiral Hahn, we received a report from a civilian freighter, the Consolidated. They picked up on their sensors at the extreme range a Romulan warbird operating in the corridor."

"We are trying to get confirmation on that, Lieutenant," Hahn said.

Buchinsky scratched his head. "You would think the Romulans would have the sense to stay out of this."

"They smell blood, just like at Icarus and Hydra," Solow said.

"If it isn't bad enough, the Klingons want a war with us. The Harrata picks a perfect time like this to issue a Challenge and now the Romulans are getting restless," Comsol said.

Turning to Hahn, "What is the status of the five Constitutions at Star base 10?"

"Three are in service and are heading for Star base 38. Astrad is nearly crewed, but Galina-NCC 1464 is having problems."

"What problems?" Solow asked.

"Galina's warp drive is acting up. They had to dry dock her and her newly appointed Captain Harvey Jellicoe is having problems crewing her and getting her ready," Hahn explained.

"Tell Jellicoe as she is ready, she will be assigned to the Romulan Neutral Zone and not join her sisters at 38," Comsol said to Hahn.

"Understood."

Comsol turned to Solow and West. "I need both of you to update the president."

Solow nodded.

Comsol and Buchinsky left.

Romulan Warbird Honor Blade somewhere in the corridor. Star date 2917.8.

"Imperial Combat diary 02251. Commander Chavernack reporting. We have successfully entered the Corridor Outer marches, evading a primitive Class Z civilian freighter. We are proceeding deeper into Federation Territory under our cloak which is set to run in conservation mode. Crew morale is high. We are the first Romulan warbird to ever reach this far."

Livinia shut off the recorder and sat back in her chair. She looked at the pictures of Keras and the black-haired beauty that was Valeria. Both were two of the Empire's greatest commanders and both had met their untimely fate at the hands of the Federation. Keras's and Valeria's families had sworn revenge against the Federation captains. Enterprise and Constitution were curse words in Romulan. Like their predecessors of the 22nd century, they continued to thwart the Empire. Between Archer and Hawke, they had denied the Empire its rightful place in the galaxy. One of her ancestors Lucius Chavernack had been killed in action when the infamous First Strike Force at the Battle of Gamma Prometheus had ambushed his fleet.

The intercom whistle sounded. Chavernack hit the button. Tal's image appeared on the screen in front of her. "Commander, our sensors have picked up a one-man civilian scout ship leaving the Klingon's sphere of influence."

"I'll be there shortly," Chavernack said as she closed the screen and left her quarters and within seconds, appeared on the bridge.

"Report, Tal."

"Sensors have identified the ship as the S.S Minnow- NC 15145. She hasn't spotted us yet," Tal explained.

"Commander, four new contacts, closing fast!" Tregar, the Honor Blades science officer said.

"On screen," Chavernack ordered

"Commander, Sensors have identified them as Constitution class. They are the Excelsior-NCC 1718, Lafayette-NCC 1720, Wasp-NCC 1721, and Littorio-NCC 1727," Tregar added.

"All stop, rig for silent running," Chavernack ordered. Honor Blade came to a full stop.

Chavernack could feel her veins pounding. Four Federation Heavy cruisers, Honor Blade didn't stand a chance if she was caught. She could see the four ships slowly come into visual range. One error and they would never see Romulus again.

S.S Minnow- NC 15145

Cyrano Jones sat at the control console of his little one-man ship. His foray into the Klingon sphere of influence had been a success. He was now heading to the Harrata Imperium to fulfill his contract obligations to a white Harrata named Barzook La Tyson.

Then back to more familiar turf at K7. His sensor alarm went off. Quickly engaging the main screen, Cyrano Jones let out a hopeless sigh. Four Federation Heavy cruisers were closing on his ship. A French-Canadian accent soon sounded through the overhead speakers. "I am Captain Jacque La Liberté of the Federation starship Excelsior. You have been identified as the S.S Minnow heave to and prepare to be boarded."

"Understood, friend Captain," Cyrano said as he complied with the order. The delivery would just have to wait.

HONOR BLADE:

"They have just locked a tractor beam on the ship, Commander," Tregor said.

"Have they picked us up?"

"Negative. All four cruisers are holding formation."

On the main screen, Livinia watched as the little scout ship was swallowed up by the Excelsior's hanger bay.

EXCELSIOR-NCC 1718:

Cyrano Jones felt himself being manhandled by two of Excelsior's security officers. Along with the security officers was Excelsior's security chief Leopold Mozart and her diminutive captain LaLiberté who Cyrano thought was a little Napoleon.

"I must protest, Captain. Can't a man do an honest living?"

"We charted your course, Mister Jones. You had left the Empire and you were heading for the Imperium. The Federation is now in a state of quasi-war with the Harrata," LaLiberté explained.

They led him around a corner to a bank of cells. Most were empty except one.

"Where shall I put him?" Mozart asked.

"In with the Vulcan."

Mozart nodded and opened the force field. Cyrano stepped in as the force field shut behind him. Sitting opposite him was a tall, imposing Vulcan dressed in plain clothes. He had a black beard that covered his entire face and radiant eyes. Cyrano let out a sigh as he sat down opposite the Vulcan.

The Vulcan immediately spoke up. "What troubles you, my pudgy friend?" the Vulcan said passionately.

Cyrano did a double-take at the Vulcan with emotions. That couldn't be possible.

"A Vulcan with emotions," Cyrano said surprised.

"Do you know of IDIC, my pudgy friend?"

"Yes, it explains many things."

"My name is Sybok and yours?" Sybok asked.

"Cyrano Jones."

HONOR BLADE:

Chavernack watched as the four Heavy cruisers jumped to warp. She could only feel relieved.

"Commander, we need to decloak and recharge," Tal said.

"Where is the nearest star system?"

"Two hundred Shevs at bearing 0300, Commander," Tal said.

"Set a course and decloak but maintain combat alert 2, Tal."

"Yes, Commander," said Tal.

Honor Blade decloaked and jumped into warp.

Tong Omarti Four. Star date 2717.10. Day One. 1131 hours.

Kirk and Kang stepped out into a clearing. A wide-open cave lay not too far from the jungle they had traversed. A path near the corners of the jungle swept over the cave to a circular abutment.

"This is perfect, Kirk. We have a perfect fortress."

"Yes, Kang," Kirk agreed as they made a wide sweep avoiding the cave and walked up the path to the circular outcropping that jutted out from the cliff. It was indeed perfect.

Kirk looked around at their future base of operations then he noticed a pile of stones that lay aside what looked to be a former campsite. Reaching down, he spotted some rocks.

Pushing aside the rocks, an old-style Starfleet solar-powered voice recorder lay on the ground.

Kang walked over. "What did you find, Kirk?"

"An old-style voice recorder Kang, early 23rd-century issue."

Kang looked around suspiciously. "Then your predecessors were here."

Kirk nodded.

"They chose a wise position; it is unfortunate that they lost their lives," Kang said. "We are in agreement, Kirk, this is the place where we will make our stand."

"Yes, Kang," Kirk agreed as he continued to look over the recorder.

"I will go find the others, Kirk. You prepare the camp."

Kirk felt his anger swelling. He didn't like to be bossed over by Klingons. But he had agreed with Robert about this. And he would keep his word.

"Understood, Kang," Kirk said as he placed the old recorder in a sunny location. First orders of business, prepare a fire and find something edible. When Bob arrived, they would start working on their weapons.

Star date 2917.12. 1715 hours.

It had been a busy couple of hours when Kang, Khod, and Hawke returned to the camp.

Hawke and Khod who had been looking for a place for them to set up camp had nearly run into the Harrata base camp when Kang had caught up with them.

Using sticks in the sand, Hawke and Khod sketched the location of the camp. It was well-placed; two streams ran near it and off to the right of the camp, a large part of the forest was swarming with Ocha plants, the Harrata's version of a Venus flytrap, only king size, making that approach off-limits. With the Nobry in the stream, it would make the approach even more hazardous.

Kirk bit into the cooked Jambat meat that Hawke had brought back with them. Khod and Kang however were bloodstained as they delve into the uncooked Jambat that Khod had captured. Kirk found it revolting.

"We only have two approaches, either right up the center or to the left," Kirk said.

"Neither is favorable, Kirk," Khod said as he finished off a raw piece of Jambat.

Hawke who was flexing a bow that he had constructed said, "We might have to use stealth to get them."

Kirk could only wonder what his hero Garth would do. Robert had his but Bob as usual was mute about his. Wiping the sweat off his face as he took a sip of water from the cistern that they had built to catch rainwater, Kirk said, "I wonder what Garth would do."

Kirk said as he played his cards. He needed to provoke a reaction from the Klingons and Hawke.

Khod jumped to his feet bellowing angrily and Kang was looking at him with blood in his eyes. Hawke however had reacted like a scalded cat.

"Jim, your dad never served under Garth. Mine did," Hawke angrily responded.

"Garth is PatQ, Kirk," Kang said angrily. "He has no honor."

Khod agreed with Kang and spat on the ground. "That is Garth."

"Jim, do you remember the live bait squadron composed of the Abukir, Hague, and Cressy during the First World War?" Hawke said. Jim needed a history lesson badly.

Kirk nodded. "All three cruisers were destroyed by a single U boat, the U9."

"Heard of the Encounter at Lea," Hawke said.

Kirk nodded.

"The victory at Das Ma Jul," Kang recalled referring to it by its Klingon name.

"Well, your brilliant leader Garth left Constitution and two Larson class destroyers at the end of his blockade line. My dad pleaded for reinforcements. Garth would have none of it, Jim. He let my dad down. If he didn't do a Cochrane Deceleration maneuver, they all would have been lost," Hawke said angrily.

"I remember it. Kirk, Khod and I were serving on the Drell 6, the Kahless, at that time, Kirk," turning to Hawke. "Your father acted like a true warrior. Colonel Koord and Admiral Morat had a say in the strategy, Kirk."

"Garth's arrogance did him in, Kirk. Garth is a denebian slime devil. He has no honor."

"Just testing," Kirk said.

"Great, Jim, now you gave me a real headache. I'm going to bed," Hawke grumbled.

"I'll take the first watch," Kirk volunteered.

"Khod and I along with Hawke will take the next three," Kang agreed.

Grabbing a handmade spear, Kirk walked slightly away from the fire and stared out into the darkness. It was going to be a long night.

CHAPTER THIRTY-THREE

January 26, 2267

"Captain's log. Star date 2918.1. Commander Spock recording. We begin the long vigil, awaiting the return of Captain Kirk."

"Captain's log. Star date 2918.2. Lieutenant Commander Thaylassa Shran recording. We are patiently awaiting the return of our captain. Our human crewmembers have evoked their various deities for his safe return."

TONG OMARTI FOUR. STAR DATE 2918 .2. DAY 2. 0950 HOURS. JANUARY 26, 2267:

Kirk along with Kang and Hawke lay flat on their chests as they looked out at the Harrata base camp. Khod had gone out scouting ahead. Kirk scratched himself. Touching his face, he could feel one day's worth of hair. With only the basics, he and the rest were making do with the Spartan conditions. They each had a set of weapons. He had a club fashioned by Kang, made from stone and wood along with some spears. Robert however had his bow and arrow and a long piece of wood shaped like a fighting staff. Both Klingons had clubs and crude knives cut out of stone. He knew from his own experience that Kang and Khod preferred to fight up close and personal. It was their own tradition. Without macro binoculars, their range of vision was limited. Moments later, Khod came scrambling back. Wiping his brow, Khod immediately laid out his findings.

"I found two dead Knabra, and their right side of the line where the Ocha are a bloodbath. All four Harratay are still alive. The Nobry are in a homicidal mood due to the presence of the Knabra."

Kang looked at Kirk and Hawke. "If we move now, our victory is assured," Kang said as he sniffed the air. "They are near." Kang suddenly began to pant furiously. Kirk realized that both Klingons were entering a bloodlust. Before he could say anything, screaming like banshees, Kang and Khod took off. Without any other option, he and Hawke ran after them. As they ran across the field, he could hear the Klingons yelling oaths as they readied their weapons.

He could hear the Harrata yelling, "Alarm! Humass! Klingonasse!" as the Harrata scrambled to get their weapons. He looked to his right. Robert was running with his fighting staff only. He had left the bow and arrows behind. Panting, Kirk felt the adrenaline rush as they approached the camp from the center.

The Harrata had started to run toward them when a screeching sound rendered the air. It sounded like a raven in pain. The Harrata suddenly stopped dead in their tracks.

Kirk, Hawke, Kang, and Khod immediately skidded to a halt. The ground started to shake. Coming out to the right of them, two Knabra slashed through the Ocha. One collapsed in a bloody heap as the Ocha consumed the Knabra. The second one however slammed through the woods and started to head for them. The Harrata broke and ran. One however wasn't fast enough and was caught in the spider-like mandibles of the creature. The Harrata screamed in pain as it was devoured alive by the creature.

The creature turned and looked at their party. Suddenly, Kang and Khod turned the other way, their bluster all gone and ran without a pause. He and Hawke broke into a mad dash. The Knabra bolted after them. It was every man for himself.

ENTERPRISE BRIDGE:

Spock was sitting in the command chair. The bridge vigil was almost morbid. With McCoy by his side, all they could do was wait. Chekov manned the science station. Palmer was at communications. Kyle and Hanson manned helm and navigation.

On the main screen, the enormous bulk of the Lothar GaZ dominated the screen with the two scout ships Noob and Hakara. Suddenly, the big monster started to move toward them.

"Oh my god," McCoy said worriedly.

And suddenly turned toward the Constitution.

"Mister Hanson, refocus on Constitution," Spock ordered.

"Aye, Sir." Hanson switched the screen over.

Enterprise's sister ship was flanked by one type 7 and one type 8.

"Constitution has gone to yellow alert," Palmer said.

Seconds later, a tractor beam lashed out, missing the Constitution and latching onto the remaining type 7, the Nesama Nama, pulling it clear of Heavy cruiser.

Chekov said as the cutting beams were slashing the ship, "The GaZ has activated her transporters, Mister Spock." Chekov added, "Gos podi!" Chekov said in Russian as the Lothar GaZ sliced the Nesama Nama up.

Spock nodded. There was nothing they could do but watch the death throes of the Harrata battle cruiser.

"Mister Spock, Lieutenant Commander Shran reports she is powering down from yellow alert," Palmer said turning to face Spock.

"Acknowledge."

"Yes, Mister Spock."

McCoy looked at Spock. "Well, Spock, so what are you going to do about Shran's insubordination?"

"Nothing, Doctor. Shran is acting like an Andorian or a Klingon would act. Acting to defend her ship as Captain Kirk had previously notified us of Captain Hawke's stand on this matter."

McCoy huffed and left the bridge. He had his belly full of this entire charade.

TONG OMATI FOUR. TONG CHAVERE. 01000 HOURS. DAY TWO:

Kirk had never run so fast in his life; Hawke had run alongside him as they both dodged and weaved throughout the forest. Trees spit and crash and the ground shook as the enormous Knabra pursued the party. He could see both Klingons running too. Runaway, live to fight another day, Kirk thought as he pushed some flowers away and leaped over a fallen tree stump followed by Hawke who hadn't given it a second thought.

Breaking into the clearing, Kirk could see the Klingons spinning about and grabbing some spears that were left behind. Hawke in his panic was heading for the cave. "Robert. no!" Kirk yelled as he sped after Hawke. The Knabra cleared the trees as Kang and Khod launched spears at it. Dodging the legs of the monster, Kirk leaped and grabbed Hawke's legs just as he entered the cave. Hawke fell with a thud at the entrance. Looking up, he thought he saw a single eye peer out of the darkness.

Kirk quickly grabbed Hawke as they swung away from the cave. Dodging the Knabras spiny legs, they could see the Klingons holding the Knabra off. Suddenly, a scream echoed from the caves. Pushing Hawke against the side of the cave, Kirk could see tentacles reach out and grab one of the Knabras legs. At that moment, Kang scored a bull's eye, hitting the Knabra's eye. Screeching, the creatures lashed out angrily slamming into the side of the cave. Rocks suddenly gave way as Kirk jumped clear of the falling rocks; Hawke however was a second slower. He had barely cleared the zone when a boulder pinned his left leg.

Hawke let out a scream of pain as he collapsed. With the Knabra fighting a losing battle against the Drachmas, Kirk followed by Kang and Khod rushed to Hawke's aid. Hawke was in terrible pain. Kirk with Kang's assistance pushed the boulder off. Hawke collapsed. Grabbing Hawke, all three of them carried the injured captain up the path to the camp. Hawke was yelling in grieving pain. "My leg! My leg!"

Setting him down, Kirk immediately removed the boot. His toes were intact. Tearing Hawke's pants, Kirk slowly made his way up Hawke's leg until Robert let out a scream. His leg was broken. "Kang, get me some splints and some water, and some Techanos sap."

Kang nodded and ran off. "Khod, hold him down." Khod looked at him and they pinned Hawke down. Moments later, Kang ran up with the required items. Kirk quickly shoved a piece of wood in Robert's mouth. "This is going to hurt, old friend," Kirk said as he could see Robert nodding. He knew what he had to do. Expertly, Kirk set Hawke's leg as Hawke let out a scream. Hawke could see the faces of Kirk and Khod looking at him as he fainted. An old memory returned.

STARFLEET ACADEMY. MARCH 16, 2252:

Third-year cadet Robert Nelson Hawke, leader of the academy flight team, Delta squad, winner of three Rigel cups, and fresh off the Exeter, quickly made his way through the academy grounds.

Atish Khatami who was graduating this year and one of his many female admirers had tipped him off that the Stack of book with legs, James T. Kirk, had been making moves on his girlfriend Samantha. Samantha was the captain of the Academy Lacrosse team.

Samantha had left him and Charlie Archer on the Exeter when her dad's ship the Hornet had rendezvoused with them near Clinton's planet. Some family matters had developed, so Brittany Mendez, Exeter's Captain, had approved.

However, he wasn't counting on that Lothario Kirk making moves on his Samantha in his absence. Bannocks Republic had dropped Kirk and Mitchell off a week ago, enough time to let the scoundrel make his moves on his Samantha.

He was fuming. He could knock Kirk's block off and get a few demerits which would only get back to mom and dad who would roast him alive for his stupidity. He could try to go and convince Andovar Drake to help him, but Drake, Waterston, and their gang were so-called Section 31s and they wouldn't help him anyway. Waterston would probably go tell him to climb a tree.

He knew one thing. Carol Marcus was in love with Jim Kirk, but Kirk never gave her the time of day. They were both in the same Academy class, and his classmate Gary Mitchell had his eyes on the blond lab technician. Mitchell was his best bet. Gary was a fellow New Yorker, even though he had moved to Seattle. Gary still joked about his Brooklyn accent which he had retained even though his parents had moved them cross country in 2244.

Making his way across the campus, Hawke stopped to admire the Golden Gate. If he guessed right, Mitchell would be serenading the ladies about Kirk's role in the Axanar Peace Mission of 2250, which even though it was a success, the Federation was already involved in another shooting war with the Klingon Empire.

The academy's commandant had already informed him about the near-fatal encounter at Lea. Luckily for him, thanks to his dad's overlooked skill, he had saved Constitution. So, he and mom were alright. Constitution was undergoing major repairs at Star base 12.

He could feel the sea breeze whip at his face. March was kind of blustery and the temperature hung in the middle sixties.

Now, if he could only find Gary. Hawke trudged his way through the Fontana Meadows and spotted the female Academy groundskeeper Sarah Appleseed. Miss Apple or Sarah App as the cadets called her was a fountain of answers to all questions. And she always handed out words of wisdom when needed.

"Miss Apple," Hawke said as he made his way to the groundskeeper who was spraying some Kaferian Shimmering flowers.

"Mister Hawke, well if it is a surprise. Tell me, Mister Hawke, you honor our academy by winning three Rigel cups in a row." Appleseed said in her heavily accented voice which reminded him of the housemaid voice on the old 1960s Disney animated movie, 101 Dalmatians.

"Thank you for the compliment." Hawke said modestly.

Appleseed immediately shoved the hose at him. "Now, spray the flowers."

"Yes, ma'am," said Hawke as he continued to spray the Kaferian plants.

"Gently, son, don't drown them," Apple said sighing. "You remind me of your dad when he was here. Blustery like the weather, he was an atypical Virgo, unlike your young man who, like your rival Kirk, are two incredibly competitive Aries. Tell me, son, are you looking for Gary Mitchell?"

Hawke nodded.

"And it concerns Kirk going after Samantha."

Hawke nodded again. He could only guess where miss Appleseed got the information.

"He and two ladies, your classmates, third-year cadets Andrea Burroughs and Grace Anne Shapiro, are over at the edge of the Roddenberry Lake. You will find him over there."

"Thank you, Miss Appleseed."

"Off you go, Mister Hawke."

Hawke smiled. "Yes ma'am." Hawke sped off. It wasn't that long of a run as he surmounted the last of the Fontana meadows and arrived at the Roddenberry Lake. The Roddenberry Lake was circular and at least four miles long. Trees flanked both sides of the boatyard. In the distance, Hawke could see the Academy Shell team led by fourth-year cadet and cadet commander Kelly Bogle. Other cadets were either sailing or using canoes or rowboats. Scanning the dock, Hawke walked over to the picnic tables.

Perched on top of one were Gary Mitchell and two females, one a strawberry blond in command yellow, Andrea Burroughs, and another in operations with nice features and radiant red hair, Grace Anne Shapiro. The girls were giggling. Most likely, Gary was talking about his and Kirk's recent exploits on the Republic. Robert walked over to them.

"Well, if it isn't the almighty himself, ladies," Mitchell said sarcastically.

"So, Bobby, what brings you down to our neck of the woods?" Andrea said.

"Just mano a mano business, Andrea."

Mitchell looked at Hawke and then at Burroughs and Shapiro. Hawke had found out about Jim's dalliance with Samantha. He had warned him not to get involved. Robert was going to ruin everything unless he found a way to wiggle out of this mess. Mitchell looked at Andrea and Grace.

"The party is over, ladies. I have urgent business to conduct with the almighty leader of our illustrious Delta Squad Academy flight team."

"Will you catch us later, Gary?" Shapiro said as she hopped off the table.

"Yes, Grace, I will."

Mitchell watched as the two females left.

Hawke hopped up on the table and sat next to Gary.

"Now there goes two works of art, Bobby. You had to ruin everything," Mitchell moaned.

"I ruined nothing, Gary. Samantha is also a work of art. You know why I am here."

"Someone spilled the beans and told you about Jim chasing after Samantha," Mitchell said ticked off.

"Right."

"That is between you and Jimmy."

"I know. I have three options. One is to cause a scene and deck Jim Kirk, which means I'll get some demerits and my parents will kill me. Two is do nothing and be called a wimp and that will ruin my reputation and three is to collaborate with someone in a nice diplomatic way and don't get mad but get even."

"Do you know Sean Finnegan and Phillip Waterston?" Mitchell said.

"I considered both but . . . Finnegan likes using me as his punching bag whenever Jim isn't around and with Phil, it is family history. No Hawke or Waterston has ever really gotten along since the 2130s. We are the Hatfield's and the McCoy's of Starfleet," Hawke pointed out.

"Why me?" Mitchell asked.

"I've noticed that you and Jimmy are terribly similar. With Jim occasionally holding an instructor position at the academy as well as dubbing as a glorified ferry captain. Kirk is busy. But so am I, Gary, I got the academy flight team and we will soon have to start preparing for graduation day for the class of 2252 as well as Federation day. This is the only window I have open to me. In less than a month, it will be gone and off to Command School."

"So, what are you proposing?"

"I heard you have an interest in the blond lab technician."

"Continue."

"Carol Marcus, who is Jim's class at the academy, is interested in Jim."

"The walking freezer unit Bobby. I didn't know she had any interest in Jim at all."

"Well, she does," Hawke said.

"So how do you plan to do this?"

"It is logical, Gary. We steer Kirk to the blond. Kirk then loses interest in Samantha."

"The blond spurns Kirk offer to marry him," Gary added gleefully.

"Carol then replaces the blond. Kirk ignores my Samantha and . . ."

"Hawke! Mitchell!" Came an Irish ditty of a voice.

"And you will take all the credit, Gary. I'll explain to Jim later."

Finnegan followed by Rehnquist and Roberts trotted up to the table.

"Well, look who we have here. Two losers. One the almighty who doesn't know exactly where he came from and the other mister lover boy," Finnegan said as Rehnquist and Roberts slapped both around.

"They are both Captain Dunsels," Robert said taunting Mitchell and Hawke.

"Go climb a tree, Finnegan," Mitchell said.

"Go kiss a Klingon," Hawke added.

Rehnquist slapped Hawke and Mitchell on the heads as Roberts made gorilla noises.

Roberts grabbed Hawke and flung him off the table. Brushing the dirt off his uniform, Hawke could feel his anger swelling. Mitchell jumped off the table. Avoiding, Rehnquist ran over and grabbed Hawke. Hawke was ready to dive in and take all three of them on.

With a maniacal smile on his face, Hawke said, "I'll take you all on." Hawke bellowed angrily.

Rehnquist, Roberts, and Finnegan started to laugh.

"Let me go, Gary," Hawke said as he tried to wiggle free of Mitchell and take Finnegan and his stooges on.

"C'mon, Bobby, we are waiting," Finnegan said as he egged Hawke on.

At that moment, James Tiberius Kirk walked up. Evaluating the situation, Kirk immediately stood next to Gary and Robert who had regained his footing.

"Finnegan, now it's three on three," Kirk said as he ran over. Earlier, he had run into Andrea Burroughs and Grace Anne Shapiro who had pointed him in this direction. Why Bobby was here, he wasn't entirely certain. But Bobby had a way of getting around. Kirk heard a scrapping sound of wood against stone. Seconds later, the Academy shell team in the academy shorts and shirts led by Kelly Bogle ran up. Mister Spit and Polish Kelly Bogle looked the epitome stereotype of a Starfleet Academy cadet.

Bogle's Shell team stepped between them. Bogle went over and chastised Finnegan and his cohorts.

On that note, Finnegan and his stooges left. Bogle turned to face Kirk, Hawke, and Mitchell.

"You three owe me one. If not now, then maybe when we are all serving together."

"Agreed," Kirk said as he followed by. Hawke and Mitchell shook Bogle's hand once Kelly and his cohorts had left.

Puzzled by the appearance of his main rival, Kirk knew he had to get to the bottom of this. Kirk turned to face Robert and Gary. On a typical day, both he and Robert would avoid each other and merely smile graciously whenever they passed by each other on the academy grounds.

"So, Bobby, what brings you here?" Kirk said cautiously.

"Got off the Exeter a few hours ago, hadn't seen Mitchell in a bit, decided to drop by," Hawke responded.

"Gary." Kirk looked at his close friend.

"C'mon, Jim, Robert is in my class. We were just catching up on some things."

"Comparing our Co's Jim Old Rollin Bannock of the Republic, versus the vivacious firecracker, which is Brittany Mendez of the Exeter," Hawke admitted. "On looks alone, Captain Mendez has Captain Bannock beat."

Kirk wanted to laugh. He never thought that his rival, the almighty leader of Delta Squad would have a sense of humor.

Hawke glanced at his chronometer and looked at Kirk and Mitchell. "Got to run. You all got to have to report to the simulator for further helm and navigation training."

Kirk checked his chronometer. If he and Gary played their cards right, they would be going out on the town with Shapiro and Burroughs tonight. He still wanted Roberts Samantha, but she was proving to be a tough nut to crack.

"Let's catch up with Shapiro and Burroughs, Gary. See you later, Bob," Kirk said as he and Gary left Hawke behind.

"Much later," Hawke said as he left Kirk and Mitchell behind.

Hawke slowly opened his eyes. His leg still hurt, but a cooling solution was keeping the pain down. Kirk was arguing with Kang and Khod. Grabbing his fighting staff, Hawke painfully lifted himself up. Kirk, spotting him getting up, dropped his argument with Kang and Khod and ran over to Hawke, who had propped himself up against the stone. Reaching for his fighting staff, Hawke pushed Kirk aside and slowly made his way over to Kang.

"I'm going to kill you both, Hawke, what is it with you, earthers? Kirk doesn't understand our ways!" Kang said angrily.

"Enough! I get injured and we have a blame game. Kang, I'll send you and Khod to Grethor so fast you will not have time to stop by Sto VA Kor!" Hawke said angrily and in pain.

"How dare you," Khod said angrily.

"Tell me, is this because of me? Because I am injured, we start the useless blame game? Kang, let's not kill each other now because, in a few months, I bet we will kill each other honorably, not on this PatQ of a planet," Hawke said as he suddenly fainted. Kirk grabbed Hawke and laid him on the ground.

"Koloth said you were formidable, Kirk, and Hawke is right. You should listen to him," Khod admitted.

"Aren't we enemies, Kirk, forced to cooperate because the Harratay have put us into this glorious situation?" Kang said.

Kirk said, "Kang, Khod, your tactics may have jeopardized Robert's life."

"If he is to die, then he will die with honor, Kirk," Kang said.

"He will die like a warrior, Kirk. He was the only Federation who stayed in our home world. The other two slunk away like denebian slime devils," Khod said as he referred to the other two Starfleet officers that left during the Interspecies Academy program.

"Our prejudices of each other are clouding our views," Kirk admitted.

"Indeed, they are, Kirk, indeed they are," Kang said.

CHAPTER THIRTY-FOUR

TONG OMARTI FOUR. TONG CHAVERE. DAY THREE. STAR DATE 2919.7. 1505 Hours. January 27, 2267.

The rain had been coming down in buckets all day long. The forest had quieted down. Early in the morning, both he and Kang had gone hunting and gathering. Khod had stayed behind to watch Hawke and monitor his condition which had improved slightly since yesterday.

Kirk watched as the Klingons devoured another live Jambat. He felt revolted as he bit on a cooked leg of Jambat. Hawke was propped up against the wall slowly drinking some arrayal juice. Kirk took another bite of the leg.

Kirk scratched his face, three days of growth, and smelled his arm. He grimaced. Three days with no shower. He and Robert probably smelled like pigs now. The Klingons were just as messy a state as he was. Kang and Khod were emitting a strong powerful body odor which Kirk found revolting.

"You look dreadful, Jim," Hawke said smiling weakly.

"You look no better yourself, Robert."

Hawke put his right hand over his face, "I need a shave."

"And a bath," Kirk admitted.

"I stink like a pig," Hawke said.

"And I stink like a skunk," Kirk said as they both started to laugh.

Kang and Khod walked over to the two Starfleet officers. Kang's and Khod's uniforms were shredded and torn. Both had lost their boots and were walking barefoot. Both his and Robert's uniforms were in a similar torn, disheveled state.

Hawke's leg was braced in a splint. Kirk had a scar running along his chest from a near-miss with an Otay. The Otay were rodent-like creatures with sharp claws. Kirk and Kang had killed one today. They were a nuisance, but not nearly as dangerous as the Knabra or the Drakma.

Kirk rubbed his hands as he tried to keep warm. With the fur from the dead Knabra, they had fashioned outer garments. The flame kept them from freezing. The temperature on this planet went from cold, blustery nights to hot, humid days. The only thing they needed to do was survive and win. By surviving, they would deny the Imperium another holy war and it would give the Federation and the Starfleet time to prepare for a conflict with the Klingon Empire.

Kirk stood up and walked away from the fire and looked out at the rain-swept forest. He could feel the rain lash his outer garments. Kang walked over. "They will not be coming, Kirk."

"How can you be so sure?"

"The Harratay like you humans have a distinct odor. We are hunters, Kirk, and warriors."

"We humans were once hunters a thousand years ago, Kang. We humans are also warriors, but we have evolved."

"Evolved?" Kang said. "You Earthers consider yourselves to be superior, Kirk. The Empire is not a confused morass of aliens in a useless Federation."

"At least the Federation is not an Empire run by a dictatorial Emperor."

"An Emperor! The Empire hasn't had a real Emperor in two hundred years. Sompeck, Korath, and Kronk were the last three emperors."

"What about Kahmmur and Kassa?"

"They are Dura's stooges, Kirk. The House of Duras along with the House of Morath have for two hundred years hoisted on the empire illegitimate emperors in their quest to control the council and the chancellor. Oreck had assassinated Durek before the Border war. The Duras tried to install another illegitimate emperor but failed. They later succeeded when Oreck died. When Sturka beat Lornak in a duel for the chancellery after the border war, the Duras used the appointment of Kahmmaur and Kassa to keep the empire in line, preventing a Klingon civil war between Sturka and Lornak. The chancellor Kirk is the true power in the empire, not some patQ emperors," Kang explained.

"And Kang, now that I know that your Empire is now run by a chancellor, the Federation is not a confused morass of aliens. We have a president and a government body elected by the citizens of our Federation," Kirk pointed out as he and Kang walked back to the fire.

He could see that Hawke and Khod were just looking at each other.

"What is it, Robert?"

"I would love to get off this god-forsaken rock and kick Khod in the you know what it is," Hawke said exasperated. Kirk smiled. He couldn't agree more.

"Just wait, Hawke. When we meet again in battle, I will be victorious," Khod said.

"Yeah, right, Khod. I sent your sorry ass running back to the Empire the last time."

Khod looked at Kang. "I cannot wait until we have a war with the Federation, Kang."

"Patience, my friend. Along with Kor, Koloth, Kazanga, and Kumara, we will all have a taste of Federation flesh."

"That will be the day, Kang. We will be waiting. Never underestimate us," Kirk said defending Federation honor. Since 2256 and 2263, the Starfleet had quadrupled in size. The much-overstretched Constitution class originals had been joined by over one hundred Bonhomme Richard, Trojan/Explorer and Achenar class ships. Kirk sat down next to the fire. He was joined by Kang.

"Then it will be glorious, Kirk. I look forward to the day we meet in battle after this wretched Challenge," Kang said.

"I'll take the first watch, Jim. I cannot sit here uselessly," Hawke said. Nightfall was coming.

"Legs better."

"Not as much pain. I'll go easy," Hawke said as he grabbed his bow and arrow and his fighting staff. Slowly, Hawke hobbled off to the edge of their camp. Kirk sat himself up against a stone and put the fur cover over him, dozing off. Kirk started to remember.

STARFLEET ACADEMY. JUNE 6, 2252:

"Gary, listen to me, the last thing I need is having Bobby Hawke as a rival when I graduate," Kirk said exasperated as he and Gary swung through the academy grounds. They were heading for Hawke Hall, the academy mess hall. Despite the technology of food processing, Starfleet Academy, just like the Federation military academy, had a full staff of chiefs.

"Did you hear the latest Scuttlebutt?"

"Tell me," Kirk asked.

"Matthew Decker is still in command of Yorktown, I heard rumors that old Admiral Fitzgerald may reassign Decker to the Constellation in 2254 and former captain of the Class J starship Goliath. Von Holtzbrinck may replace him."

"Holtzbrinck, didn't he command the Sulaco, an old Mann class ship at the battle of Donatu Five?" Kirk asked.

"That's the one. I heard that Evan Foster of the Thomas Paine will replace Holtzbrinck."

Kirk remembered that the T.P was one of ubiquitous Miranda class starships. Two Mirandas were built for every Constitution.

Matthew Decker along with Robert Wesley had been two of his instructors at the academy. Wesley had taken an interest in him since he had joined the academy in the same way that Decker had shown a keen interest in Hawke.

"Didn't Robert's dad have a say in Matt Decker going from security to the command track, Gary?"

"Right on the money, Jim. Matt Decker was serving as chief of security aboard the old Class J Constitution back in 2240 before she was retired. After that, he was chief of security on Star base 6 until his transfer to the command track was approved in 2241."

Kirk recalled that Joe Hawke who was the old Class J's last captain and Admiral Jefferies had joined up with Robert April, the former captain of Tiberius that year to start work on the Constitution class design project.

"So, Gary, did you figure out which ship you might serve on after you graduate next year?"

"Enterprise, Constitution, Saladin, or Bozeman are my choices. Joe Hawke, Robert's dad, recently transferred from Constitution to the brand-new Essex. Fredrick Augenthaler his XO for many years may succeeded him as her commanding officer, but I think that Garth might get his way. And what are your choices, Jim?"

"Farragut, Enterprise, Constellation, and Intrepid," Kirk mentioned.

"So, it's Garrovick, Pike, Armstrong, or Satak. Tell me, Jim, why do you want to serve on the Intrepid?"

"A better way to understand the Vulcans, Gary, the ship is 100 percent Vulcan, unlike Eagle which is 90 percent Andorian. But most likely, I'll wind up on Farragut."

"Want to hear your rival's choices."

"Shoot."

"Robert put in for Constitution first but then he forgot about regulation 255. Then he put in for Farragut, but Captain Garrovick, like his dad, wasn't so pleased about that Kolvoord starburst maneuver he pulled off successfully on Federation day. Then he put in for Constellation, but rumor has it he might be going to Defiant under the command of David Aaron L.T Stone," Gary said.

L.T. is otherwise known as Left Tackle Stone, from his years as the top defensive tackle in the Starfleet academy football team history.

Stone was captain of the Defiant, the newest of the original Constitutions. He had replaced Commodore Anton Magill last year as her CO. Stone was a formable commander not known for his patience with new officers. Robert was in for a hell of a time under his command if rumors were true. Kirk could only smile. Robert had gotten the short end of the stick.

Kirk and Mitchell entered the expansive mess hall. Portraits of famous starship captains dominated the wall. Jonathan Archer, Alexander and Nicole Hawke, Travis Mayweather, Stuart Mann and William Larson, Malcolm Reed from the 22nd century, William Jefferies and Robert Justman, Torel Shran, Robert April, and Kevlar Garths—their portraits representing the 23rd century up to this point were on the walls. Joseph Edward Hawke's portrait was hung up in committee waiting for a vote.

Kirk and Mitchell went over to the food dispensary. Kirk grabbed a chicken soup and ham sandwich with black coffee. Walking quickly, he and Mitchell weaved by their fellow cadets.

Kirk watched as Jonathan Taylor Esteban was sitting with and talking to Carmen Ikeya, Clark Terrell.

John Blackjack Harriman was talking to Michael Walsh.

Turning to the right, he could see trouble. Phillip Waterston and Andovar Drake were talking with two starship captains Captain Lance Cartwright of the Indomitable and Captain Vaughn Rittenhouse. Andovar Drake gave him a nasty look.

"Mind if I join in?" Hansen said to Kirk.

"No problem, Barry," Mitchell said.

Barry Hansen Jr. was the son of Commodore Hansen, like his dad George Kirk had been assigned to the ill-fated Hell Spawn outpost set up to improve Federation-Harrata relations on the border. The outpost had been attacked by the Children of Lothar, wrecking all chances of full relations with the Imperium. Hansen was following in his footsteps and was soon to be posted at Star base 10.

Kirk and his party finally arrived at Hawke's table. Charlie Archer who reminded him of a slightly heavier version of Jonathan Archer was deep into his studies. Beautiful Samantha Reynolds with her long flowing black hair was peering over at Robert who was as thin as a rake and still a bit hyper in his mannerisms at times as he was reading an old-fashioned hardcover book. Kirk glanced at the title Subway systems of the World circa 2100.

"Bobby, do you mind if we join in?" Kirk asked.

Hawke looked up. "No problem, Kirk."

Kirk and his group sat down. Kirk took a bit of his sandwich and could see that Hawke was still ignoring him. Mitchell reached over and grabbed the book out of Hawke's hand causing an uproar as Samantha Reynolds cussed at them. "Don't you have any manners, Gary?" Samantha said angrily.

Hawke reached over and grabbed the book back from Mitchell almost tipping his bowl of soup over.

"I got his attention," Mitchell said to Kirk as Hawke angrily slammed the book on the table causing Charles Archer to mutter some curse words under his breath. Archer looked at Mitchell, Hanson, and Kirk. "Let's hope Mister Kobayashi Maru has something good to say because we all deserve an apology from Bannock's brats."

"Look who's talking the gang from the Exeter, the Exeter's three stooges," Hansen said.

Hawke turned to Charles and Samantha. "Enough already."

Kirk looked at Mitchell and Hanson. "Gary, Barry, enough of this nonsense."

Hawke looked at Kirk and folded his arms together. "Well? We are waiting, Jim," Hawke said clearly annoyed.

Kirk looked at Hawke, paused, and took a breath. "Bob, I want to call a truce. The last thing I need in the service is a rivalry between us. You gave as good as you got."

Hawke put the book down. "If you weren't so annoying, Jim, we could all be good friends, but you're shipping off at the end of this month. All three of us next semester has to do our required one year at command school."

"I know, Bob, it is well worth it."

Kirk suddenly heard a commotion and what sounded like a confrontation. An Andorian female cadet was getting harassed by Drake's gang. Jim Kirk leaped from his chair followed by Robert Hawke.

"Jim, don't," Mitchell pleaded.

"Robert, don't get involved," Samantha warned.

Hawke kissed her on the head. "Duty calls, dear."

Kirk and Hawke marched over to the table. Captain Cartwright and Captain Rittenhouse were sitting back and letting Drake and Waterston harass the Andorian female. Kirk stepped between Waterston and Drake as Hawke pulled her clear.

"Back off, Jim," Drake warned.

"No."

"Leave the female alone," Hawke added as he protected the Andorian.

Waterston moved up next to Hawke. "This is none of your business, Robert."

"It is mine if some decide to use prejudice against a fellow member of the Federation, Phillip."

Cartwright stepped up. "She doesn't want to serve on Indomitable. It is insubordination."

"I want a transfer. I am not happy serving on your ship, Commander. As a cadet, I have my rights," she said.

"She has to go where she is posted by the academy," Rittenhouse added.

"But isn't there a rule in Starfleet for serving academy cadets that if they are not happy with their original assigned ship, they can be reassigned?" Kirk said.

"Regulation 254, no cadet, officer, or crewmember can be allowed to remain onboard a ship, outpost, or Star base which he or she is having conflicts of interest with said officers and it is detrimental to the readiness of said unit," Hawke said quoting chapter and verse.

Rittenhouse and Cartwright exchanged glances. "We will get right to it, cadet."

"Cadet Thaylassa Shran, my father's portrait hangs on these walls. He is Torel Shran Ambassador to Earth. You both will be hearing from my father," Shran said as she pointed to her father's portrait.

Cartwright, Rittenhouse, Drake, and Waterston made a quick exit. Kirk soon found them joined by Mitchell and the rest of Bob's group.

Shran turned to Kirk and Hawke.

"I am Thaylassa Shran."

"James Kirk."

"Robert Hawke."

"So, I finally get to meet the infamous stack of books with legs and mister almighty himself," Shran said laying it in as she smiled.

"Tell me, Thaylassa, are you that big of a handful at times?" Kirk asked.

"You both can call me Thay," Shran said. "Yes, I am." Shran looked at the group. "My good fortune knows no end. I finally get a chance to meet the Exeter Three and Bannocks boys."

Kirk pointed to Mitchell and Hanson. "Thay, this is Gary Mitchell and Barry Hansen."

Hansen was beaming and Mitchell just smiled.

"And this is Samantha Reynolds and Charles Archer," Hawke said.

Samantha smiled. "You really got them, girl."

Thay could only agree. "I really did get them," Thaylassa said awkwardly.

Charles Archer who had been pretty mute up to this point said, "I think we have a problem."

Heads turned as everyone did double-takes at Archer's ambiguity.

"What problem, Charlie?" Hawke said puzzled.

"Where?" Kirk looked at Hawke equally puzzled.

Archer smiled. "For two hotshots, both of you are really dim."

Kirk pointed at himself. "Dim?"

Hawke did the same. "Oh, get over it, Charles."

"Charlie, what are you angling at?" Samantha said frustrated by Charles' lack of specifics.

"C'mon, Charles, what is on your mind?" Mitchell said.

Archer paused. "Today, we just witnessed a revolution. The unspeakable has happened," Archer said dramatically. "I never thought I would live to see the day that James Kirk and Robert Hawke would put aside their differences and rivalries and actually work together."

"Heaven help the Federation and the Starfleet if these two works together," Gary Mitchell said.

"I got an idea," Hansen said. "If you guys aren't busy, let's all go to the 602 club and get blasted."

"I agree," Shran said. "Tomorrow is the weekend."

Hawke paused. He had come to a point of decision.

"Robert, I think they are right. Time to put away your differences with Kirk. We have no more classes, so?" Samantha said.

"What do you say, Bob?" Kirk said as he put out his hand. Hawke grasped it and smiled. "What the hell."

Together, they all marched off.

PRESENT DAY. Day Three. 2000 hours.

Kirk felt a tapping on his foot. Shaking off his stupor, he could see Robert towering over him.

"You're up, Jim," Hawke said. Kirk could feel his bones aching as he got up. "Any sign of them?"

"No, Jim. None."

"Leg any better."

"Still hurts somewhat, but I'll live."

Kirk gathered his weapons as Hawke eased himself into a sitting position next to the fire.

Walking out to the edge of the camp, Kirk began his long vigil.

CHAPTER THIRTY-FIVE

January 29, 2267

Tong Chaevere. Day Four.

U.S.S Ptolemy-NCC 3801 orbiting Planetoid X. Star date 2920.1.

Sarek sat in the guest quarters provided by Captain Waterston. Sarek sat back and tried to meditate. He couldn't fathom the illogic of the Harrata calling for negotiations while the Challenge was still on.

The Harrata race was known to have an emotional excess of religious fanaticism. Like the Vulcans, they too had a schism in their ancient history. The great Crusade led to the Harrata race having a civil war.

Thousands of years ago, the Harratas who lost the war and followed Pong and the other twelve original deities left to form the Harrkonen Empire. Harrkonen translated into standard meant true or pure Harrata. The Harrkonen Empire was a thorn in the side of the Romulan Star Empire and it also acted as a bulwark against the rumored ISC.

Freedom probe one launched early in the twenty-third century had passed through Harrkonen space only to be wrecked by the ISC. The Harrkonens had sent the damaged remains back to the Federation, but the Empire wanted nothing to do with the Federation. Because the Federation had failed the so-called challenges, they thought the Federation was composed of weaklings and fools. The doorbell chimed.

"Who?'

"It is Torel Sarek."

"Come."

Hravishran th' Torelhi's, also known as Torlyk Shran, imposing figure entered his quarters. Shran was wearing the typical Andorian Ambassadorial cloths with the classic breastplate in front. On it was the old insignia of the Eagle which he had commanded back in the 2220s during the Second Federation-Harrata war.

Shran started to pace Sarek's cabin. Sarek could see he was clearly frustrated.

"What troubles you, Torel?"

"Captain Waterston, Sarek. I just can't place him, but I did encounter him once before."

"His father was Vice Commodore Arthur Waterston who commanded Outpost eight destroyed by the Romulans. He is a captain of little accomplishment and ability when one compares him to Captain James Kirk or Captain Robert Hawke," Sarek said.

"Any word from the Harrata, Sarek?"

"None since the last message we received. The second part of the challenge is always the longest and the most demanding of one's physical prowess."

"Tell me, Sarek, have you heard anything from Sybok or Spock?"

"Spock is on the Enterprise, Torel. He still disappoints me with his enlistment in Starfleet against my wishes and Sybok, he is continually stirring trouble up with his quest for Sha Ka Ree," Sarek said. "And what about your three children, Torel?"

"My oldest Hravishran ch' Shareli is with the First Imperial Guard corp. at Star base Alpha. We both know that my middle child Hravishran zh' Thaylassa is serving with Hawke on the Constitution. My youngest Hravishran sh' Tellessa, she is the governor of the Beneicia colony."

Shran was shortly interrupted by the intercom. Sarek got up and went over to the screen.

"Yes."

Captain Waterston with his wavy blond hair appeared. "Ambassadors, the Harrata have signaled that they want to resume negotiations."

"Agreeable, Captain, have the transporters standing by."

"Yes, Mister Ambassador." Waterston's image faded.

Shran looked at Sarek. "Another round of pointless negotiation leading nowhere, Sarek."

"Pointless. Yes, Torel, but somehow, we will find out a means to end the Imperium's illogic."

Torel nodded. It was pointless, but they would eventually find a reason for Harrata's insanity.

Sarek and Torel left the guest quarters.

Honor Blade near the Delta Construction sites. Star date 2919.5,

"Telemetry is coming back, Commander," Tal said.

"It is confirmed, Commander, two Klingon fleets of 100 ships each are right across the border."

"Then why don't they attack the Federation? It is a perfect opportunity," Bacakra said.

"Fool, the Klingon dogs also have challengers taking part in the Challenge," Tal admonished Bacakra.

"Tal is right, Bacakra, the Klingon dogs will follow the honorable way of their great warrior Kahless unless our lapdogs the Duras make an overt move at the council and take it over," Liviana reminded Bacakra. "Long-range sensors sweep, Tal."

"Yes, Commander," Tal said as he swept the sector. "No contacts."

"Do we have that Intel provided by the Tal shiar?"

"Yes, Commander," Tal said as he overlaid the screen. "This is the information stolen by the Tal Shiar agent from Star base 41."

On the main screen, an overlay of the entire sub quadrant lay before them. Livinia looked the screen over and decided. "Lay in a course for this system and activate cloak in the conservation mode."

"Commander, need I advise you that our orders do no cover for that section of Federation space? We are already deep in the outer marches alone and out of contact with our people. We may lose our route of escape if we penetrate too deep into Federation space."

"I understand, Tal, but our praetors Vrax and Gaius have ordered us on this mission. We need to ascertain the stratus of the Harrata and the rest of the Federation forces. The Empire needs a full accounting of this so we can decide if we are to go to war with the Federation."

"Commander, my younger brother Tel served as Valeria's first on the Van Hashem and they did not return."

"Understood, Tal, but Valeria overreached. She could have attacked more outposts along the line but instead, wound up penetrating deep into Federation space and was run down by the sister ship to the Enterprise. Remember, Tal, our duty is to the empire and it is our obedience to the Praetor. It is what makes us strong," Livinia said.

"Understood, Commander. Lay in a course for system C115, engage cloak alert condition two," Tal said.

Honor Blade shimmered out of existence.

January 28, 2267

STARFLEET HEADQUARTERS. ADMIRAL HERBERT SOLOW'S OFFICE. STAR DATE 2920.6:

Solow looked up as West continued to pace the floor. It was getting annoying. His analyst was spinning like a top before his eyes.

"Lieutenant West, please sit down," Solow said as he motioned to the chair in front of his desk. Patrick West stopped pacing and sat down at the admiral's request.

"What's bothering you, Lieutenant?" Solow asked.

"I wish my father hadn't retired and he instead of that deskbound paper pusher Hancock was in command of the Fourth Reserve."

"Hancock is a capable officer, Lieutenant, in 56 when the Klingons were losing the Four Years' War and tried to open up a second front. Hancock got the needed ships necessary to blunt the final Klingon offensive of the war," Solow said. "Hell, I was there with Jose Mendez who commanded Maine. I was in command of the London at the time."

"My dad never liked the Hawkes."

"C'mon, son, are you going to stoop to that petty rivalry that split the twenty founding families or are you going to forgive and go on with your life? Joseph Hawke is a fine man. Hell me and Justman served with him early in our careers. Look how quickly he nipped that conflict with the Shelliack corporate in 57. Because of that, Starfleet was able to prevent that second front from opening. Your father is a fine man and both he and Garth with the help of Hawke, Bannock, and the rest saved the Federation at Axanar and solidified it during the Four Years' War."

"But, Sir. I am entitled to my own opinion."

"Tell me what your opinion of James T. Kirk is." Solow asked.

"An overrated showoff, too young to be given command of a Heavy cruiser class starship. Like his fellow competitor, that dashing, swashbuckler Hawke, another overrated prima donna. They both should have stayed in command of the Miranda and the Sacagawea, which is better suited to officers of their age group," West finished.

"You are very harsh, Lieutenant," Solow said.

"Yes, Admiral Solow, but as an analyst, I see nothing but problems from these two."

"Even though Jim Kirk and Bob Hawke are two of the most highly decorated officers in their age group," Solow explained. "Did you check their service records before coming to this conclusion?"

"No."

"Check it; their records speak volumes about their careers, Lieutenant, any more Intel on that Romulan Warbird."

"No, Admiral, none."

The intercom buzzed.

"Who?"

"Ensign Sarah Dahbany, Admiral, I have some important news."

Solow mused, so his aide de camp had something important after all.

"Come in, Ensign."

The officer doors swooshed open and Sarah Dahbany stepped in. She had classic Yemenite Jewish features.

"What do you have to report, Ensign?"

"We have had an incursion into Federation space."

"Who? The Tholians, the Naussicans?" West asked.

"No, Sir, the Kzinti."

Solow shook his head. That the Kzinti would take advantage of the Challenge to launch a preemptive strike on the Federation and be so stupid in its timing surprised him.

"Ensign, what information do you have for us?" Solow asked.

"According to intelligence provided at main missions, the Kzinti launched a preemptive strike at the Weyland outpost line. Luckily for us, the starships Hood- NCC1703 under the command of Glen Barton, Dauntless-NCC 1697 under Captain Mark Turner, Indomitable-NCC 1685 under Captain Rudolph Alava, and the Scovil- NCC 1598 under Captain Arthur Kincaid intercepted them near Weyland One and obliterated fifty out of the sixty Kzinti vessels. Fleet Commander Comsol wants to give Barton a Silver Palm and the other captains will receive Starfleet Command honor roll citations."

Solow was relieved three of the ships were of the Constitution class type, one the less successful Pyotr Velikiy type. Along with the old Caracal-Palomar, Apache class cruisers, the Marklin class and Detroyat class destroyers and the Pyotr Velikiy class had proven to be less than successful and were dead ends in design and had been built only in limited numbers.

"Anything else?"

"Yes, Sir. Hood, Dauntless, and the Indi were severely damaged and had to return to Star base 11 for repairs. Scovil, Monitor, and Merrimac are holding security patrol in Kzinti space."

"There goes Stone's command," West mused. With Star base 11 designated as a fallback for all non-assigned ships during the Harrata conflict, Eleven was going to be filled to the maximum with ships. And that meant other star bases would have to fill in the slack. Alpha, Trafalgar, 41, and 38 already had fleets assigned to the conflict and were unavailable.

"We need to report to the president our intelligence," Solow said. "Good job, Ensign."

"Thank you, Sir."

Solow, West, and Dahbany left Solow's office.

CHAPTER THIRTY-SIX

Tong Omarti Four. Tong Chavere, Star date 2920. 10 1200 hours.

Kirk followed Khod and Kang as they trudged through the shattered forest that had been obliterated by the Knabra two days prior. Leaving Robert behind to watch the camp, they had set off to once and for all finish off the three surviving champions. Kirk scratched himself. Three days of this and he felt terrible. His uniform was in tatters, both of his boots were gone, and he hadn't shaved in three days.

The Klingons were in an equally desperate state, but Kang and Khod weren't showing it. The sun was relentless as they made their way toward the Harrata camp. For all he knew, the Harrata were out. Once and for all, they would end this part of the Challenge alive or dead. Kirk could feel his feet sink in the mud. The ground still had not dried up from the storm last night. All three of them had fanned out and were within visual distance of each other.

"Alarm! Humass! Klingonasse! Attar!" Out of the woods, three raggedy Harrata burst forth heading for Kang. Kirk took off and joined up with Khod. Kang had knocked two of them over, buying time for him and Khod to engage the Harrata. It was the reverse of their second day on the planet. The tables were turned. Khod quickly

441

engaged a Harrata captain. Kirk found himself faced by Fakari. Fakari had a maniacal look on his face. The calm, older Harrata he had spoken to at the feast of champions had become an animal. Fakari swung his spear at Kirk as he evaded the Harrata, using the fighting staff that Robert had given him.

"You will not fulfill the prophecy, Kirk!" Fakari yelled at him. Kirk, using the staff, blocked another thrust. Kirk pivoted and hit the Harrata in the back, knocking him over. The Harrata captain rolled down the hill. Kirk lost his balance and tumbled down the hill. Kirk rolled out and quickly tried regaining his footing as the Harrata captain dropped his spear and tried to choke him. Kirk quickly flipped him over. Reaching for the spear, Fakari punched him in the face. Kirk reeled over. He looked to see the Klingons charging Fakari. They were yelling Klingon oaths. Khod stopped to pick Kirk up. "We are victorious, Kirk. Two dead Harratay."

Kirk could see Fakari disappearing into the bush. Kang walked up.

"We'll finish him tomorrow, Kirk, let us celebrate our victory."

Kirk nodded. "I agree, Kang."

They all headed back to the camp.

"First officer's log. Star date 2920. 11. Commander Spock recording. We have entered day four of the Tong Chavere. We patiently await the return of Captain Kirk."

"First officer's log. Star date 2920. 11. Lieutenant Commander Shran recording. Four days and still no word from the captain. We maintain a silent vigil on Constitution. We all hope and pray for Captain Hawke's safe return."

U.S.S ENTERPRISE-NCC 1701 ORBITING TONG OMARTI FOUR. STAR DATE 2920.12:

Spock watched from the science station as the enormous Lothar GaZ swung away and headed for the Klingon battle cruisers, stopping next to the Klingons. Two tractor beams lashed out grabbing two of the Harrata battle cruisers, the Alas Ja Booma and the Gomesh Al Antarie and swinging them away from the Suvwl and the Vorcha. The deadly cutting beams lashed out striking the ships as the transporters were activated. Within minutes, both ships were dead hulks. Without a pause, the Lothar GaZ jumped to warp.

The monster ship was towing both hulks to the Lothar system, where they would rest amidst the other dead ships of the graveyard. The GaZ would be back before the day was through.

"Well, Spock, what are you contemplating?" McCoy said

"The ends of the Tong, Doctor. The Harrata are more irrational than humans. They slaughter their own people when they fail and issue illogical challenges."

"At least, for once, I could agree with you, Spock. This Challenge, this test of champions, is starting to wear thin on me."

"What about the crew?"

"They are all on edge, Spock. They are worried about Jim. If he doesn't survive, then we are all finished."

"And Constitution?" Spock said.

"Doc Russell tells me that the crew is in the same state of anxiety. I just wish we could be done with this circus and go home already," McCoy grumbled.

"Circus?" Spock asked.

"Didn't you ever go to Ringling Brothers or Big Apple or Cirque de Soliel, Spock?"

"No, clowns and acrobats do not interest me, Bones."

"They are a form of entertainment, Spock. You never seem to want to have a good time, Spock. You are always too wrapped up in your work," McCoy responded clearly irritated by Spock's response.

"Doctor, I thank you for your concern. But if I don't stay wrapped up in my work, we may not survive."

"You have a point, Spock. I'll see you later," McCoy said as he departed the bridge. Spock turned around and resumed his research at the science station.

TONG OMARTI FOUR. TONG CHAVERE DAY FOUR. Star date 2921. 18. 2015 hours. January 29, 2267.

Kirk sat alongside Hawke as Kang and Khod bellowed out Klingon songs of war and glory. Robert translated the words into the standard for his benefit. The songs clearly reflected the culture. Music was always a way to ascertain the way of the people and culture behind it.

The campfire crackled and sputtered as it lighted up the four figures sitting next to it.

Kang came over to him. "Kirk, Hawke, join us. We must celebrate our victory over the Harratay."

Kirk looked at Kang. "I would like to celebrate, Kang, but one Harrata still remains at large."

"And we will vanquish him tomorrow, Kirk."

"And what about you, Hawke? You used to participate with us during your stay in the home world," Khod asked.

"Khod, I'm just too tired and irritable. The leg still bothers me. And I speak for us all. I wish this damn Challenge would be over already," Hawke responded. "So, Jim and I could get back to our mandate of exploring the galaxy at large."

"And Khod and I could return to our duties of protecting the empire," Kang said.

Kirk got up. "I will take the first watch, Kang."

Kang nodded as he and Khod went back to singing Klingon songs. Robert however had curled up next to the fire and had gone to sleep.

Kirk stared out into the darkness. The alien sound of the various creatures filled his ears.

One item dominated his thoughts. His thoughts drifted to the Enterprise, Spock, Bones, Scotty, and the rest of his crew. He was never going to give her up, never lose the Enterprise. He loved Enterprise more than his previous commands, the two Miranda classes Starships Oxford and Lydia Sutherland. Hartford was an old Baton Rouge class cruiser and his little Sacagawea, his primary command, was Hermes class scout.

His third command was the Lydia Sutherland that had a comical history. Starfleet had built two of her sister ships prior to her construction in 2250. The Lydia and the Sutherland, the dockyard boss at Utopia Planetia suggested that they combine both names together to form the Lydia Sutherland.

The Oxford was a whole other story. Oxford had the misfortune of being plagued with dockyard disasters and had been shoddily constructed at Riverdale Shipyard. He later had to transfer off Oxford to the old Hartford. Oxford had needed complete reconstruction.

Her first two captains had died tragically on various missions and Carmen Ikeya, her present commanding officer, was hoping to transfer out by the year's end. Carmen just didn't like the feel of the ship.

Kirk stared out into the darkness and wondered what Carol Marcus was doing right now. He hadn't seen her since he took command of the Enterprise.

Kirk paused and realized that this had been the first time he had thought about Carol in years.

Sometimes, he envied Robert and Samantha.

Starfleet had decided to team up both ships when necessary and at shore leave together. The last he had heard was eight months prior at Star base 27 when Robert was given a competency hearing on his readiness to command the Constitution thanks to an unspecified event. Robert had survived and avoided a court-martial.

Kirk wrapped the fur closer to him. This wasn't one of the worst planets he had ever been to. But it ranked up there as one of the worst ever.

If both he and Robert survived, it would be a first, but how long until the Harrata issue their next Challenge? And two more unfortunates would have to go through this ordeal. One way or the other, these challenges had to end. The Harrata had to listen to reason, but how was he going to get through to them?

Kirk could hear some footsteps behind him. Carrying a torch, Kang walked up to him. "You stand relieved, Kirk."

Kirk got up. Time on his watch had passed quickly.

"Thank you, Kang."

Kang looked at Kirk. "Tomorrow's victory."

Kirk could only nod in agreement as he silently walked off back to the camp. He still hadn't been able to get the old voice recorder working. When he got back to the Enterprise, he would let Spock take a crack at it.

Hiding in the woods, Fakari watched the cycle of watches of the Humass and the Klingonasse. There was no way he could kill Kirk or the two Klingons, but the one named Hawke was vulnerable due to his injury. He would get his revenge and prevent the fulfillment of the prophecy. Silently, Fakari made his way away from the camp. He had to prepare for tomorrow.

TONG OMARTI FOUR. TONG CHAVERE. STAR DATE 2922. 5. DAY FIVE. 1400 hours. January 30, 2267.

Kirk slowly made his way through the forest. He was making a wide sweep near the camp.

Kang and Khod were making flanking maneuvers near the Harrata camp. Robert remained behind to watch the camp for obvious reasons. And he had a feeling that the remaining Harrata, Flolitor Commander Fakari, would go after Robert. He was obviously the choice. Kirk immediately swung himself closer to the camp. If Fakari was here, he would soon know.

Floli C Fakari watched the camp closely. The other three had left. He could see Hawke hobbling. Looking into the cave, he thought he spotted an eye or two peering out of the darkness. The Drachmas were clearly agitated. Fakari knew just what he needed to do. Chiss would be proud of him.

Robert Hawke propped himself on a rock overlooking the cave and the forest. Very soon, he hoped to be back on his ship and with his beloved crew. Dirty, tired, and still in a little pain from his leg, he couldn't wait to get back to his ship, shave, wash up, take a shower, and have Doc tend to his wound.

In a few days, if all went well, his ship would be at Star base 11 for a long overdue shore leave, upgrade, and overhaul. Stone his old commander had promised him a month due to the amount of work his ship needed. His crew had more than earned their keep. Hawke lay back for a moment contemplating the scenario when his solitude was shattered. "Chissary!" came the cry.

A bed-ragged Harrata was charging up the hill. Staggering up, Hawke grabbed his fighting staff. If it wasn't for his leg. "Jim!" Hawke yelled out as the Harrata slammed into him knocking his fighting staff clear, slamming into the ground. Hawke desperately tried to fight back. Fakari pummeled him with punches. Fakari hit Hawke across his jaw and the Starfleet captain went limp. Grabbing the Humass, Fakari dragged Hawke down the path. Soon, he would have victory.

"Jim!" Kirk faintly picked up Hawke's voice.

"Kang! Khod!" Kirk yelled out. No response came back. Kirk dashed back to the camp. Making his way into the clearing, he could see Fakari dragging Hawke toward the cave. Three single eyes appeared out of the blackness. The Drachmas were up and Fakari was going to sacrifice Robert to even the odds.

"Fakari! Don't!" Kirk yelled.

"You can't stop me, Kirk! I will not spend eternity in Lothar's grasp! The prophecy must not be fulfilled!" Fakari yelled back as he dragged Hawke closer to the cave's opening.

Kirk ran forward and slammed into Fakari, throwing the Harrata to the ground. They were too close to the cave. Kirk staggered up and grabbed the now-groggy Hawke and pulled him away from the cave just as some tentacles flew out of the cave searching for victims.

Kang followed by Khod burst through the forest into the clearing. Launching their spears, the Klingons hit one of the Drachmas that let out a cry of pain as it disappeared into nothingness. Fakari wasn't so fortunate. His childhood nightmare of being swallowed by the Drachmas was coming true.

The old Harrata monster story of the Drachmas plaguing Harrata children's nightmares was coming to pass. Fakari let out a scream as a tentacle grabbed him and dragged him into the cave. The last thing he saw was a single eye and an open mouth full of death. He screamed.

Kirk, Kang, and Khod heard Fakari's death scream. They remained in silence until Hawke, who was still lying flat on his back, tugged the remains of Kirk's uniform pants. Kirk looked down to see Robert giving a faint smile. "We did it, Jim." Kirk bent over. "We did, Bob. Just hang on, old friend," Kirk said as he grasped Robert's hand.

Seconds later, the air was filled with a roar. A Harrata shuttle appeared overhead and landed near them. Hittay and two Harrata soldiers of Lothar's Legion exited the shuttlecraft. Kirk, Kang, and Khod walked over to the Harrata.

"Only three, where is the fourth?" Hittay asked. "Dead."

Kirk responded, "Bob, give us a sign."

Hawke raised his arm, put the thumbs-up signal, turned toward them, and gave a faint smile.

Hittay pulled out his communicator. Within minutes, the air was rendered by sounds of transporters materializing. Kirk turned to see McCoy, Spock, and Chapel approach him. Nearby, Doc Russell, Nurse McCall, T'Pau, and Shran were hovering over Hawke.

The Klingons however had broken out in traditional war songs again.

McCoy grumbled as the Klingons continued their celebration. He never cared for the bombast of Klingon opera or Klingon ceremonial music. It was too militaristic for his taste.

"You look like hell, Jim," McCoy said as he ran his medical scanner over Kirk and checked his medical tricorder.

"Feel like it, Bones."

"It is fortunate that you have survived, Jim. Starfleet cannot afford to lose an officer of your talents," Spock added.

"Very funny, Spock," McCoy added.

Kirk turned around to see Doc Russell looking at him.

"Did you set Robert's leg?" Russell asked.

Kirk nodded.

"Good job, Doctor Kirk."

"And Robert's condition, Doc."

"He'll survive, Jim. He got a slight concussion from the blow he took in the head and with a little stitching and rest, he'll be on his feet in no time at all."

Shran and T'Pau came over as Russell and Hawke disappeared.

"I can't thank you enough, Jim," Shran said happily. It was the first time he had seen Robert's XO smile in a long time.

"Captain Hawke is a valuable asset to Starfleet. His loss like Kirk's would be a tragedy," T'Pau said.

"What is it with you, Vulcans and assets?" McCoy grumbled. "First, Spock, now T'Pau. Your captain is a human being, young lady. Not an asset."

T'Pau looked at Spock.

"I stand corrected. I am most appreciative of Captain Hawke's and Captain Kirk's fortune."

T'Pau said correcting her vocabulary.

"Are you satisfied, Bones?" Spock said blandly.

"Yes, Spock."

"Hate to break up the party, ladies and gentlemen, but I need a shower," Kirk said as he scratched his dirty, ragged uniform flipping open the communicator that Spock had given him.

"Kirk to Enterprise."

"Is that you, Captain?" came Scotty's happy voice.

"It's me, Mister Scott, three to beam up."

"Aye, Sir."

Kirk smiled as he watched Tong Omarti four disappeared from view. For all he cared, he never wanted to visit this place again.

CHAPTER THIRTY-SEVEN

U.S.S. Constellation- NCC 1017, flagship of FSF Charlie near the Gibraltar Star system. STAR DATE 2922.9.

Matthew Decker sat in his quarters. He had a moment of solitude from the demands of being a Starfleet Commodore.

He had come a long way from his days at Starfleet Academy, specializing in security. His first assignment out of the academy had been a rare posting to an antique from the last century. The old NX class ship Avenger had been returned to service in haste during a brief border flare-up with the Tholians. As fortune would have it, the diplomats resolved it. With that, he transferred to Hera. The old Icarus ship had just been recently lost at Caron. Nothing remained forever. Decker thought.

After serving as Class J Constitution's Security Chief from 2239-40 before that ship was decommissioned, Joseph Hawke was recommended that he transfer from security to command which went through in 2241. During that interim period, he served on various starships and outposts as temporary (aka replacement) first officer in the reserve first officer's pool.

In 2244, he was at Donatu Five commanding the old Patton, a relic from the Romulan War which commanded until 2246. In 2246, he served as Chief of Security on Star base Four before transferring to the brand-new Constellation under Ran Armstrong as first officer. when the massacre at Tarsus had happened, Ran had gotten sick and he was in temporary command of Constellation during that crisis. Constellation, Constitution, and Enterprise had been the only ships fast enough to reach Tarsus.

Transferring off Constellation, Decker with his brevet captaincy and full commanders rank commanded three survey vessels over the next three years. They were the Bougainville, Cook, and Magellan. Later, Decker taught at the Academy and was given command of Yorktown which was filled in as a training ship during his stay at the Academy and was being overhauled during that period. At Starfleet Academy, along with classmates Jacque LaLiberté and Robert Wesley, all served as instructors. In 2254, Admiral Fitzgerald made his captaincy permanent, surprising everyone, and he was given command of Constellation.

With that done, Matt refocused on the image of Willard Decker. A few months earlier, he had been an adjunct to Admiral Brock. Now, he was XO on the Miranda class Cruiser Boston-NCC 142, under the command of Captain Fox.

Willard had wanted XO duty on a Constitution class starship, but Starfleet couldn't build those ships fast enough. The Mirandas however were the next best thing. Decker could count his luck. Captain Fox along with Captain Reynolds of the Soyuz were the two best upcoming captains of Soyuz, Miranda class ships. Miriam Fox had previously served with him on the Constellation. Will was sitting in his quarters on the Boston.

"So, Will, how are you liking the job of XO?" Decker asked.

"Never had so much work to do," Willard moaned.

"A good XO knows how to keep the captain focused and doesn't become a yes man. I was lucky the two have had two outstanding females Anne and Hiromi, Will. It sucks that Anne retired from the fleet. I was lucky enough to find Hiromi when I became a full captain instead of a brevet when I was given Constellation in 54. Hiromi was serving as Second officer, Charles Osgood. Ran Armstrong's old XO had retired. So, I promoted her to first. She knew the ship and the crew, Will. Ran Armstrong was then promoted to Rear Admiral and commanded the Second Reserve Fleet before being assigned to the council."

Will Decker looked at his father. His father had some interesting tales, he thought, and asked, "Didn't Robert Hawke follow your example? But Jim Kirk didn't."

"Bob like Miriam are two of my protégées, Will. We all know what happened with the Sargon. But I warned Jim that he and Gary were too alike. At least Robert and Thaylassa are opposites. That is why Starfleet accepted Shran as XO on Constitution and Gary had to become second on Enterprise yielding to Spock."

"Have you heard from mom, Captain Dad," Will said as he reverted to his old familiar tone.

"Mom is doing fine. She's hoping to meet me at Star base 27 within a month," Decker said as he thought about his wife of many years.

Her father Neil Hopkins along with Robert Fox and Sarek and Shran were the greatest Federation Ambassadors of the last half-century. Will had been born a year later in 2241.

Willard had graduated from Starfleet Academy in 2262.

He was looking forward to shore leave on Star base 27. Constellation and Constitution home ported at that base since their commissioning.

At the other end of the Klingon border, Enterprise and Lexington since their commissioning were home ported at Star base 12.

For all he knew, maybe Jim Kirk and the Enterprise would stop by. He always considered Jim to be a good friend, but Bobby Hawke was almost family. Not many security officers ever became starship captains. Along with medical officers, they were the least likely to get a command. Command track cadets followed by engineering and science officers always stood a better chance at the center seat.

The intercom buzzed. "Hold on, Will."

Will Decker nodded.

"Decker here."

Will's image faded and was replaced by his XO Hiromi Takesheweda.

"Matt, we have a Spedy class scout ship identified as the Noob approaching us at high warp. She has white running lights."

Decker knew what the white stood for. "She's the same ship that contacted Samantha Reynolds' Soyuz a few days ago."

Hiromi nodded. "The same one, Matt."

"Bring FSF Charlie to yellow alert and have Lieutenant commander Regina MC Catskill contact the Ari, I need to speak to Harry Morrow immediately."

"Understood. Takesheweda out." Hiromi's image faded and was replaced by his sons.

"Something up?" Willard asked his father.

"Yes, Will, got to go."

"Boston out."

"Constellation signing off," Decker said as he sped from his cabin.

Matthew Decker sat in the high-backed command chair on the bridge of Constellation. To his right was Takesheweda and to his left Doctor Rosenhaus who had replaced his old doctor Lennon a few months earlier. On the main screen was the image of a man of similar age and experience. Harry Morrows' mustache was standing out.

"Harry, I want you to take charge of the fleet and rendezvous with the rest of the FSF."

"Matt, remember what happened the last time with Sam Reynolds. The Star force almost laid a trap for XY 75847," Morrow warned.

Decker nodded. Harry was right. But he really doubted the Star Force would pull the same act again. It would be a bad strategy.

"Good point, Harry. But the fleet is yours. We'll meet you at the Gaugamela star system as planned."

"Don't get foolish, Matt."

Decker smiled. "You know I won't. Constellation out," Decker said as the screen was replaced by open space.

"Mister Tellaya," Decker said to Constellation's female Andorian navigator. "Plot a wide-sweeping course to clear the fleet, Mister

Stoll, warp four," Decker said to Constellation's male Vulcan helm officer.

Stoll nodded silently and engaged the course.

Constellation swung to starboard to port Excelsior and her three other heavies held formation as Constellation cleared Excalibur Intrepid and Defiant.

Matt Decker could see Harry Morrows, Ari, and three other Constitutions in formation. As Constellation cleared the last of Charlie, Ann Toroyan Kongo as well as the Yamato, Asimov, and Tori, swung into view.

At the very end of the fleet, Fleet Captain Mary Ann Rice's brand new Achenar's, the Achenar, Sol, Jupiter, and Rigel Kenataurus, appeared.

All four ships were barely a year old. Their untouched, gleaming hulls, brand spanking new compared to the Constellation's well-worn looks.

Constellation left the fleet behind. Moments later, Constellation jumped to warp. Seconds after Constellation disappeared into warp space, the remaining Heavy cruisers of FSF Charlie jumped to warp.

MINUTES LATER:

Constellation closed in on the minute Harrata scout vessel.

Decker watched from his command chair as the small Speedy class scout ship came into view.

"Commander, the bridge is yours," Decker said as he turned the bridge over to his XO.

Takesheweda nodded and replaced him in the captain's chair.

CONSTELLATION TRANSPORTER ROOM TWO:

Decker watched as a plain-looking Harrata female Nav Commander stepped down from the transporter alcove. She handed him a tape.

"For your leaders," the nav commander said in plain English.

"Nav Commander, do Captains Kirk and Hawke live?" Decker asked.

"They live," Nav Commander said as she returned to the transporter alcove.

That was all Decker needed to know. "Whenever you are ready, Mister Running Bear."

"Yes, Sir."

The Harrata female faded from view.

Decker hit the intercom. "Bridge any contacts."

Takesheweda's voice came back, "No, Matt."

"Set a course for Gaugamela warp six."

"Aye, Sir."

Constellation jumped to warp as the Noob returned to Harrata space.

CHAPTER THIRTY-EIGHT

SECOND INTERLUDE

FIRST STRIKE FORCE-TASK FORCE ALPHA. GAUGAMELA STAR SYSTEM. STAR DATE 2922.12.

GEORGE KIRK'S QUARTERS:

Fleet Captain George Kirk flipped through the pile of tapes he had on his desk. Being chief of Staff wasn't easy. It was like being a XO again magnified by one hundred. He could just envy his son Jim.

Jim only had one ship to manage. He had one hundred and fifty not including the Eighth and Ninth fleets as well as the Fourth Reserve to worry about.

But he had a job to do and he would do it. He had heard nothing from the Harrata since the first part of the Challenge. He worried like all parents would. He had contacted Winona, Sam, and Aurelian about the Challenge. None of them had taken it well considering the last two times the Federation had failed. The doorbell buzzed.

"Who?"

"It's Joe George."

Admiral Joseph Hawke entered George's cabin. He could see his old friend poring over a set of tapes at his desk. Next to his desk were ship models of the Kelvin, Constitution, Enterprise, and the old Drexler class ship the Ames.

George could see that Joe was smiling.

"Good news."

Joe nodded. "Matt Decker rendezvoused with the Noob. He sent the rest of Charlie to Gaugamela. Jim and Robert are still alive."

Kirk jumped out of his seat and he and Joe exchanged high fives.

"I heard a rumor that one captain was injured."

"That's my son, George. He had his leg broken and a mild concussion but thank the lord for your son, Jim. He pulled him through." Joe had a tear on his cheek. "They both might have been trouble at the academy, but Robert has exceeded my expectations."

"And so has Jim." If he hadn't nearly lost his life at Hell Spawn, he would have been there for his son's graduation.

"Jim was always trouble, Joe. Always getting into trouble despite being a genius."

"And so was Robert, never could sit still for a moment. Always running off and not listening to me and Dina."

George nodded. Those two were so alike. No wonder they worked so well together as starship captains.

"George, I am reassigning Rachel Hunter's squadron, the Aerfen, Trident, Will o wisp, and Courier be needed by Admiral Connors, sector 5 at the Romulan neutral zone. With that Bird of prey somewhere in the corridor, Connors wants to play it safe. Hahn has ordered that the Fifth fleet be mobilized just in case. I argued with Mattea over it. But she said that since I now had Charlie with those additional Constitutions, Hunter was needed elsewhere," Kirk said.

"She's a fine CO, Joe, one of the best."

The Kirov's red alert siren sounded off.

Joe hit the switch.

The silver-haired form of Commander Nicolas Sherman appeared.

Nick Sherman was reliable and somewhat boring. He was Scheer's XO. He was fourth in command after him and George Kirk and Fleet Captain Scheer in the command structure of the Kirov.

"The Paladin has picked up two Harrata battle groups. Echo and Foxtrot, they are heading our way."

"Two?"

"Yes, Admiral."

"Get the fleet out of the system. And bring us into a parallel course. Get me Robau and Harari."

"Yes, Sir."

George and Joe sped out of Kirk's cabin.

By the time both officers arrived on the bridge, two senior admirals were on the split-screen. One was a bald Starfleet officer of Cuban descent who had age lines showing. George immediately recognized his old CO from the Kelvin, Richard Robau.

The other was in her early fifties. Her once-long hair had been trimmed and showed traces of grey. Michaela Harari, former CO of the Hood in the late 2240s and early 2250s, had been Hoods first CO.

"Richard, Michaela, what is your status?"

Harari shook her head. "We are pursuing Battle Group Alpha. They are heading for the Hell Spawn system. There is no way we can support you, Joe. We'll never arrive in time," Harari admitted.

Robau then spoke, "We are pursuing Battle Group Golf near the Islandana system. We are trying to head them off before they reach Star base 41."

Joe looked at George. "And the Fourth Reserve."

George shook his head. "At least another week according to Admiral Hancock."

"And the Seventh."

"Hahn wants to keep the Seventh on standby at 27. Along with the Sixth at 12, both fleets are needed to watch the Klingon and Romulan borders."

"Admiral," came the voice of Kirov's Andorian science officer Commander Zarick th' Chan.

"Echo has turned our way. Foxtrot is heading for the Federation-Klingon neutral zone. Two Klingon battle groups are moving to intercept."

Joe could feel the gears in his head churn away. Echo was to delay them. So, the Harrata could finally engage the Klingons in one Challenge battle.

"We better get going. Good luck, Joe," Robau said as his image faded. Michaela just nodded as her image faded to be replaced by the stars on the main screen.

"Tactical," Joe called out.

On the tactical image, two masses were heading in different directions. Across the border, two Klingon fleets were stirring.

"All ships hold formation until contact and then attack opposite numbers," Joe ordered.

The First Strike force closed on the Harrata Battle group Echo.

HONOR BLADE:

Livinina had been studying the reports coming in. They had gone to C155 and found nothing. Now they were heading under cloaks for the system designated Gaugamela.

Chavernack couldn't understand the Terran's predilection for name systems after Earth battles. Some human called Alexander the Great had defeated a king named Darius many eons ago. There was even a star system called Midway which was supposedly between the two outer marches frontiers. Named after some obscure Terran sea battle, she could thank the elements that Romulans were much more practical. She never understood humans. They were illogical, overly passionate, and prone to extreme excess and yet they could join races like the Vulcans, Andorians, and Tellerites into a Federation. Chavernack closed her eyes for a moment. Seconds later, the alert siren went off and her quarters were bathed in a green glow. Alert condition one had sounded.

"Commander Chavernack, report to control central!" came Tal's urgent voice.

"What is it, Tal?"

"Two Harrata battle groups are heading our way, Commander."

"Rig for a silent approach."

"Yes, Commander."

Chavernack left her quarters in a hurry, arriving control central moments later. She looked at the screen.

"One Harrata battle group is heading for the empire. The other is maintaining station within two shevs of the other commander," Tal said.

"Commander, another contact."

"Who or what, Tal?"

"A Federation fleet, one hundred and fifty ships, could be the Ninth, Eighth, or the infamous FSF."

"Tactical."

Converging on her lone ship, she could see the Harrata Battle group and the Federation fleet converging on her lone command. They were right in the center.

"May the elements preserve us," Chavernack said. "Control officer, begin Keras Evasive pattern Thalus once the Federation fleet hits."

"Yes, Commander."

"Tal, sound off names as they come. We will need this information if we survive for our praetors."

"Yes, Commander," Tal said.

Honor Blade suddenly weaved and dodged as she evaded the massive fleet. Invisible, she swung through the mass of Federation vessels. Tal began chanting names as they came in. "Kirov, Star League, Federation, Compactat, Unificatum, Defender, Roger Young, Arizona, Divine Wind."

Chavernack watched as the rumored Federation battle cruisers and dreadnoughts slipped by. The empire had nothing comparable.

"Apache, Sioux, Zulu, Samurai, Ninja, Franklin Delano Roosevelt, William J. Clinton, Barack Obama, Theodore Roosevelt, Hill Street, Jefferson Heights, Division, South Ferry," Tal continued.

Honor Blade swung to the center of the Federation fleet. They were lucky so far. Just a little bit more and they would be free of the enormous fleet.

"They haven't picked us up."

"No, Commander."

Suddenly, the familiar yet classic form of a Federation Heavy cruiser loomed out of the masses. The ship was heading straight for them. Chavernack could make out the name—U.S.S Constellation-NCC 1017 on her primary hull.

"Emergency maneuvers five!" Chavernack yelled out.

Honor blade swung violently over the cruiser's primary hull. She had just cleared the primary hull, but the circular form of the starboard nacelle loomed up.

"Emergency evasive, cloaks emergency reserve!"

Honor Blade contacted the Constellation's starboard nacelle. The shields protecting the nacelle flared as the Blade bounced off the nacelle. Constellation's nacelle began to sag under the impact.

The nacelle flared red hot.

CONSTELLATION:

Matt Decker watched with eager anticipation as his ship one of one hundred and fifty closed to engage the battle group.

The proximity alarm suddenly went off. "Collision Alert! Collision Alert!"

"Masada."

"Unknown contact bearing."

"Commodore, something just bounced off our starboard nacelle!" Constellation's chief engineer Shoshanna Najjar warned.

Decker felt the Constellation suddenly drop out from him. The lights flickered. Something had hit his ship. Constellation plunged toward the Excalibur.

EXCALIBUR:

"Captain. The Constellation!" Terise Lo Brutto warned as she turned from her console facing him.

"Collision Alert! Collision Alert" came the proximity alarm.

"Mister Ogden, Z- 10.000, full power decent!" Harris yelled.

Howard Ogden expertly manipulated the Helm controls.

Excalibur swung further down as Constellation's secondary hull bounced off the rear end of the primary hull scraping and denting the rear primary hull and the impulse engines.

Harris held on for dear lives as the battered Excalibur plunged clear of her sister ship.

"Port your helm, Ogden! Level off. Damage reports all decks!"

Excalibur wobbled and began to drift.

CONSTELLATION:

Decker had grabbed the helm console. Quickly and expertly, he punched in some commands into the Helm. Constellation's secondary hull had bounced off Excalibur's primary hull. Swinging to starboard, the form of the Intrepid loomed up on the main screen. Decker hit the helm controls again as Constellation's secondary hull contacted with the Intrepid hanger bay, smashing her aft running light and stoving in the hanger bay doors.

INTREPID:

"Collision alert! Collision Alert!" came the proximity alarm.

Satak looked at his wife, first officer, and helm officer.

"Hard to Starboard!"

T'Lena activated the controls.

Intrepid swung away just as Constellation's secondary hull impacted on the Intrepid shuttle bay.

Satak felt his entire command shutter as Constellation banged along Intrepid now mangled shuttle bay.

DEFIANT:

Thomas Blair watched in disbelief.

First Constellation, then Excalibur, and now Intrepid were damaged. Blair had swung Defiant clear of Intrepid avoiding any mishaps.

He watched as the rest of the First Strike Force continue its way to engage the Harrata Battle group.

In his long career in Starfleet, he had never witnessed such a calamity. Prior to commanding Defiant, he had commanded the Coventry class frigate, the Dahlgren, for nearly ten years.

He had been promoted to captain at age forty, after serving as XO aboard the Hornet under Captain Arthur Reynolds. He was now the fourth person to command the Defiant. She had been launched in 2246 along with the Lexington, Yorktown, and the Excalibur, and Exeter had all been finished that year. Her first captain was Captain

Commodore Anton Jarv McGill who had been succeeded by David Aaron L.T Stone. Stone had then been replaced by Captain Josiah Serling in 2260. He had replaced Serling in 2265.

"Ensign Hogawa, signal Kirov. Constellation, Intrepid, and Excalibur were damaged in multiple collisions with an unknown object. Defiant will remain behind to aid."

"Yes, Sir, message sent."

"Mbunga, get damage control and medical parties ready. We are going to assist."

Commander Kamau Mbunga nodded.

Blair walked up to the science console where Lieutenant Commander Erin Sutherland was busy analyzing the data.

"Damage report."

"Constellation's Starboard nacelle is fried. She has damage to her lower secondary hull and there is a gash along her secondary hull. Excalibur's primary hull aft is a wreck. She has no impulse engines. Intrepid shuttle bay doors has been damaged." Sutherland said as she completed the scan of Defiant's sister ships.

"Captain Blair, Admiral Hawke sends his approval."

"Tell the admiral thank you."

Hogawa nodded. "Yes, Sir."

Blair glanced at the main screen. Constellation and Excalibur were drifting. Intrepid was limping along under impulse power.

"Mister Sanders, take us in one quarter impulse power. Mister Devane, nice and straight line. Don't waste any time."

Both officers nodded as Defiant closed in on her three helpless sisters.

"Commander Sutherland, scan for cloaked ships."

"Aye, Sir."

Mbunga came alongside Blair. "Commander Stevok has damaged control teams standing by and Lieutenant commander Jane Hamilton has medical teams standing by and is ready to receive casualties."

"Captain Blair, Commodore Decker is on," Hogawa said.

"Put him on."

Defiant's screen changed from the visual of three Heavy cruisers to a smoke-filled bridge. Dim emergency light was on. Decker was discussing something with his XO, who he immediately recognized as Commander Takesheweda.

"Commodore," Blair said.

"Drop the formalities, Tommy. I need you to render assistance to all three ships and then I want you to scan the area for a cloaked Romulan bird of prey," Decker said as he wiped his face clean.

"A Romulan out here."

Decker nodded. "Didn't you read the latest reports?"

Blair shook his head. "We came here and joined your squadron from Vanguard Matt. There were reports of a lone bird of prey operating in the Taurus reach two years ago. Nothing about the Romulans operating in Federation space. That would be rare and even daring."

"Well, according to Lieutenant Masada and collaborated by Lieutenant Commander Lo Brutto, both our ships have picked up Tachyon emissions and a residual quantum singularity signature. We will transmit the information to Defiant."

"We are receiving it now," Blair said as he looked at Sutherland. Sutherland nodded back, confirming the receipt of the information.

"Damage control parties and medical teams have beamed aboard Constellation and Excalibur. Captain Satak has refused any help. He says he will watch the Constellation and Excalibur while we pursue Romulans," Mbunga said.

"We'll stay in contact. Defiant out." Decker's image faded. "Lieutenant Sanders, I want a wide search pattern and coordinate with Commander Sutherland since she may have been crippled. She might not be that far. Ensign Devane, one quarter impulse."

Defiant began her long sweep as she swung away from her sisters.

HONOR BLADE:

Chavernack put a bandage provided by the ship's chief medical officer Tomak to her head. Next to him stood Takvi, the ship's Master engineer or First Engineer as well as Tal and Bacakra.

"Tal."

"Cloaks are holding on emergency reserve. We have two dead and six injured."

"Mainly from engineering," Tomak added.

"The quantum singularity drive is offline. I need at least five hours to repair and realign. However, I have shut the drive down and closed external dampers. Feeding all reserve power to life support and cloaks," Takvi said.

"Any residual tachyon, anti-proton or quantum singularity emissions?"

"Yes, we emitted some when we hit the Constellation," Tal said.

"Commander, the Defiant, she is beginning her sweep," Bacakra warned.

Chavernack watched as Defiant-NCC 1764 began her sweep.

"May the elements protect us."

DEFIANT:

"Anything," Blair said impatiently to Sutherland.

Erin Sutherland shook her head. "The tachyon traces, anti-proton, and the residual quantum signature end less than a couple of hundred meters from where Constellation fell out of formation. Radiation from the Constellations damaged warp drive and Excalibur's damaged impulse engines are flooding the area interfering with our scans."

Blair was frustrated. The Romulan was going to getaway.

"Do the scans match the ones taken by Enterprise and Constitution during their encounters?"

Sutherland shook her head. "In both cases, Romulan warbirds were using the older versions of their cloaking device. Not as efficient as this one, however. The anti-protons' trace elements from the new cloaking device are less and not as pronounced."

This was really getting to be frustrating. Blair thought.

HONOR BLADE:

Chavernack watched as the Defiant slowly closed on Honor Blade's hidden position.

"She's scanning," Tal said quietly.

"Anything?"

"Negative."

On the Honor Blade's screen, Defiant stopped and turned around.

Chavernack felt a wave of relief rush over her.

DEFIANT:

"Bring us about. Take us back to the squadron, Mister Sanders. Ensign Hosagawa, contact Starfleet command. I need to issue the following report."

Sanders and Hosagawa nodded.

"This is so frustrating, Kamau."

Defiant's XO could only agree.

STARFLEET MAIN MISSIONS. STAR DATE 2927.19:

Mattea Hahn looked around as the Main Mission control center bustled with activity. Comsol, Solow, and West were back. Buchinsky had other matters to attend to and wasn't present.

"We've just had three battles. The Ninth engaged Golf at the Islandana system. The Eight had engaged Alpha at Hell Spawn. The FSF engaged Echo near Gaugamela. But Foxtrot entered Klingon space and was confronted by Task Force Korrd and Kerra. In each of the cases, the Harrata suffered grievously. They lost a total of fifty ships. Foxtrot is completely wrecked as a fighting unit. Echo, Alpha, and Golf are still effective," Hahn filled the officers present on the fleet's status.

"At least we know that Kirk and Hawke survived the second round," Solow mentioned.

"Amen to that," Comsol said. "Mattea, did we suffer any losses?"

"No. About forty ships from the fleets engaged suffered varying degrees of damage. Alpha, Trafalgar, 38, and 41 are seeing to their needs."

"What about that cosmic pile-up that Decker's squadron XY 75887 of FSF Charlie suffered before the battle of Gaugamela?" Comsol asked.

"According to Captain Blair's report, Decker's ship was hit by a cloaked bird of prey which caused a chain reaction, sending Constellation piling into Excalibur and Intrepid. The tugs Anaximander, Keppler, Hayashi have already been dispatched. In addition, Excelsior and Kongo were damaged during the battle of Gaugamela. Admiral Hawke wants to send all of these Heavy cruisers to Star base 11."

"Have you contacted Stone?"

"Yes, he says he is running out of dock space. With Exeter, Lexington, Indomitable, Hood, and Dauntless already occupying half of his dock space, he only has enough room for four more ships."

"Send Excelsior, Kongo, Excalibur, and Intrepid to Star base 11," Comsol said.

"Admiral Hahn, Admiral Nogura from Vanguard wants a word with you," a lieutenant said.

"Put him on," Hahn ordered.

Nogura's formidable appearance appeared on the screen. He wasn't pleased.

"What can I do for you, Hiro?" Hahn asked.

"Potemkin and Coronado are nearly finished with their missions. Do you know when I can get Defiant back?"

"Defiant will be towing Constellation to Star base 27, Hirohito. Then we'll send her to Vanguard."

"Okay, do you need me to dispatch Potemkin and Coronado to the combat zone?"

"That would be most appreciated, Hirohito. Is Endeavor ready?"

"She's all ready to go. But I wish I could have had the assistance of Enterprise or Constitution. Both those ships know the Taurus reach as well as Endeavor and Defiant."

"Well, so far, Kirk and Hawke have survived the second round, Hiro. The stars seem to be with us so far," Comsol said.

"Not like in 2220, Robert, we paid with blood back then," Comsol said remembering. He and Nogura had graduated from the academy that year, just in time for the war to break out.

"Indeed, we did, Hiro."

"If there is nothing else, Vanguard out." Nogura's image faded.

Comsol looked at Hahn. "Which fleets is presently not engaged in any conflict?"

"The first to the fourth, the tenth to the fifteenth."

"What about that excuse, the thirteenth?"

"According to Commodore Florida, no action at all," Hahn explained.

Comsol thought for a moment. With Hancock getting the fourth Reserve back into fighting trim, they needed another fleet to fill in for the over-stretched FSF, Ninth, and Eight fleets. The First had been deployed to Kzinti space after the incursion. The Second was on alert near Nauissican territory. The Fifth, Sixth, and the Seventh were also on alert status near Klingon and Romulan space. All other fleets were on standby status except for the infamous Thirteenth.

"Tell Florida at Star base 29 to dispatch fifty of his sixty ships. They are to report to brevet rear admiral, Captain Lance Cartwright at Star base Alpha, and act as a backup for the other three fleets."

"I don't think Carlos would like that, Robert."

Comsol gave Hahn a look. "Mattea, that fleet just sits around and collects cobwebs. They are the only fleet in the Starfleet that has no battle honors. They were too late to be deployed during the Tarn conflict of the 2160s, and they missed the First and Second Federation-Harrata war. They saw no action during the Tholian border skirmishes of the 2230s. They missed the Four Years' War. They were only engaged during the Shenzhou extension of the Four Years' War in 2257 at the Battle of the Binary Star. They are the opposite of the FSF, a totally useless bunch of colonel blimps trying to avoid each war. Now I want that fleet deployed," Comsol insisted.

Mattea nodded. Comsol had a good point. It was time for the thirteenth to pull their own weight.

"Ensign George, get me Commodore Florida Priority."

"Yes, Sir."

Moments later, an aging Hispanic Commodore appeared on the screen. He was far different from the young lieutenant who piloted the newly launched Enterprise out of the dock in 2245.

"Now Mattea, what can I do for you?" Carolos Florida said kindly.

"Carlos Comsol wants your fleet deployed fifty out of sixty ships. You are to send them to Alpha for orders."

Florida slumped in his seat. It really was happening. The Thirteenth was finally getting deployed.

"No problem, Mattea. No problem."

HARRATA STARFORCE SPACE CONTROL CENTER. CITY OF HOGASH. STAR DATE 2922.20. MAIN CONFERENCE ROOM.

Vorrad Flolitor Dalomey along with Vorrad Shara has Gomany. Chief of Space Control looked at the esteemed figures that faced him. The chancellor and the vice chancellor were present as well as the fourteen high priests and priestesses of the thirteen deities and the Shawazee.

They were all present in the conference room that flanked the Harrata equivalent of the Federation's Main Missions, Space Control. On the walls were portraits of prior commanders of Space Control.

"Harr Chancellor, Herr Vice Chancellor, and noble ones of the holies. We stand at a crossroads. The prophecy appears to be coming true," Dalomey said as he addressed the group present. Gasps and conversation broke out amongst the chancellor and vice chancellor while the priests and priestesses remained quiet.

"Vorrad Gomany will fill you all in," Dalomey said as he turned the meeting over to the chief of Space control.

A medium-sized middle-aged Harrata female took over. She had blue skin with white hair that covered her head in a half-circle and a bald top. Gomany began with the usual formalities and then energized a three-dimensional hologram that appeared in the center of the conference room table.

"We have suffered grievous losses. Battle group Fohari was mauled by the Klingonasse at Hotat de back. Islandana and Hell Spawn Battle groups Echosy and Gofaldan have been damaged. In addition, Alp and Betraka have suffered earlier losses. We also know that the Federank are interning all Star force Subjective command merchant ships and are refusing them the right to return to the Imperium.

In addition to those honored ones, the thirty-seven Star force ships that were outside our borders, twenty have been interred by the Starfleet, six are known to be destroyed, including an episode where the Neparah class, type 6 cruiser Masday de Far was destroyed by the Naucass while a Federank ship, the Stargazer, looked on at Wolf 359. The remainder have made it home."

"We must punish the Naucass," High Priest Jama De Bal of Lothar demanded.

"How, Noble, are we supposed to do that?" the Herr Vice Chancellor asked. "Our fleets are tied up in the Challenge phase. The realm must be defended."

"Lothar demands vengeance against the Naucass Herr, Vice Chancellor."

"Lothar always demands vengeance, Noble De Bal. But it will be Gom the almighty who has the final say," High Priestess Shara de Napari said looking directly at De Bal.

"There will be a time of reckoning, Noble Napari."

"When the book of prophecy foretells it, Noble De Bal, not when Lothar demands it," Napari reiterated.

"Honored and noble ones, we have only hope. Commandants Don de Bari of the Hajj ba Hajj and Hari de Bogash of the Gom de Zek are last remaining hope, honored, and noble ones," Dalomey mentioned. "Our Hogar class types 8s is superior to the Klingonasse D7s and the Federank Constitutions. Surely, the Imperium must prevail over the Federank and the Klingonasse."

Dalomey could hear voices of agreement emanating from the room. Seconds later, Shara de Napari got up and looked at the assembled group.

"Noble and honored ones and protectors of the realm. We are Harrata, the children of Harr, we differ from our misguided brothers and sisters of the Harrkonen Empire who still follow the pagan Pong and the original twelve that divided our planet for centuries. We are not Harrkonen. We are the pure Harrata. We survived the Ikonan and the Tkonasi and the evil Horror from beyond our galaxy and grew stronger with each trial. We are the chosen race of this galaxy. Let us now pray for the success of Bogash and Bari against the Federank and Yamak O Toole and Separi Ga Hinney against the Klingonasse. Viktwa Harratay!"

The whole room resounded with the chant. "Viktwa Harratay!"

"Now let us pray."

The conference room was suddenly filled with thirteen different prayer styles reflecting the diversity of the Harrata race. Shari stopped her chant to Gom and smiled. They have all reunited again.

CHAPTER THIRTY-NINE

TONG PART THREE. TONG OMARTI FOUR. TONG SPAC CHE. THE FINAL CHALLENGE. STAR DATE 2923.3. February 1, 2267.

"Captain's Log. Star date 2923.3. Captain James T. Kirk recording. In less than two days, both Enterprise and Constitution face the final hurdle of the Challenge. The infamous Space battle, ship-to-ship combat at code one conditions. No quarter, no mercy is the Harrata way. I expect Commanders Kang and Khod will perform in their usual Klingon manner. I also expect that Bob Hawke and the crew of the Constitution will perform in their usual manner, which is a credit to the Starfleet and the Federation. Both Robert and I know the odds in this final match. We must prevent a full-scale war from breaking out. There is no other way, no going back. The Federation cannot afford a two-front war. We must succeed."

"Captain's log. Star date 2923.4. Captain Robert N Hawke recording. Two days, it will all be over. We will survive or there will be war. I have every confidence in Jim Kirk and the Enterprise. I also have the highest respect and confidence in my crew which has performed admirably for eight months with no shore leave. The crew and this ship have earned their place and their keep. I expect that Khod and

Kang will make their Empire proud. If the news I have been hearing has been correct, then there is hope. Hope that there will be no war, hope that maybe, just maybe, we may actually open up full relations with the Harrata."

CONSTITUTION-NCC1700 WITH HAJJ BA HAJJ HIS 24500 IN ORBIT OF TONG OMARTI FOUR:

Kirk materialized in one of the transporter rooms on the Constitution. As he stepped off the pad, he was met by the lanky figure of Lieutenant Renee Dorvil, Constitution's Haitian Creole transporter chief.

"Welcome aboard, Captain," Dorvil said pleasantly. "Can I contact Commander Shran for you?"

"No, Lieutenant, just coming to pay a courtesy call on your captain."

"He's in sickbay, Doc. May be discharging him today, rumor has it."

"John Kyle says hello."

Dorvil smiled. "That's Johnny for you. He was my roommate at the academy, Captain. Never could beat me at cards."

"I heard you are one mean card player."

"Best on the ship, Captain. Remember, Captain, we don't play poker, mainly Gin Rummy and blackjack."

Kirk smiled. He indeed remembered he had to hold his own against the card sharks on this ship. Constitution had a mean reputation in that regard.

"I even beat the captain once," Dorvil said. "But then our captain never was a great card player."

"Did he hold anything against you?"

Dorvil shook his head. "No, the captain never does. We'd follow him to hell and back if he said so."

It was almost the same with him. He didn't dominate his crew. Both he and Robert led their commands with camaraderie and Robert knew he led his ship by setting his own example. He however led by the front. And Robert unlike him would sometimes send Shran down instead on certain missions.

They both were different ships and different crews led by two different captains. Different folks and different strokes, the old axiom went.

"It was a pleasure talking to you, Lieutenant," Kirk said.

"It was a pleasure too, Captain. Au Revoir, Borchas mon Capitane."

"Same," Kirk replied as he stepped out into the corridor. As he made his way to the turbo lift, he spotted a few Enterprise crewmembers that were walking and chatting with their opposites on this ship. Kirk responded in kind as he got responses from his own people and Robert's. Entering the turbo lift, Kirk signaled "Sickbay," and in moments later was deposited on the correct deck. Swinging around the corner, he entered the main doctor's office. Doctor Russell was chatting with two other doctors. A screeching noise came from the back of the office.

"Nurse McCall, please feed the Denobulan lemurs."

"Yes, Doctor," McCall said as she hurried over to the cages that were in the back of the office. Kirk walked over to one of the wall outlets and opened it up. Instead of finding a trove of liquors, Kirk found that the lower shelf was stacked with old-style hard-cover books with such titles as Edible Seafood and Shellfish of Alpha quadrant, Comparative Alien Physiology, Comparative Human Physiology, Grays' Anatomy Human, and Known Alien Species.

The Plight of the Starship Medical Officer by... Kirk smiled. Even McCoy had a copy. Donald Russell had written that book and it was a bestseller. He looked up at the upper shelf wall. It was stacked with various exotic liquors but no saurian brandy.

"No Saurian brandy, Doc," Kirk said to Russell.

"No, Jim, Bob, and I hate the stuff, but we do have Orion whisky or Andorian ale and Harrata Pogash."

Russell said as he turned from both doctors he was talking with.

Kirk grabbed the bottle of Orion whisky. It was of a reddish color and he had never really got to taste it. Grabbing two glasses off the nearby shelf, Kirk walked over to Russell and the two doctors.

"Jim Kirk, I would like to introduce you to my two assistants Doctors Early and Brackett."

Kirk shook the hands of both doctors. Russell then led all of them into the Diagnostic Examination room. Early and Brackett split up taking care of both patients with the assistance of nurse McCall.

In the background, he could hear Robert's voice coming from the other room. Stepping into the ward, he could see Robert conversing with a Tellerite male and a human female. Hawke spotting Kirk immediately changed the tone of the conversation. "Look what the cat dragged in," Hawke said sarcastically.

Kirk smiled. Robert was being a pain in the neck as always, which was a good sign. He was clean-shaven and was wearing his medical smocks. He had the screen on and on his bed were tablets. Sometimes, he always knew that Robert took his work to bed with him.

"What are you reading, Robert?" Kirk asked as he handed a glass to Hawke who flipped the screen in his direction.

"The Four Feathers by AEW Mason," Kirk said as he poured himself and Robert a glass of Orion whisky. Kirk took a sip of it. It was strong yet exhilarating in its flavor.

"Unlike you, Jim, I don't mind Shakespeare but my tastes in literature are more 19th and 20th century."

Kirk took another swig of the Orion whisky.

"How's the leg?"

"Better. Doc said he will discharge me later today. Tell me, did you find anything on that recorder you found?"

"Not much, but it was quite graphic, Robert."

"I bet a Knabra got Captain Rayburn."

Kirk nodded. "The recorder was still on when we heard his screams."

Hawke leaned up against the bedpost. "Jim, I envy you."

"Why?"

"You are like me. We are part of the eternal brotherhood and sisterhood of starship captains. You know the problems we face every day. The never-ending mountain of decisions we have to make. The pomp, the circumstance, and the diplomatic ass-kissing we must do, the compromises. And our all-important oath we took as captains."

Kirk could only agree. Robert was never as philosophical as him, but he had his moments.

"What is worrying you, Robert?"

"The final battle, those types 8s, my ship, and my crew."

"I have the same worries, Robert."

"But at least, your crew had shore leave two months ago at Star base 12. We haven't had it in eight months. I couldn't even find a decent place for us to have shore leave, Jim. I need to get this ship and crew to Star base 11. It is imperative," Hawke said betraying his worries.

"Relax, Robert. We will prevail, just like at Savo and Ghihoge in 63. You always came through for me and my people."

"Yeah, but you got all the acclaim, and everybody forgot about the part I played."

Kirk could see Robert's point, no matter how good Robert and his people were, and he and the Enterprise would always tower over them. And his reputation would outshine even Robert's acclaim.

"Strangely enough, Robert. After Garth and me, you are the greatest commander in the fleet. You even beat out Matt Decker, Ron Tracey, Bob Wesley, Iglor Khan, and Jacques La Liberté on that list."

Hawke smiled. "I know I am even beating the record my dad accomplished on this ship when he commanded her." Hawke took another sip of the Orion whisky. "What do you expect of me, Jim?"

"By tomorrow, I need your entire senior staff to be there."

"All of them."

Kirk nodded. "All of them, Robert. We'll meet in the Enterprise briefing room at 1300 hours."

Kirk took another drink of the Orion whisky. Kirk handed the bottle to Hawke. Hawke however gave it back to Kirk. "We have extra, Jim, on the house. Keep it."

"Jim Commander Spock needs to see you on the Enterprise," Doc Russell said.

"Tell Spock I will be there shortly." Turning to Hawke, "Got to go, Bob, duty calls."

Hawke raised his glass. "To duty, Jim, we'll be there."

Kirk sped out of sickbay and back to the Enterprise.

Sulu, Uhura, and Desalle made their way down the corridors of the Constitution. Uhura felt bored; Sulu and Desalle were engaged in guy talk and in this case, the boring statistics and differences between both starships. How only four ships of the original twelve had Constitution's blue scheme while the rest had Enterprise's green scheme and that all Bonhomme Richard, Achenar, and special configuration Trojan class ships and the new building Tikopia's had a blue scheme. Nyota could only sigh. She couldn't wait to talk to Mariko and Barbara when they joined them in one of Constitution's recreation rooms.

Uhura spotted Pavel Chekov and Daniel Harris and gave them a wave. Chekov and Harris waved back. Hikaru and Vincent however were oblivious and kept up their boring guy conversation.

Arriving at the recreation room, except for some minor differences, a few more plants and some paintings, the recreation room resembled the one on her own ship.

Sitting in the corner were Mariko Shimada and Barbara Desalle. Next to them was Morgan Bateson, Constitution's Chief Navigation officer who was talking to a familiar figure. She immediately recognized Daniel Paris. Paris had a mustache and was of medium-built.

Nyota followed Vincent and Hikaru over to the food slot and grabbed her dish. She then sat down opposite Morgan Bateson and Daniel Paris.

"Welcome to the Constitution," Bateson said.

"On behalf of the Enterprise, we thank you, Morgan," Vincent said.

"So, tell me, Nyota, what you think of our fine ship," Mariko said.

"She's nice, Mariko, but no Enterprise," Uhura said indifferently.

Nyota could see Mariko and Barbara giving her a cold stare. Paris was slack-jawed at her response.

Morgan looked at her. "No Enterprise! Doesn't the rest of us in the fleet count? This ship next to yours is the finest in the fleet. If it wasn't for the Four Years' War and the Axanar war, aka rebellion, we would have discovered as many worlds as Enterprise. Added to that, Enterprise, Constellation, and Yorktown were the only Constitution class ships that weren't even deployed during both conflicts. The rest of the class did all the heavy lifting," Bateson pointed out.

"Our captain served for two months under Pike as her temporary XO Uhura. And he along with Andovar Drake was in line for command of the Enterprise. And didn't Jim Kirk spend some time on this ship if memory serves?" Barbara Desalle said sarcastically.

"Nyota, she has a point," Sulu agreed. He loved the Enterprise too. But he could agree with his fellow crewmembers from Constitution that Enterprise wasn't the center of the universe.

"You're all suffering from the rest of us poor slobs in the fleet called Enterprise mania," Bateson said.

"Hell, I could have served on Enterprise, Vincent, but Augenthaler gave me an offer and I grabbed it," Barbara Desalle said.

Vincent nodded. "We were both serving on the Lafayette, Constitution class, not her decommissioned Larson class predecessor under Ron Tracey. Barbara went here and I went to Enterprise."

"C'mon, Uhura, didn't you serve under Captain Martin Callas on the Potemkin before going to Enterprise?" Mariko asked.

"And you served under Captain Igor Kranowsky on the Merrimac, Mariko. I do remember that was after that stint of yours at SI at Star base 27 after serving on the Anton after you graduated," Uhura mentioned.

"I never liked the Potemkin. Callas was always such an arrogant ass. I was glad to go to the Enterprise under Pike," Uhura admitted, sighing.

Daniel Paris smiled. "Why do you all think they called him Callous Callas?"

"Well, dear, Igor Kranowsky was no knight in shining armor. Why do you think they call him crabby Kranowsky?" Mariko said as she took a drink from her cup.

"So, Sulu, where did you start?" Bateson asked.

"I was supposed to get the Aerfen, but since I was initially trained as astrophysics in addition to my command track training, they gave me the Enterprise and I didn't want the Enterprise."

"Well, that's a revelation, so you wanted to join the Starfleet Border patrol, the Coast Guard."

"Yes. Morgan, the Soyuz, Aerfen, Detroyat class starship gang, the border patrollers. But my attitude has changed since then. I enjoy being on a Heavy cruiser. And you?"

"I lucked out. I got the Constitution right out of the academy and have been serving on her since 2260. First with Fredrick Augenthaler, then Robert Wesley, and now our present captain and I did a brief stint on the Enterprise before returning to Constitution."

"There were rumors circulating that Wesley was supposed to command this ship until 2270, but something came up," Uhura mentioned.

"That was what we were supposed to believe, Nyota. With Rousseau retiring, Starfleet was going to give our present captain the Lexington, but Wesley I heard wanted Lexington and since he was senior to our less senior Captain, Wesley got his way. And Bob Wesley always gets his way," Barbara Desalle mentioned.

"Either we were going to get your Jim Kirk who was now no longer available or Robert Nelson Hawke, Nick Silver, or Phil Waterston," Mariko added.

"And I am glad we got Bob Hawke. Like father like son, he knows this ship, and he's not like the great almighty Garth who intermittently interfered with Joe Hawke's command or that disaster Page.

Augenthaler did this ship proud. And I am glad that Nicolas Silver became captain of Defiance. Silver we all know is a bit of a martinet and I would have left this ship if that idiot Phillip Waterston took command," Bateson admitted.

"I heard Waterston is a decent officer," Uhura said.

"Yeah, right, I had to serve with him on the scout ship Batidor during my academy days. He as XO ran the cadets hard, Nyota. You mention to him our captain's name or the name of this ship and he goes into a rant and raves about how he hates our captain and that this ship is his and his alone," Bateson explained. "Something I heard about a feud that has been going on between the Hawkes and the Waterston's since the old Earth Starfleet days."

"Yeah, Waterston was a fool. Like Morgan, I served on the Batidor when I was a cadet at the academy," Paris pointed out agreeing with Bateson.

"Are you related to Rear Admiral Howard Paris of Star base 38?" Sulu said.

"The one and only," Paris said.

"We thought you were on duty, Dan," Barbara said.

"To give Alpha and Beta some rest for the upcoming final battle, Shran is using Gamma shift. She is rotating between Belker and Catalan on the bridge, giving the youngsters a chance to take a spin in the big time."

"Sounds like Spock. Occasionally, he does something like that with our youngsters," Vincent Desalle said.

"Shran and Spock, two peas in a pod. We'll all be lucky if we make XO, much less becoming captains of our own ships," Mariko Shimada admitted. "It's all of you command track officers who stand the best chance, not us lackeys in engineering and communications."

"Now hold on, Mariko, there is a Captain Benson who used to be a former Communications officer and look at Commodore Stone. He started out as an engineer before switching to command. Hell, from what I heard, your Lieutenant Commander Shran started out in engineering," Sulu said.

"Good point, Sulu," Paris chimed in.

Sulu turned to Paris. "Tell me, Dan, so how did you wind up on this ship? I know that you and Uhura here served on the Potemkin."

"I was gamma shift navigator on the Potemkin. Uhura worked the same shift."

Uhura nodded in agreement.

"So, how did you wind up here?" Vincent Desalle asked.

"Well, it's a long story. When I graduated from the academy in 2261, I was assigned to the Miranda under Captain Lori Ciana. A year later, I transferred to the Potemkin under Captain Martin Callas and stayed on that ship until 2263. In 2264, I transferred to Excalibur and in 2265, I transferred to the Endeavor under Captain Sheng," Paris said.

"What caused you to transfer to the Constitution?" Sulu asked.

"You heard about Erilon," Paris said.

"Something about a race called the Sendai," Vincent Desalle recalled.

"To make matters short, we barely got out of them in one piece. A few crewmembers wanted to transfer off and newly promoted Captain Khatami granted our request. According to Fleet Scuttlebutt, nothing was available on a permanent basis. It would at least be a few months until we received reinforcements and with Defiant temporarily reassigned. Commodore Reyes wanted Enterprise, Farragut, or Constitution to fill in temporarily. Only Constitution was available, so I transferred to this ship when she made a return visit to Vanguard and I am hoping to spend the rest of her five missions on this ship if everything works out."

The wall screen lighted up. A Korean female appeared. Sulu looked surprised. Enterprise had gotten rid of all her recreation room wall screens.

"My Beta shift relief," Mariko said.

"Is there a Lieutenant Sulu, Uhura, and Desalle here?"

"We are here," Sulu said.

"I am Lieutenant Janice Park. Captain Kirk needs you three to report back to Enterprise immediately."

"Understood," Sulu said as he, Desalle, and Uhura got up. "Well, it was an experience," Sulu added.

"Indeed, it was," Bateson said. They all hugged and shook hands as the Enterprise gang left the recreation room in a hurry.

Bateson gave a yawn and stretched his arms. "I don't know about you, ladies, but I'm turning in," Bateson got up.

"I couldn't agree more," Desalle agreed.

"Same," Shimada said.

Paris looked up. "And what about me?"

"You'll find someone to talk to, Dan. You always do," Barbara Desalle said as she left the recreation room. Scanning the room, he found no one he could really talk to until Paris picked up his meal and walked over to Lieutenant T'Pau.

T'Pau looked up at him. "Yes, Lieutenant."

"I was seeing that you were alone, I figured..."

"Mister Paris, your repute on this ship as a ladies' man is well known. As you can see, I am quite busy. Captain Hawke and first officer Shran need my evaluation on the capabilities of the Hogar class type eights. I really do not have the time," T'Pau said coldly.

"But Lieutenant, since I am the assistant helm officer, it does concern me, maybe I could assist you in the evaluation of the type 8s' capabilities from a helmsman's point of view."

"I will let you assist as long as you do not make a pass on me."

"Scout's honor, T'Pau."

T'Pau's eyebrow arched. She still didn't fully understand humans even at this point.

"Very well, Mister Paris, you may assist."

Paris smiled, sat down, and started to look over T'Pau's data.

CHAPTER FORTY

HONOR BLADE NEAR THE GAUGAMELA SYSTEM. STAR
DATE 2923.5:

Livinia watched as Charete showed her the repairs that he and his
staff had completed on the Honor Blade. For the past two hours,
they had been decloaked.

Charete showed her the newly repaired Quantum singularity
energizers. The two energizers dominated the engine room. They
were also hooked into the Honor Blades' impulse drive. Charete went
over to the master control station on the far-left side of the room.

"Whenever you are ready, Master Engineer," Livinia said.

Charete nodded and activated the energizers. The room started to
rumble as the quantum singularity energies flowed into the Honor
Blades' warp drive.

"All system nominal, quantum singularity is functioning within
specifications."

Chavernack smiled, walked over, and activated the wall intercom. "Tal, we have warp drive back."

"Course, Commander."

"Home. All decks to alert status one."

"Yes, Commander."

The alarm went off and engineering was bathed in a green glow.

Charete turned to Chavernack. "Let's hope the elements favor us, Commander."

"That is all we could hope for, Master Engineer," Chavernack said as she left engineering. Until they cleared Federation space, the game wasn't up yet.

Planetoid X. Star date 2924.7.

ToZak looked at Shran with comical amusement, unlike the cool, calm, unruffled Sarek. She knew how to get an Andorian mad. It was as easy as feeding Gagh to a Klingon. All warrior races had this macho prediction of superiority and even though the Andorians were members of the Federation, they could still be led on a leash. She had negotiated with many of the major and minor races in her one hundred years as a diplomat in what the humans called the Alpha and Beta quadrants.

"We will not divulge why we are here, Torel, until the Challenge has run its course. The Imperium has its reasons and as the humans say, it is none of your business."

Torel looked at ToZak and decided not to respond. In his experience, it was easier dealing with the Harratas' cousins, the Harrkonens.

Torel and Sarek had the good fortune to meet the Harratas' estranged brothers and sisters almost eight years ago.

In 2259, Excalibur under the command of Captain Anton Harris with his first officer Lieutenant Commander Robert Nelson Hawke had been ordered by the Federation council to make overtures to the Harrkonen Empire.

Escorting Excalibur was the Eagle under the command of Captain Roger Botwin with his first officer Lieutenant Commander James Kirk.

They had met two Harrkonen. Te Gold class battle cruisers Pong Pa Ra and the Omar outside Federation territory in unclaimed territory.

All four ships had rendezvoused at the star system T900 which contained a little-used Harrkonen outpost, set up in secret to monitor the Harrata Imperium.

The Harrkonens had come merely to satisfy their curiosity about the losers of the Federation who couldn't even beat the evil Tong.

Both he and Sarek tried to convince the Harrkonen delegates of the advantages of a treaty with the Federation but to no avail, the Harrkonens were not convinced. Until the Federation finally beat the Harrata in the blasphemous Tong, it was a no-go.

The Excalibur and the Eagle later rendezvoused with the Intrepid and the Eagle and both ambassadors went their separate ways.

If Kirk and Hawke succeeded, they would be getting a call from the Harrkonens.

Torel folded his arms and sat back in his chair.

"If it is not any of our business, then why are we talking at all?" Shran replied.

"I concur with my colleague Ambassador ToZak. It is illogical to confer day in and day out with no logical conclusion in sight. We both find these negotiations to be fruitless and never in history has the Imperium called for talks during the Challenge time. The last two times you called for talks, the Federation was involved in two wars."

Sarek continued, "And you never called for talks during the previous centuries when the Confederation of Vulcan and the Andorian Empire were involved in the Tong. Only when you wanted to end the Andorian-Harrata and Vulcan-Harrata wars," Sarek explained. None of this made any logical sense.

"We would like an honest answer," Shran demanded. Enough was enough.

ToZak looked at her fellow ambassador, Hattari. They quickly exchanged words in Harratese instead of Standard. After a few heated minutes, ToZak looked at Shran and Sarek and said in Standard.

"This is our last assignment as diplomats, my friends. We are being replaced by our successors who will carry the Imperium through the dark times into the 25th century. According to the Book of Prophecy, the evil will return, the dark forces will come. We in the Imperium must change our ways. The next three centuries will be a time of testing for our people. The Imperium will reunite with our heathen brethren, the Harrkonens, and begin the rejoining of our people. Because of the two humass Kirk and Hawke, the anointed ones will finally beat the Challenge and set in motion the events that will rock both quadrants of the galaxy for the next three centuries," ToZak warned.

"Ambassador Shari Ben Gazari Fahiri did mention it during our meeting with Ambassador Korvat and President Westcott," Shran said.

"Are you referring to the Daklenah, the Borgara, and the Iconians?" Sarek asked.

"And the unmentionables, the lords of the spheres," Hattari said in his wheezing voice.

"What about the Horror?" Shran asked.

"Not in our lifetimes will they return," ToZak reassured as she got up. "We will await the final part of the Tong, Sarek, and Torel. Then we will meet once more, either to lay the groundwork for the inevitable or declare war on the Federation if the Book of Prophecy is wrong, which never has been."

Sarek and Shran got up. ToZak and Hattari bowed. Sarek and Shran did the same. As Sarek watched them leave, he understood that everything comes to an end. Very soon, they will find out if they would be at war or not.

ENTERPRISE-NCC 1701 WITH THE GOM DE ZAK-HIS 24501. STAR DATE 2923. 5.

ENTERPRISE'S BRIEFING ROOM. 1300 HOURS:

In his entire career as a starship captain, even when he commanded Oxford and Lydia Sutherland as a captain, he never really cared too much for briefings. Kirk sat back in his chair and scanned the briefing room.

In addition to the group from the past two meetings, he could see Sulu, Vincent Desalle, Barbara Desalle, Bateson, Uhura, and Shimada conversing on the chairs that were added before the briefing. Robert had brought his feline Maxine with him and he was in high spirits.

Kirk smiled. He recalled that Hawke had irritated Captain Custer just before the Battle of Savo by bringing Maxine into the briefing aboard the Pegasus. He couldn't help but laugh at the thought. As he watched the officers of both ships socializing, Kirk knew it was time to get down to business.

"Ladies and gentlemen let's start this meeting," Kirk said as he turned to Spock.

"We all know that for the past week, our ships have had plenty of time to run simulations against the Hogar class Type 8. Both Constitution and Enterprise come up short," Spock said. Spock engaged the tripod viewer. "Technically, the Hogar class is the old Earth Starfleet NX design modified through years of service. It was originally a two-nacelle design until the type 4s, then it became a three-nacelle design with the type 5s. With the Type 7s, it matured into its present four-nacelle design stage adding in the neutronium hull plating on the vital areas, making this ship a formidable opponent."

"Starfleet Intelligence believes the Harrata have mined neutronium from the extinct star system Hoshar deep in the Imperium," T'Pau added.

"We are technically outmatched and outgunned," Hawke said voicing his concerns.

Kirk could only agree. They were out of their league and all of this would come to naught if they did not survive the final battle.

"Jim, we also have other problems," Hawke added.

"Like what, Robert?" Kirk said concerned.

"Last year in 2266, we were supposed to rendezvous with our supply ship the Antares. We were late because we had just ended the century-long conflict that engulfed the Nakarat alliance. Spock's father Sarek was onboard and after it was concluded, we rendezvoused with the Intrepid. Due to a whole lot of complications, we missed our rendezvous with Antares. I don't know what desk jockey decided to send Antares into the Thasian system. We were scheduled to do a survey of the system after our rendezvous with her. But later on, we found out that Antares blew up after rendezvousing with this ship."

Kirk could only pity Bob. Charles Evans had cost Captain Walter Ramart the lives of his crew and endangered his own ship if only Constitution hadn't been late from her assignment. Robert was far more capable than he was and probably would have not abused Charlie like Ramart and his crew did.

"We had run out of spares and Antares had our spare parts. So, Starfleet ordered the ship to a supply depot at Talax Six. All Constitutions use a type 8 warp core. We are stuck with the older type 6 warp core and other antiquated parts we salvaged at the depot," Andrews added.

Scotty looked at Andrews surprised. "A type six, Andy, how did you get that old thing to work on ye ship?"

"It took a lot of elbow grease and adaptation to get it running, Scotty," Andrews said.

"Robert, you could have asked us for a spare type 8 warp core. Why did you wait to tell me this?" Kirk said angrily at his fellow starship captain.

"We never would have had the time to install it. Plus, Talax Six had an old dry-dock that fitted my ship and you must power down the ship to install it," Hawke said.

"Jim, Captain Hawke is correct in his assumption. You need a dry-dock to install a new warp core or replace the nacelles. It cannot be done in the time allowed on this mission," Spock added.

"That is correct, Mister Spock," Scotty said agreeing with the point made.

"How fast can your ship go, Bob?"

"We max out at warp 7. Our phaser power is cut by ten percent with the smaller core. Our shielding is also reduced by fifteen percent."

So, Constitution's capabilities were reduced slightly, but not enough that she couldn't be an effective combat unit, Kirk thought.

"Spock, what about Harrata tactics?" Kirk asked.

"The Harrata ships are equipped with plasma torpedoes and disruptor batteries. They will use the disruptors on us to weaken our shields and reduce our capabilities. Then they will send boarding parties to disrupt our operations and then finish us off with plasma torpedoes."

"Giotto, Martinez, all security teams on Enterprise and Constitution should be on full alert," Kirk said looking at his and Robert's security chiefs.

"We should also have all ships' personnel armed with phasers to repel the boards, Jim," Hawke suggested.

"Sounds a strategy, Robert," Kirk agreed. He had read reports dating from the first and second Harrata wars of the Harrata boarding a starship to disorganize the enemy and then sacrifice them when the Federation ship was destroyed at the end, martyring themselves to their various deities.

"Jim, you and Bob need not worry, Dave and I will have our sickbays ready for whatever you throw our way," McCoy said.

Russell nodded in agreement. They were going to be ready hell or high water.

The intercom whistled. Kirk hit the switch. Palmer's image appeared on the desk screen.

"Yes, Lieutenant," Kirk asked.

"Ringmaster Hittay says both you and Hawke have five hours to prepare. The final Challenge will begin then."

"Tell Hittay we understand his instructions."

"Yes, Sir," Palmer said as her image faded.

Hawke looked at Kirk. "There goes the baby out with the bathwater."

Spock and T'Pau's eyebrows both stood up simultaneously.

Kirk looked at Spock. "Spock, don't even think of responding to this."

"Indeed, I will not, Captain."

Hawke looked at T'Pau. "T'Pau, ignore what I just said."

T'Pau folded her shoulders and looked at her commanding officer.

"One does not respond to such a colorful metaphor. My captain's colorful language has always left me wanting."

"Does anybody have anything else to mention?" Kirk asked. Kirk scanned the briefing room; there were no takers. There were none. "This meeting is adjourned."

Kirk watched as Hawke's people left the briefing room. In a few hours, they were either going to be dead or alive. Kirk sat back in his chair alone. He needed to formulate a strategy that would help them win. Running through every scenario he could think of, he kept coming up with snake eyes. The Enterprise would be destroyed. There had to be a way out. There just had to be a way out of this. Scratching his head, Kirk gave up and headed to his quarters.

"Captain's log. Star date 2924.9. Captain James Kirk recording. Within the next hour, we face the final part of the Challenge. It is do or die. If we do not survive this, I would like to say that I never served with a finer crew in my entire career. They and this ship do me proud."

"Captain's log. Star date 2924.9. Captain Robert Hawke recording. In sixty minutes, we begin the final Challenge. As we roll the dice, we will see where they fall. If we don't make it through, I just want to say that this crew has been the finest I have ever served with."

ENTERPRISE:

Jim Kirk stood in the turbo lift as it made its way to the main bridge. He had just completed a complete ship tour from stem to stern as the old naval adage went. He had visited every vital section from the rear phaser room commanded by Madge Sinclair to auxiliary control where young Pavel Chekov manned the station, to the ship's computer core where Ben Finney was stationed. He even stopped by his usual haunts' sickbay and engineering and a few of the ship's recreation rooms to check on his crew. The turbo lift doors opened, and Kirk stepped on the bridge. Everybody was where they were supposed to be. Kirk walked down and sat in his command chair.

"Lieutenant Uhura, open up inner ship communications."

"Yes, Sir, channel open."

"This is the captain speaking. In less than fifteen minutes, we will face the final part of this Challenge. We will face it as a united crew along with our fellow Starfleet personnel aboard our sister ship Constitution. This is a battle to the death. If we win, we would have succeeded in stopping a full-scale war that the Federation cannot afford. If we lose, we all know the consequences. We have the best ship and crew in the Starfleet. History will not forget the name Enterprise," Kirk finished. Uhura closed the channel.

"Get me Constitution, Lieutenant."

"Yes, Sir."

CONSTITUTION:

Robert Hawke swung his command chair around observing his bridge crew. He had done a tour of his command. Satisfied, he looked at their tired faces. Once they finished this, off to Star base Eleven. They had all earned it. He was not going to let them down. They were too important to him.

"Lieutenant Shimada, addresses inner ship."

Shran walked down from tactical and stood by his side as she had always done since their first command together.

"Aye, Sir," Mariko Shimada said. "Channel open."

"This is Captain Hawke speaking. Soon, we will be facing the final part of this Challenge. This is our final test of this crew's extraordinary mettle and stamina that we have endured for eight months. We are all united in this final struggle, united with our fellow Starfleeters aboard the Enterprise. You are an extraordinary crew and the finest in the fleet bar none. This ship has a proud name and heritage. Let us not forget the name Constitution. She surrounds us and endures with us. Let's make her proud." Hawke turned to Shimada who instinctively closed the channel.

Before Shran could speak, Shimada had swung back. "Captain, the Enterprise is signaling."

"Put Kirk through."

Shimada nodded, the view screen shimmered, and Kirk's image appeared on it.

ENTERPRISE:

"Give the word, Jim."

"The word is given. Good luck and god speed."

"Same, Constitution out." Hawke's image faded from the screen. Approaching the Enterprise was the Lothar GaZ and the four remaining type 8s. None of the ships had their shields up.

"Spock."

"Captain, Constitution is now starboard of the Enterprise. The Suvwl' and the Vorcha are now on our port. In addition to the Lothar GaZ, four Hogar class types 8s is behind her and are dead onto each of our ships," Spock said as he looked up from his science station.

Kirk nodded. He was wondering what his opposite number aboard the Gom de Zek was thinking.

"Captain, the Lothar GaZ is signaling," Uhura said.

"On visual," Kirk said.

Moments later, the bulk of the GaZ shimmered and faded and was replaced by the same dark dreary bridge. Kirk could see Hittay and the Gaz's admiral. Also, present on the bridge was a Commandant, probably the ship's commanding officer. Hittay stepped forward.

"I welcome all of you to this final round of the Challenge. As for the Humass and the Klingonasse, I praise you for your skill and fortitude in getting this far. We stand at a crossroads, one race the Harrata will war against and one we will not. Or we may fight both races in glory or neither will have a conflict with us. It is the will of Gom and the deities and glory to the Book of prophecy that has brought us here," Hittay said relishing each word. "The rules are simple. The entire engagement must take place within the confines of the Tong Omarti system. If you attempt to flee, the GaZ will destroy you. It doesn't matter to us if you have your ship, wrecked, destroyed, or rendered a lifeless hulk. A loss is a loss. If you survive, the GaZ will render all assistance to your ship and as a courtesy, tow your ship back to the Harrata home world for final post-Challenge ceremonies and then, we will tow you back to our borders as a courtesy to the victors."

Kirk looked at Uhura. "Uhura, maintain a continuously open channel between both ships, scramble it, and put it on a secure channel."

"Yes, Sir."

Hittay continued, "To the victors, the spoils, may you all receive the blessings of the thirteen." Hittay's image faded revealing the enormous bulk of the GaZ

"Constitution has acknowledged, Captain," Uhura said.

Seconds later, the GaZ swung away revealing the four Hogar class type eights.

"Red alert. All hands, man your battle stations," Kirk said. The Enterprise jumped to life.

Kirk holstered his phaser two.

"All decks report ready," Spock said.

"Mister Sulu, give me some maneuvering room. Bring us to 112-mark 15 full impulse."

"Aye, Sir, 112 mark 15, full impulse."

Enterprise followed by Constitution swung away from Tong Omarti Four. The Klingon battle cruisers veered off in the opposite direction.

"Captain, two type eights have swung clear. The Hajj and the Gom are in pursuit."

"Aft view, Mister Sulu."

"Aye, Sir, aft view."

"Robert, we'll head for the asteroid field. Break formation when we enter it."

"Understood," Hawke said through the open commlink.

"Approaching the asteroid field," Spock said.

"Standby to go to half impulse, Sulu. Mister Desalle, stand by on aft phasers and photons."

Sulu and Desalle nodded. Enterprise suddenly gave a jolt.

"Shields holding at ninety-five percent, minor damage to aft shield," Spock said.

"They don't want us going in there, Spock."

"Indeed, Captain."

"Constitution reports her shields are down to eighty percent," Uhura said.

"Now, Sulu."

Sulu immediately reduced speed. Constitution broke off swinging to starboard of the Enterprise. The Hajj continued in pursuit of the Constitution while the Gom pursued the Enterprise.

"Now, Mister Desalle, target her warp engines, after phasers' fire."

"Aye, Sir," Desalle said as he hit the firing button. Enterprise's phasers lashed out at the Gom striking her shields which flared under the barrage.

Enterprise shook again as the Harrata ship returned fire. Kirk looked surprised as the form of Constitution suddenly swung in between the Enterprise and the Gom. Her aft photons were firing on the Hajj as her starboard phasers hit the Gom and she swung by both ships. Robert was flying his ship like a madman through the asteroid field. The Hajj was in dead pursuit and unleashed a volley at Enterprise. Enterprise shuddered under the volley.

"Hard to port, Mister Sulu, bring us about."

Sulu nodded as he swung the Enterprise around.

The Hajj and the Gom were trying to line up on Constitution. Kirk knew he wouldn't be too late. The bulk of both Hogar ships came up in a wide-open tract of the field.

"Now, Desalle, fire at will all banks!"

Enterprise let go a salvo of photon torpedoes and phasers who hammered the Hajj. Another salvo hit the Gom.

"The Hajj has lost her aft shields, Captain. Number one warp engine is damaged. Gom's aft shields are down fifty percent."

"Robert."

"Our aft shields are faltering, Jim. Auxiliary power to aft shields! Seal off decks five and four. Divert all power from those decks to shields," Hawke said over the open mike.

"Line up on the Gom, Sulu. Mister Desalle, photon torpedo spread fire!"

Enterprise fired on the Gom. The photons slammed into the battle cruiser's aft shields. The Hajj launched a disruptor salvo at the Enterprise, Enterprise staggered under the assault.

"Our forward shields are down to twenty percent."

"Give me some maneuvering room, Sulu. Take us out of the asteroid field."

Sulu nodded.

"Constitution is following," Spock said as he quickly checked his viewer.

Constitution launched another salvo at the Harrata ships as both ships cleared the asteroid belt. Harrata ships buckled under Constitution's salvos.

"Captain, Constitution is emitting plasma from both of her engines," Spock said.

"How long till the Harrata exits the field, Spock?"

"We have two minutes maximum."

"Uhura, give me a visual.'

"Aye, Sir."

Constitution's smoke-filled bridge filled the screen. Hawke was bellowing out orders, "Shran, get down to engineering. Assist Andy in tying down those plasma relays. Mister Bateson, take over tactical. Mister Harris, take over at navigation. Desalle, keep formation with Enterprise."

"Hanging in, Robert."

"We just lost our warp drive, Jim. If we keep up at this, they will pound us to pieces at the rate we are going."

"One minute, Captain, the Harrata ships will be exiting the field."

"I know this is insane, Bob."

"You said it, but I am not giving up. We just can't go toe to toe with them. They will pound us into matchwood," Hawke admitted.

There had to be a way, but Kirk was at a loss of ideas.

"It is not going to end here, Bob," Kirk said.

"No, but I bet that you think your team of Sulu and Desalle is better than mine. I'll bet you a bottle of Klingon blood wine," Hawke said challenging Kirk.

"A bottle of Romulan ale, Bob, on my end."

"Forty seconds."

"Let's play chicken, Jim," Hawke suggested.

A light bulb went off in Kirk's head. That was it. Robert had done it again.

"Agreed," Kirk said.

"Ten seconds," Enterprise shuddered under the Harrata attack.

"Full impulse, Mister Sulu."

"Aye, Sir," Sulu said as Hawke's image faded from the screen. "Aft view."

Sulu nodded. Enterprise's port nacelle was starting to trail plasma.

"Mister Desalle, assist Scotty. Spock, get me Chekov."

"Yes, Sir."

Desalle left his post and was met by young Pavel Chekov exiting the elevator. Chekov immediately took his place at navigation.

"Mister Chekov, plot a nice, wide course."

"Aye, Keptin," Chekov said.

They had to play it close to the vest; the Harrata did not need to know what they were planning.

Enterprise swung wide away from Constitution which had swung wide in the opposite direction.

Kirk leaned over to check the astrogator. Constitution had done her job. She was swinging around and lining up with Enterprise.

"Mister Chekov, emergency power to aft shields, aft phaser fire."

"Aye, Sir!" Chekov said as he released a barrage of fire at the Gom.

"She's taking the bait, Captain," Spock said.

"Robert, are you still there?"

"Yes."

"I'll go port, you go starboard," Kirk suggested.

"Got it."

"Mister Sulu, standard magnification on view."

"Aye, Sir, standard mag."

"Scotty."

"We have damage to our warp drive from the last attack. Desalle has secured the port nacelle."

"Give me everything she has, Scotty."

"Aye, Sir, ye will have it."

"Chekov, Sulu, it will be close. Standby." Too soon and they would be in irons. Too late and both ships would collide. They, not the Harrata, would die.

The vague form of Kirk's old ship Constitution swung into distant view.

"500 miles and closing," Sulu said.

Kirk could feel his palms sweating.

CONSTITUTION:

"Andy, give me everything the old girl has."

"Aye, Sir, you got."

"Mister Desalle, Mister Harris, it will be close."

"Mister Bateson, pummel that Harrata with everything you have."

"Yes, Sir," Bateson said from tactical which was next to the science station.

Bateson opened fire with everything they had.

Hawke watched as the Enterprise loomed on the screen. It was going to be close. Robert looked around at his crew. He would not trade them for Jim's crew if the whole universe ceased to exist.

ENTERPRISE:

"100 miles and closing," Sulu said. Constitution's form loomed up on the screen.

"Fifty miles," Sulu said.

GOM DE ZAK:

"Harr Commandant, the Humass must be crazy," Ober Commander Oscar Vi Altary said.

"They are Ober C. The victory will be ours. Signal Hajj full power ahead! Enough with these games!"

"Yes, Harr Commandant."

ENTERPRISE:

Kirk watched as the Gom surged ahead. They had taken the bait.

"Push her for all she's got, Sulu."

"Aye, Sir. One mile and closing."

Constitution's form almost dominated the main screen. They were almost on top of each other.

Enterprise shuddered again.

"Aft shields are failing, Captain," Spock warned.

"Half a mile," Sulu said. His palms were sweating. "A quarter-mile."

They were almost out of maneuvering room. Kirk did a slow count in his head from ten.

"Captain," Spock warned. "Jim."

"Now, Sulu! Hard a port Z plus 10,000 full power ascents!"

Sulu activated the controls. Enterprise swung to port as Constitution rolled to starboard on a decent. Kirk watched as Constitution's secondary hull swung by Enterprise's secondary hull. Kirk could make out Constitution's NCC 1700 on her primary hull as she plunged downward.

Gom de Zak.

"Harr, Commandant!"

Commandant looked in surprise as both Federation ships did a ballet swinging in different directions away from each other.

"Emergency evasive!"

It was too late. The Gom De Zak was too close as the silhouettes of the Federation ships disappeared only to be replaced by the Hajj ba Hajj.

Commandant de Bari shielded his eyes as both ships at full impulse slammed into each other.

The Tong Omarti star system lit up as matter and antimatter collided. Both ships exploded like a supernova going off.

ENTERPRISE:

Kirk and his bridge crew shielded their eyes as both Harrata ships exploded into a fireball which turned the night into day. The flash faded as space returned to normal. Kirk's bridge crew exploded into cheers.

Spock came down to Kirk's side, "Well done, Captain."

"Yes, Spock. Well, done. Robert. you and your people did a great job."

CONSTITUTION:

A tired Robert Hawke stood next to the turbo lift. He was patting the ship's dedication plaque which said:

U. S.S Constitution –NCC 1700

Starship class, First of her class

San Francisco Navy yards

To Boldly Go.

Hawke smiled as Shran returned to the bridge. Shran smiled back.

"We did it, Robert," Shran said.

Hawke smiled. He was so relieved.

"Yes, Shran, we did."

T'Pau came up. "Truly extraordinary, Captain."

"Yes, T'Pau, it was."

Kirk's voice came through the intercom.

"Well done, Robert, you and your people did a great job."

"And so did yours, Jim. It was a draw."

"Indeed, it was, Robert."

ENTERPRISE:

McCoy had come on the bridge. The Enterprise had been lucky—only fifteen injured, nobody killed.

Scotty had stood by as Kirk looked at his chief engineer.

"I need to take the engine's offline captain. The warp core was damaged severely during the attack."

"Understood, Scotty."

"We'll need a space dock to do repairs, Sir. Figure five-day repair."

Kirk nodded. In front of Enterprise was the battered form of Constitution. Robert's ship had it worse. They had lost all warp power and both nacelles were badly scarred. He could see a hole in the aft section of the secondary hull and another in her dorsal section. Kang's battle-scarred Suvwl was next to her and Khod's equally damaged Vorcha looked nearly as bad as Constitution. Enterprise was the least damaged of the entire squadron. But the Harrata had lost all four of their vaunted type eights. The hull plating had proven to be a bane. It had turned the usually fast-turning Hogars into ships that maneuvered like garbage scows and had completely negated the advantages.

"Captain Kirk," Uhura said. "Ringmaster Hittay expects you alone on the planet for the final discussion."

Kirk nodded. "Understood, Uhura, I will be there in a half an hour."

"Yes, Captain."

Tong Omarti Four. Final day. Star date 2925.10. Council of Tong. February 2, 2267.

Kirk and Hawke stood in front of the fourteen priests, priestesses, and Hittay. Hittay read out the Harrata law.

"By the law of the Tong, any challenger who spares the life of a champion and refuses to kill one in combat must take into one's family the wife and children of the said champion."

Kirk thought about Carol, what she would really think. He could not really manage this.

"Hittay, this is binding," Kirk asked.

"Yes, Ober C Kirk, it is."

Kirk looked at Robert, but he couldn't figure out what his old friend was thinking. Robert looked tired and exhausted. Kirk liked children, but did he have the nerve to take on this new responsibility? At that moment, Hawke stepped into the conversation.

"Honored Hittay, and holy ones of the deities, I would like to assume responsibility under Harrata law for Kirk's as well as my charges."

"You are truly wise, Ober C Hawke. You and Kirk have similar destinies, but different fates. You honor your ancestors who came before you. You will be the light in the darkness that will come."

Hittay said, "Kirk, do you agree?"

Kirk looked at Hawke. Hawke looked at Kirk. "Remember, Jim, you now owe me one."

"Yes, Hittay, I agree."

"It is done. The Challenge is over," Hittay said.

Enterprise officer's lounge:

Kirk let out a roar of laughter as the Klingon blood wine slogged around in his glass.

"How can you drink this horrid stuff, Bob? It tastes like bilge water."

Hawke slapped Kirk on his back. "Bilge water! This Romulan ale tastes horrible!" Hawke slurred his words as he took another slug of ale.

Kirk rolled over laughing. Hawke wobbled a bit as he got up from his chair and plopped over next to Kirk.

"You could never outdrink me, Bob," Kirk admitted as he laughed.

"I could never hold my liquor," Hawke said as he chugged down another glass of Romulan ale.

"You're right," Kirk said as he stretched his words out. Kirk heard the doors of the officer lounge open. Spock, McCoy, Shran, T'Pau, and Russell were all standing there. Shran had her hands at her sides and McCoy had folded his.

"Didn't I tell you, Spock, they are both drunk as monkeys?" McCoy admitted.

"Indeed, Doctor, your assessment is correct, considering the stress both of our captains have been under lately. You have come to a logical conclusion," Spock agreed.

"Never thought I would see the day Bobby gets stoned," Russell huffed.

"He is usually a moderate drinker," Thaylassa said.

"Jim Kirk is the same. This Challenge got the better of both of them," McCoy summarized.

"What should we do?" Russell asked.

"The last thing this crew and ours need is to see our captains wasted, Doc," McCoy added.

"Correct assumption," T'Pau added.

"Let's put both of them in the guest quarters to sleep it off," Russell suggested.

"Logical, Doctor Russell. Doctor McCoy with me," Spock agreed.

Spock and McCoy went over to Kirk. Kirk looked up at both.

"Jim, I think you and Bob have had enough to drink."

"I have not, Bones."

"Yes, you have," McCoy said as he grabbed the bottle of Klingon blood wine and the glass from Kirk. Kirk tried to grab it back, but Spock stopped him.

"Let's go, Jim," McCoy said as he and Spock grabbed Kirk and walked him to the door. Russell and Shran followed behind holding an equally drunk Robert Hawke. T'Pau checked the deck.

"Quickly, efficiently," T'Pau said.

Kirk felt himself being hauled to a guest quarter, not his own. At the next door, Shran, Russell, and T'Pau were leading Hawke into the adjoining guest quarters.

"I want to go to my quarters, Bones," Kirk protested.

"Not in your state, Jim. You and Robert have been through the meat grinder in this case. You are both drunk and cannot command your ships."

"The doctor is right, Jim. Enterprise is in good hands," Spock said as he and McCoy laid Kirk out on the bed.

"Now get some rest. Doctor's orders," McCoy ordered.

Kirk couldn't respond. He felt his eyes close as he fell asleep.

McCoy and Spock rejoined Shran, Russell, and T'Pau.

"We'll just tell our crew that our captain must not be disturbed until we reach the Harrata home world," Thaylassa said.

"Logical, Thaylassa. We will tell our crew the same thing," Spock said.

"Bridge to Captain Kirk."

"Spock here. Lieutenant Uhura, make it known that Captain Kirk must not be disturbed until we reach the Harrata home world for the final ceremonies."

"Yes, Mister Spock, but I want to inform you that the GaZ is ready to begin towing procedures on both of our ships."

Spock looked at the visiting Constitution officers.

"Time to go," Shran said.

"Transporter room standby to beam Commander Shran and her party back to Constitution."

"Yes, Mister Spock," Kyle's voice came back.

"Lieutenant Uhura, notify the GaZ we will begin towing procedure as soon as Constitution signals she is ready."

"Yes, Sir."

Spock turned to see Shran and the visitors from Constitution heading for the turbo lift.

"Doctor."

"I'll stay here and watch both of them, Spock."

Spock nodded and headed for the bridge.

Within a few minutes, the enormous bulk of the Lothar GaZ released her tractor beams one at a time, latching onto Vorcha, then Suvwl'. Enterprise was next followed by Constitution. The monster swung away from Tong Omarti four and accelerated out of the system. Reaching the end of it the system, GaZ activated her warp drive. Her four massive nacelles flared as the GaZ jumped into warp.

Kirk watched this all on the guest rooms' view screen. He then fell back to sleep. The last thing he remembered was thinking good riddance to that planet.

PART FOUR

"We're going home." Kirk. By any other name. Star date 4657.5.

CHAPTER FORTY-ONE

THE FINAL INTERLUDE

PLANETOID X. STAR DATE 2925.12. February 3, 2267.

Sarek sat patiently watching the two opposite numbers from the Imperium discussing among them. The arrival of the Noob, which was traveling to meet up with the First Strike Force and Battle Group Hotel, had been an unexpected change in routine for them. Because of this, they had been summoned from the Ptolemy and had arrived down here promptly. In a few minutes, they would know if the Federation would be at war with the Imperium or not. Hattari and ToZak stopped chatting in Harratese and turned to Sarek and Shran.

"We regret to inform you that there will be no war between the Federation and the Klingon Empire. The book of prophecy was correct, and our government formally requests that we begin testing the waters between us. The Imperium would like to open our borders to trade relations with the Federation," Hattari said.

"This is the first of many discussions, Sarek, Shran. In a few months, we would like to meet to discuss further matters that concern both of our governments," ToZak said.

"The first order of business that concerns all members of the Federation is the recovery of the dead and the lost starships that perished during the Tong over the centuries," Shran said.

"It can be accomplished. We need to contract the chancellor and the high priestess of Gom to clear it, but in the interest of interstellar cooperation, it can be done."

"We also need the Federation to release all Subjective Command Merchant ships that have been interred and all interred Star force vessels must be released."

"We agree, Hattari. The Federation will comply," Sarek said.

"When will we see the dismantling of your battle stations, ToZak?"

"Not those, Shran. The Federation can maintain their outposts along our borders unless your people have something better to use them for."

"We will also allow you to regain control of the old Hell Spawn outpost," Hattari mentioned.

"And the problem with the Children of Lothar?" Sarek asked.

"That is a separate issue, Sarek, Shran, and extremely sensitive to the Harr or as you refer to us as the Harrata. We will discuss this later, Sarek."

"Our replacements will be with you the next time you are summoned, old friends," ToZak added.

"We need to contact our government to clear these matters. We are honored to have had both of you as competitors in the game of diplomacy all these years," Hattari said as she and ToZak put their fists together and with their staff bowed.

Sarek and Shran and their staffs did the same.

"Live long and Prosper Dana D Tozak and Akara Val Hattari," Sarek said as he made the appropriate Vulcan symbol.

"Honor, faith, and clan," Shran added as he closed his hand into a fist and pushed his arm in the air making the appropriate Andorian symbol. "ToZak and Hattari both responded in kind to both ambassadors." Peace and long life and honor, faith, and clan, Sarek, Shran."

As the Harrata stepped out, ToZak paused for a moment and looked back at Shran and Sarek. "Sarek, don't forget about the Ligarians as will be foretold in the book of prophecy."

Shran looked at Sarek. "Ligarians, who are the Ligarians?"

"Don't stress yourself out, Torel. One day, we will find out who they are."

"You're right, Sarek, but I am already starting to miss those two."

Sarek paused for a moment. Torel was right. He was going to miss those two.

"Let us return to the Ptolemy and contact the council. We have much to discuss."

Shran nodded as both entourages filed out of the room. A new day had dawned between the Federation and the Harrata Imperium.

13th FLEET NEAR THE SALAMIS STAR SYSTEM. STAR DATE 2925.18. BRAHE-NCC 1305. FLAGSHIP: 13TH FLEET:

Lance Cartwright wandered around the strange bridge that was his new flagship the Brahe. Until the Ark Royal had completed repairs, he was stuck here. The Brahe had been the first additional authorization Constitution class Heavy cruiser constructed between the completion of the original Constitution class and the Bonhomme Richards in the 2250s. Brahe had been used to test all sorts of experimental components. She was fitted with a third nacelle which later led to the construction of the Proxima and Federation class dreadnoughts.

It also led to the three-nacelle version of the Constitution class Heavy cruiser. The Sovereign class composed of twenty ships. All twenty were outfitted as battle cruisers. The Sovereign had been lost at Ghihoge.

But that was beside the point. The thirteenth was an odd hodgepodge of ships. Twenty of the fifty Detroyat class destroyers had been assigned to this fleet as well as ten Marklin class destroyers. In addition, the rest of the fleet was composed of old reactivated Caracal class cruisers, Drexler and Bode class scouts, and the heavy hitters, the four Sovereign class cruisers the Star stalker, Brahe, Argo, and Serapis.

It was a step up from old Fourth Reserve, but not counting the Sovereigns, the fleet was bordering on obsolescence. No wonder this fleet was considered a joke. No one in their right mind would put this collection of freaks on the front line. However, it was still a step up from the antiques of the Fourth Reserve. Cartwright could only sigh as he sat back in his new captains' chair.

"Well, Lance, what do you think of our much-maligned fleet?"

Cartwright looked up to see Fleet Captain Ian Hazard looking at him. Hazard was Brahe's commanding officer and had made his reputation years ago during the Tholian border skirmishes during the 2230s and later serviced during the Four Years' War. Now, he was an old veteran officer counting down his days to retirement.

"Things are going to change, Ian. I am tired of this fleet being the laughingstock of the Starfleet. This ship and her sisters will see a lot more action when all of this is over with and I intend to redeploy the fleet more aggressively."

"Rear Admiral Cartwright."

Cartwright swung his chair to face the science console. Brahe's Denobulan science officer looked at his new CO nervously. "Long-range sensors are picking up a massive fleet approaching."

"Confirmed, the Marklin scouting ahead signals a fleet of one hundred and fifty ships heading our way."

"Recall the Marklin and have the fleet reverse course. Which fleet is the closest?"

"The First Strike force," Hazards said.

Cartwright cursed under his breath. It had to be the FSF. Out of all fleets, it had to be that cesspool of liberal idealistic dreamers. He was only glad that Joseph Hawke and George Kirk didn't know of his section 31 connection. He and Vaughn were keeping the charade up. The fleet had no inkling of what would happen in a few years. They didn't have a clue.

"Where is the FSF?" he asked.

"Near the Salamis star system at last update."

"Signal all ships scramble coded, follow my lead, head for the Salamis star system, and get me Admiral Joseph Hawke. Tell him we have encountered Battle group Hotel composed of one hundred and fifty ships and we are heading your way."

Brahe's communication officer nodded. "Transmitting." Moments later, the communication officer looked back at Cartwright. "Admiral Hawke acknowledges. Proceed to Salamis. We will join you there."

"Sir, Battle Group Hotel is less than a parsec away from us. They have found us and are closing," Brahe's science officer said.

"All ships, this is Cartwright emergency warp. Jump now!"

The thirteenth jumped to warp. Moments later, Battle Group Hotel jumped into warp pursuing the Federation fleet.

First Strike Force-Task Force Alpha, near the Salamis star system. Star date 2930.19.

George Kirk turned from the communications station.

"They are on their way."

"ETA."

"Less than fifteen minutes."

"Signal the fleet, battle stations."

"Yes, Admiral."

"Standard magnification on screen, Mister Wojohowitz," Hawke ordered.

"Yes, Admiral, standard mag."

"Admiral, I have a lone contact shadowing us at ten thousand kilometers. It's a Harrata scout ship," Kirov's science officer mentioned.

"Could be a scout from Hotel," Fleet Captain Scheer said.

"What is her trajectory?"

"Sir, the Guadalcanal signals that she has the thirteen on visual. Behind them is battle group Hotel."

The Guadalcanal was a Paladin class destroyer.

"Her trajectory indicates her course came from the Imperium, near Planetoid X and the Tong Omarti system."

"Sir Cartwright requests orders."

"Tell him to take position next to FSF Charlie."

"Yes, Sir."

"Admiral, the Harrata scout is the Noob. She is the one who contacted the Soyuz and the Constellation earlier," Kirov's Andorian science officer said.

"Admiral."

Hawke turned to see the little scout ship park herself right between the oncoming fleets.

"She's crazy," George exclaimed.

Hawke cursed. They were down to eighty ships. The Defenders were giving trouble again. And he only had ten combat support vessels trailing his fleet and five Moran warp tugs backed up by the Keppler and the Ibn Daud reassigned from Star base 41.

"What is the strength of Hotel?"

"Two Vorrath class type 1 battleships, six Marga class type 1 battle cruisers, ten Hegar class type 1 Heavy cruisers, twenty Hogar class type 8s, twenty Hogar class types 7s, numerous Neparah, Spedy class ships supplemented by the new Chiss class type one light cruisers. The Vorrath, Marga, Hegar, and Chiss were the Star force's latest edition to their fleets, along with the new Hogar class type 8s. Unlike Alpha to Delta, Hotel had the latest new design class of starships.

"Joe." Kirk warned.

Hawke turned to see the Harrata fleet suddenly come to a halt.

"Signal all fleets. Do not engage. Hold position." Hawke ordered.

Out in space, the FSF along with the 13th fleet stopped and held a position facing the one hundred and fifty ships of Battle Group Hotel.

"Admiral, the commander of Battle Group Hotel wishes a truce to confer," Kirov's communication officer said.

"Put him on."

"Yes, Admiral."

Moments later, the screen of space showing the distant enemy ships was replaced by the familiar gold, blue, and red triangular bridge. A red-haired Harrata officer wearing the traditional Mohawk haircut and the blue cast color stepped forward. He had mutton chop sideburns and was slightly overweight.

"I am Vorrad Baruta Kelalo Jafary, commander of Battle group Hafaz. Of the Harrata Imperium, who am I addressing?" Jafary said in high-caste Harratese English.

Joseph Hawke got out of his command chair. "Vorrad Jafary, I am Admiral Joseph Edward Hawke, commanding officer of the First Strike force-Task Force Alpha representing the United Federation of Planets."

"Our scout ship the Noob has important information concerning the outcome of the Challenge. We would like to confer on neutral ground."

"Agreed. We should move our flagships to the Noob and confer aboard this ship if that is acceptable," Hawke suggested.

Jafary turned away from the screen and began to confer with his officers. Seconds later, he turned back. "It is agreeable, Vorrad Hawke."

"A half an hour."

"Yes." The screen went blank only to be replaced by space.

"Mister, I want Vice Admiral Fairchild in the Praetorian, Commodore Morrow in the Ari, and Rear Admiral Cartwright in the Brahe to join me with their ships in neutral ground between our fleets"

"Yes, Sir."

"George, get us ready for a welcoming committee. We will soon know the fates of our sons and if we will or will not be going to war."

"No problem, Joe," George said. He had a lot to do in less than half an hour.

535

ONE-HALF HOUR LATER:

Slowly but surely, the Kirov, Brahe, Ari, and Praetorian moved clear of their fleets.

Opposite them in one battleship, one battle cruiser along with two familiar Hogars left the Harrata fleet and rendezvoused with the Federation ships.

KIROV'S BRIEFING ROOM:

George Kirk was sitting at the library computer station in Kirov's secondary briefing room which was the standard type of room on his sons Enterprise. Next to him was Joe Hawke, followed by Vice Admiral Louis Fairchild, Commodore Harold Randolph Morrow, and finally representing the 13th was Captain Brevet Rear Admiral Lance Cartwright temporarily estranged from the Ark Royal assigned to Brahe sat at the end.

Moments later, the briefing room door swooshed open. Kirov's chief of security Captain Louis Santiago led the five Harrata officers in. Simultaneously, they each took their seats opposite them.

"Admiral," Santiago asked.

"Standby outside and wait to escort our esteemed officers back to the transporter rooms when we are finished, Captain."

Santiago nodded. "Yes, Sir."

"On behalf of the united Federation of planets, the First Strike force, and the thirteenth fleet, we welcome you," Joe said.

"On behalf of the Harrata Imperium, Battle group Hafaz, and Special group Lothar representing the Noob, we accept your welcome," Jafary said as he got up and his officers clenched their fists together, placed them together, and bowed.

Joe and his party got up and returned the gesture. Quickly, both groups returned to their seats.

"Nav Commander d' Taz has information for you," Jafary said.

The plain-looking female Harrata stood up. She was wearing the feminine version of the gold jumpsuit with the required blue sash. She had the two full stripes and one broken strip in blue on her collar representing Nav commander, the equivalent of Commander in the Starfleet.

Kirk could feel his palms sweating. He could see that Joseph was also uneasy. D'taz looked at the Federation officers. It was time to get it over with. Clearly, the Admiral and the Fleet Captain were the fathers of the two challengers. The other three officers however sat mute.

George could feel himself screaming inside. He didn't want a repeat of Tycho. Not again, not this time.

D'taz broke the silence, "Ober Commanders Kirk and Hawke have survived."

Kirk felt a rush of relief spread over him. Jimmy had done it. Soon, he would contact his beloved Winona and George Jr. and his family to tell them the good news.

"I will notify my government of what has transpired, Vorrad Hawke. We will withdraw all our forces."

"And we will do the same, Vorrad Jafary." Hawke hit the button. "Captain Santiago, please escort our guests back to the transporter room."

"Yes, Sir," Santiago said as he came in with his security detail.

Hawke and the officers got up, followed by the Harrata contingent who immediately departed the room.

Cartwright blew a sigh of relief. "That was short and swift."

Morrow smiled. "Congratulations, Joe, George, looks like the great bird of the galaxy was with us today," Morrow said as he shook Joe Hawke's and then George Kirk's hand. Fairchild patted them both on the back.

"All's well that ends well," Fairchild mused.

"Admiral," came the voice of the Kirov's communications officer. "The Harrata delegation has beamed back to their ships and they are returning to their fleet."

"Admiral," came the voice of Kirov's executive officer Nicolas Sherman.

"Yes, Commander."

"The Harrata ships are powering down their shields."

"Order all ships in both fleets to stand down from red alert and go to condition green and get me Starfleet Command and the commanders of the Eighth, Ninth, and the Fourth reserve fleets."

"Yes, Sir."

Hawke turned to Kirk. "Let's start demobilizing, George, until the next crisis comes."

Kirk nodded. It was time to put the fleets back on a peaceful standing and release ships that were needed elsewhere. The FSF was going to fall back to its prewar strength of fifty ships instead of the original one hundred and fifty it had during the crisis. That meant releasing the Miranda, Soyuz, Anton, Saladin, Hermes, and Constitution class vessels. The others would have to stay until Starfleet ordered them elsewhere. Only Kirov and the original assigned fifty would stay.

Kirk blew a sigh of relief. "I am glad this is all over with, Joe."

"Same, I can't wait to see my son Robert again. I have to contact the rest of the family and notify Dina my ex-wife at Starfleet Command and her husband Steven who is the commander of the Starfleet Flight Command Division Charlie at Star base 27 of the news."

"And I have to do the same."

"See you later," Kirk said as he and Joe went their separate ways on the Kirov. Kirk was so happy he jumped for joy in front of some startled Kirov crewmembers and did a little jig as he made his way back to his quarters.

Starfleet Operations. Main Missions. Star date 2925.20.

Admiral Herbert Solow stepped into Starfleet operations to find the place had the atmosphere of a party.

Comsol, Hahn, Buchinsky, Solow, and the rest were all dancing for joy.

Something momentous had happened. The usually stark, professional operations center was completely bonkers. Mattea Hahn ran up to him and gave him a surprise hug. Solow was startled by Mattea Hahn's reaction.

"What's going on, Mattea?"

"Didn't you hear the news Kirk and Hawke survived? There will be no full-scale war, and we did it!" Comsol and Buchinsky walked up.

"Herbert. Robert, Marcus. Herb."

"Isn't that great, Herb, no war with the Imperium?" Mattea said.

Comsol walked up with a bottle of Champagne.

"Vintage 2177, Bollinger," Comsol added.

Solow grabbed some glasses and passed them out. Comsol shook the bottle and popped the cork. Buchinsky caught some of the liquid. Mattea got the rest. Comsol filled each admiral's glass up.

Raising his glass, he said, "To Captain James Kirk and Captain Robert Hawke. We honor you."

Glasses clanked and there it was announced. A sigh of relief filled the room.

STAR BASE 11. STAR DATE 2925. 23. COMMODORE STONE'S OFFICE:

Stone looked over the Vulcan and the pudgy human. Behind them stood Captain La Liberté of the Excelsior and his Tellerite First Officer Bork and Security Chief Commander Leopold Mozart.

A star base commander's job never ended. Serving fleet commanders, if a fleet was assigned to the base, relations with colony governors if a colony had been built at a base.

The never-ending stream of requests from Federation Starfleet and Merchant ship captains and the irritation from their private counterparts added to the exasperation.

Commanding the Defiant, Stone thought was so much easier than this. Dealing with these two was probably going to be the easiest part of his day. He had a backlog of ships, not enough dock space, and Constitution and her CO were going to be in for a shock when they finally arrived here from the Harrata Imperium in four days. He had no place to put Hawke's battle-damaged ship. And that ship needed more work than just repairing her battle damage.

He had already contacted Starfleet Command that Constitution would require a minimum of six weeks to get her back into service. That included overhauling her, upgrading the ship's computer system, new nacelles to replace her odd ball original ones, and major weapons in case the Starfleet had to face the Defense force. Added to that, he would have to deal with Hawke's worn-out crewmembers.

Stone got up and looked at the pudgy human and the Vulcan who was smiling. Stone figured this Sybok was doing it just to irritate him. He however was no ordinary Vulcan but a son of Sarek and he had to treat him with kid gloves. The trader Cyrano Jones was one of the better ones of his kind.

"I would like to inform you that quasi-war between the Federation and the Harrata Imperium has been concluded. Both of you may go on your respective ways," Stone said.

"Thank you, Commodore, thank you, friend," Jones said exuberantly.

"We are returning your ship, Mister Jones, as for Sybok. You cannot return to the Pengus colony. If you do you, you will be arrested by the authorities and sent to jail," Stone warned.

"I know you are a son of Sarek, Sybok, but those are my orders from Starfleet and T'Pau of Vulcan," Stone added.

Sybok bowed his head; he knew the consequences of his actions on Pengus.

Jones raised his pudgy hand. "Commodore Stone, I will take Sybok to wherever he needs to go. I must first meet a Harrata businessman at Domar Amid three near Fillapadous before I return to more familiar surroundings of K7."

Stone paused for a moment. Jones did have a good point.

"Commodore, you can't be serious," LaLiberté exclaimed.

"Very well mister Jones I put Sybok in your care. I will forward you a list of colonies. Where Sybok cannot be left off at. And as a precaution, I will send an all-points fleet bulletin to every ship, base, and outpost of your whereabouts mister Jones. One does not renege on your promise to me or I will put the full might of the Starfleet on your tail." Turning to LaLiberté.

"Is that satisfactory, Captain?"

"Yes, it is."

"Then that is it. You may leave gentlemen."

La Liberté and his officers followed by Jones and Sybok left the Commodore's office. Stone hit the intercom. "Commander Cooper has maintenance crew D shifted from Lexington to Intrepid. I want orbital dock four to be free for Constitution by Star date 2947 at the earliest. She is a top priority repair, upgrade, and overhaul candidate."

"Commodore, but what if she arrives before 2947?"

"Then they will have to wait."

CHAPTER FORTY-TWO

ENTERPRISE RECREATION ROOM 3:

Kirk tossed the food he had on his plates as he slowly ate his ham and eggs because he still had a slight hangover from drinking that awful Klingon blood wine. He had settled on decaf coffee. He had woken up and went back to his quarters for a shower and a change into a clean uniform.

Orders had come through from Starfleet that once the final ceremonies were concluded, Enterprise was going to rendezvous with Commodore Harry Morrow's recovery and salvage fleet near Hell Spawn. From there, Enterprise was going to be towed to Star base Trafalgar for repairs. And he and Robert were going to go their separate ways again, with Constitution due at Star base 11.

The recreation room doors snapped open. Hawke entered the recreation room saying, "This isn't my ship," trying to be funny.

Some Enterprise crewmembers laughed at the joke. Hawke went over to the wall unit and ordered his breakfast. Moments later, he sat down opposite Kirk. Kirk noticed that his fellow captain had a similar breakfast. He however had substituted bacon for ham.

"I had forgotten the kick that Romulan ale has, Jim."

"Well, I never knew that blood wine would taste so awful," Kirk admitted.

"Well, at least I like the Pogash you gave us Bob. The crew really likes it."

"Same for the Tranya, Jim."

"Remember the inter-academy games," Kirk said remembering.

"How could I forget? You led your team to victory one year and I won the next year. We really wiped the floor with those beetle crunching grunts of the Federation Military Academy," Hawke remembered.

"We sure did." Starfleet's basketball, football, soccer, and hockey teams had to face their opposite numbers from FMA. It also included boxing. And he and Robert both had participated in the Commando course against their rivals. Kirk remembered. "Who is Starfleet Academy's all-time boxing champion?" Kirk said.

Hawke smiled. "That's easy. Matt Decker academy class 2239. He holds the record of 20-0 and between 2235-37, he beat the hell out of all the FMA challengers in the inter-academy games. And who led the academy to the most Polo wins."

"Bob Wesley," Kirk said. "Same academy class."

The intercom cut their conversation short.

Kirk flicked the switch. Spock's image appeared on the screen. "I trust you and Captain Hawke are sobered up, Captain."

"We are, Spock."

"We just entered the Harrata Star System. The government signals that we will participate in the final Parida in four hours. And Miss Jennings wants to interview both you and Captain Hawke one last time."

Kirk could hear Hawke sighing. The last thing they needed was another interview. But they had to maintain good public relations with the public at large.

"She added that she would like to hold it on the Enterprise this time," Spock said.

"Not my ship, Spock," Kirk said exasperated.

"And not mine," Hawke protested.

"Then where?" Spock said.

"Ask Finnegan that we would like to do the final interview on his ship instead," Kirk said.

Spock's eyebrow went up. "That seems to be a logical choice, Jim."

"Tell her within one hour."

Hawke had quickly finished his breakfast and got up.

"And have the transporter room beam Robert back to his ship."

"Affirmative, bridge out."

Kirk finished up his breakfast too. And he joined his fellow starship captain.

"I'll see you within an hour, Bob, on the Cortez."

"I will be there," Hawke said as he left the recreation room. He had a lot to finish up when he got back to his ship. Kirk got up and headed for the bridge. He needed to catch up on a few things before the interview and the Parida.

Omarz Allah Orbiting Harrata Four. Star date 2925.5.

Omar Ek watched the three screens along with the three humans from section 31 with deep concern. The humans instead of being happy at the survival of the two Starfleet ships were angry and sulking at the sight of the enormous Vorrad Class Battleship towing Enterprise, Constitution, Suvwl, and Vorcha surrounded by the Kotcha class gunboats escorting them into the standard orbit of the Harrata home world.

"This cannot be, no human has ever survived the Challenge," the female agent said exasperated that both ships survived.

"We could have had Waterston and Tutakai in command of their successors and we would have had our revenge against the Hawke family for opposing us in the beginning," one of the male operatives said.

"Rittenhouse has cabled us that Waterston will be ready by 2268. We just must find a way to replace either Kirk or Hawke without arousing suspicion. And Rittenhouse said that due to delays, the Star Empire will not be finished until 2270," the other male operative said.

Ek looked at the humans. "Do you want to stay for the parade?"

"No. Take us back to Minotaur five. There we will make our rendezvous with the Spetsnaz."

Ek nodded. Good. Now he will finally get paid well for this.

The Omar Ek sped out of the system.

Cortez-NCC 536, flanked by Kotcha class type 6 gunboats Allay-HIS 00245 and Dog-HIS 00233 Orbiting Harrata Four. Star date 2925. 6.

Kirk and Hawke followed Finnegan and Jennings, as he laid out the history of Cortez's predecessors. After the portrait of Hernando Cortez, Kirk spotted the Verne class Cortez, lost under mysterious circumstances, followed by the Intrepid class Cortez lost at the Battle of Wolf 359 with the FSF only to be succeeded by the Bonaventure class Cortez, hijacked by Romulans in 2180.

In one of the three known incidents that predated his and Robert's battles with Romulans in 2266 during the Romulans-forced isolation after the Earth-Romulan war, Cortez was destroyed by Constitution, her sister ship.

They then arrived at the Nelson Class Cortez which had been decommissioned due to her commanding officers' disgraceful actions, followed by the Larson Class Cortez which due to severe battle damage was also decommissioned, and Cortez's immediate predecessor, the Miranda class Cortez, was hijacked by renegade Vulcans and destroyed by the Enterprise.

Somehow, Kirk thought that some ships with names like Valiant, Gallant, Cortez, or Alexander never got any break. Cortez's sister ship Alexander had been rescued by the Tori in 2258.

Alexander had suffered so much damage that she too was decommissioned. He could recall that Scuttlebutt was going around in the fleet at the time that they were planning on giving Alexander to him. But everything fell through and he was put back in the temporary first officer pool and reassigned.

With the pleasantries finished, Kirk took his seat in between Hawke and Finnegan.

Jennings and Victor checked their equipment. Martin, Finnegan's chief communications officer, had done a good but adequate job of tying them into the Harrata Subspace array.

And just like the last interview, they would receive this final one in the same way as the first. Somehow, Jennifer wished that the interview could have been conducted on Enterprise or Constitution again. But Hawke and Kirk were adamant about it. So, now she missed the skills of Starfleet's two top Chief Communications Officers Uhura and Shimada. Richard Martin was adequate. Maybe now she would, and the public learns why there was such a discrepancy in the fleet between the Imperial Guard like Heavy cruiser fleet and the poor slobs who manned the little ships.

"In three, two, one," Victor said.

"Live aboard the U.S.S Cortez, this is a special report by Jennifer Jennings. Federation one Harrata Imperium Zero. I am here in the briefing room aboard the destroyer Cortez. With me is Captain James Tiberius Kirk, Captain of the Enterprise, Starfleet's Flagship, Captain Robert Nelson Hawke and Captain of the Constitution, which is sometimes known as Starfleet's other flagship, and finally, Commander Sean Finnegan, captain of the Cortez," Jennifer Jennings said finishing her introductions.

She looked at the commanding officers and decided to settle on Kirk.

"Tell me, Captain Kirk, what is your conclusion of this Challenge? What are your views and your opinions?"

Kirk suddenly felt like she had shoved him into a corner. He had to do this diplomatically no matter how much it bothered him on the inside.

"The Challenge is brutal, barbaric game fostered upon all other races in the Alpha quadrant in the name of piety. Robert and I had some close calls. The game is personal to a point. Unless you have been through it, you cannot understand."

"Captain Hawke, the same question."

Hawke paused for a moment. This was going to get tough, he thought.

"It took all our skill to get through this," Hawke said. He wanted to keep it short and sweet. The sooner this interview was over, the sooner he could get back to more important things.

"Robert, I, and Sean here all swore an oath to protect the Federation, Miss Jennings. By surviving the Challenge, we did protect the Federation and her citizens," Kirk said.

Hawke nodded in agreement. "I also believe that both Jim and I have changed because of this experience. We both have grown up and our friendship as fellow Starfleet officers and captains has now reached the next level," he explained passionately.

"Indeed, we have, Bob, no more games, no more childhood antics," Kirk admitted.

"I concur, Jim," Hawke said.

"Commander Finnegan, what do you have to say about these two? You were at the academy at the time that both were enrolled. What is your view?"

Finnegan looked at Kirk and Hawke. "I always figured that these two were meant for great things. Don't get me wrong, Jimmy and Bobby. I only hazed you two to try to get both of you out of your prima donna attitudes," Finnegan said and looked at Kirk. "I mean, Jim, why do you think we called you a stack of book with legs? You were so dour you made my hair wilt."

Kirk smiled embarrassedly by Finnegan's remark.

"And mister almighty over here." Finnegan pointed to Hawke. "Lord of Delta squad, mister self-righteous. I had to bring you back to earth, Bobby. A couple of good challenges I gave you brought you down from Mount Olympus and maybe gave you some compassion," Finnegan said.

Hawke also smiled. Hawke shifted in his seat uncomfortably. Did Finnegan have to reveal all?

Finnegan joined in and smiled.

Jennifer Jennings looked at Hawke, Kirk, and Finnegan. It looks like the interview, unlike the first, was going to be short and sweet.

"Anything more to add Captains Kirk, Hawke, Commander Finnegan?"

She received a chorus of noes.

"In closing reporting from the Cortez orbiting Harrata Four, this is Jennifer Jennings signing off."

Jennifer got up out of the chair followed by Hawke, Kirk, and Finnegan.

"Well, gentlemen, that was short and sweet."

"There really wasn't much to talk about, Jennifer," Kirk said. "And don't worry about the Tranya. I'll be sending you a case of it."

"Captain Hawke," Jennifer asked Hawke, "And my Pogash?"

"I haven't forgotten, but I will match Jim's offer and send you a case of Pogash as promised."

"Thank you, Captain." Jennifer checked her chronometer. "I have to run, with you and Robert participating in the final Parida. Victor and I must head for the embassies and interview the ambassadors. Until the next time, Captains." Jennings said as she and victor left the briefing room.

Finnegan turned to Hawke and Kirk.

"It is still good to see both of you again. And I just want to tell you both that we may be seeing more of each other in the coming years," Finnegan said.

"How much more, Sean?" Kirk said concerned.

"I just received orders from Starfleet command. Starfleet is transferring the Jenghiz, Sargon, Cortez, and the Shaitan to Star base 27 from Star base 6. We have been reassigned to try to fill in the gap in the patrol line that merges on Enterprise's and Constitution's patrol routes along the Federation-Klingon border. That planet Amasov. We'll be using it as a jumping-off point for our patrols fanning out toward 12 and 27. So, Jimmy, if you and Bobby ever need help, just holler and good old Cortez will come to both of your rescues," Finnegan said smiling enjoying every minute of it.

Kirk could only shake his head. "What did we do to deserve this, Bob?"

Hawke could only raise his hands to the ceiling. "Why us, Jim?" he said hopelessly.

"I see we are all in agreement," Finnegan finished off. He had finally gotten the last word with both.

CHAPTER FORTY-THREE

HARRATA FOUR. CITY OF TOMAR. FINAL PARIDA AND CLOSING CEREMONIES. STAR DATE 2926.8. February 6, 2267.

"Mild, Spock? This heat is mild. It reminds me of Georgia," McCoy said to Spock as they observed the dignitaries give one boring speech after another.

"It might remind you of Georgia, Doctor, but it hardly fits the temperatures experienced on Vulcan."

Kirk looked at McCoy and Spock. "Bones, Spock, enough of this," Kirk said slightly frustrated. He looked around the massive podium which held all the Harrata government officers. To his left, he made out the cabinet officers sitting below the military staff.

Above them were the Imperial Supremes, the Harrata version of a supreme court. Above them sat a few representatives of House of Harratay, the lower house, and above them were the House of Lords, the upper house.

The female vice chancellor was making her speech. Soon, the chancellor would make his speech and the final Parida would begin. Looking behind him, he could see Khod and his people sitting above him. Kang's people were above Khod's and Robert sat below him.

Each of them had been awarded a sash of honor. Kang's had four colors, Khod's three, his was two, and Robert's had been a single color. Kang had scored the highest with Robert scoring the lowest due to his injury in the second part of the Challenge. After all this was finished, he had intended never to wear this again but to keep it as a cherished memento.

Kirk could now hear Chancellor Vardeck de Banari making his speech. It was almost time.

"Harratay! A Salutay Klingonasse, Humass," Banari bellowed out.

In front of them, Kirk watched as all the civilian Harrata, the multicolored mass suddenly prostrated themselves. The High Order Corp and the Middle Order Corp knelt as did all the government officers. The banging started in unison as the soldiers of the corps banged the disruptor lances against their energy shields.

Hittay, the ringmaster, came down. "By order of sash, you may begin."

Kang followed by Khod led the way. Soon, he, Spock, and McCoy followed finally by Robert's people marched down the stairs onto the Boulevard of the Imperium and headed for the temple of the deity's way.

THE LEGATIONS:

Jennifer Jennings and Victor along with Ambassador Burroughs and her aide Andrew watched the spectacle unfold before them. She had been more successful this time with the interviews. She had a successful interview with Élan, Dohlman of Elas, and the Troyan ambassador Sezak. The Tkarians had reluctantly come to their senses. She was also able to get interviews with the Mirak and the Orions. The Kzinti ambassador due to the blunder they had committed was nowhere to be found.

She had a very engaging interview with the Xindi ambassadors and even got one from the Klingon ambassador.

"So, mister ambassador, all is well that ends well."

"Yes, Miss Jennings, and the good news is that my successor ambassador Burg gah Mesh is traveling to Harrata Four as we speak. He will be arriving aboard the Isshasshte and then back to Earth."

"Congratulations, Madam Ambassador," Jennings said as she watched the champions of the Federation and the Klingon Empire walk by the silent masses of the Harrata Imperium. Once all of this had concluded, she would be heading for her next assignment. The Federation's luck had finally changed.

Kirk looked up at the Legations. Spock was on his right, McCoy on his left. None of them were speaking. And everything was silent as a tomb.

Once this circus was finished, he was looking forward to getting back to Enterprise's primary mission, of exploration. He glanced back at Robert. Hawke smiled in return.

There was none of the old bluster that he had known from his old academy rival. It was as though he and Hawke had matured. It was now a new phase in their friendship, and he felt that the next time they met again, it would be on a new more mature level. They both had grown up.

Kirk watched as they left the Boulevard of the Imperium and entered the Temple of Deities' way. He could see the many priests and priestesses lining up next to their temples. The majestic temple of Gom dominated the very end of the way. An elegant female High priestess made her way down the stairs as they approached the temple of Gom. Kirk felt relieved that the Tong was nearing completion.

ENTERPRISE COMPUTER CORE:

Lieutenant Commander Benjamin Finney watched the parade in silence, his anger growing inside of him. He was still glad to be alive but just hated the sight of Kirk marching like a triumphant conqueror in that damned parade. During the Challenge, he had slowly begun to formulate his plan of revenge. He was at the top of the roster to be assigned the next pod assignment when an ion storm hit. He needed to falsify the actual log and find a place to hide. The initial place to hide would be the lower cargo holds on deck 24 with supplies to last him a few days. He would not be missed, only if the ship was evacuated would he move up to the main engineering on deck 19.

"Enjoy your triumph while you can, Kirk. It will be short-lived," Finney said to himself with satisfaction.

TEMPLE OF GOM:

Kirk followed Khod's and Kang's group as they entered the Temple of Gom. Compared to the Temple of Lothar, it was like night and day. The corridors glittered from the colorful jewels that lined the walls acting as a natural lighting system as they lighted up the corridor. In the distance, Kirk could hear the rumble of thunder and lightning. Spock was adjusting his tricorder to pick up data on the event. He looked back to see T'Pau conversing with Robert as her tricorder was also analyzing the incoming data.

"Never seen the likes of this," McCoy said surprised. "The care they put into this temple is like the complete reverse of that Temple of Lothar back on the Lothar system."

"Since Gom is like Zeus or Jupiter doctor, its temple would resemble a palace befitting the chief ruler of the deities," Spock added. Double-checking his tricorder, Spock's eyebrow went up.

"Something wrong, Mister Spock?" Kirk asked.

"Yes, Captain, my tricorder readings are correlating with the readings we received at the barrier a few years ago. My sensors say something is there, but my scanners say there is nothing here," Spock said as he looked back at T'Pau. "Lieutenant, are you receiving similar readings?"

T'Pau nodded. "Yes, Spock, sensors and scanners are acting the same way they did when we did encounter the barrier four days later, Spock. We received the same readings; this is not logical."

"Indeed, it is not, T'Pau."

Chanting echoed through the temple as they approached the end of their journey. Suddenly, as it began, the lightning and thunder stopped. A lone voice suddenly echoed out, "Gom!"

All was silent as they turned the corner and reached a circular room. In the rear stood the dais where the priests and priestesses did their praying. The high priestess marched them up alongside the circular hole. Kirk looked down into the wide chasm. Energies not so different from the barrier collided in furious chorus of energy.

"Spock."

"Captain, all of my tricorder readings correlate with the ones we received when we encountered the energy barrier. If Gom is what it is, then the barrier maybe a living entity."

"You are correct, Mister Spock," Napari, high priestess of Gom said. "The loss of your S.S Valiant back when you began your interstellar warp age was a warning. But you and Captain Hawke over here persisted. Only one could finally be let into the intergalactic darkness. Gom chose your sister ship, Kirk. The book of prophecy felt that you were not ready for the mantle of responsibility that you now face today. You were hit by the demons of the Q continuum when you entered the barrier and paid the price."

Kirk looked at Hawke. "What happened out there, Robert?"

Hawke bowed his head. "You don't know the half of it, Jim, and we are all sworn to secrecy for the sake of the survival of the Federation. When we are finished with this, never ask me this question again." Hawke looked at Kirk. He had the look of a condemned man on his face.

"While you shine in greatness, Kirk, your equal and friend here will work in the shadows. He is as great as you are, Kirk, but he bears a burden which you will never have to bear. He will be laughed at, called crazy, but when the time comes, what he did will make him nearly as great as you in the eyes of future generations. This part of his mission will not be revealed for another six centuries when humankind is now advanced enough to deal with the threat that lies beyond our galaxy," Napari said answering Kirk's question.

Anadaria/Gom came over to the group.

"One must join with me," came the male/female voice from Anadaria.

"Thy will be done, great one," Napari said as she bowed and stepped aside.

Anadaria/Gom ignored Kang and Khod and moved over to Kirk.

"You went to find the missing and lost your friend," Anadaria/Gom said.

Kirk nodded as he stared into the cat's eyes of the Harrata priest.

"You are not due, Kirk, you will be touched in the future by others, but not today," Anadaria/Gom said as she moved from Kirk over to Hawke.

Anadaria/Gom pointed at Hawke. "He's the one." Anadaria/Gom suddenly jerked with a mighty spasm and collapsed.

Hawke screamed and toppled over.

Anadaria then stood up and flung herself into the mealstrom as Kirk ran over to his friend.

Napari flung herself between Kirk, blocking him and everyone else. "Do not interfere," she said as she was joined by more priests and priestesses that formed a wall between them.

HAWKE:

Robert could hear voices, but he was falling into a void, an endless void that never ended. Something or someone had possessed him.

Kirk glanced over at the prone figure of Robert Hawke. McCoy and Russell were trying to talk reason with the priests and priestesses, but nothing came of it. Hawke suddenly stood up. His eyes glowed as they shimmered in a cat-like radiance.

McCoy quickly checked his tricorder and his medical scanner; Russell was doing the same.

"Oh, god," Russell said as he stared at his readings. Humans were not meant to be possessed by this entity.

McCoy realized the same. "You are going to kill him. Humans cannot take Gom's energy, high priestess. He'll burn up."

"High priestess, my friend cannot take what you are doing to him," Kirk pleaded with Napari.

"He will die if we don't do something soon."

"Let me meld with him," Spock said.

"No, Spock, I must do it," T'Pau said as she came up to Spock. "You have never melded with him, but I have."

"If you insist, T'Pau kam."

"It is my right, Spock."

"High priestess, let T'Pau meld with her captain. It will stabilize him."

"Very well," Napari said as she ordered the priests and priestess to part ways.

"Let McCoy and Russell through to monitor them both."

Napari nodded. "Agreed."

T'Pau, McCoy, and Russell rushed forward. T'Pau paused for a moment to meditate as Russell ran his scanner over Hawke. McCoy monitored T'Pau's readings. T'Pau focused on Hawke. Her hand reached out and touched her captain's face. "My mind your mind. My thoughts to your thoughts. We are merging, we are one," T'Pau said.

A flood of images filled her mind. She let out a scream and then calmed down. She was in. She found herself floating in a void of blackness, which suddenly started to form into space. She found her captain floating in space as she reached out and grabbed him. They both stabilized as Hawke stopped falling. Events started to form around them as the history of the Harr race known as the Harrata and Harrkonen began.

Gom/Hawke/T'Pau got up. Napari and the religious retinue stepped aside as Kirk walked up to face them.

"You are being honored, Kirk. Only the first champions are honored," Kang said.

Gom/Hawke/T'Pau faced Kirk and said, "We honor you as champions, Humans and Klingons." Gom said in a perfect human male/female voice through the receptacle that was Hawke.

Kirk could see the cats' eyes glaring at him.

"We are sorry that we did not understand the fragility of your race. The Harr are a chosen people who existed long before your world could support life, Captain Kirk. The Challenge is merely used to test your worthiness and your standing in the universe. The dark times are returning, and we must be certain all races in these two quadrants can sustain the assault that will come."

"Will there be further challenges, Gom?" Kirk asked.

Gom/Hawke looked at Kirk. "No. All challenges of this reality are done."

"Reality as in more than one?" Kirk asked.

"Yes, this T'Pau is fascinating at such a young age she may have opened the door to a wider understanding of reality and your Mister Spock will also contribute to this in his own way."

Spock raised his eyebrow at the compliment.

"We came in peace, Gom."

"And you may go in peace. But Kirk, we will meet again." Gom/Hawke reached out and touched him. Kirk could feel the power of Gom surging through him and he could now hear Hawke and T'Pau's voice in the distance. A flash of images flooded through him. It was overwhelming Kirk started to feel woozy. Kirk watched as Hawke and T'Pau collapsed. Everything went black. The last thing he heard was the voices of Spock and McCoy.

CHAPTER FORTY-FOUR

Qunos. Klingon Home world. Chancellor's residence. Star date 2925.9.

Gorkon walked into Chancellor Sturkas residence as Kesh, Logash, and Koval all walked out.

He didn't trust any of them. All were in striking distance to become the next Chancellor. Kesh was slightly mad, Logash was a power-crazed control freak, and Koval hated the humans so much it blinded his judgment. All were probably plotting Sturkas demise. At least, Sturka was stable like Tomec. Neither had been influenced by the Duras family that he firmly distrusted.

"Councilor Gorkon, what brings you here today?"

"Good news and bad, Chancellor."

"The bad first."

"The Duras family has rammed down the council's mouth, another phony emperor."

Sturka grunted. The Duras never learned. "Who?"

"Kahmmaur Setai and his wife Kessa Setai."

"Of house Morath, isn't there a lord Kruge related to them?"

"Yes, Chancellor."

"And the good."

"Kang and Khod survived the Challenge."

Sturka sat down as Gorkon sat opposite him.

"And the humans?"

"Kirk and Hawke have survived."

Sturka grunted very annoyed at this development and threw his glass of blood wine against the wall missing Gorkon who had to duck out of the way.

"The Harratay have ruined everything! Now they are ready for us! In six months, we will have war with the Federation!" Sturka moaned.

"We still have to avenge the humiliation of Donatu Five Chancellor. Our honor and our standing in the galaxy demand it," Gorkon said.

"Indeed, it does, Gorkon. The battle of Star base 42 was a warning to the Federation. Despite this setback of ridding our Empire of the Starfleet's two most infamous starships, we will prevail. I will not have us further humiliated by the Federation. Unlike the border war, Gorkon, this conflict will run up and down our borders and the Federation. We will engage them everywhere and anywhere. They cannot be everywhere at once. They have to watch the patQ

Romulans and the Tholians and still have to deal with the Naussicans, Tkarians, Orions, and the Kzinti pirates and raiders."

"And what about the other powers?" Gorkon asked.

"The Mirak, Lyrans, and Hydrans are friendly to the Federation. So are the Xindi. The useless, nearly bankrupt Ferengi, thanks to the Harratay's Tong Va Gar are too far for real contact with Federation borders. The patQ Cardassians are in a similar situation. Only the Gorn which is close enough to Federation space may help us and work to our advantage."

"Starfleet has yet to contact them, Chancellor."

"Notify our ambassador to the Gorn to make overtures and I want our ambassador to Romulus to put out feelers for an alliance," Sturka said as he got up. Gorkon stood up as Sturka turned to face him. "Who is the present chancellor of the Romulan Empire?"

"According to imperial intelligence, the Romulans are in transition. Vrax will be stepping down and Gaius is in waiting," Gorkon said recalling the latest directive put forward by Imperial Intelligence. "Vrax is tough and suspicious. Gaius, Imperial Intelligence believes could be manipulated by us."

"What about that unfounded rumor about the Duras family being lapdogs of the Romulans?"

"Just rumors, nothing proven."

"I do not trust the Romulans, but their strengths are our weaknesses and vice versa," Sturka said cautiously. "Let us propose this idea to the Council. I want to gauge their reactions to an alliance with the Romulans, Gorkon. We both served in the Defense force and we did a little time in the diplomatic corps as well. The rest of the council is filled with self-serving lords and money men and women who can easily be bought with the right baubles. Go, Gorkon, we will meet again."

Gorkon bowed. "Yes, Chancellor," Gorkon said as he left the chancellor's residence.

ROMULUS (RIHANNSU). PRAETOR'S RESIDENCE. STAR DATE 2926.11:

"When you succeed me, Gaius, you must do all you can to placate the Preatorate class as well as the wandering ship clans. If you do not, your Preatorate will be short and you will jeopardize the royal family's appointments of Emperor, Empress, and Legate. The Preatorates would like nothing better than bringing back the Preatorate of three out of seven," Vrax said as he looked at his young successor. "You are Praetor in name only. In one year, you will succeed me. The senate is a nest of scum. Any sign of weakness and you will be overthrown."

The desk monitors buzzed. Vrax got up and answered it. "Yes, of course, send the Commander in."

"Pardeck, I assume," Gaius said.

Vrax nodded. "Correct."

The doors parted to the living room as one of Vrax's aides said, "Commander Pardeck."

Pardeck walked in.

"And what do you have for us today, Commander?" Vrax asked as he leaned back in his chair.

"The latest Intel and I would like to report that Shiarkiek has been made the new Emperor and T'Reihu the new Empress."

Pardeck said as he handed both Praetors two tablets containing the latest Intel.

"Sit down, Commander," Vrax said as he looked over the report. "It seems that the Harrkonens have fought us to a standstill again."

Pardeck nodded. "Yes, Praetor. Admiral Vin couldn't match them ship for ship."

"Then he will be executed as an example of failure and be made an example to all," Vrax said as he continued to look at the report. "Then we will also make peace with the Harrkonens." Vrax continued to look over the long extensive report. "I see that Commander Chavernack has survived and brought us a wealth of intelligence on the Federation."

"She believes that due to the Harrata conflict, the Federation and their Starfleet are now prepared for any future conflict."

"I see that she caused the damage to three Federation Heavy cruisers without firing a shot and evaded the Starfleet."

"She evaded a Federation Heavy cruiser on her return, identified as the Galina-NCC 1464.

The captain thought he had her but Ael and Miral's warbirds gave him a surprise at the borders of the outer marches. The Galina beat a retreat back into Federation Space, Praetor," Pardeck explained as he sat back in the chair opposite both praetors.

"Then she will be properly rewarded. Have fleet central dispatch the warbirds Snipe and Remus to join up with her."

"Yes, Praetor," Pardeck said.

"I heard a rumor that you are leaving the fleet, Commander. Is it true?" Vrax asked.

"Yes, I decided to run for the senate. I have had my fill of the fleet, Praetor."

"You would have made a fine admiral one day had you stayed, Pardeck, but I accept your choice. You will make a fine senator."

"Thank you for your vote of confidence, Praetor." Pardeck bowed and left.

Vrax nodded. Pardeck would help cut down the discourse in the senate. Fleet officers were such pragmatists.

Vrax got up and stretched his old bones. "I'm turning in, Gaius. We have another busy day tomorrow at the Senate."

Gaius got up. "I will return to my residence, Vrax. Until tomorrow," Gaius said as he left.

"Until tomorrow," Vrax said as he left the room.

Q. STAR DATE 2926.12, 7683.3, 9999.5, 10433.9, 40777.6, 54667.8, 9888997.325:

Nothingness was nothingness as three orbs of light appeared in the nothingness.

Claymore grumbled, "Why did we have to go to the mirror universes? We exist in all realities like the Q."

"I needed to check up on their status, Claymore. The mirror universes are such barbaric places. This reality is so much better," Alybourne said.

"Terrible, just terrible," Trefayne moaned.

"You got poor Trefayne upset, Alybourne," Claymore pointed out.

"Sorry, old chum, but we had to check up on those realities," Alybourne said to Trefayne.

"Terrible, just terrible," Trefayne continued to mutter.

Alybourne looked around to see that they were standing on a long road, mountains were in the distance. They had now assumed human form courtesy of the Q. Together, they marched up the road until they came up to a gated community. A guard post was unmanned, but there was a sign on the entrance.

PROHIBITED: NO HUMANS, ORGANIANS, METRONS, EXCALBIANS, AND THASIANS ALLOWED.

Next to the sign stood a poster.

WANTED FOR HIGH CRIMES AGAINST THE CONTINUUM: (*), O, Z, GORGON!

IF YOU KNOW THEIR WHEREABOUTS, PLEASE CONTACT THE Q AT THE GUARDPOST.

ALL INFORMATION WILL BE KEPT STRICTLY CONFIDENTIAL.

Flashes suddenly appeared around them. The beings had arrived. So, had Thasians Aramis and Charlie Evans. Next to them stood two male and one female Metron.

"I don't want to be here, Aramis," Charlie Evans moaned.

"Now be good, Charlie. After what you did to the Enterprise and the Antares, you should be grateful that I am taking you here. No human has ever been too—" Aramis was cut off by a resounding clap of thunder.

A short little Organian wearing a striped suit and a fedora was chomping on a cigar and leading a tall regally attired Q in eighteenth-century clothing appeared.

"Charlie isn't the first faded one a Captain Ah H was here. That is why the Q changed the sign," the little Organian said.

"Now, Polwheal, you apologize to Aramis right now," Claymore said.

"I will not, Clays."

Claymore huffed. "Well, I never."

Alybourne walked up to Polwheal and looked down. "Still nurse-maiding for the Q, Polwheal?"

"Yeah, you don't know what I have to go through with Trelayne over here. He ran away from his parents and I chased him through the continuums and dimensions. From Galactica to the Galactic Civil War via Jupiter 7 and Moon Base Alpha and all the way to the end of time and the end of the universe where I ran into this lord of time, some crazy doctor who had this outlandishly long scarf. Pops," Polwheal said as he chomped on his cigar in frustration.

"You are out of uniform, Polwheal," Claymore said.

Polwheal looked at his clothes. "Don't like the suit, better than that rag that we Organians have to wear."

"Tallyho go get them, Pols," Trelayne said smiling.

"My boy and one hell of a pain in the neck," Polwheal said proudly, still chomping on the cigar.

"You and Enowil are such embarrassments to us," Alybourne said. "Don't follow the rules and you run off and do your own thing."

"Oh, please, Alybourne. Enowil is nuts, he got his crazy planet, and he's worse than that Q, Trelayne, or even Charlie Evans."

Aramis turned to Charlie Evans. "See, Charlie, some of us do appreciate you."

Evans folded his arms and continued to pout.

A flash and a clap of lightning resounded. Suddenly, the coalition of the light was surrounded by the Q. Two were tall and lanky. One male, another female, one male had blond hair. One was a female Q with curly hair and high cheekbones and the other male looked vaguely familiar.

"I see you found Trelayne Polwheal," the female red-haired Q said.

"Yes, well, at least I finally get a chance to meet you. You remind me of that babe on Platonius."

"Enough, Polwheal," the other male Q said.

"And you remind me of the Enterprise's chief engineer," Polwheal said to Trelayne's dad.

Trelayne's father huffed. "If you weren't so good at finding, Trelayne, we never would need your services. Plus, Trelayne has a fancy for you."

One of the big male Q suddenly stepped in, "I hope the family reunion is over because we have to deal with the coalition of the lightheadedness."

Q's comments provoked a lot of discord among the various higher beings.

The Metrons looked completely pissed off at Q's remark and the Thasians were looking at Q with murder in his eyes.

Not to be outdone by the rest, the Organians were furious at the Q.

"Oh, please, members of light. You are all on Trelayne's level. Children among us higher beings," the tall female Q said.

"You should mind your manners, Q, and be more respectful to us," Yarneck said pointing a finger at Q.

"Listen, stone quarry," the blond Q said. "You are nearly as bad as Gom and his gang. You like to play with whoever drops by your planet and get your jollies out of the spectacle."

"And the Them, the Immortals and the Infinite who live in the Barnards galaxy, are higher than you," Aramis, the Thasians said.

"The Immortals and the Infinite haven not yet concluded their millennial war. From what I hear, the Immortals are winning," Q said.

"The Infinite does not pose a threat to this galaxy at this time. What transpired 50,000 years ago was a fluke. That the primitives chose to Challenge the Infinite on the opposite side of the barrier was laudable. It gave us the time to rally and stop the Infinite in their tracks," Trelayne's mother said.

"Which brings me to another point," Q said as he looked around. Looking down, he found Polwheal and walked over to him. "Polwheal, now tell me. I am still fuming over that idiot move you did with that Federation starship the . . ." Q tried to recall its name.

"Constitu…." Polwheal began to speak but was cut off by Q.

"Yes, that one. Flinging into the Gamma and Delta quadrants for what a joy ride."

"Now, wait a minute, Q. You could fling the Enterprise D from the future into Delta quadrant, but I cannot fling a ship from this era around the galaxy."

"Do you realize the repercussions of your act, you pint-sized dimwit?" Q said looking down at the little Organian.

"I am not a pint-sized dimwit," Polwheal said as he pointed the stub of his cigar at Q.

"No Federation ship has ever been to those quadrants. Your brilliant move may have confirmed the Dominions' opinions about the Federation and alerted the Borg to the existence of the Federation," the tall female Q said.

"The Federation and the rest of the Alpha and Beta quadrants not counting the Harrata are blissfully ignorant of what lies beyond. That is the way it should stay. They are not ready," the blond Q said.

"They are not ready to face what lies beyond those quadrants and not ready to face what lies beyond the barrier. That three foolish ships attempted to go beyond. It shows the stupidity and arrogance of the ape-like human race," Q said.

"Humans are not apes, Q, they possess significant flexibility which will help them evolve and maybe even Challenge us one day," Polwheal said.

"Not until the 29th century will they even be mature enough, Polwheal. Until then, try not to interfere in human affairs. We know of your violation of Organian contact rules," Trelayne's father said.

"It is not fair that you Q could do full form first contact while we Organians have to do that icky possession stuffs," Polwheal said as he recoiled at the thought of doing that again.

Q looked at all the other super beings, all in their own way omnipotent like himself. Maybe they were being too elitist. It was time to do a change of face.

"Fellow Q, Organians, Thasians, Excalbians, and Metrons. We Q have been too elitist. Maybe it is time for a change of view. I propose this change."

Q pointed at the Prohibited sign and waved his hands.

PROHIBITED: NO HUMANS OR ORGANIANS ALLOWED.

"All the rest are now welcome," Q smiled deviously. The troublesome Organians and the ape-like humans would have to wait.

"Good idea, Q, but we need to approve it with the Q council."

"I will make them understand, dearest."

Alybourne looked at Polwheal, Trelayne, and Claymore.

"Are you coming with us, Polwheal? We are still not wanted here," Alybourne said as he watched the rest of the super beings join up with the Q.

"No, I am still responsible for Trelayne Alybourne."

"Very well, Q."

Q looked at Alybourne. "Yes."

"Polwheal will be the council's liaison to the Q. Is that acceptable?"

"Yes, now go," Q said as he waved his hands. Everything disappeared.

The three orbs of light then disappeared. Nonexistence remained.

CHAPTER FORTY-FIVE

VANGUARD STATION. STAR DATE 2926 .15. 1701 hours.

Nogura made his way through the habitat ring. Instead of going directly to his quarters, he had to go visit Carol Marcus at her quarters.

He had contacted Khatami about Bobby Hawke surviving on subspace. Endeavor had left 47 for her next assignment and Defiant was returning to 47 for shore leave and mini overhaul.

Potemkin and Coronado had been reassigned since the so-called Harrata Conflict of 2267 had now ended. The Intrepid as soon as she was fully repaired at Star base 11 was going to be temporarily reassigned here until Constitution was ready after six weeks of work. Both were going to do further survey and star-charting work near the Tholian and Klingon borders.

Then both ships were to release for further service elsewhere. Starfleet had also notified him that the new Galina and Astrad would be posted at Star base 46 which was nearing completion near the Taurus Reach. 46 was going to be 47s back up base. 46 was more of a relay point and was going to build as a Watchtower class station.

Commodore David Aaron L.T. Stone was going to be given command of the new base.

Stone had a reputation for no-nonsense and he would be a good backup if needed. Nogura arrived at Marcus's quarters. He paused for a moment and rang the bell.

"Who?" came Carol's voice.

"Nogura, Carol."

"Come."

Nogura stepped into Carol Marcus's quarters. Like most star base quarters, they were three times larger than the quarters on most Federation starships which were more like cubicles to save as much space as possible.

"Nice quarters, Carol."

"I like things simple. Hirohito, want a drink?"

"No thanks, I'll be turning in soon."

"Mom."

"Yes, David." Carol turned to see her son David walk in. He was carrying a school data pad and was typing in some information. David looked up to see Nogura looking at him.

"Admiral."

"David."

"Now what are you writing about, David?" Nogura asked.

David paused nervously.

"David Hirohito is not going to bite," Carol cajoled David.

David reluctantly turned the pad over to Nogura.

Scanning the contents. "Interesting. You are writing the history of the development of Protomatter and why it was banned. Tell me, Dave, how do you like the 47 school?"

"I like it a lot more than some of the others. At least, 47 doesn't have no fool instructors unlike Malvern Research Admiral," David said. "You're not here to update us on that overgrown boy scouts that mom knew at the academy and on the Eagle, are you?"

Nogura nodded. "That is why I am here," Nogura said as he looked at Carol.

"Jim Kirk and Robert Hawke both survived the Challenge, Carol. I don't know how they did it but they both pulled a rabbit out of their hats and saved the Federation from an unnecessary war."

Carol breathed a sigh of relief. But it still didn't change anything between them. Why couldn't she and Jim have a relationship like Robert and Samantha had? Those two had patched up their differences back in 64 after not seeing each other since 55.

She and Jim never got around to do that and if the rumors were true that Kirk was acting like a galactic lover boy, then she wanted no part of Jim's present life. David sure as well wasn't going to join the fleet. She had seen enough of that.

Her father was presently serving as Vice Admiral, Commander at Federation Border Patrol, Starfleet's Coast Guard Division at Starfleet Command. And her time on the starships Lexington, Endeavor,

Saratoga, and Eagle had made her wary of Starfleet. She had had her fill by 2260 and had resigned at the end of the year and taken up a career in research and gave birth to David.

"Thank you for telling me, Hirohito."

"Just doing my duty, Carol. Good to see you, David."

David nodded.

Carol let Nogura out of her quarters and breathed a sigh of relief.

ELBA TWO. FEDERATION PENAL COLONY. STAR DATE 2926.16. 1840 HOURS:

Doctor Cory made his final daily rounds of the facility as he prepared to go to his quarters. Walking through the corridor, he could see all the lights off except for one. Garth's was still on. Cory walked up to the cell. Garth was sitting on his bed. His facial expression was blank.

"What do you want, Cory?" Garth said as he got up and walked up to the force field.

"Both ships survived the Challenge, Garth."

Garth said nothing—no rage, no anger. He was hiding something, Cory figured. No rage or temper tantrum that Garth had done almost three weeks earlier.

Garth looked at Cory and pointed a finger at him. "There will be a reckoning, Cory. Mark my words, there will be a reckoning," Garth said as he hit the light switch and the lights went out in his cell. The lighting dimmed overhead as the colony began night protocol.

Cory shrugged his shoulders and went to his quarters.

CHAPTER FORTY-SIX

STARFLEET COMMAND. OFFICE OF MEDIA AND PUBLIC RELATIONS.

STAR DATE 2926.18. 2300 HOURS:

Herbert Solow stepped into the office. All the duty stations were unmanned. Only one office light remained on. Solow walked up to see Roddenberry finalizing some news media.

Roddenberry looked up to see Solow watching him.

"Doing late-nighters, Gene?"

Roddenberry nodded and handed him a pad.

Solow looked it over. "Kirk triumphs again," Solow read out loud and scanned the rest of the document.

"You don't give much credit to Hawke or the Klingons, Gene."

"If Hawke commanded the Enterprise, I would feel different, but he doesn't. He's the other guy, Kirk's only real competition and trouble. They laugh at both kids when they send their reports in.

But only one can be number one and if what happened at the barrier is true and not Apocrypha that happened to Constitution, then we must bury that ship and put Enterprise out in front. It is as simple as this, Herbert. April, Pike, Kirk over Jefferies, Joe Hawke, Garth, Augenthaler, Page, Wesley, and Robert Hawke. The Constitution must be buried along with the rest of her sisters for the good of the fleet and the service," Gene explained.

"And what about the rest of the fleet? There are some brilliant and gifted Starfleet officers like Bob Hawke and others who will never have their stories told."

"Name one."

"Ron Tracey."

"Too confrontational."

"Matt Decker."

"A security grunt who due to good fortune wound up on the command track."

"Robert Wesley."

"Experienced, but Starfleet has other plans and like the above, getting old."

"Samantha Reynolds."

"The hellion of the border patrol fleet. We don't need to be bothered with them. The rest of the fleet does border patrol with more pizzazz."

"Rachel Hunter."

"Ship too small, another hair raiser from the border patrol."

"Michael Walsh."

"Boring, commands the Anton."

"Andover Drake."

"Keeps the fleet up at nights with his crazy actions. Makes Hawke look like a choir boy."

Solow could go on and on, "Robert Hawke."

"Second in everything except the first officer, beat Kirk in 58 to the promotion to first officer, youngest in Starfleet history. First in a few other less mentionable achievements, brilliant, solid kid, Herbert. Possible Admiral material like Kirk if he doesn't screw up. The ship he commands is too controversial, next to Enterprise, the finest ship in the fleet. Good family, solid connections, and excellent well-earned service record. But he like the rest must toil in the shadows, Herbert. There can only be one number one and her name is Enterprise," Roddenberry explained as he got up.

"Well, it is time to call it a night."

"You made your point extremely well, Gene," Solow said as he and Roddenberry walked out of the office.

"Yes, I have, Herbert. I did it with a fine-tooth comb."

PALAIS DE CONCORDE. PARIS, FRANCE. OFFICE OF THE PRESIDENT.

STAR DATE 2926. 20. 2300 HOURS:

Westcott popped the bottle of Bollinger champagne 2244 and poured the contents out to the guests in his office. Among them were Vice president Lorne McLaren, Prime Minister Bormenus, Federation Military Forces, General-in-Chief Norman Scott, Starfleet Commander-in-Chief Robert Comsol, and Starfleet commander Marcus Bull Buchinsky.

"To James T. Kirk and Robert N. Hawke and the crews of the Enterprise and Constitution. We are forever in their debt," Westcott said as he raised his glass.

As their glasses clanked together in unison, a chorus of cheers resounded through the office as everyone present took their seats.

"I heard a rumor that the Imperium wants to open their borders to us," Bormenus said.

"It is true," Westcott confirmed.

"In three months, we will be sending a delegation back to the Imperium," McLaren added as she sat up in his chair.

"Which starship are we going to send?" Buchinsky asked.

"Let's let the Imperium make the request," Comsol said to Buchinsky.

"Sarek and Shran have contacted us from the Ptolemy. They are heading to Star base Alpha, then to Star base 11 and Vulcan and Andor. Bozeman is providing escort," Comsol added.

"Not having the Harrata Imperium as a major nuisance will be a great relief to all Federation forces. We might even now have a good chance to contact the ever-elusive Harrkonen Empire. They are still giving the Romulan Empire a run for the money," Scott said.

"At this moment, Commodore Harry Morrows Salvage and Recovery fleet are traveling to the Imperium. They should be rendezvousing with the Lothar Gaz, Enterprise, Constitution, and the two Klingon battle cruisers near the abandoned Hell Spawn outpost by tomorrow," Buchinsky mentioned as he poured himself a second serving of champagne.

"That fleet is going to the Lothar system?" Bormenus asked.

"It is," Buchinsky said.

Bormenus felt a rush of relief. One of his ancestors had failed the Challenge and his ship along with her entire crew had perished. Now there was a chance of a proper burial for his ancestor.

"From what I heard was that Lothar made quite a protest but was overruled by Gom," Scott said.

"I envy Morrow. He has a thankless job," McLaren admitted.

"Morrow's second five-year mission in command of the Ari is going to come to an end in 2268. He will be spending the remaining year with this operation and Ari will be temporarily assigned as Starfleet's liaison ship to the Star force. After that, Morrow is to be promoted to rear admiral and reassigned to Starfleet command," Comsol explained to all.

"Who were you thinking of as his replacement?" Westcott asked.

"Robert Hawke, but I believe that kid is going to want to stay with Constitution," Comsol said. "Maybe even Jim Kirk, but he is going to want to stay with Enterprise."

"Those two are not going to budge from their ships. We might have to look elsewhere, like the commanders of the Border patrol and the transport tugs to get a replacement for Morrow," Buchinsky said.

"Who do you have in mind?" Scott asked.

"Transport tug captains Waterston, Strohman, Albertson, Masada, or Border patrol captains Samantha Reynolds, Rachel Hunter, or Eugene Roddenberry," Buchinsky explained.

"I'd go with Roddenberry who commands the Soyuz class ship the Retaliation. Samantha and Rachel should be backup choices. Phil Waterston and Henry Strohman are about average. We don't need average commanding a heavy. Masada and Albertson are still lieutenants and don't have the years or the rank," Comsol explained. Westcott checked his chronometer. It was nearly 2400 hours or 12 midnight. "I'd hate to spoil the party, gentlemen, but it is time to call it quits," Westcott said as he got up. The rest of the guests got up.

"Good evening, gentlemen," Westcott said as he left the room. The admirals, general, and V.P all responded in kind as they too left the office.

CHAPTER FORTY-SEVEN

Enterprise with Constitution, Suvwl with Vorcha, and Lothar Gaz at Federation—Imperium border. Star date 2928. 7. February 10, 2267.

"First officer's log. Star date 2928.7. Commander Spock recording. We have reached the border. We are awaiting the arrival of Commodore Morrow's fleet. The crew is relieved that we have survived the Challenge. Captain Kirk is still resting in his quarters recovering from the stress of this experience under the able care of Doctor McCoy. Mister Scott predicts that he could have Enterprise up and running by Star date 2943 at Star base Trafalgar. The crew will be getting an additional shore leave time at that base."

"First officer's log. Star date 2928.8. Lieutenant Commander Shran recording. Constitution, Enterprise, the Lothar, and the two Klingon ships are now at the border. We await the arrival of Commodore Morrow's fleet. Captain Hawke is in his quarters resting. Lieutenant T'Pau is in deep meditation. Both are under Doc Russell's able care. After eight months in deep space, the crew is looking forward to exceptionally long shore leave. The minimum is six weeks. Constitution needs everything—battle damage repair, upgrading, as well as a heavy system overhaul and modernization. As I look at Enterprise from Constitution's ready room, I sum it up for our captain. We are going to miss those guys on the Enterprise as both ships go their separate ways."

ENTERPRISE:

"Mister Spock."

"Yes, Mister DePaul."

"Long-range sensors are picking up a fleet of thirty-one ships on approach."

"Mister Harrison."

"Sensors identify them as the starship Ari, cruisers Anton, Soyuz, Reliant, Miranda, two Wayfarer class ships the Gallant and Hortense, tugs Thales, Aristarchus, Pythagoras, Eratosthenes, ten hospital ships, ten Moran class warp tenders, and two mobile dry-docks, the Cyclops and Pluto," Harrison said.

"Mister Spock."

"Yes, Mister DePaul."

"I have picked up three Klingon battle cruisers trailing the fleet. One is the Klothos and two are D10s, the Sompeck and Kronk."

"They are here to take our Klingon adversaries home, Mister DePaul. I do not believe they intend any hostile action."

"Mister Spock, Commodore Morrow requests visual," Palmer said.

"Put the commodore on."

KIRK'S QUARTERS:

Kirk relaxed as he sat back at his desk. An hour earlier, he had finally woken up, took a Sonic shower, and got dressed. He was now having a late breakfast and was catching up on the latest reports. He had picked up quite an appetite and hated to imagine how hungry Robert was going to be. The doorbell buzzed.

"Come."

McCoy walked in. "Well, it's nice to see that you have returned to the land of the living," McCoy said smiling.

McCoy walked over to Kirk and ran his scanner over him.

"Your opinion, doctors," Kirk said to McCoy. He was still trying to make sense of the wave of images he had received when Gom/Hawke had touched him.

"You are fit, Jim, to return to duty," McCoy said as he checked the scanners' readings out.

"History buff, Jim."

"Decided to look in on the NX or Constitution class."

"You mean Columbia class."

"That was the one point where Jonathan Archer and Alexander Hawke disagreed. They did agree that Constitution became the next Starfleet flagship starting in 2165."

"And so, it remained until 2245, Bones. NX/NCC 00 was lost the next year and the year after that, NCC 400 was lost. When 1007 was launched in 2169, she remained flagship until 2200."

"And she was succeeded by 0700 which was flagship until 2240," McCoy said.

"And in 2245, Enterprise took over," Kirk finished. "Bones, let's go to the bridge."

Kirk and McCoy left his quarters and within a few minutes arrived on the bridge.

Spock turned to see Kirk and McCoy arriving. "Captain."

Kirk nodded at Spock and faced the viewscreen. Harry Morrow's image was on the screen. He was wearing his gold command uniform, with the rank of Commodore and the lion's head insignia detonating the Ari.

Ari's crew was predominately African, African-American, and West Indian. She was built as a present to the United States of Africa, the same way the Intrepid and Eagle had been for Vulcan and Andor.

"Harry."

"Jim," Morrow said. His mustache dominated the view since Morrow was right up against Tori's main screen, blocking the view of the rest of the bridge.

"Nice to see you up and about. Thanks to you, Bob, and the Federation ambassadors, you have just opened a new chapter in Federation—Harrata relations," Morrow said.

"It wasn't all about the Enterprise, Harry, Constitution did her share. And I wouldn't be here if my number two hadn't given me some good advice."

"You mean Spock, Jim."

"No, Harry. In this case, I mean Robert Hawke. This was a captain-to-captain scenario and my wingman backed us up all the way."

"I am dispatching Anton commanded by Michael Walsh to tow Enterprise to Star base Trafalgar. Soyuz will tow Constitution to her overdue appointment at Star base 11. Ari out."

The screen switched over as the fleet rendezvous with the Lothar. Anton and Soyuz broke off from the fleet.

"Mister DePaul, prepare for towing procedure. Lieutenant Palmer, contact Anton and tell them we are ready."

"Yes, Sir."

Kirk sat back in his command chair and watched as Anton approached. In the distance, he could see Samantha Reynolds' Soyuz closing on Robert's battered Constitution. It was good to be back in command, Kirk thought.

ROBERT HAWKE'S QUARTERS:

The doorbell buzzed repeatedly. Hawke finally got out of bed. What he had gone through had been a hell of a once-in-a-lifetime experience. With doc fussing over him like mother goose, he was surely going to heal himself. Grabbing a T-shirt, he put it on and went to the door.

"Who?"

"Samantha, dear."

Hawke released the lock. Samantha came in and nearly threw herself on him. They kissed and hugged for a few minutes before he released her.

"Don't tell me. I heard rumors about these two Harrata women. Both you and Kirk spared their husbands' lives and you inherited them for marriage," Samantha said almost broken up.

Robert held Samantha close. "Not entirely true, Samantha. You don't understand what we went through."

Samantha looked up and noticed a few strands of grey in Robert's hair.

"You changed. You aged a bit since I last saw you," Samantha said as she brushed his black hair that had traces of grey in it.

"I am still the same, Sam. Just a bit more mature."

"And those two Harrata women!"

"According to Harrata tradition, if you spare the life of the champion in the Challenge and the Harr are supposed to kill them, by rights, you adopt the champion's wife and children. They become part of your family. You do not have to marry them."

Samantha absorbed the information.

"I only want to marry you, Samantha," Hawke said. "No one else."

Hawke kissed her on her cheek.

"I will back you up, dear. Once we arrive at eleven, I must proceed to Earth and meet with Ambassador Shari ben Gazari Fahiri and Loona et Omardy Van Sant at the Harrata embassy in Sausalito."

"That is merely a formality dear, you are still my number one," Hawke said as he and

Samantha began a round of passionate love-making.

IKS SUVWL:

"Milord, the Klothos is signaling," Konar said.

"Put Kor on."

Moments later, Kors image filled the screen.

"So, Kang, another great day for the Empire. You succeeded in keeping the Empire's honor intact," Kor said.

Kang nodded.

"Commander Knash of the Sompeck and Commander Kritza of the Kronk will tow you and Khod back to the home world where Chancellor Sturka wants to honor both you and Khod with an opera dedicated to your glory," Kor explained. "You will also take temporary command of the CHARGH, Captain Kang. Suvwl will go into the dock for a heavy refit at the Ham puch shipyard."

"There has been traffic along the net that we may be going to war with the Federation, Kor," Kang asked.

"It is true. Within a few months, we expect. However, we now believe that the Harratay have gotten the Federation out of its slumber. They are now better prepared," Kor admitted.

"Indeed, they are, Kor. The humans are now better prepared to face our onslaught but we will have so much more glory when it begins," Kang said.

"Indeed, we will. Keplach, Kang."

"Keplach, Kor."

Kors image faded in the distance. He could see the Enterprise and the Anton heading away in one direction, Constitution and Soyuz heading in another.

"We will meet again, Hawke and Kirk, we will meet again."

Sompeck towing Suvwl and Kronk towing the Vorcha both engaged their warp engines.

Enterprise NCC 1701:

Kirk sat in his command chair. The Klingons were departing and in the distance, Soyuz was towing Constitution to Star base 11. Kirk smiled as fate would have it. In the future, he and the Enterprise would probably run into Hawke and the Constitution again.

"Mister Spock, ETA to Trafalgar."

"18 hours, Captain."

Anton and Enterprise disappeared into the realm of space.

ENTERPRISE-NCC1701. STAR DATE 2942.5. FEBRUARY 20, 2267.

Kirk sat in his quarters. The repairs at Trafalgar had taken longer than necessary.

Enterprise was heading for her next assignment—rendezvous with Kelly Bogle's Farragut for star charting. Kirk left his quarters and headed for the bridge. Arriving on the bridge, Kirk sat in his seat. At that moment, Enterprise gave a violent shake. He knew the sensation. They had encountered an ion storm.

EPILOGUE

STAR BASE 11

COURT MARTIAL 2.0

STAR DATE 2943.6 to STAR DATE 2945.9 CONSTITUTION

STAR DATE 2943.7 to STAR DATE 2945.9 ENTERPRISE

FEBRUARY 21-23, 2267

CONSTITUTION-NCC 1700. OUTSIDE ORBITAL DOCKYARD 3:

Hawke stood on the primary hull in his EVA suit alone as he focused his Canon Eos Holocron Mark 320 Holo camera on some of the ships that passed below him and above them. Since he had been a kid, he loved to take photos. Hawke focused the camera's zoom as he panned around the area. In the distance, he could see Intrepid finally leaving Orbital Dockyard 3.

He carefully swung the camera following Intrepid as she swung around the planet.

"Captain."

Hawke hit the communicator. "Yes, Shran."

"We are now cleared to move into number 3, Commodore Stone wants to see you and mister Andrews in his office in 30 minutes."

"Give me five minutes, Shran. Tell 3 to stand by and tell Stone I will be there."

"Understood."

Hawke scanned the horizon of the planet and looked to his left. Refocusing his zoom, he spotted the Antares class freighter Yorkshire and the Intrepid. Quickly, he knocked off some photos and swung further to the left. Another Constitution class ship had just entered the orbit. Quickly, he zoomed in and recognized the contract number.

"No, it can't be," Hawke said as he snapped off a few photos of the Enterprise and the Intrepid.

"Hawke to Constitution, energize."

Hawke disappeared from the primary hull as Constitution entered dockyard 3.

COMMODORE STONE'S OFFICE HALF AN HOUR LATER:

Robert Hawke and Thomas Fredrick Andrews sat opposite Stone. To the left of him was Commander Rory Goldman, Star base 11 executive officer, and to the right was Commodore Steele from Starfleet Engineering.

"We have looked over on your recommendations, Captain. Constitution will be upgraded from Mark 2 to Mark 3. We will however keep a single rear phaser and photon bank as a test. She will be the only Mark 3 with forward and aft weapons," Steele said.

"Constitution's original non-standard warp drive nacelles as well as her external phaser batteries and those old-fashioned recreation room screens are to be replaced," Cooper added. "The Androcous has left San Francisco Navy yard with your new nacelles."

"Bob, we are sorry that even though you were a priority, we had to keep you outside the dock for three days," Stone said. "Your crew has been granted a full six-week shore leave at Star base 11 if some of your people want. The Astral queen will be arriving to pick up some Starfleet personnel for a trip to Wrigley's pleasure planet."

"I would like to supervise the refit, Commodore," Andrews said.

"That is out of the question, Mister Andrews," Commodore Steele said. "Constitution will be the last ship to receive the upgrades. We just completed Exeter and Lexington," Steele said and continued.

"This refit required special knowledge, Mister Andrews. Your reputation as one of Starfleet's most brilliant engineers proceeds you. But Commander Cooper's people will oversee the refit. If you want to observe, you may go right ahead. But your ship needs everything—battle damage repair, upgrading, and an overhaul as well as the new warp nacelles and the refit of the upgraded phaser and photon batteries. Don't get me wrong, Mister Andrews. I admire your conceptual ship designs and you have added to the manuals a lot of new procedures, but in this case, we cannot rush your ship's repair. In six weeks, Constitution will be a brand-new ship," Steele explained in her Scottish brogue.

"Aye, understood," Thomas gave in.

"Commodore. My science officer wants to join her parents on the Intrepid and Thaylassa as well as our other two Andorians wants to hop on the Ptolemy when she arrives and go back to Andor."

"That could be accommodated. And you?"

"I'll be joining my family on Risa for three weeks. Masao is on her way. We could also take about sixty from my crew if they want to vacation there," Hawke said to Stone. "And Dave, why is Enterprise here?" Hawke asked curiously.

"She left Trafalgar and ran into an Ion storm, took damage, Robert, and lost one of her crew. Kirk should be arriving here shortly," Stone said.

At that moment, the transporter hummed. Jim Kirk materialized and hopped off the transporter.

"Speak of the devil," Hawke said as he and Kirk shook hands. "I didn't expect to see you so soon, Jim."

"Same here, Bob."

"We're here for six weeks, Jim. Next time we meet, you won't recognize old battlewagon."

"Captain Hawke, I have urgent business with Captain Kirk," Stone said.

"No problem, Sir."

Thomas looked at Hawke. "Captain, I would like to discuss the upgrades further with the commodore and the commander."

"Go right ahead, Tom."

Andrews nodded and left with Steele and Goldman. As he looked back, he could see Kirk beginning to discuss some urgent matters. Hawke opened his communicator. "Constitution, one to beam up." Hawke dematerialized.

Transporter room one. A few hours later.

Hawke stormed into the transporter room, fuming. After all that he and Kirk had gone through, Kirk was now accused of murdering Ben Finney. The ship was powered down with the crew already reporting to Shran for their shore leave destinations. Work had already begun on his ship. The quartermaster had finally been issued the proper insignias to outfit the rest of his crew with Constitution's proper half arrowhead insignia. Exeter, Hood, Kongo, Ticonderoga, and Defiance had also had the same problem—not enough proper ship design insignias, so they had to make do with Enterprise's.

What really ticked him off was that four people from his ship had gotten into an argument with Kirk over Finney at Larson's, one of the many officer's clubs at the base. Kirk had contacted him about what had happened.

"Whenever you are ready, Mister Dorvil."

"Star base 11 to Constitution six to beam up," came the voice from Star base 11.

"Understood." Dorvil activated the controls. Six crewmembers materialized. Four were male, two female—Ensign Hannah Grainger and Johanna Moore.

Mike Hannah, Adam Timothy, Jack Corrigan, and Mark Teller immediately realized what was happening. Hannah muttered under his breath, "Oh, hell."

"Timothy, Hannah, Corrigan, Teller, front and center," Hawke said. "Mister Dorvil and Ensigns Grainger and Moore are dismissed."

Dorvil, Grainger, and Moore quickly left the premises.

Hawke looked each one in the eye as he paced back and forth. "You know why you are all here. Do you?" Hawke said angrily as he pointed at all four officers.

"That little incident with Kirk, Sir." Hannah admitted.

"I recall that we attended the academy at the same time. And the rest of you were a year behind of me in Kirk's class. We all had high regard for Ben Finney. But after what we all recently went through at the Imperium with our crewmates on the Enterprise," Hawke said as he went face to face with Corrigan. "I figured you would show some discretion on a matter like this." Hawke's voice was trembling with anger. Corrigan looked away.

"Face me, Lieutenant Corrigan."

Corrigan looked back up and faced his CO.

"Good," Hawke said. "Since we are now having a long overdue shore leave, I will not punish any of you for this. Everyone in this crew is too tired, combative, and edgy after what we went through over the last eight months. Report to the quartermaster and get those insignias replaced and then report to Shran if you don't want to spend six weeks here. You have a choice. You can either go to Wrigley's Pleasure planet or come with me and my brother on the Masao. We are going to Risa for three weeks."

All four of them nodded meekly.

"You are dismissed," Hawke said. As the officers filed out, Hawke waited until the last one left. He let out a sigh of relief. Thank god, that was all it was. Without a second thought, he left the transporter room.

KIRK'S TEMPORARY QUARTERS ON STAR BASE 11:

Kirk and Sam Cogley pored through the many books Cogley owned. Kirk smiled. Books had so much of a real solid feel to them computer disks and unemotional computers couldn't convey. The doorbell buzzed.

Kirk got up and answered it. Robert Hawke was there, and Kirk let him in.

"Took a while to find this place," Hawke said as he entered. Noticing that Kirk was in his dress uniform, "I see they got you in your dress uniform," Hawke said as he introduced himself to Sam Cogley.

"Aren't you the CO who was put up for a competency hearing eight months ago?" Cogley said.

Hawke nodded. "I was cleared, and we didn't go to court-martial proceedings. Plus, the nature of the hearings was classified," Hawke said as he was skimming through one of Corley's many books, smiling. How did Cogley found out about it? He didn't want to know.

Kirk was relieved that Hawke was being raked over the hot stove instead of him.

"Anything to report, Bob?" Kirk asked.

"Scuttlebutt, it is that you don't stand a chance. They want to hang you, Jim. I know Stone. He is merciless when it comes to lawbreakers. I should know. After my fling on the Jovian run, I wound up on Defiant instead of Constellation. Stone flayed me alive for my brilliant maneuver, the Kolvoord Starburst." Hawke remembered. "He will hang you, Jim."

"Nice to know." Kirk figured Stone had a reputation when he was a starship captain, that he didn't suffer fools gladly. Either you shaped up or you found yourself shipping out to another assignment.

"And Jim, I cleared that other matter up. And I believe you are one hundred percent innocent."

The incident in the officer's club. Hawke must have roasted his crewmembers alive. They all were former academy classmates, but they were Robert's people and his responsibility.

He would have done the same if he had been confronted with a similar incident.

"I'd hate to break up the lovefest here, but Kirk and I have to go. It was a pleasure meeting you, Captain Hawke," Cogley interrupted.

"Ditto, Sam," Hawke said as he shook Corley's hand.

Kirk and Cogley left.

Hawke wandered around the base and found himself at a bar named Old Peculiar. As he entered the establishment, he could see the trial being broadcast on the screen.

"Hey, hotshot," came a familiar voice.

Hawke turned to see Rudolph Alava, Captain of the Constitution class, Indomitable, walk up to him. Alava was heavy set, built like a bull with a full black beard.

"Rudy," Hawke said surprised.

"Bobby, your old showoff. Both you and Kirk saved us from an unnecessary war with the Harrata and now Kirk's neck is on the line," Alava said. "You just missed Harris, Tracey, and Wesley," Alava said in his Basque-accented English. "Sit down, my old friend."

Hawke joined Alava at the table and quickly ordered some Centaurian oysters and Centarian mood ale. Alava placed his order for Andorian tapas and some good old Sangria.

"You look five years older, Robert," Alava said noticing the trace of grey in Hawke's hair.

"Tell me, Bob. What happened during the Challenge, my friend?" Alava asked.

"You don't want to know, Rudy. It was however a once-in-a-lifetime experience."

"Your old science officer Thelin, your former science officer on the Miranda, and me present chief science officer says hello."

"Tell Thelin the same, Rudy."

The waitress brought over the food. Both officers dived into their dishes.

"Have you seen Erin, Rudy?"

"Erin is on the Defiant, Bobby. She transferred there in 2264," Alava mentioned as he took a sip of Sangria.

"She was my first science officer on the Sargon. However, no matter how much Erin liked me, I was her CO and I couldn't really get involved with her."

"But you and Samantha are back together again. Doing that doesn't make anything different," Alava said as he stroked his neatly trimmed beard.

"No. There is nothing in the regulations that says about two captains getting involved."

"Well."

"Well, what, Rudy?"

"Nothing, Bobby. What is your take on Kirk?"

"He's innocent, one hundred percent innocent."

"He's guilty, Bob, since that incident on the Republic. I bet he holds a grudge."

"Not from my point, Rudy. Sure, Jim was a snitch."

"You're damn right. He once spilled the beans on me in our junior year. I never forgave Kirk for that," Alava said ticked off.

"I had to hold our classes' pride up, Rudy. Do you think those three Rigel cups were so easy to do? I had to counter Kirk and his class of 2254s with the pride of our class of 2253. So, what if Kirk was a snitch? He was better than Finnegan and those two stooges Rehnquist and Roberts."

"That doesn't change my opinion, Bobby."

"Well, I worked with Jim a number of times since then. He has changed and he once told me that he really regrets being a snitch."

"Then he should apologize to me, Bob. I just hope that the Indi is not paired with Enterprise."

"Let's change the subject. I saw the Hood and Kongo are here."

"Your old CO Glen Baron from the Hermes is going to new construction and being replaced by Joaquin Martinez, Captain of the Austerlitz. Anne Toroyan your old CO from the Geronimo had to report back to Earth. Rumor has it Toroyan may be getting a Federation class dreadnought or a star base command in two years," Alava said.

"Captain Hawke, is there a Captain Hawke here?" a voice said.

Hawke looked up to see a young female Ensign looking at him.

"I am Captain Hawke, Ensign."

"Commodore Stone wants to see you in his office immediately."

"Got to go, Rudy."

"Until the next time, hombre."

Hawke and the female ensign left.

COMMODORE STONE'S OFFICE:

Hawke walked in to see some old familiar faces in their dress uniforms discussing matters.

Stone was along with two other starship captains who he immediately recognized—Igor Kranowsky of the Merrimac and Nensi Chandra from the Monitor. Next to them was old Samuel Lindstrom of New York fame. Lindstrom served as an aide to Admiral Noguchi at Starfleet Command headquarters. Rounding out the group, he could see Nicolas Nick Silver of the Defiance and Areel Shaw.

Hawke made all his introductions and got acquainted with the group. Hawke kissed Areel on the cheek.

Hawke sat down next to Silver. Silver was tall and thin as a rake.

"Now that we are all here, let us get right to the point. Robert, both you and Andover were on the list to command the Enterprise. Well, we believe that you are the best choice since we are about to hang Kirk," Stone explained.

Hawke could feel his jaw go slack.

"Nick Silver will replace you as captain of Constitution."

Hawke nearly flipped out and leaped out of his seat. "No, wait a minute, Commodore. After what Kirk and I went through at the Imperium, you want me to stab Kirk in the back, take his ship, and give up Constitution?"

Kranowsky and Chandra were shocked at Hawke's reaction. Shaw stood there mutely. Stone was fuming and Silver was pissed.

"Yes, Captain. The service demands that," Stone said. "You are doing it for the good of the service, Robert. You go where you are assigned."

"There is nothing in the regulations that says I could refuse a command," Hawke said to Stone looking at Silver. "Sorry, Nick, but I didn't spend this long getting Constitution just the way I like it to turn her over to another captain. Plus, you have Defiance and you didn't spend an equal amount of time getting that ship up to your specs."

"He has a point, Commodore. I am perfectly happy with Defiance. Don't want that broken-down rust bucket Hawke has," Silver admitted. Silver then looked at Hawke. "No harm intended, Bob."

"No taken, Nick."

Stone looked at Hawke. "Robert, what am I going to do with you? You are back to being that young insubordinate lieutenant I knew fresh from the academy."

"I just want to stay with my ship, Commodore. Thank you for the offer, but I am happy where I am now."

Silver cut in, "So am I, Commodore Stone."

"Then that leaves one more candidate, Phillip Phil Waterston of the Ptolemy," Stone said as he looked at Hawke. He could see Hawke recoiling at the name. Those two never got along. As soon as Kirk was sacked, he would contact Waterston. Stone checked his chronometer. "We have to go, the court-martial has to reconvene. Good luck, Robert, Nicolas."

Stone said as the entire board left.

"You have a way with people, Bob, I will never figure you out. Turning down the Enterprise, the flagship of our fleet, and having all that gall," Silver said.

"No one's perfect, Nick."

"Good luck with that old rust bucket, Bob."

"Good luck with the Deaf I ants," Hawke added using Defiance's nickname.

Both captains went their separate ways.

ENTERPRISE-NCC 1701. STAR DATE 2949.9:

Kirk watched McCoy depart the bridge and Spock move back to his station. He was still clutching the book Sam Cogley had given him. He was glad that he had been absolved of all guilt. Rumors had it that Robert had turned down command of Enterprise.

Well, so much the better, Kirk thought. It was a big galaxy and there were always plenty of situations when two captains would meet and challenge the scenarios. Enterprise was going to resume her original mission with the Farragut- NCC 1729/1647. Bogle was the opposite of Robert and was by the book.

"Captain, the Masao is contacting us," Uhura said.

"On screen," Kirk said as Uhura switched over.

Robert was standing on the bridge of the Masao. Next to him was his younger brother Commander Richard Hawke, Masao's captain.

"Congratulations, Jim."

"Thanks for not taking my ship from me."

"Never wanted Enterprise, Jim. Off to Risa for a three-week vacation. Heard you are rendezvousing with Farragut."

Kirk nodded.

"Well, there goes the fun, Jim. Kelly is so serious he takes the fun out of command."

Kirk laughed at Hawke's opinion.

"See you around the galaxy, Bob."

"Borjouney Mon Ami Kirk. Au Revoir. Masao out."

The screen went blank, replaced by space. Masao jumped to warp.

"Mister Spock, take us to our next destination ahead warp 6."

Spock nodded. "Helm make course 234-mark 45 ahead warp 6."

Enterprise jumped to warp. Only the stars remained.

TU ET FINI.

ACKNOWLEDGMENT

The Challenge fills in a gap leading up to the episode Court Martial, with the famed list of starships in Commodore Stone's office. Nothing had ever been explained why so many Constitution class starships were present at the star base.

To make this novel work, I liberally borrowed characters from future and some novels that took place prior to the Challenge. And to fill in some gaps, some fanon material was used as well as references to the Star Trek comics.

I would like to thank my mom for helping me—Gene Roddenberry who created the wonderful universe of Star Trek that inspired a four-year-old boy who woke up in 1968 and found his parents watching the original series in black and white.

The list of authors:

Kevin Ryan, Alan Dean Foster, Michael Jan Freidman, S.D. Perry, Howard Weinstein, Dean Wesley Smith, Vonda McIntyre, Diane Carey, Diane Duane, David R. George 3rd, William Shatner, aka Captain Kirk, David Mack, Greg Cox, Margret Wander Bonaano, Bernd Perpiles, and Christopher Humberg.

Greig Jeins list, Starfleet Technical Manual, Federation at 150, Starfleet Space Flight Chronology, Starfleet maps, all versions.

Memory Alpha, Beta, and the Expanded universe.

And finally, I would like to thank the fan sites and the DC, Marvel etc. comics which I borrowed references to round out and complete this novel.

There is also a brief mention of Star Trek Discovery to bring the novel up to date.

9 781957 220635